ONCE UPON A CURSE

17 DARK FAERIE TALES

DEVON MONK ❧ ANTHEA SHARP

CHRISTINE POPE ❧ YASMINE GALENORN

C. GOCKEL ❧ DONNA AUGUSTINE

ANNIE BELLET ❧ AUDREY FAYE

JENNA ELIZABETH JOHNSON ❧ TARA MAYA

ALEXIA PURDY ❧ PHAEDRA WELDON

JULIE CRANE ❧ SABRINA LOCKE

JENNIFER BLACKSTREAM ❧ ALETHEA KONTIS

Fiddlehead Press

ONCE UPON A CURSE

ISBN: 9781680130881
Copyright © 2016 by the respective authors
Published by Fiddlehead Press

CONTENTS

YARROW, STURDY AND BRIGHT
DEVON MONK

THE TOWN'S BELLS RANG IN STRANGE HARMONY, MOURN-
ing the last light of dusk and filling Yarrow's heart with fear.

Tonight, at the rise of the winter moon, she would go into
the woods. Tonight, she would find the tailor's son and bring
him home. Tonight, they would be together again, and there
would be no darkness to fear.

He had promised her, on a summer's kiss, that he would
return in a month. He had held her hand so tightly that the
thimble on his finger had pressed a small pattern into her skin.

He had promised he loved her.

But it had been a year and more, summer was gone once
again, and so too, autumn. The world was covered in snow,
trees plucked down to bony limbs by the bitter wind.

She loved the tailor's son, his kind golden eyes, his quiet
words, his beautiful, graceful hands. Yarrow knew she was not
beautiful or graceful or quiet. Rather, she was sturdy and bright
and strong, like the flowering weed that bore her name.

But here, in this trembling moment between day and darkness, she did not feel strong, did not feel brave. Beyond the edge of the forest, with the wild mountain rising at its back, was a twisted magic.

Something dangerous.

Something dark.

Something that had taken the tailor's son.

The wild mountain had always made her feel safe, protected. But tonight it was a bitter shadow, warning. Warning her to return to her little house where her mother and old aunties slept. Return to the safe hearth of her grandmother.

She was done waiting. Done wishing. She was done with endless days without the tailor's son's laughter, his voice, his touch. She was done being alone.

She pulled her grandmother's red cloak closer around her shoulders and stared at the forest's edge. In one hand she clutched a lantern, in the other a silver dagger.

The dagger had been a gift from her grandmother who had watched her with a knowing eye as Yarrow came home from the forest's edge each night.

Her grandmother had given her the dagger wrapped in a soldier's kerchief.

"This will light the shadows, sweet Yarrow," she had said, pressing the dagger into Yarrow's palm. It was warm, as if a fire smoldered within it. "This will burn the heart of the piper."

Yarrow had fitted her fingers around the dagger's black hilt and wondered at how well it was balanced to her. "Was it grandfather's? Did he carry it in the great battle?"

Her grandmother's eyes went distant as the firelight from the hearth brushed her softly in gold. There was more than memory in her eyes. There was steel. "No," she said. "I did."

Yarrow saw then, not an old woman before her but an old warrior, strong beneath the creases and wrinkles of age. Patient, clever, and sad. "We could not stop him then, the piper. Could not stop him from taking them away from us. So many. So many."

"What?" Yarrow asked, aching for tales of the great battle she had only heard in whispered snatches. "What did the piper take?"

"Our children. Every child old enough to crawl. Drawn into the night by his call, his music. And we with our strong arms, our mighty shouts, our clever weapons, could do nothing to stop him, to break his song, to turn our children home."

"Did you hunt him?" she asked, her pulse beating too fast. "The forest is not too deep. It is not too dark."

"He didn't take them to the forest, dear Yarrow," her grandmother said. "He took them to the mountain, and the mountain swallowed them whole."

A shiver tripped down Yarrow's spine. The cozy hut suddenly felt cold.

And still her grandmother spoke. "The piper is a wicked creature with wicked needs. No matter the gold we threw at his feet, no matter the riches and comforts we gave to him, all he wanted, all he hungered for, was our children's souls. He promised he would return when the stars fell from the sky and his hunger grew great enough. We have watched. We have waited. All these years."

Yarrow held her silence. Held her desperate questions. She did not want the truth stolen away by her grandmother's regret. She wanted to hear the words no one in the town dared to speak.

But finally, she could not wait. "Did he return? The piper?"

Her grandmother shook her head, her snowy hair catching the yellow shadows of firelight. "He never returned. Just as our children never returned. Just as the tailor's boy will never return."

Yarrow felt fear scratch into the spaces between her heartbeats.

"You must find the tailor's son." Her grandmother gripped both of Yarrow's shoulders with strong, warm hands. "Or he will be lost forever."

"Perhaps he is still looking for the ivory key that will unlock the mountain and destroy the piper," Yarrow said, anxious for the comfort of hope. "Perhaps he hasn't yet found the piper."

"Oh, child," her grandmother said softly. "I am sure that he did. Otherways, he would be home. Tonight, the stars will fall. Tonight, the piper will slip free of the mountain and feast upon our souls."

"No," Yarrow said. "I will find him. I will stop him."

"Then you must promise me three things."

Yarrow nodded, caught by the tears that pooled unshed in her grandmother's eyes. She had never seen her grandmother cry. From the fierce expression on her grandmother's face, she never would.

"Take the silver dagger. Carry the copper lantern. Wear a cloak the color of blood. When you find the ivory key, you will find the tailor's son. He will lead you to the piper so that you can cut out his wicked heart."

The old woman rose and drew a folded bolt of rich, thick cloth from the shelf hidden in the corner. This she shook out around Yarrow's shoulders, a cloak the color of blood.

"How will I know the piper?" Yarrow asked.

"By his voice. By the magic within it."

"And if he is silent?"

"There is a mark upon his neck." Here, she drew one finger beneath her own chin. "Just below his jaw, a jagged scar that leads to his heart."

"How do you know?"

A glint of fire sharpened her eyes. "Because I am the one who scarred him. And you, my child, must be the one who ends him."

Her grandmother's voice echoed in her ears as she stood here, now, at the edge of the forest where no paths could be found. Yarrow ached for the warmth of her grandmother's house, for the safety of her own room, her own bed.

The bells had long gone silent, smothered beneath the weight of snow. The swollen yellow moon rolled over the edge of the sky.

Here, in this dark night, here in this stillness, the moonlight seemed weak, a faint and far-away glow that did not quite touch the land. A light too fragile to break the deep darkness of the forest.

She patted the crust of bread she had tucked in her pocket, and with a final glance back at the warmth and safety of her town, of her family, of her home, Yarrow walked into the woods.

The shadows were so still, her own breathing sounded like an ocean, her boots in the snow like sand sifting through waves. The lantern in her hand burned a pocket of light around her, but it was only bright enough to reveal a few steps ahead.

Soon, she knew she was lost. But she did not stop. Could not stop.

The shadows drifted near, then dragged away, as if the entire forest were breathing, as if her feet were its heartbeat, as if she were the only thing alive in the world.

Until above her she heard the faintest of wings and a soft hollow voice called out. "Who walks these woods of silence and darkness?"

She held the lantern high overhead and saw a beautiful tawny owl with strange eyes the color of snow.

"I am Yarrow, sturdy and bright, a weed of the field. I am looking for the ivory key."

The owl blinked, then tipped its head greatly to one side. "The ivory key is lost, is lost, but if you give me your cape to warm my nest, I will take you to one wiser than I."

Yarrow didn't want to give away her grandmother's cloak. She didn't want to break her promise that she would wear it. But she had a sturdy coat beneath the cape, and did not fear the cold.

She carefully unknotted the ties and the owl flew to her, lifting the cloak away and flying slowly deeper into the woods.

Yarrow followed, her lantern high. It seemed she had walked swiftly behind the owl for hours before they came upon a small creek that crinkled like hammered pewter.

There, beside the creek was a raven, black feathers glossy and soft as a summer's night. Its eyes were the colors of beetle wings.

"Who stands by this creek of frozen stone?" it asked in a voice like a rusted gate.

"I am Yarrow, sturdy and bright, a weed of the field. I am looking for the ivory key."

The raven strutted away from the edge of the creek, walking a full circle around her before pausing. It tipped its head the other way, black eyes piercing. "The ivory key is lost, is lost, but if you give me your lantern that shines so pure, I will take you to one more clever than I."

This too, her grandmother had made her promise to keep. But her eyes had grown used to the darkness, and she didn't need it. She extended the copper lantern to the raven who launched in a flurry of wings, clutching the lantern in its claws.

Yarrow ran to follow the swift bird, the glittering yellow light flitting just out of her reach like the fae wisps of old. Her breath came more quickly, her cheeks burned from the cold of night, and still she ran, deeper into the forest.

Finally they came upon a hollow tree, the roots of which were gnarled and black, covered in tufts of spongy green moss.

There in the roots sat a rat, fur the color of fog, eyes glinting like wet agate.

"Who stops at my hollow tree?" the rat asked in a voice like a child's whistle.

"I am Yarrow, sturdy and bright, a weed of the field. I am looking for the ivory key."

The rat twitched its pink nose, long whiskers shivering. It scampered up to Yarrow's feet, then lifted on its back legs, one tiny hand softly braced on her boot.

"The ivory key is lost, is lost, but if you give me the bread in your pocket, I will take you to your heart's desire."

"The ivory key is my heart's desire."

"No," said the rat. "There is something you desire more."

Yarrow wanted to ask if it was the tailor's son. Wanted to speak his name. But the shadows of the forest leaned in, breathing cold against the back of her neck.

The silence was listening.

She gripped the silver dagger tighter, felt the heat of the hilt against her palm. The bread was all the food she had. If she gave it to the rat, she would surely become too hungry and weak to find her way home.

Still, she drew the bread out of her coat pocket and handed it to the rat.

"Here," said the rat, as it ran up upon a tumble of boulders each covered in thick moss and snow. "Follow me."

Yarrow climbed the boulders, her hands soon covered in wet and slick, her boots sliding against the ice that crackled beneath her toes and heels. It was a tall pile of stones, ragged and old, as if the tears of giants had fallen and frozen here at the mountain's feet.

At the top of the pile, in front of a small opening, waited the rat.

"Only in the full winter moon can this door be found," the rat said, its voice a soft peeping. "The first touch of morning's light will seal it away for a year full of days."

The moon had already traveled the ocean of sky, a baleful blind eye nearing the other horizon. And like glimmering sparks stirred by a heavenly wind, the stars began to fall.

She had so little time left.

"Thank you," she said, as she crouched down. It was dark beyond the opening. Darker than the forest around them.

The rat patted her face exactly where the tailor's son's fingers had last touched her, then scurried away before Yarrow could ask any questions of what, exactly, lay within the mountain.

She had to find the key. With it, she might find the tailor's son before the moon was gone and the sun burned the heavens from black to blue.

She walked into the mountain. It was so dark, she felt as if she were wrapped in a fold of velvet, blinded. Still, she made her way forward, one hand dragging lightly across the cold stone wall, the other holding the dagger close to her chest.

The stones leaned closer and she had to turn sideways to ease between the walls that crowded in. If she had been wearing her red cloak, it would have caught here and she would have been trapped.

Instead, she slipped easily through the narrow opening.

Her breath echoed back to her, a chorus of hush and sighs. Then the narrow passage opened into a small chamber no bigger than her grandmother's hut.

There was no light here, but her eyes, so long without the lantern, had finally become used to this darkness. If she had been carrying her lantern, she would be blind and could never have seen the truth of this place.

The truth was horrifying.

The walls were covered in bones. Some of them small, some of them large. They were not the bones of animals. They were the bones of people.

At first, she thought the bones were draped in gauzy cloth that shifted slightly in the deadened air. Except the gauze was not cloth. It was the tattered souls of all the missing children of the town, lured away by the piper, swallowed by the mountain.

All the ghost eyes watched her. All the ghost hands reached for her. All the ghost mouths moved with words barely more than a sigh, warning her: "*Run, run away from these cursed stones. The piper hungers for your bones.*"

But she did not need warning.

In the center of the room stood two figures. One was a slim, tall man, with dark hair and eyes that glowed green. He wore a patchy suit that reminded her of her auntie's quilt, stitched of bits of bright-colored fabric. In his hand was a pipe made of bone. When he brought it to his lips, the sweetest music she had ever heard filled the room, filled her head, filled every breath of her lungs.

"And who are you, my brave child?" the music seemed to ask. "Who has come to hear my song?"

Yarrow struggled to look away from the man. She wanted desperately to see the other figure in the room—the man she knew as well as her own heartbeat.

The tailor's son stood quietly. He didn't look afraid, only curious. He was not bound or tied, his face was clean, the curl of his hair combed. He wore the same coat, trousers, and boots that she remembered him wearing a year ago, and yet, he looked as if he hadn't aged a day.

"I am Yarrow, sturdy and bright," she said. "A weed of the field. And I am here to take my true love home."

"Of course," the piper said. "Of course you are. And there he is, waiting for you."

Yarrow stepped toward the tailor's son. He smiled. "My beautiful Yarrow," he said, golden eyes shining. "Stay with me here, where the fields are green and skies are blue. Where summer never ends."

The music played softly, and as the tailor's son spoke, the chamber around them faded and became instead the vision of his words. Green fields rolled resplendent with flowers. Trees heavy with fruit offered perfumed shade, and the sun shone warm between fluffy clouds.

There were no bones nailed upon cold stone walls. There were only children, a hundred or more, some of them small, some of them large, laughing, dancing, frolicking in the field.

"Stay with me," the tailor's son said again, his voice oddly that of a flute playing.

The children danced by and one tugged at her sleeve. Yarrow did not see laughter on the girl's face. She saw terror.

She thought she could hear soft words on the breeze: "*Run, run away from these cursed stones.*"

But the music played louder, and she forgot the terror, forgot the words.

"We will marry, you and I," the tailor's son sang.

Another child tumbled past her and as he rolled, his mouth formed around words she could barely hear: "*The piper hungers for your bones.*"

But the music played louder, and she forgot the warning, forgot the words.

"Take my hand and we will be together forever." The tailor's son held out his hand, his eyes shining.

Yarrow looked from his warm eyes down to his hands. Familiar hands. Kind hands. But there was no thimble on his finger. She had never seen him without the ivory guard. Never known him to put it away.

A third child skipped past her, brushing her wrist, and Yarrow felt a heavy heat burning in her palm.

She was carrying a dagger here in this beautiful field. Even though the music played louder, the dagger remained solid in her hand, sturdy and bright, reminding her of her grandmother, reminding her of her home.

No matter how loud or how sweetly the piper played, she knew in her heart this was not her field, this was not her summer, and this was not her tailor's son.

She lifted the dagger and with a steady hand, plunged the blade deep into the tailor's son's heart.

The music stopped. The children stopped. The wind and sun and clouds in the sky all went still.

A great shrieking rose from all around her—a wind that was more than a wind. It was voice, it was power, it was fury. The tailor's son who still stood in front of her melted away like hot wax, revealing instead another man.

He was the tall, ragged coated man. A thick white scar carved a path from beneath his chin toward his heart. He was the piper, a flute of hollowed bone clutched in his hand.

Off at a distance, the other man who had looked like the piper wavered and changed into a sight so familiar, her heart caught. The tailor's son.

"You are nothing," the piper hissed, his eyes glinting green, pupils long and narrow like a snake's or a demon's. "You are no one. You are nothing but a weed in the field."

"I am brave, and strong, and alive," Yarrow said. "Just like a weed in the field. And I am your end."

The final fragments of the piper's illusion shattered. She was once again in the deep and dark cavern. Once again surrounded by walls hung with bones, souls pinned in tatters against them.

The piper's blood pooled around the dagger. As drops fell to the rocky ground, they hissed and caught the stones on fire.

With each drip of blood, the ghosts against the wall began to move, unfastening themselves from their bones like buttons sliding free of holes.

The ghosts surged forward, surrounding the piper, pulling, pushing, snarling. They fed their bones like dry kindling into the fire at his feet.

And the piper screamed.

Yarrow fought her way through the weaving ghosts, fought her way through the smoke and fire filling the small cavern.

The piper screamed and screamed as the fire devoured him whole.

She had to find the tailor's son.

Her eyes watered, her lungs hurt from the sting of smoke. She knew she would have to leave the mountain before the fire burned her up too.

She knew dawn was moments away from sealing the mountain for another year.

Just then, she felt a warm hand clasp her own. Familiar fingers threaded together with hers.

On the end of one finger was the cool, heavy press of an ivory thimble.

"Yarrow?" said the tailor's son, his voice rough and unused from a year trapped in the mountain.

"Run." Yarrow held tight to his hand and ran, guiding him through the narrow corridor, through the dark of the cave, and then out onto the pile of rocks. Smoke gushed out of the cave as Yarrow made her way down the stagger of stones.

She glanced back only once, and saw the ghosts of all the children flying free of the mountain, their laughter and joy like bells shivering in the star-tumbled sky.

The tailor's son followed her down the boulders. He did not once look back, his hand locked tightly with her own.

When they reached the forest floor, she finally turned to him.

He looked tired, thin. A year trapped inside the mountain had taken some of the light out of his eyes and the blush from his cheek. But when he smiled at her, she knew with her heart that he was indeed the tailor's son.

"I'm sorry I broke my promise," he said. "I'm sorry I didn't return."

"I know," Yarrow said. "Now that I've found you, we will make new promises."

Yarrow looked around at the trees. Even though dawn was just beginning to bring light back to the sky, she was still lost and didn't know how to find her way through the forest.

"There," the tailor's son said, pointing with one hand. He would not let go of her other hand slotted so closely with his that she could feel his heartbeat. "Breadcrumbs."

The breadcrumbs had been dropped by the clever rat. If she had not given the rat her bread, she would never find her way through the forest, and would be lost.

They followed the trail through the forest as dawn rose and the bells of the town rang out in jubilant harmony. The wise owl and thoughtful raven winged above them like heralds announcing royalty. All the ghosts followed in their wake.

The town rejoiced at their return, and a celebration was held to honor the children who had been lost.

The ghosts attended the celebration, families finally reunited after long, long years. There was dancing, and singing, and music, though no one played the pipes. Stories were told, memories shared, loving words given and received.

Yarrow watched, her heart full, as her grandmother, old aunties, and friends laughed and danced with the spirits of those whom they had never stopped loving.

Before they left, the ghosts promised they would return in a year to celebrate with their families again. Yarrow did not know if her heart could be happier.

But it was not yet the happiest time.

The next summer on a full and beautiful moon, Yarrow and the tailor's son exchanged their own promise of love. While many might offer a ring to seal a vow, Yarrow and the tailor's son instead gave each other an ivory thimble.

They wore them that day and wore them on their fingers forever more.

When they kissed, when they searched each other's eyes and saw hope and trust and kindness there, they knew their love was sturdy and bright.

And it would last forever, happily ever after.

FIN

About the Author: Devon Monk is a national bestselling writer of urban fantasy. Her series include Ordinary Magic, House Immortal, Allie Beckstrom, Broken Magic, and Shame and Terric. She also writes the Age of Steam steampunk series, and the occasional short story, which can be found in her collection *A Cup of Normal,* and in various anthologies such as this one. She has one husband, two sons, and lives in Oregon. When not writing, Devon is either drinking too much coffee or knitting silly things.

Want to read more from Devon? Find all her books on her website: www.devonmonk.com.

FAE HORSE
ANTHEA SHARP

IF THE MEN CAUGHT HER, THEY WOULD TIE HER TO THE stake and set the fire.

Eileen O'Reilly crouched beneath a hawthorn tree, her heartbeat dinning in her ears so loudly it nearly drowned out the sound of her pursuers. Torchlight smeared the night, casting fiendish shadows over the hedgerows. She clenched her hands in her woolen skirt and gasped for air, trying to haul breath into her shaking lungs.

She had heard there was no worse agony than burning alive.

The flames would scorch and blister her skin before devouring her, screaming, as her bones charred. Eileen swallowed back bile.

Shredded clouds passed over the face of the half moon. One moment, sheltering darkness beckoned; the next, the newly-planted fields were washed with silver, her safety snatched away.

"I see her—there, across the field!"

Cursing the fickle moon, and her fair hair, which had surely given her away, Eileen leaped to her feet and ran. She crashed through a thicket, heedless of the thorns etching her skin with blood. In the distance she heard the pounding waves below the cliffs of Kilkeel.

Better a death by water than by flame. There was no other escape.

Five months ago, when the new vicar came to town with his fierce sermons and piercing gaze, she had not seen the danger. She'd lived in the village most of her life, first as apprentice to her aunt, then later taking on the duties of herb-woman and midwife.

But Reverend Dyer sowed fear and superstition—an easier harvest to reap than charity and love, to be sure.

Eileen stumbled, falling to her hands and knees in the soft soil. *Get up, keep running.* She must not give in, though her side ached as if a hot poker had been driven through it, and the air scraped her laboring lungs.

"There's no escape, witch!" The vicar's voice, deep and booming, resonated over the fields.

The stars above her blurred, and she tasted the salt of her own desperate tears. She risked a glance over her shoulder.

If she did not find a hiding place, they would catch her before she reached the cliffs. She veered toward the remains of the ancient stone circle that stood beyond the fields. Only two of the stones remained upright, the rest tumbled and broken. Still, she might find some shelter there.

She reached the ruin, and a figure loomed before her, large and dark. Lacking the breath to scream, Eileen staggered to a halt. What new enemy was this?

Four-legged and blacker than the shadows, it let out a soft whicker. A horse, untethered, with a rope halter dangling from its neck.

Blessing her luck, Eileen caught the rope. It stung her hands, as though woven of nettles, but she did not care. Hope flared up, painfully bright. She might yet live to see the dawn.

"Easy now," she whispered, forcing back the panic pounding through her.

The horse was tall, and lacked any saddle or bridle. She gazed up at it and choked on misery. Her escape was in her hands, but she could not mount it unaided.

"Quick, lads!" the vicar bellowed.

Now, she must go now. For a strangled second she considered kicking the horse and holding fast to the rope, letting it drag her to her death.

A faint glimmer of gray caught her eye—a fallen stone tangled in the tall grasses. She tugged, and the horse followed her to the stone. Fingers trembling, trying to ignore the pounding footsteps of the men of Kilkeel, she scrambled onto the stone and pulled the horse close.

"Grab the witch!" That was Donal Miller, whose advances she had spurned. "She's summoned her familiar. Stop her!"

Torchlight flared orange and red against the horse's glossy hide. It rolled its eye, the white showing, and whinnied, high and strange.

The men were almost upon her. With a cry, Eileen tangled her hands in the horse's mane and heaved herself up.

"A devil steed! Catch it!"

As if only waiting for her to mount, the horse leaped forward. Hemmed in by the men, it let out a shrill whinny and rose up, hooves flashing. The coarse mane cut into her palms as she clung there, half falling. She must not slide off.

The horse stamped and feinted. She heard the thunk of hooves on flesh, and two of the men cried out in pain. Then they were through, bowling past the grasping hands and shouted curses. Eileen held on as the jolting pace smoothed into a gallop and the cries of the men grew distant.

Slowly, her breath returned, the stark edge of her fear blunted. She had escaped—for now.

But what of Aidan? His name was a knife through her chest.

Did her true love still live?

When Young Sean, the village simpleton, had come to tell her that Aidan had fallen into a fever, she'd gathered her herbs and charms and raced to the cottage he shared with his mother. The widow had grudgingly opened the door, her eyes narrowed in animosity. Eileen had handed the woman the herbs for a soothing tisane. Then, as planned, Young Sean caused a racket, freeing the widow's chickens and chasing them about the yard.

The moment Aidan's mother went to tend her fowl, Eileen darted into the cottage and rushed to Aidan's side. His dark hair was plastered with sweat to his forehead, and he shivered uncontrollably beneath the blankets. She dropped a kiss on his brow, flinching at the heat rising off him. As she slipped the charm over his neck, his skin scorching her hands, he mumbled. A coughing spasm shook him. When it finished he lay in a stupor, breath wheezing in and out of his lungs.

"Peace, *mo chroi*," she said, then softly wove the words to send him into a healing sleep.

'Twas perilous, to take a person to that between place, but Aidan was gravely ill. Even a few minutes of that enchanted rest would do much to ease the sickness. Her charm would protect him while his body fought for life.

However, if he slept too long the connection would fray, then break. Aidan's soul would slip free, and death would bear him away into the West.

She began singing the song to draw him back.

"Eileen," Young Sean whispered at the window. "Reverend Dyer is coming, fetched by the widow. Go!"

Fear stabbed through her, but she must remain. She must finish the song and draw Aidan back to the waking world.

"Witch!" The vicar slammed into the cottage and grabbed her by the hair.

Her scalp burned and tears pricked her eyes from the pain, but she continued to sing. Nearly done. One more phrase...

Reverend Dyer clapped a hand over her mouth, his skin stinking of onions. To ensure her silence, he pinched her nostrils shut. Eileen clawed at his arm, her cries muffled by his meaty palm.

"Do not think to ensnare me with your spells," he said.

"Cast her out," the widow cried, her face twisted with hatred. "Keep her away from my son."

"We will do better than that." The vicar grasped Eileen's arm, his fingers digging into her flesh. "We will burn her."

Panic gave her the strength to whip her head free. "No! You must let me wake Aidan. The danger—"

"Aiee!" The widow had gone to Aidan's side and spied Eileen's charm. Now it dangled from her wizened fingers, broken.

"Proof," she spat. "This evil creature has had dark designs on my boy since the day she set eyes upon him. Look, she has cursed him."

Eileen writhed in the vicar's grasp.

"He will die," she gasped. "I must—"

"Out!" the widow shrieked. "Take her!"

"I'll lock her in my cellar until the pyre is built," Reverend Dyer said, shoving Eileen before him.

She stumbled over the threshold, then caught her balance. Though she knew it was hopeless, she broke free of his grasp, gathered up her skirt, and ran.

The vicar would have retaken her, but for Young Sean. He threw a chicken at the vicar's face, granting her precious time to pelt from the yard. He would likely be whipped for it, poor man.

Now Aidan's spirit was in terrible danger, spinning out into the mist. She must turn her mount back toward the village and wake her beloved, before it was too late.

The black horse galloped madly through the night, avoiding every obstacle with uncanny precision. The ground blurred beneath them with sickening speed.

"Turn," she cried, yanking at the coarse mane.

Once. Twice. Thrice, until her hands stung, her muscles burning with effort.

The horse did not respond. Eileen might as well be a gnat on its hide for all the notice it paid. For one mad moment, she considered throwing herself off. But the risk was too great. She could not return to save Aidan if she broke her leg, or worse.

Over the thud of her mount's hooves come the boom and crash of the surf.

Oh, no.

They were racing straight for the cliffs. Ahead, the stars were a veil reaching down past the horizon, disappearing into the dark Irish Sea.

"Stop! Please, stop." She pulled back with all her strength.

Her mount did not slow. Below them, the sea glimmered and heaved.

Eileen tried to release the horse's mane, but the strands were wrapped tightly around her fingers.

"Let me go!"

Heart pounding, she yanked. Her hands would not come free. She attempted to leap off, but her legs were bound fast to the horse's sides. She screamed and thrashed in panic, banging her elbows against the horse's shoulders.

They reached the cliff's edge.

Eileen's stomach churned as grass turned to empty air. Then they were falling, plummeting to their doom.

She found that, after all, she rather desperately wanted to live.

The water swirled restlessly beneath them. Eileen squeezed her eyes shut. She could not bear to watch the surface coming closer, closer. Or worse, the teeth of the hungry rocks, waiting to crush her body and spit it into the sea.

They hit the water with a crash. She gulped in a breath as the sea grabbed her legs, her arms, then closed relentlessly over her head.

She tightened her legs around the horse, the only warm thing in a world of shivering salt. Its withers bunched as it swam. They must be close to the surface. They *must*.

Lungs clenching with the need to breathe, she tipped her head back and opened her eyes, blinking past the sting and blur.

The wavering moon lapped the water, high overhead. The horse was not struggling toward the surface. Betraying its fey nature, it swam strongly downward, untroubled by the need for air. The surface glimmered, receding, and she could not free herself.

So, it was to be death by drowning after all.

Eileen released her breath in a silver stream of bubbles. They raced away from her lips, uncatchable. Crying, though she could not feel the tears, she laid her cheek against the water horse's neck. In another moment, she must gulp in the harsh tang of salt water. It would fill her, smother her—but at least it would be a quick end.

"You are brave, for a human." The words sounded in her head, the voice low and amused.

It was the uncanny creature she rode, speaking to her; or it was her own mind, conjuring up visions as she descended into her doom.

"Release me!" She aimed the thought at the black head bobbing through the water in front of her. "Or do you want a sodden corpse bound to your back for a blanket?"

She must breathe—her body demanded air. Against her will, Eileen's mouth opened and she gasped in the cold seawater. Choking, she doubled over on the horse's back as the water invaded the warmth of her throat and stopped her lungs.

Cold, and bitter, the weight of the sea lay heavy on her chest. She was dimly aware of silver spattering the surface above her head.

Then, with a thrust, the horse burst into the air, spray flying in a mighty gout. Eileen leaned over her mount's neck and heaved up water. She coughed and vomited, the agony in her lungs like a thousand stabbing pins.

Finally, teeth chattering and fingers numb, she pulled in a breath of sweet, sweet air. The horse bore her strongly through the heavy wash of the sea, no longer seeming intent on drowning her.

"Thank you," she whispered into its thick, black mane.

Her mount veered, swimming toward the rocky beach. Low, shadowed hills rose behind, and further down the coast the cliffs shone. Eileen coughed again and huddled against the horse's burning heat as the waves shoved against her.

"Do not thank me yet, human girl," came the reply. "The night is not ended."

The voice she'd heard beneath the water had not been her imagination. It held the echo of terror, a darkness she did not want to heed too closely.

"What are you?" she asked. "A kelpie?"

Even as she spoke the word, she knew it to be untrue. A kelpie would have taken her directly to the bottom of the sea, delighting in the drowning.

"Nay."

"Then you are a *púca*."

Her aunt had raised her on tales of the fair folk. Indeed, she should have realized her peril far sooner, but fear had blinded her in one eye, and hope in the other.

"Not just any *púca*. I am Tromluí, shredder of sanity, waker in the night. The longer you remain astride me, the more of your mortal soul you will lose. You should have chosen drowning, girl."

Eileen shuddered, cold to her marrow.

Better to be trapped on a kelpie's back. But no, she was astride the NightMare. She might live to see the dawn, but only as a madwoman, chased by stones and suspicion from village to village, cackling in the grip of her lunatic visions.

The mare strode up from the sea, hooves clattering against the stones of the beach. Overhead, the half moon shone, a bowl of whitest milk. At first the air seemed warm, but in moments Eileen's skin prickled with gooseflesh. Her hair hung in a soggy plait down her back and saltwater dripped into her face, stinging her eyes.

"Will you let me go?" she asked, despairing at the answer.

"Shall I?" The mare's voice was ice and midnight. "I might climb into the stars and release you there, high above the earth. For a short time you would know what it is to fly."

The copper taste of desperation flavored Eileen's mouth. Indeed, she rode a dreadful creature. But she was not dead. Not yet.

Possibilities, sharp and painful, brought her upright, her mind racing. It was perilous to bargain with the fey folk—beyond perilous—but this night was full of wild chance. Already she had escaped death by fire, then by water.

"I will remain upon your back," she said. "But I demand a boon."

The NightMare turned her neck, regarding Eileen with an eye the color of moonbeams.

"It amuses me to hear your request. What is it you desire?"

Eileen swallowed and forced her voice to steadiness. "Help me save my beloved, Aidan."

She had sent his soul spinning from his body, and she must return it. No matter how dire the consequences.

"This is no small thing you ask," the mare said. "There will be a price, mortal."

"I will pay," Eileen said recklessly.

The horse gave a high whinny. Through the clear, still air Eileen heard the ring of chimes.

"Our bargain is sealed," the mare said. "Now hold fast, for we have far to journey 'ere the sun rises."

The NightMare leaped forward, muscles bunching beneath Eileen's legs. The rocky clatter of the beach fell behind as the mare galloped up the long rise of hills, leaping low stone walls and skirting tangles of briars. Eileen ceased shivering as the night wind dried her dress and the NightMare's heat seeped into her body.

With every stride, something burned away in Eileen's blood. She could feel her earliest memories shred and tatter, but she clung tightly to every thought of Aidan.

Near the top of the highest hill, the mare slowed, her hoof beats no longer the frantic race of a pulse but the slow stutter of a dying heart. A dark maw gaped in the side of the hill; the doorway to a barrow grave. Starlight picked out the gray stones outlining the opening, but within was sheer blackness.

As if aware of their presence, a dank wind moved from the depths of that hole. Eileen, her hands freed from the NightMare's mane, covered her nose at the stench of old, dead things.

A large, flat stone scribed with spirals marked the threshold. The mare raised one hoof and brought it sharply down upon the stone. Bright sparks skittered, followed by a distant, booming echo. Twice more the mare knocked, and each time the sound grew closer, until it vibrated Eileen's very bones.

The air of the doorway wavered, like a pond stirred by the wind.

"We pass now into the Realm," the NightMare said. "You must remain on my back, no matter the sights you see or the danger you face. Are you ready?"

"Yes." The syllable floated up from Eileen's mouth, a fragile moth lost in the night.

The mare stepped forward. As they passed over the threshold, Eileen felt a terrible pain, as though angry wasps swarmed over her. She bit her lip and drove her fingernails into her palms, determined not to cry out.

Inside the barrow a pallid light spread, illuminating a stone-lined corridor with a corbelled roof. Rank fungus, pale and misshapen, grew along the edge of the flagstone floor and clumped in crevices on the walls. The stinging pain passed, but the clammy air lay heavy against her skin.

She cast a look over her shoulder, straining for one last glimpse of the night sky before the mare bore her deeper in. The stars were tiny pricks of light, washed dim by the moon. Then the opening was blocked by a shambling figure. The barrow light illuminated its skeletal form, ancient skin shriveled tight against the bone. Tattered rags hung from its limbs and a golden torc encircled its neck, marking it as a chieftain of yore.

From the skull-like face, empty sockets regarded her. Deep within lurked a spark of eldritch fire. The corpse opened its mouth in a soundless laugh.

Eileen pivoted away and leaned over the mare's neck, hoping her mount might hurry, but the NightMare continued her measured pace down the corridor. Another memory untangled itself from Eileen's mind, flared and burned down to ash.

The echo of hoof beats was soon muted by the slither and scrape of dozens of footsteps.

Throat dry, Eileen glanced behind her again, and smothered a scream. The dead followed, patient in their stalking. *Your beloved will soon join us,* their tongueless mouths seemed to say.

"No," she whispered.

The barrow amplified the sound, turning it into a long "*ohhh*" of despair.

"Quiet," the mare said. "Or do you wish to bring the *bean sidhe* for a visit as well?"

Eileen had been afraid before, but this slow, creeping terror held her nearly paralyzed. What if the NightMare chose to stop and allow the restless corpses to touch her with their rotting fingers? Would they merely stroke the resilience of her living flesh, or would they gouge great handfuls, feasting on her in a vain bid to regain their own vitality?

From the avid lights in their eye sockets, she very much feared the latter.

The mare bore her past an opening to her left, filled with the tang of blood and the sighing of the sea. Then an opening to her right, where noxious vapors swirled. Eyes stinging, Eileen buried her face in the crook of her elbow and tried not to inhale. Her heart beat hard and fast, knocking against the fragile prison of her ribs.

She did not need to look back to hear the following dead.

At length, her mount brought her to the central chamber. The pale light revealed crumbling treasures in the corners: rotted linens, tarnished silver set with dully gleaming gems, a golden goblet with one side crushed in as though it had been used as a weapon in some vicious fight.

In the center of the room lay a stone slab, and upon that slab...

"Aidan!"

She swung her leg over the mare's broad back, and only a shrill whinny of warning made her halt. Mere inches from dismounting, Eileen scrabbled back onto the horse. The dead hissed in disappointment behind her.

Hands trembling with impatience, she forced herself to be still as the NightMare stepped up to the slab.

Aidan lay as if asleep—or lifeless. His eyes were closed, and he was dressed in the raiment of an ancient king, with gold armbands encircling his biceps and thin circlet set upon his brow.

Digging her fingernails into her palms, Eileen watched his chest, straining for a sign of breath. At last, it rose in a long, slow inhalation. She slumped back, tears pricking her eyes.

"He lives," she whispered.

"Not for long," the mare replied. "You may step down now, but stay upon the marble verge. Should your foot touch the flagstones, you will be lost, and your love as well."

Eileen slipped down, placing her feet with care. She cupped Aidan's cheek.

"Wake, beloved," she said.

He made no response.

"Aidan, please wake."

She took his shoulders and shook him, gently at first, then harder as he continued his enchanted slumber. A kiss did not wake him, nor a shout. The echoes of her cry woke strange shadows that skittered across the ceiling, but Aidan slept on.

Throat choked with tears, she turned to the mare. "What shall I do?"

"He has dreamed too long, too far from the mortal world. *Tír na nÓg* calls to him strongly."

As if confirming the words, the dead lined up in the chamber stirred and rustled. The fallen chieftain took a step forward. Soon, Aidan would be among their number.

No. She refused to let him slip away.

Eileen gazed at his strong, beloved face. Her heart had long belonged to Aidan, since the first time she met him while picking herbs. He was brave and kind, and deserved a long, full life. And he was lost to her, now, whether she lived or died.

"Lie beside him on the slab," the mare said, "and take his hand."

The stone chilled her side, but Aidan's fingers were warm in hers. She watched the excruciatingly slow rise and fall of his chest. With one finger she traced the slope of his nose, the line of his jaw.

She must sing him back.

Pulling in a breath of grave-cold air, she began. His spirit had traveled far down the road to the West, and the simple waking chant would not be enough. It must be a call home, back to the human world.

Her voice filled the chamber as she sang the heat of summer, the call of the thrush, the taste of ripe berries on the tongue. Every warm, vital memory she once owned, she gave to him, spilling it forth. Each word carried more of her humanity out of the shell of her body and into his. The golden plait over her shoulder leached of color, the strands turning an eerie white.

Slowly, the dead began to dissipate, fading under that mortal onslaught.

Eileen sang of fresh-baked bread, a child's laughter. The humming feel of her hand clasped in his as they laughed together above the ripening fields.

Aidan's breathing sped, his cheeks flushed with warmth and color.

Three of the dead remained. Then two. Then only the chieftain. It stared at her, bony fingers wrapped around the golden torc at its neck. The cold malevolence of its will dampened the song, chilled the air to ice.

Shivers gripped her, but she raised her voice, defiant. This time, nothing would stop her.

The last syllables faded. The dead chieftain took another step forward, and Eileen caught her breath. Had she failed?

Then Aidan opened his eyes. Turning his head, he smiled at her so freely she felt her heart break in two. From that crack, the last of her mortal essence seeped. The dark form of the NightMare struck her hoof against the slab.

"Eileen?" Aidan asked, blue eyes clouded with confusion.

"Live well," she said. "Live long, and happily. I will never forget you."

"Why would you need to? I'm here, beside you."

She shook her head, her chest aching with sorrow. "There is no future between us, my love. We must part."

"No! Marry me, I don't care about—"

She stopped his words with her lips, a last kiss to carry her into the night. He tasted of apples and sunlight; everything now lost to her.

The dead chieftain howled. The mare's hoof boomed against the stone. And between one heartbeat and the next, Aidan was gone.

Weeping, Eileen bent her forehead to her knees. The breath of the NightMare was hot upon her nape and the stone beneath her wet with salt, with blood.

Yet she remained.

Wondering, she sat and lifted her hand, curling her long, wraithlike fingers. Had she a mirror, the reflection would bear little resemblance to the human features she had once called her own.

"The price has been paid," the NightMare said. "And I have a new rider. Come."

The far wall of the barrow clattered down to reveal a night rich with shadows and starlight, and a wild, fey wind that called them to ride.

Eileen-that-was rose from the stone, her body hollowed nearly weightless, freed of memory, freed of hope. She mounted the black horse.

Together, they flew forward into that sweet dark.

FIN

❧━━◦━━☙

About the Author: Growing up, Anthea Sharp spent most of her summers raiding the library shelves and reading, especially fantasy. She now makes her home in the Pacific Northwest, where she writes, plays the fiddle, and spends time with her small-but-good family. Find all of Anthea Sharp's books at her website: www.antheasharp.com

Anthea also writes historical romance under the pen name Anthea Lawson. Find out about her acclaimed Victorian romantic adventure novels at www.anthealawson.com.

THE QUEEN OF FROST AND DARKNESS
CHRISTINE POPE

"IT IS A PITY THAT YOUR BIRTHDAY FALLS IN MIDWINTER," said the Countess Anna Feodorovna Godunov as she pinned the last of the hothouse gardenias into the intricate curls of her daughter's honey-colored hair. "Still, I believe there will be a most respectable turnout."

"If you think so, Mama," Galina Andreevna replied demurely. Truth be told, if no one but Karel showed up, she would still count the evening a success. It seemed silly to be going to all this fuss to launch her into society, when everyone knew that the young Baron Karel Ivanovich Saburov and the daughter of Count Andrei Mikhailovich Godunov were as good as engaged. But she supposed the forms must be followed.

At least there had been a break in the harsh January weather, and three nights in a row where the sky was so clear that the stars sparkled like the diamonds in the lavish parure her mother wore to only the most formal occasions. Those diamonds glittered now at the Countess Anna's throat and ears and in the careful coils of her graying fair hair, which was discreetly supplemented by a good number of switches and false braids in order to achieve the required effect.

Galina had no need of such artifice; her own luxuriant tresses reached nearly to her waist. Indeed, her hair felt quite heavy pinned up as it was now, with carefully arranged curls falling about her shoulders and a tiara of pearls and diamonds tucked into the tall braided mass at the crown of her head. She thought she looked quite grown-up now, what with the hair and the evening gown that showed off her shoulders and just the slightest curve of her breasts. Yes, she and Karel had known each other since they were children, and were so intimate that they often could finish one another's sentences, but he had never quite seen her like this. Perhaps he would be so moved by her new elegance that he would ask for her hand in marriage right away; after all, she was eighteen now, and it was time to leave the schoolroom behind. Such an offer would be a fitting cap to the grand evening her parents had planned, and she thought they would be very glad of it.

Her mother made the minutest adjustment to Galina's tiara, then said, "It is time. We must be ready to receive our guests, and it is almost eight."

The countess swept Galina out of her rooms and down the wide marble staircase with its carved gilded balustrades, on past the foyer and into the grand salon. Despite the wintry weather outside, the room bloomed with more hothouse flowers—orchids and lilies and more gardenias, their perfume combining to quite make Galina's head swim. She did shake it, just a little, to clear her thoughts. Any more than that, and she risked dislodging her tiara.

She took the designated position between her father and her mother, and waited for the first guests to arrive. With any luck, Karel would be one of the early comers. He did tend to be somewhat punctual—as long as he wasn't delayed for some reason at his club. She often wondered what could go on in such places to make them so endlessly fascinating to men, but when she'd tried to ask her mother to enlighten her on the subject, she'd only gotten a curt reply that properly brought up young ladies shouldn't be troubling themselves with such matters.

But here was Karel, looking very fine as he took off his evening cloak and handed it to Gregor, the butler. Blue eyes dancing—and in such striking contrast to his coal-black hair—Karel bowed to her and her parents, then said, "Everything is quite *en fête,* is it not? Tell me I am not the first here, though."

"You are," the countess told him. "But you should not trouble yourself, Karel Ivanovich. Your promptness does you credit."

"And now you have saved everyone else from the shame of being the first to arrive," Galina put in, "which makes you quite the hero of the evening."

Both her mother and father shot stern looks in her direction for this piece of impertinence, but Karel only smiled and said, "Then as I am first to arrive, may I also claim the honor of the first dance?"

Of course Galina smiled and nodded, and her parents appeared relieved that he had taken no offense. Then the Count and Countess Stroganova appeared, followed by the Galitsyns, and the evening was off and running.

As it turned out, Karel claimed not only the grand march that opened the dancing, but also a waltz, and then the mazurka. Galina knew she should not monopolize her old friend for the evening, but really, he danced so beautifully, and looked so dashing in his tailcoat with the white rose fastened to his lapel, that she found it difficult to turn him down. And very likely they would be engaged by the end of the evening, or soon after, so what difference did one tiny bit of impropriety make? Certainly none of her other prospects for dance partners were half as appealing.

The mazurka had just ended, and Karel had departed to fetch her a glass of champagne, when a sudden hush fell over the company. Heads turned toward the entrance of the ballroom, and Galina peered past the assembled guests to see what could have drawn their attention so.

A woman stood in the entryway, framed by matched floral arrangements of trailing white orchids and elegant lilies. But she made the flowers appear as if wilted and yellow, so brilliant was her beauty. Her snow-fair hair was topped by an icy coronet of sparkling diamonds, and her flawless skin was equally as pale. She wore white worked in silver—something that should have been an egregious *faux pas,* as only the guest of honor should wear white at her *début,* but something in the woman's air seemed to say that she couldn't possibly be seen in any color but white.

With one elegant hand she reached out, and at once one of the servants hurried over to place a champagne flute in those long, kid-encased fingers. She smiled; her teeth were as white as her skin and hair.

"Who is that?" Galina whispered to her friend Ekaterina Borisovna. "Have you ever seen her before, Katya?"

"It's the Princess Tatiana Vasilievna Zakharin," Katya replied, looking flummoxed. "She has lived in Moscow for some time, but I heard Papa say something about her buying an estate not too far from St. Petersburg."

Galina couldn't quite understand why such a personage was attending her small coming-out party—but there was her father, forging forward and bowing over the unexpected arrival's hand. And if the Count Andrei Mikhailovich Godunov appeared rather red-faced and common next to the princess' lily-fair beauty, at least he had broken the tension somewhat by welcoming her to the party.

The crowd began to flow normally again, and Galina realized she had quite lost sight of Karel. Then she heard a throaty laugh, and looked over to see her friend amongst a crowd of other young men, all of whom had clustered around Tatiana Vasilievna like little bits of iron drawn to a magnet. Karel stared down into the strange woman's face with an intensity Galina quite disliked.

A tinkle of broken glass, as Princess Tatiana's glass of champagne slipped from her gloved fingers and crashed to the marble floor. She cried, "Oh, how clumsy of me!"

Karel winced, and blinked, and Galina watched as he raised one white-gloved hand to touch the corner of his left eye, as if something there had pained him. But then he smiled and extended the glass of champagne he held—the champagne which was supposed to have been Galina's—and said, "Accept this, Princess. And do not call yourself clumsy, for of course that is an impossibility."

Princess Tatiana smiled and accepted the glass, and Galina bit her lip and forced herself to look away. If Karel wanted to make a fool of himself over the woman, there was very little she could do about it. And really, the Princess must be quite a bit older than he, for all her beauty, and so he would look doubly a fool after she passed him by and bestowed her attentions on someone more equal in age and rank.

Still, seeing him smiling foolishly at the other woman made the blood in Galina's veins run just a little hotter, and she murmured an excuse to Katya and went over to Karel, who hovered a few inches from Tatiana Vasilievna's elbow.

"Karel, hadn't you promised me the next waltz?" she inquired, in tones she hoped were sweetly beseeching. It wouldn't do to look desperate, of course, even though she wished she could take him by the elbow and haul him away from the icy beauty's orbit.

He turned and stared down at her blankly, as if he had never seen her before. Then his eyes narrowed a bit, and he replied, "I think you have danced enough, Galya. Your forehead is shiny, and your nose quite red."

Galina raised a hand to her brow before she could stop herself. True, she had been dancing a good deal, and perhaps she had acquired a bit of a "glow," as her mother would have put it. But it was quite unacceptable for Karel to be mentioning such things. A gentleman never brought up a lady's shortcomings, whether real or imagined. As for her nose —

"And if we dance some more, I suppose I will get shinier and redder," she retorted. "I never noticed that such things bothered you before, Karel Ivanovich."

"Well, they do now," he said carelessly, and turned half away from her, his gaze resting on the Princess, perfect and pale between the men who were clustered around her. "I don't wish to dance."

The words "with you" remained unsaid, but they hung in the air between them. Hot tears started to Galina's eyes, but she blinked them away and raised her chin. She would not let him see how much he had upset her.

"Very well," she replied. "Anatoly Andreovich has been pestering me all night for a dance. I shall give him yours." And with that she flounced off in search of a surprised but very gratified Anatoly. That individual, although never someone Galina could take seriously as a suitor due to a deficiency in height and an even more deficient fortune, rose higher in her esteem because he at least seemed to have escaped the spell of Princess Tatiana. Or perhaps he had simply decided that if he could have no success with someone such as Galina Andreevna Godunov, then the Princess was as far out of his reach as the stars in the sky.

Whatever the case, Galina did not lack for partners for the rest of the night, although she did not have the only one she wanted. From the corner of her eye, she watched him dance with the Princess, or bring her champagne and caviar, or stand in a corner and chat with her much more intimately than their short acquaintance should have allowed, and through it all Galya felt a tightening in her stomach that had very little to do with the close-fitting rows of whalebone which encircled her slender waist. When the soirée finally ended in the small hours of the morning, she could only think of how differently she had thought the evening would turn out. She had thought Karel would finally speak, that she would have ascended these stairs with the touch of his first kiss thrilling her lips. Instead, she sat mute as her maid Oksana undid the laces on her gown and then on her corset, and helped her into her nightdress and brushed out the heavy masses of her hair before braiding it for the night.

Galina said nothing through all these ministrations; she feared that if she opened her mouth to speak, a sob would escape instead. So she sat, tight-lipped, and avoided Oksana's questioning eyes, until she could finally go to bed and put the dreadful day behind her.

The next morning—or rather, the next afternoon, as Galina did not rise from her bed until the morning was quite spent—Oksana was unable to hold her tongue any longer, and informed Galina that apparently Karel Ivanovich had had the most dreadful quarrel with his mother, and had gone riding off late that morning to goodness knows where and hadn't come back. The Dowager Baroness had not attended Galina's coming-out party, as the older woman suffered from a degenerative condition that had left her quite unable to walk, but her condition apparently had not prevented her from learning everything there was to be learned, including how dreadfully he had treated Galina Andreevna and how he had fawned over Princess Tatiana, who was a horrid woman who'd broken hearts right and left in Moscow and had apparently only moved on to St. Petersburg because she desired fresh sport.

Even the news that Baroness Natasha Alexandrovna Saburov supported Galina and not her son did little to lift Galya's spirits, as, after all, it mattered very little what the Baroness said or thought; it was not she who would ask for Galina's hand, but her son. And with the Princess now on the scene, it seemed as if that day would never come.

"What's more," Oksana said in confiding tones, as she cleared away Galina's supper tray, "I've heard it said that the Princess is not a real woman at all, but a sorceress who's sold her soul for beauty and wealth. So no wonder she bewitched all those poor young men."

Galina wished it were that easy. Better to blame Karel's defection on diabolical intervention than on the simple sordid fact that he preferred another woman to her. She had no doubt that he had gone to the Princess, or at least somewhere near her property. Perhaps they had eloped. He had certainly seemed besotted enough to do something that foolish.

At this dreary thought, the tears finally did come, dropping down Galina's cheeks and falling onto the patterned silk of her quilted dressing gown. She had told her parents she was over-tired and quite indisposed, using that as an excuse to stay in her rooms. No doubt they had guessed the real reason for her hiding herself away, but as they tended to be indulgent, they had not asked any questions or demanded that she join them for supper.

"Oh, my poor lamb," said Oksana, who produced a handkerchief and proceeded to blot the tears from Galina's cheeks.

"It's no small thing, to have a witch steal your young man away from you."

"He's not my young man," Galina replied. She took the handkerchief away from Oksana and wiped her eyes, then balled up the piece of linen in her lap. "And if he thinks the Princess is so fascinating, he can have her."

"What he thinks can't be trusted. One only had to look at him to see that he was bewitched."

"And how would you know that? You weren't at the ball."

Oksana's full cheeks flushed a little. "As to that, I was watching from the landing upstairs. I saw him leave—with her. And shouldn't I know that young man's expressions almost as well as I know yours, seeing as he's been almost a part of the family for both your lives?"

Galina, who had hidden herself away in the smaller salon with Katya and a few other sympathetic friends, had not known that Karel had escorted Tatiana Vasilievna from the party. Once again she felt her stomach clench. Perhaps Oksana was right. After all, what other explanation could there be for Karel's odd behavior, save that a witch had somehow cast a spell over him?

"And what if he is bewitched?" she demanded. "What on earth do you propose I do about it?"

"Why, you go get him, and fetch him back. Black magic can't prevail against true love. And he loves you. Everyone knows that."

Everyone except Karel, apparently. But Galya had felt sure of that love up until last night, and so had her family and friends. It had to be a spell that had altered him so, some dark magic that had erased the pure love she and Karel shared. If only she could see him, be alone with him, she might be able to remind him of how their spirits had always seemed to be one, even if the connection between them had not yet been sanctified by the church.

"And how am I to go, when you know I never leave the house alone?" Even as she asked the question, some small part of her quailed. For it was one thing to be brave in her own rooms, in the company of the maid who had known her since she was an infant, and quite another to go out into the wide world and confront a witch.

"As to that, we shall go out together, saying you are calling on your friend Ekaterina Borisovna. No one will think anything odd in such a visit—indeed, your parents would think it only natural that you would seek the comfort of a friend after suffering such a shock as you did last night."

So it was settled, and Galina allowed Oksana to help her into her best walking-out suit, the cinnamon wool one that went so well with her honey-colored hair and brown eyes. The Princess' eyes, she recalled, had been a glinting pale gray, almost silver. Quite otherworldly, as one might expect from a witch and a consort of the Devil.

The weather still held fine, although a line of dark clouds to the northeast seemed to signal that the odd extended clear spell would soon be over. Oksana had Gregor call a hired carriage for Galina; luckily, the Countess was also visiting that afternoon, and so no one saw anything untoward in the daughter of the house and her maidservant setting forth in a hired hack.

They drove to the edge of town, for the intelligence Oksana had gleaned indicated that the Princess' estate lay some miles to the south of the city. Where exactly, no one seemed to know, but Galina supposed it was better to have a direction than nothing at all.

The driver would take them no farther than the outskirts of the city. Oksana began to scold him, but Galina laid a hand on her arm. "We cannot ask the man to drive all over the countryside. He has shortened my journey, at least."

"*Our* journey, you mean."

Galina shook her head. A feeling had been growing all during the ride here, the knowledge that she must go to seek Karel alone. Knights errant did not set out on their quests accompanied by maidservants, after all. "No, Oksana. You must stay here, and let my parents know what I have done if—" She hesitated; while she somehow knew what she must do, still that didn't keep her from being afraid. In all her life she had never been alone, and now she proposed to set forth by herself, into the dark and the storm. It was madness, but as surely as she had known Karel loved her, she knew she could only save him if she did so alone.

"But miss—"

"My mind is quite made up, Oksana." Galina spoke firmly, and pressed Oksana's hands. "Take the carriage back to the house, and try not to be seen. The longer my parents don't know I am gone, the better. And don't you dare let them blame you, whatever they might say. You must tell them that I ordered you back home."

Apparently Oksana didn't quite know what to do with such a suddenly masterful and commanding mistress, for she hesitated, and wrung her hands, then said, "If you think that is how it must be—"

"I do. Now go, for the driver is becoming impatient."

So he was; he shifted from foot to foot and scowled at the two of them, and cast a jaundiced eye at the lowering skies overhead. Galina fished a coin from her reticule and pressed it into the driver's hands. He pocketed it at once and climbed up onto his seat without giving either her or Oksana a second look. It seemed quite clear that he was ready to drive off without either one of them if they tarried much longer.

So she opened the door to the carriage. Oksana paused, then gave her charge one final glance before heaving a resigned sigh as she climbed into the passenger compartment. "How I will ever explain this—"

"Don't bother," Galina replied. "I'll explain it all myself, when I come home."

And with that she shut the door and turned away from the carriage, facing into the bitter wind. True, she wore her new mink-lined cape and its matching hat and muff, and even her hands inside the muff were covered in warm fur-lined gloves, but all that did not seem much of an shield against the biting blast from the east. However, she had decided her course, and she would follow it, no matter what happened.

At least since it had not snowed recently, the road was easy enough to navigate. From time to time a carriage or wagon would rattle by, more often than not with its occupants giving her increasingly puzzled stares, but Galina kept on, following the route as it wound away to the south and east.

She tried to tell herself that it was not so very cold, not really, but after a while she only put one foot in front of the other because she knew that was what she had to do, not because she could really feel those feet anymore. The light began to fade, and then the first snowflakes gently started to fall—one by one at first, and then in flurries, and finally in billows of white. By that time Galina had given up any pretense of following the road, or even of knowing in what direction she was headed. She only blundered forward, hands clenched inside her muff, her entire being focused on Karel. The thought of him would be enough to keep her alive.

So intense was the storm, and so complete the darkness, that she was shocked to hear a female voice cry out suddenly, "Hold!"

Galina stopped, and saw the flare of a torch bobbing through the white-shot darkness. Her heart began to pound. Had the icy princess discovered her quest?

The voice had sounded far rougher than the sweetly chill voice of Tatiana Vasilievna, however, and the personage who revealed herself now was obviously no princess. Rough furs muffled her form so that one could barely discern her sex, and the tip of the nose that protruded between the fur hat she wore pulled low on her brow and the muffler which covered most of her chin had a distinct spot of soot on it.

"Who goes there?" demanded this apparition. She held her torch up high and gazed into Galina's face. The strange woman—or girl, as something in her shape seemed to suggest that she was not much older than Galya, if that—cocked her head to one side and said, "Are you mad?"

"No," Galina answered, although she wondered even as she made the denial if perhaps she had gone mad, to push on into the heart of the storm after a man who perhaps did not love her as much as she thought he did.

"Hmm," said the rough young woman. "I think you must be mad to be out in this."

"You are out in it as well, aren't you?"

The stranger appeared to consider. "True...but I was on my way home, and I know that you live nowhere around here."

"No, I don't," Galina admitted. "I'm seeking the palace of the Princess Tatiana Vasilievna Zakharin."

"The Queen of Frost and Darkness?"

Somehow Galina knew that this Queen and the Princess must be the same person. For how else could one describe a woman of such outward icy beauty, yet with such a black heart beating within her perfect breast?

She nodded, and the young woman said, "And I believe I know why. Only this morning a fine young man went riding to the Princess' estate and never came back. Someone you know, I presume?"

Galina nodded, but found herself quite unable to reply, for her teeth had begun to chatter so violently that she could not get a word out. The stranger cocked her head and said, "I know the way. But we cannot stay out in this—let me take you to my home, and we shall see if the morning gives us better weather."

To this suggestion Galya could only nod, and she bent her head in thanks. The young woman took her by the arm and led her off into the swirling snow. How she could possibly find her way in this, Galina did not know, but after what felt like an eternity but was most likely less than a quarter-hour, they blundered out of the storm and into a cave opening half hidden by a stand of dark pines.

Inside were a score or more of men, ruffians and robbers by the look of them, and Galya shrank back against her guide, quite certain she had been led astray on purpose. But the young woman called out, "I am here with a friend. You would do well to look elsewhere!"

And the men turned away, and Galina found herself led to a smaller chamber outfitted with quite a warm bed piled high with furs, and a brazier that served to take some of the chill from the air.

"You—you are very kind," she stammered, and the strange young woman only smiled and replied,

"As to that, I expect payment for my assistance. That muff you carry is quite fine; I think that should do nicely."

Something in Galina quailed at the thought of giving up the muff, which had protected her hands so well, but perhaps the storm would have blown itself out by morning, and she would no longer need it quite so badly. Besides, what was a muff, compared to shelter and the prospect of finding Karel on the morrow?

"Of course," she said, "but I will give it to you only after you have brought me to Tatiana Vasilievna's palace."

"Well enough," replied the young woman with a grin. "It's good that you have some spirit. You will need it."

And with that she settled herself into her bed, and gestured for Galina to join her. They slept, safe and warm in the heart of the robbers' stronghold.

The next morning they set out for the Princess' palace, which Sasha the robber girl claimed lay only a few miles off. The storm had moved on, and the countryside was blanketed in white, dazzling under a pale morning sun. Galya squinted against the glare as best she could and trudged along after her unlikely companion. An hour or so later, they reached a border of dark hedges half-buried under the snow, which Sasha said marked the border of Tatiana Vasilievna's property.

"And here is the gate," the robber girl said, and produced a rather fine set of lock picks from her belt. Within a moment she had dispatched the heavy padlock that held the gate shut.

"You are very clever," Galina said quite honestly. It seemed quite a fine skill to have, and she smiled as she pulled the muff from her hands and gave it to Sasha. "You have earned this, and more."

"That I have. But I shan't leave you here—let me take you to the back door."

How Sasha had gained this knowledge, Galina didn't know and felt sure she couldn't ask. But she followed the other girl around the outskirts of the house, which took some time, as it truly was a palace, and not just a fine country house such as the dacha Galina's family stayed in every summer. There seemed to be no one about, not even a footman or a scullery maid. As they approached the rear door, which was covered by a small portico, an odd little flurry of snow rose up from the ground and surrounded the two girls. For a few seconds, Galya felt as if she might be blinded by the driving flakes, but she murmured the words of the Lord's Prayer under her breath, and asked the Holy Father to protect her and Sasha. As quickly as it had risen up, the snow fell to the ground.

Sasha stared at her with wide, dark eyes. "I thought you were mad," she said, "but perhaps you are only touched by God."

Was it God's hand that had guided her so far, which had brought her here so far unharmed? Galina thought that more likely than simple blind luck, but she merely lifted her shoulders. "I cannot say. I only know that I must bring Karel back to me. If God has guided me so far, then let us pray that He will continue to do so."

Her companion made a clumsy sign of the cross on her breast, and then she pushed the door inward. "You first. I fear I do not have the same protection that you do."

Galina did not bother to argue. After all, this was her quest; Sasha was only an unexpected—if very welcome—attendant. She stepped inside, the robber girl at her heels, and made her way into the Queen's stronghold.

It was a very elegant palace, all marble and gilt, but so cold within that Galya's breath hung as clearly in the air as it had outside. She did not begrudge Sasha the muff she now carried, for the other girl had earned it and more. Still, it was so very, very cold.

There was no movement, no sign of life. The two girls peered into room after room, from salons and drawing rooms to dining rooms and libraries, and yet they did not see Karel, nor Tatiana Vasilievna, nor any retainers or servants.

Perhaps this wasn't the Princess' palace at all, but rather the home of some unknown Count or Prince, retired for the winter months to the sunnier climes of Italy or Greece. Galina would not rebuke Sasha, not when the girl had been such help, but she worried that somehow she had guided them to the wrong house.

But then they passed through a great hall, where an icily perfect portrait of Princess Tatiana Vasilievna stared down at them from the damask-hung wall, and beyond that hall two enormous double doors yawned into a space which let forth an exhalation so icy that Galya was sure it had come straight from the North Pole itself. She shivered, even as Sasha sent her a questioning, frightened glance.

Somehow Galina knew she must go forward alone. She held up a hand, indicating that Sasha should wait in the hall, beneath the Princess' pale, freezing stare.

"No worries," Sasha said at once, and sat herself down on the marble floor, hands still tucked improbably into the muff.

It is for Karel, Galya told herself. She held the image of her friend in her mind, a stray memory from a summer sunlit day, when his eyes as he smiled down at her had put the blue of the sky to shame. He had brought her wildflowers that day, in bunches so large she could barely wrap her fingers around them. And it was the memory of that warmth which held her up as she strode forward into the freezing chamber.

The floor was ice, stretching before her as smooth as the rink below the walls of Novodevichy Convent. At its very center sat a chair so grand it could only be called a throne, carved all of wood dark as ebony, with an ice-blue cushion. And below the chair, crouched on the ice, Galina saw the dark, huddled form of a man.

She knew at once that man was Karel, and so she ran out onto the ice, even though her boots slipped and caught and threatened to throw her to her feet with almost every step. But she would not give up now, not when she was so close.

At the very end she did stumble and fall, but she merely slid along the icy floor until she was only a few inches away from Karel. Even then he did not look up, but kept sifting pieces of what looked like thin shards of ice, setting them together very much as one would the pieces of a puzzle.

"Why, Karel," Galina said. Somehow his odd concentration on such an inconsequential task frightened her more than the blizzard the night before, more than the robbers who had crowded the cave where Sasha lived. "Whatever are you doing?"

Finally he lifted his head and stared at her, although she saw no flicker of recognition in his eyes. "She said I should do this, that if I could spell the proper word I might be hers for all eternity. But I cannot find all the pieces, as you can see."

Galya's heart was wrung then, for she saw at once that he truly was bewitched. "Who said that? Princess Tatiana Vasilievna?"

He nodded slowly, still watching her with those uncomprehending eyes.

"Dear Karel," Galina began. She hesitated, trying to decide what on earth she could say to break the spell, to have him truly see her once again. At least he was looking at her, instead of those incomprehensible pieces of ice scattered around him.

Then it seemed so very clear. She must do the one thing that would remind him of warmth, of light and sunshine.

Of love.

She leaned forward, and carefully removed the gloves from her hands. Still he watched her, even as she raised her hands, now bare to the cold, and placed them on either cheek.

His skin felt scarcely warmer than the frigid air of the chamber around them, but it was enough. It had to be.

She drew closer, then laid her mouth against his.

At first he did not move, but only sat there, immobile, as if he had finally succumbed to the freezing air. Slowly then, so slowly that at first Galina was not sure she hadn't imagined it, his lips pressed against hers. And he lifted a hand, and another, and then it was him touching her face, his mouth exploring hers as a heat she could never have imagined flooded through her body.

"Galina," he choked. His eyes shone with tears, and she watched as one slid down his cheek, glinting in the pale light that slanted through the chamber's tall windows. On that cheek flashed something diamond-bright, something she knew was not a tear.

She reached out and caught that glittering speck, felt it sharp upon her fingertips. A drop of blood welled up against her skin, shockingly red in the white glare of the ice-filled room. *So that is how you caught him,* she thought, and deliberately bent down and wiped her finger against the icy floor, leaving a thin trail of red against the white.

"Will you come with me?" she asked.

Karel blinked. "Of course," he said, and got to his feet. He extended a hand to her. "How did I come to be here?"

If he truly did not remember, then Galina saw no reason to task him for his defection. It had not been his fault, after all, but the black spells of the woman Sasha had called the Queen of Frost and Darkness. "A mote in your eye," she said lightly. "But it is gone now. Are you ready to go home?"

"Yes," Karel said at once. Then he paused, and looked down at her with eyes that once again recalled summer and a warmth she had almost forgotten. "That is, if I can share that home with you. Would you, Galya?"

It was not the proposal she had imagined, back in her rooms as she prepared for her coming-out ball. She had thought he would go down on one knee and say something exceedingly flowery. But that didn't mattered. Nothing mattered, save the look in his eyes.

"Yes, Karel Ivanovich," she replied. "Yes, I would."

FIN

❦

About the Author: A native of Southern California, Christine Pope has been writing stories ever since she commandeered her family's Smith-Corona typewriter back in the sixth grade. She is the author of the bestselling Witches of Cleopatra Hill, Tales of the Latter Kingdoms, and Djinn Wars series, among others. She now lives in Santa Fe, New Mexico, with her husband

and the world's fluffiest dog. For information on all her books, including her novel-length fairytale retellings, Tales of the Latter Kingdoms, visit her website: www.christinepope.com.

BONES

YASMINE GALENORN

TEAL, PRINCESS OF THE WOODLAND KINGDOM, STARED out of her bedroom window into the early morning light. A quiver of excitement ran through her breast. She gazed over the broad forest of oak and maple that stretched for miles around the castle. An ancient wood it was, and filled with secrets and legends and ghosts, but she knew every inch of the copse, had traveled every pathway, and yet, the glen always called her back.

Today was her birthday, she was almost a grown woman, and this time next year would see her taking her place beside her parents, learning how to be Queen when it came time for her to ascend to the throne. She would put away her childhood and face the mantle of her duty. It was the way—it was always the way.

Seventeen years she had passed in this castle, under the watchful eyes of her parents. Seventeen years she had listened and learned and obeyed their every command, as a good daughter should. Today, however, she longed to race into the woods, unescorted, to romp through the trees and find...find... she didn't know what she wanted to find. An adventure, perhaps? Something wild and free, untamed? After all, one turned seventeen only once in their lives.

Teal turned back to her dressing table and brushed her long, flowing hair. Golden as sunlight, golden as the shimmering necklace that embraced her throat, her hair streamed down her back to kiss her waist. A beautiful contrast to her sea green eyes. Her mother had named her Teal because of the color of her eyes. They were like sea foam, her mother said—wild cresting waves that never rested.

Teal dressed quickly in a billowing green skirt and a light silken chemise, then wrapped a shawl threaded with silver strands around her shoulders. Today she would go wandering. The castle was silent, still slumbering, and she craved to feel the wind kissing her face, the taste of summer heat on her tongue.

Teal had never been beyond the borders of her land before. Her parents said when she became Queen she would take journeys and meet neighboring heads of state, and find a prince to rule by her side. But there was plenty of time for that, and she was not to worry herself about other places and other peoples. Their kingdom was safe and peaceful, but danger lurked beyond the borders, and her parents repeatedly warned her of venturing too far.

Usually, she acquiesced, as she always did, and contented herself with walking through the forests and picking flowers and occasionally listening to the King and Queen dispense their wisdom and justice from the Court, bedecked with honeysuckle and roses.

*But today...*today she wanted more than a garden journey, more than a chaperoned excursion into the fields to gather flowers. She passed through the silent corridors, aware of the heavy gray stones surrounding her. They bore the weight of her family lineage, and every step she took through the echoing halls reminded her of her duty, her heritage, her life to be.

Two guards watched over the mammoth doors that allowed passage in and out of the castle walls. They bowed as she lingered at the gate.

"Lady, let us call an escort for you," one said, but she shook her head softly.

"No, I will go unescorted today." She flashed them a smile, trying to sooth their worries. "This is my birthday. This is my wish, my will. Be kind and do not wake my parents, they need their sleep and I am only seeking a breath of fresh air and a walk in the sunlight."

The guards looked at one another. Her will was law and there was nothing they could do. They nodded and backed away, allowing her free passage.

"She is beautiful," one of the men whispered behind her.

"That she is, but child-like still. The King and Queen do not see that she is almost a woman. They have not prepared her for life. I wonder that they allow her to go walking about alone like this," the other replied.

The first guard shook his head. "No one in the land would hurt the Princess."

As she meandered through the forest, Teal thought about what the guards had said. Truth be told, they were right. No one within the forest kingdom would even think of raising a hand to her. She was their prize, their beloved jewel who shone brilliantly in the dark paths of the wooded glen. Even the poorest farmer knelt before her without a grumble.

The Princess looked at all the paths spread out before her. She had explored far along each and each today seemed too tame, too familiar. Startled, she realized that she knew the Kingdom as well as her parents, her long walks had given her a fine perspective on the borders of the land.

"So I have been learning something," she whispered. "But where should I go today?"

A rustle in the grass caught her ear. There, between the trees, was a narrow path that she had not seen before. She chewed on her finger for a moment. Had she simply overlooked it, or had it had magically appeared?

But magic was rare in the Kingdom these days. The Dragon had long ago been slain by a brave knight who married her grandmother's aunt, and as the land grew more peaceful, the witches had less inclination to use their powers for anything besides bits of healing and entertaining small children.

She must have overlooked it, she finally decided. Her parents would not like her traversing an unknown road by herself. They would fret and worry, but then it occurred to her that in another year, she would be of age. She should start making some of her own decisions now, as much as she valued her mother's wisdom and her father's heart. Indecision warred within her. She wanted to explore, to run free like a farmer's daughter. She knew her duty, but for one day, one hour, she wanted to cast it off and be truly seventeen, free and full of fun and not caring about what dangers might lie on the trail.

Finally, unable to resist, she hiked her skirt up on one side and knotted it to keep it from dragging on the ground, then set off down the narrow path. She had been walking for over an hour when she noticed that the trees were thinning out. The light made her wince, and she shaded her eyes as she picked carefully through the briars and brambles creeping out of the soil.

The forest soon opened out onto a wide plain, scorched and barren, with soil so compacted that it cracked and peeled upwards like old paint on a fresco. Teal blinked against the glare of the sun and an uneasy feeling crept over her, as though she were gazing upon something she was perhaps not meant to see. She searched her memories for any mention her parents might have made of a neighboring land like this, but nothing came to mind. What should she do? Go home? She yawned, tired and hot, as she realized how sore her feet were.

"Maybe I should rest a bit before I turn back," she said to herself, suddenly wanting the comfort of a voice. She looked around, hoping to see a stream she could sit by, or a tree she could sit under.

But there was no water here, and the trees had grown dark and twisted. Feeling more uncomfortable by the minute, Teal shifted her weight from foot to foot. The heat from the wastes filtered up through her shoes and burned the delicate soles of her feet. She decided to turn back now, before she grew any more uncomfortable. She turned back, but the path had disappeared under a tangle of wild matted brambles and thorn-bushes.

"It's not possible," she whispered. "It can't just have vanished."

Teal paced along the borders of the wood, but could find no inroad. She tried to ford her way through the undergrowth, but the foliage was so thick and thorny that her arms and legs were soon tattooed with long, bleeding scratches. Finally, she gave up and turned towards the barren land.

The King and Queen had expressly forbade her to cross over the borders of the Woodland Kingdom, but there was nothing else she could do. Perhaps someone along the way could help her find her way home. She began walking across the barren land, wincing as the relentless sun burned against her skin. If only she had brought some water or some food. Her throat parched, her stomach empty, she wept as she forced herself along. She wept out of fear, wept out of anger and hunger and wept because today was her birthday, and birthdays should never be dismal or frightening.

"Am I going to die?" The thought of death flashed through her mind, and for the first time in her life, Princess Teal was afraid. She had never questioned her own mortality. She toyed with the thought, wincing as she realized if she died, it would mean no coronation, no balls or games or laughing children calling her Mama. Her hand fluttered to her throat. She had never seen anyone die and didn't know what to expect. But princesses didn't die in faerie tales—she knew that much. Surely someone would come along to help her. But until then, she realized she was on her own, lost in the middle of a desert with neither shade nor water and no one knew where she was.

"There's nothing for it, I have to buck up and survive until either some prince, or my parents come along." Teal strained her eyes, searching the horizon for any signs of life, but nothing stirred in the parched, arid land surrounding her. Weary from both the heat and fear, she decided to seek shelter behind a large rock about fifty yards away. It offered shade from the burning sun, and she lie down behind it, grateful for the respite. Within moments, she slipped into unconsciousness.

Karamak the Dark, King of Wraithland, led his band of riders out onto the burning plains that separated the land of the dead from the land of the living. He was stately in form, with a strong silver aura enveloping the bones of his body, and his eye sockets glowed with opaline flames. A silver crown bedecked with sapphires and opals sat atop his skull, and a long purple cloak flowed gently from the outline of silver surrounding his shoulder blades.

He led his band of riders atop skeletal horses which, during life, had been their faithful mounts. They traveled across the great plains as they so often did in search of wanderers who had strayed too far from the land of the living. Some they would send home, no worse for the wear than a minor scare. Others, in whom the spark of life was but a faint glimmer, they took back to Wraithland. The King enjoyed this diversion, it gave him satisfaction and occupied the unending days that passed in the land of immortality.

They were out this day, riding, when one of his companions pointed towards a boulder that sat against the floor of the valley. Behind the rock lay a young woman. She was beautiful and radiant, and life bloomed full within her, still, and her hair gleamed like spun gold. Karamak stared at her, enchanted.

"She is like a spring morning," he murmured. He motioned to his riders and they gently picked her up and began to head towards the land of the living.

"No," the King said, wind whistling through his mouth to become the breath of his voice. "No," he said again as his riders looked back at him, waiting.

"But she is young and still filled with life. We should return her to her land. No doubt her parents will be worried."

Karamak swung off his mount and strode over to them, his purple cloak fluttering behind. He looked down into the woman's sleeping face. Blood coursed through her veins, plumping her cheeks and filling them with a rose blush. Breath whispered from between her full pink lips. Karamak silently reached out one bone-white finger and stroked back the golden strands that covered her face.

"Bring her," he said quietly. "Bring her back to the castle."

"But she is alive, Your Highness," one of the riders said.

"I know," Karamak answered. "I know."

When Teal awoke, she found herself in bed in a dark hall. She was nude under a scratchy blanket that irritated her flesh. Confused, she sat up, propping herself on her elbows, and surveyed the room around her. The furniture was stark, heavy and dark with age and the pillows and bedclothes were old and tattered, though at one time they had been exquisitely embroidered with gold threads.

Teal pushed herself out of bed, wincing as her feet hit the floor. She pulled them up again and examined the blistered soles. Her shoes and clothes were nowhere to be seen.

She was about to knot one of the sheets around her shoulders into a tunic when the door opened. Teal held her breath, expectantly. Into whose kingdom had she had unwittingly stumbled? And then, she forgot her nakedness as fear rose up in her throat.

A skeleton, surrounded by pale blue light that took the rough shape of a body, entered the room, carrying a tray. On the tray was a bowl of fruit, withered and sickly. The creature set the fruit on the nightstand and turned to the Princess.

"You've woken," it said, and its words were like the pale wind. "The King will be relieved to hear that you survived your misfortunate trip."

Teal bit back a scream. She was a princess and that, in itself, meant she had to show courage. She straightened her shoulders, and quietly draped the sheet around her like a cloak. One look at the fruit told her she would never eat it. A worm burrowed out of the apple and her stomach lurched.

"Who are you? Where am I? Can you help me find my way home?"

The creature seemed reluctant to answer.

She tried again. "My parents will be worried about me. I am Princess Teal of the Woodland Kingdom." She shivered, her skin rippling in the chill. The hall was as cold as the desert plain had been hot. "Where are my clothes? I demand my clothes."

"Climb back under the bed covers. Your things will be brought to you soon. I will tell the King you've woken and he will answer your questions." When the creature spoke, Teal could hear the faintest hint of disapproval in its voice. "Eat, if you will." Then, it turned and left the room.

The Princess stared at the molding fruit for a moment, then looked around the room. A window near the bed hid behind shutters so old they had cracked, and at her touch, they fell to the dust-laden floor with a crash. She jumped back, holding her breath, but in the silence that followed she realized no one had heard. She looked down onto the plain below. Twilight made it difficult to pierce the shadows that surrounded the castle. She tossed the fruit out of the window, not wanting to appear ungrateful by leaving it on the plate.

There was a pitcher of water on the armoire and she raised it to her lips but stopped when the smell of vinegar rose to cloud her senses. The liquid was black, briny, and she quietly set the pitcher back in place without taking a single drop. She had barely crawled back into bed when the door opened.

The King. She had expected a real King, a flesh-and-blood liege and her disappointment washed over her like cold rain. A flash of bones and silver light. What nightmare had she stumbled into?

"So you are a Princess?" he asked, striding into the room. "I am Karamak, King of this land."

Teal looked once into the opaline eyes for a moment, searching for any sign of humanity, and then hung her head. "Yes," she whispered. "I am Princess Teal, from the Woodland

Kingdom. I was out for a walk and seem to have gotten lost. Today's my birthday," she added helplessly.

Karamak settled himself on the bed next to her. She drew away, pulling the covers up to her chin. When he spoke, there was a new gruffness in his voice. "You should know better than go walking unattended."

"In my kingdom, no one would hurt me," she countered, not liking his tone. He was far too close for comfort. She straightened her back, summoning up what dignity she could. "We are a peaceful people. Our last Dragon was slain years ago and the brave knight married my grandmother's aunt. I had no reason to fear walking alone."

"Then yours is an unusual land. Have you no murderers? No rogues?" He spit out the question so harshly that the Princess pulled back against the headboard.

She looked at him through half-closed eyes and said, "Once in a while those things happen, but it's rare and usually strangers are involved. My parents deal with the criminals quickly and efficiently, as will I when I am Queen."

Karamak stood, towering over her. He looked at her with a fierceness that made her quiver. She had seen the same look, that same flash of light, in the eyes of a few men in the Woodland Kingdom and it always made her feel appraised, weighed and measured, and tied up with a pretty bow. She couldn't help but notice that the silver light of his aura burned fiercely near his pelvis.

He leaned over her and with one jointed ivory finger, pointed at her. "Princess Teal of the Woodland Kingdom, you are a lovely woman. You should not cover yourself in shame, but display yourself with pride."

"I want my clothes," Teal cried out, angry now and blushing. She wanted to slap away his bony hand but was too afraid of what he might do.

Karamak nodded as he started towards the door. "I will order them brought to you immediately."

Somewhat mollified, Teal rearranged the covers her and asked, "Are all your people like you?"

He paused and his voice was puzzled when he spoke. "What do you mean?"

"Are all of you...bones without flesh?"

"Oh," he said. "Yes, we live in bone and fire instead of bone and flesh."

"What land is this?" Teal called out but Karamak had vanished out the door. Within moments, the servant who had brought the fruit returned with Teal's clothing and helped her dress but would answer no questions.

The second day, Karamak again visited Teal. They discussed her mother and father and her kingdom and how much she loved and missed the wooded glen. She hoped that he might help her find her way home but every time she approached the subject he waved her fears away.

"I've sent a message to your family," he said. "They know you're safe."

Teal did not trust the skeletal King and she hated the dark castle with its shadows and perpetual gloom. No morning light showed through the windows, only the cloud and mist-shrouded plain through which she could barely see. Her heart ached for the sound of her mother's voice. Once more, she tossed the fruit out of the window, but gnawed on the stale bread until she began to choke and was forced to swallow the brackish water, which set her stomach on fire. After that, she decided not to eat or drink at all.

When he left her the second day, he asked, "Is there anything I can give you?"

"A safe passage home," was all she said.

Karamak turned and left the room in silence, bolting the great door behind him.

On the third day he told her he loved her. "Stay with me," he pleaded. "You are like the golden sun, radiant and beautiful. I may have no flesh on my bones but my fire can take substance and I can love you like a man loves a woman."

Teal stared at him, horrified. "Love? What would you know of love? How dare you imprison me? My family will destroy your kingdom to get me back."

"But yours is a peaceful people. Have you an army ready to ride? They don't even know where you are." The dread king laughed.

Teal burst into tears, her dreams of escape dwindling as each moment passed. "You said you told them. I knew not to trust you." She had suspected him of deceit, and now she knew she was right. As he reached for her, she screamed and flailed against his ivory embrace.

"Let me go! Don't touch me!" A tidal wave of hatred and fear rushed over her, the first time Teal had ever hated anyone. The feeling sent her reeling with its strength.

The King pulled her to him, the silver fire swirling like a vortex. He tried to kiss her, to press his mouth against hers, but she fought him, shrieking, cutting herself on the sharp edges of his bones. He was stronger than she, but then—a glimpse of her bloodied face stopped him. The fire died down to a muted flicker.

Teal managed to break away from him and stumbled back as she looked for a weapon.

Karamak reached for her, then stopped. "Teal, please don't be afraid of me." The breath of his voice trembled.

She looked into his ivory face and knew that he wanted to comfort her. "Let me go home. That will be the only comfort you can give me, you wraith of bones and fire."

He paused, then silently turned and left the room. A few minutes later, two servants entered and though Teal protested weakly, they stripped away her clothing and dressed her in a gown that had once been golden but was now faded and threadbare. After they left, Teal tried to bar her door, then crawled into bed and cried herself to sleep. Hellish nightmares plagued her dreams.

"Can it be done?" Karamak demanded.

Rennard shrugged, the bones of his shoulders grating as they lifted. "I can give you that illusion, but will it do any good? You have terrified her. What makes you think she will ever trust you?"

Karamak pounded the table. Dust flew into the air where his fist landed. The castle was thick with it, but the King and his company never seemed to notice. It made no difference in Wraithland, where shadow ruled.

"I have to try. I must try." He unfastened the heavy cloak and laid it aside. He was about to remove the crown when Rennard stopped him.

"The King must never be without his crown," the magician said softly. Karamak nodded. "I have to speak now. This is folly. You cannot expect this to work, Your Majesty. I warn you," Rennard continued, "she is of flesh and blood. How long do you think she can last here? Our land is for the dead, not the living."

"We feed her, she has air to breathe. She will live as long as I want her to live," Karamak said.

"You have seen the fruit lying below the girl's window each morning. She wastes away."

"Will you give me the illusion or must I find another magician to aid me?"

Rennard shrugged. If not he, another would provide the King with what he wanted. "Very well," he said. "But I do not think it will do any good."

The Princess stared out the window towards the land of shadow below. She still didn't know where she was, but she was starting to entertain the thought of climbing out the window, and trying to scale the castle wall to the ground below. From there, she might be able to make her way out of whatever land this was.

The cuts on her face had crusted over, and she had bruises where he had gripped her wrist too tightly, but the fear had taken to her bone deep. Every time she closed her eyes she could see Karamak's ivory skull bearing down on her face, the fire in his eye sockets burning with pale lust. She shuddered, trying to cleanse herself of the feeling that insects were running over her body. As she scratched her arms, she noticed that the dress he had given her was loose and she cinched it up with one of the swags that tied back the curtains. She was losing weight from not eating.

As the lock sounded, Teal backed away from the window, not wanting to give herself away. She moved to stand by the table, keeping it between her and the door. To her surprise and relief, a young man strode in.

He was flesh and blood, like her, with long red hair and a full beard. Wearing a faded tunic that had once been royal purple, and trousers, he might have been handsome, but then she noticed the silver crown of Karamak set atop his head and her heart sank.

"What new horror is this that you visit on me? You wear the crown of Karamak and yet you are mortal?"

The King quietly crossed the room. He stood at arm's length and said, "You cannot love me as I am. I thought, if I were to look like you...if I were mortal, you might accept me and accept my love." He reached out for her and pulled her into his arms.

Teal struggled against his icy embrace. "Your touch is still the touch of death, and you stink of all that is faded and old and long, long dead. You imprison me against my will and expect me to love you?" Her stomach twisted as his hands slid over her body.

Karamak felt ashamed, but still he forced his mouth on hers and kissed her deeply, his tongue leathery and dry against her moist own. She beat against his chest and he finally let her go. As he left, he warned her, "You leave me little choice."

"Let me go home," she said.

"You will not love me, even in this form?"

"You are repulsive in any form," she said, throwing the pitcher at him. It crashed against the floor, shattering into a thousand shards as the brackish water spread across the boards. "As long as I live I will hate you!"

He slammed the door as he left.

Rennard was waiting for the King. Karamak looked at him and shook his head. "Remove the illusion."

"Then you will let her go home?" Rennard asked. "Your Majesty, take pity on the girl."

"She has no pity for me." Karamak settled back into his bones, watching the illusion fade with just a faint hint of regret. It had been so long since he had been mortal that he no longer missed it. "I don't know what to do."

"You must do something, Your Highness. She is wasting away. She refuses the food you give her each morning. She will die of thirst soon because she only sips at the water."

Karamak stared at the magician. "She said she will never love me as long as she lives. And, how can she? I am the King of Wraithland and she is mortal. We are worlds apart."

"Your Highness, I beg of you to stop this folly. Your obsession clouds your judgment." But his words were lost on the

King. As Karamak waved him away, he added, "I warn you, you will be sorely disappointed."

But Karamak wasn't listening.

The cold was almost more than Teal could bear. The dampness had gotten into her lungs and she coughed now, a painful shudder that wracked her body. When Karamak entered her room on the fifth morning, she turned quietly. She had almost decided to try her luck at climbing down the castle wall but then she stared into the gray mist and a wave of helplessness engulfed her and she realized at last just how far away her home was. She had climbed onto the ledge, willing herself to jump, but at the last minute couldn't bring herself to do so, and so she fastened the windowpanes again and settled herself at the writing table.

The room held nothing to interest her, no books, no games. If there had been any paper in the desk, it had long ago vanished into dust. So Teal sat alone with her thoughts and when Karamak entered, she stared up at him silently, waiting his next torture.

Karamak gently crossed the room. "You are in Wraithland, you know."

Teal stared at him, silently accepting the sentence. She knew then that she was doomed. "The land of the dead," she whispered. "Am I already dead?"

"No," Karamak answered. "Not yet. I could send you home again. You have the spark within you that still speaks of life. But how bright you are in my kingdom of shadow. How beautiful and radiant, like the sun you bring light into my world." He ran his finger over the empty fruit plate. "Every day the plate is emptied and yet you grow thin. Why won't you eat?"

"The fruit is full of worms and the bread is stale. The water is brackish, full of brine," she said.

"Ah, that explains it. We don't notice things like that here. We have no need for food."

"Are you going to let me go home?" Teal asked, one last spark of hope rising up. She wanted to fall on her knees but her body was too weak and tired. Anyway, she was a Princess, born and bred never to beg.

Karamak leaned across the desk. "I thought I might, but now I see how bright you still are, how beautiful and full of sparkle and I know I cannot. I love you, Princess Teal of the Woodland Kingdom. I love you and I will not let you leave me."

"I don't want you . . . I don't love you," she said.

"Not with the gulf that lies between us. I was a fool to think my illusion could capture your heart. It was still illusion. But there is a way. If we are the same, then you will have no reason to fight me."

He reached out and took her chin in his hands. Teal knew then that he was going to kill her. She straightened her shoulders and closed her eyes, trying not to cry out as he snapped her neck. As she slumped back in the chair, Karamak waited, watching the energy of his land work on her body.

Within minutes, the bones lay clear and gleaming, and a brilliant sea green fire surround the Princess as she stood, shrugging away the draperies that had been her dress.

Teal looked down at her bare bones and the thin line of sea foam flames that surrounded them. She looked back at Karamak and now he did not look so frightening. She had no more hope, no more reason to run. She stared at him unblinking.

"You have won the battle, King of the Dead. You own me. Will I be your dark queen, now?" The wind that was her breath and voice whistled like a hot summer breeze blowing through the reeds.

Karamak stared at her in horror. The brilliant beauty, the pale skin and bright eyes, the spark of life that had promised joy and desire to his soul, it was all gone and in its place, stood simply another wraith of shadow and fire and death.

"No," he whispered, stepping back. "No. Where is my sunlight? Where is my radiant Princess? What have I done?" he cried. "Your will and your passion! Where have they gone?"

Teal laughed then, bitterly, for she saw his repulsion and suddenly understood. He fell to his knees as she turned. With her bones clicking gently, with her fire crackling quietly, she strode past the grieving King, stopping to lift the crown from his skull and set it atop her own. Then, without a single look back, the dark queen entered the shadowed kingdom that was her new home.

FIN

❦━◦━❦

About the Author: *New York Times, Publishers Weekly,* and *USA Today* bestselling author Yasmine Galenorn writes paranormal romance and urban fantasy. The author of over forty books, in the past, she has also written paranormal mysteries, and nonfiction metaphysical books. She is the 2011 Career Achievement Award Winner in Urban Fantasy, given by *RT Magazine*. A shamanic witch and priestess who collects daggers, crystals, china, and corsets, she lives in Kirkland, Washington, with her husband Samwise and their cats. Yasmine can be reached via her website: www.galenorn.com.

Magic After Midnight
C. Gockel

I

"ARE YOU SITTING DOWN?" THE VOICE AT THE OTHER end of the phone asks.

Feeling herself go cold, Marcia pushes a chair away from the table, and slowly eases into it. Marcia exhales. "I am now," she whispers. Why, oh, why, had she picked up the phone? Because she'd expected it to be Cindy...

"It's inoperable, I'm sorry. If you need— "

"Mom!" Joshua calls from the bathroom. "Mom, Alicia is going to do your hair."

"I have to go," Marcia says.

She takes a deep breath and smells the reek of trash, the trash that Cindy was supposed to take out.

"Ma'am— "

"I've worked in an oncology department for the last ten years, I know what this means," Marcia says quickly. *Why did I have to answer the phone?*

"Mom!" Joshua calls again.

Marcia hangs up, and walks the short distance through the apartment to the master bath. Alicia and Joshua beam at her as she walks in. Maybe it's the perfect vanity lighting, making their skin exceptionally golden and their dark eyes sparkle, or maybe it is the soul-crushing news casting the moment in sharp contrast—their health next to her illness—but they look especially beautiful and handsome. Alicia is wearing a green silk sheath dress with an amazing gold and pearl belt. Joshua has dyed his roots purple and the ends pink. He is wearing a gray suit with pink triangle cufflinks, a blue shirt and a lighter gray—what had he called it? A choke tie. Something that is popular in the realm of Vanaheim—or is it Svartálfaheim, land of the dwarves? Her children are so perfect, and Marcia laughs despite everything, or perhaps because of everything. She feels tears come to her eyes and spill over.

"Mom, what's wrong?" Alicia asks, a brush in her hand. Her thick dark hair is upswept and held back with pearl pins. Her dark eyes are wide and caring.

"It's the suit," Joshua says, "I shouldn't have worn dad's suit, but it's in style again, Mom, and you said..."

She shakes her head and hugs him. "No, no, William would have wanted you to wear it." The suit Joshua had worn just a few months ago no longer fits, as his shoulders seemingly grew three inches broader overnight. When the surprise invitation had come, he'd turned to his father's—stepfather's—old clothes in desperation. After some adjustments, the suit fits surprisingly well, and hides the fact that Joshua doesn't have a lot hanging on those wide shoulders.

Turning to Alicia, Marcia says, "And you look beautiful." She feels tears hot on her cheeks again. Her daughter is slouching; she always slouches. Marcia isn't sure if that is due to the weight of the world on Alicia, her oldest, most responsible child, or if Alicia just feels eclipsed by her siblings. Cindy is more conventionally beautiful, and Joshua is so loud. Maybe it's both. Marcia swallows. The cut of Alicia's garment is just right for her broad shoulders and arms toned by swimming. And the green is beautiful against her golden skin. Marcia says to her son, "You did such a wonderful job on the dress."

Joshua flushes from his neck to his forehead. "I told you those curtains were worth keeping."

"Mom, you're still crying," Alicia says.

"I'm just emotional," Marcia says, wiping her eyes and silently willing, *don't ask, don't ask.*

Alicia's brow pinches, but she gestures to a stool in front of the mirror and says, "Sit down."

Marcia takes a seat and Alicia starts brushing her hair back. The dress Marcia wears is something she pulled out of the closet from better times. Joshua had declared that the floor length black gown "doesn't match Alicia's green, but at least it is so old it is new again." Marcia frowns at the lines at the corners of her mouth, around her eyes, and in her forehead. She looks as old as she feels. She glances up at her children. Joshua is just fifteen, Alicia is only seventeen. They're too young to lose their mother so soon after losing William. She closes her eyes. Oh, but they'd lost more than that. Marcia's first husband had died when they were five and three. William had been like a real father to them...to lose two fathers, and now a mother.

"That gray streak through your black hair makes you look like Cruella Deville." Joshua cackles. "Fits your evil stepmother reputation."

Marcia's eyes spring open.

"Joshua," Alicia hisses, tugging Marcia's curls tight against her head.

He flicks a wrist. "She knows I'm only joking."

Marcia's phone rings. Joshua looks over at the counter where she'd put it down. He scowls. "Speak of the devil..."

"Cindy's not the devil," Marcia says. "She's—"

"Going through a tough time," say her children in unison.

"Pick it up," Marcia says, wiping her eyes.

Sighing, Joshua picks it up and walks out of the bathroom.

Arranging Marcia's hair into a bun at the nape of her neck, Alicia asks, "Is your stomach feeling better, Mom?"

"Yes," she lies. She smiles and more tears fall out of her eyes. What is she going to do? Can she make it just three more years, to see all her children come of age? Who will look after them if she doesn't?

Joshua tromps back into the bathroom, rolling his eyes. "Cindy's hair-styling-dress-fitting date with her fairy god-mother is running late and she's going to take her godmommy's chariot to the ball."

"At least we're still invited," Alicia says.

Joshua snickers. "We still get to embarrass our stinking rich snobby relatives!" He fist bumps Alicia. "Ugly step-sister powers activate!"

Marcia's eyes go wide, and not at her son's declaration of himself as a 'sister.' "You're not the *ugly* step-sisters!"

Alicia huffs, "Of course not, Mom. Fairy tales aren't real."

"Mom," Joshua says, "you're losing weight again." He picks at the dress as they walk through the grand foyer of Marcia's in-laws, or former in-laws, or whatever you call the family of a widow when the controlling members of said family never really liked her. "I should have taken it in."

"It's fine," Marcia says. Normally she would bat his hand away, but she's too tired. She tells herself not to think of what that exhaustion means as they walk toward the main reception room and the buzz of conversation.

"I know that we're probably only here because some event planner made a mistake on an invitation that was probably only supposed to be for Cindy," Alicia whispers.

Marcia's jaw sags. She'd actually thought exactly that...but her children had begged her to accept the invite. She'd thought they'd thought the offer had been genuine.

"But I'm still so excited!" Alicia gushes. "We'll probably be hustled off to a corner like the last time we were here, but still—"

"We'll be the only people at school who've seen Night Elves up close," says Joshua, his voice bubbling with excitement.

Marcia rubs her temples, partly at the memory of the last time, partly because she feels like crying again and wants to hide her eyes. She has to give them this. One last night of excitement, hope, and magic. Not everyone gets to meet elves, even since the opening of the realms. They tend to remain in

Alfheim. But the Night Elves, a minor kingdom allied with the Light Elves, are interested in trading minerals...for what, she's not sure. Clutching her side, she rubs her temples. Her wealthy, well-connected in-laws made their fortune in commodities futures; of course they'd have maneuvered to have the Night Elves come to call.

They step into the reception room, the swirl of voices, and the press of bodies. Her flamboyant son whispers dramatically, "Oh, my God. I think I just got pregnant."

Alicia gasps. "They're...they're..."

Marcia drops her hand from her face. She looks around. There are male and female elves intermingled through the crowd. They have pointed ears and too-perfect faces. They're tall, elegant, dressed in silk brocades that are elegant and alien and...

"They're beautiful," Alicia whispers.

"Vampires," Marcia whispers at the same time. She can see fangs peeking between their lips as they speak, plop hors d'oeuvres in their mouths, and take sips of their wine.

"Beautiful," Alicia whispers.

Joshua snorts and whispers, "We know our stepfamily are all bloodsuckers. Don't worry, Mom, we'll be careful."

Alicia sighs and squeezes Marcia's arm. "How could Dad have been so nice when his family is so evil?"

They hadn't all been evil. William's parents had been lovely...but since her mother-in-law was put into a nursing home, and her father-in-law's passing, the fortune had fallen into the care of Cindy's godmother. Marcia doesn't remind the children of this. She's too petrified. Is she hallucinating? She turns slowly in place, dreading what she might find—that she is going mad, or that her hallucinations are real. She finds herself staring at a man standing so close he could reach out and touch her. He's one of them, tall, with olive skin and dark hair curling in ringlets around his pointed ears. His eyes are light brown flecked with yellow, and his cheekbones are very sharp. His lips are slightly parted, as though in surprise, and his fangs are glinting in the light. He must have heard her. Swallowing, she takes a step back and blinks.

And the fangs are gone...

She's hallucinating. The news of her disease has sent her into shock. She has to hold it together, just tonight. One more night.

"Yoo-hoo!" an older woman cries from behind Marcia.

Alicia grumbles, "And here comes Cinderella and her fairy godmommy."

"Stop calling her that," Marcia says, weakly stamping her foot.

Alicia and Joshua have already turned around.

"Oh, my God," Joshua whispers. "Those are Vera Wang gowns made with elven silk. My heart just broke. I feel so shabby; I think I lost my insta-baby."

"She looks beautiful," sighs Alicia resignedly. And there is no doubt that Cindy is beautiful. Along with her blonde hair, she has enormous blue eyes, a delicate nose, and a mouth shaped like a bow. And Cindy knows she is beautiful. She often complains that, if she were "just a little taller," she could be a model.

"You both look beautiful too," Marcia protests. She tries to turn, but feels a sharp pain in her side. She takes a breath.

"It's okay, Mom." Joshua says. "We're not the kind of girls who get swept up by Prince Charming. We've accepted our fate...but we can enjoy the ride."

Putting a hand to her side, Marcia manages to turn, and there is Cindy with her aunt and godmother, Deidre. Cindy is wearing a gown of sky blue that glows with unearthly magic. It has a diaphanous white train that flutters like a cloud. Above the sweetheart neckline her pale skin and golden hair are like the sun. Deidre wears a dress of black that seems to have stars woven into the fabric. Above the black, her silver hair is like the moon. Even next to elves, the two seem celestial. Marcia bites her lip. What a world her children are coming of age in; one where magic is real. Their possibilities seem endless.

Seeing Marcia's threesome, Cindy and Deidre walk over. They're not six feet away, when, looking at Alicia's dress, Cindy exclaims, "You're wearing our *old* curtains!" Her voice is so loud it rises above the gentle murmur of the crowd. Marcia feels all eyes on Alicia. Her daughter's shoulders slump further. Marcia closes her eyes and reminds herself that there is a fifty-fifty chance Cindy didn't mean to be hurtful.

"That suit and that dress look familiar," Deidre says. Marcia opens her eyes to see Deidre looking her up and down with a clear expression of disdain on her face.

"Real class never goes out of style," Marcia says through gritted teeth.

"Burnnnnnn..." whispers Joshua, but Marcia notices his eyes are a little too wet after the curtain comment.

Deidre sniffs. "If you say so." Guiding Cindy away, Deidre says, "Cindy, let me introduce you to the prince."

The three of them watch them walk off, and Alicia gulps. "You were right, Mom, they really are vampires."

Marcia hears a cough. Her eyes slide to the side, and she sees the man she'd seen before. His gaze meets hers, and for an instant she has x-ray vision. She can see his fangs behind his lips. She gasps and blinks. And then he is gone.

Marcia sits just outside the main reception area, now filled with people dancing. She is in a hallway open to the back veranda, behind a potted plant, on a chair one of the very nice waitstaff have brought for her. She looks at her watch. It's only 11:50, but she wants to go home. She peers beyond the plant and sees Joshua and Alicia dancing the foxtrot. They look like they're having a grand time, and she doesn't want to make them leave. They're doing quite well on the floor—William had insisted they learn ballroom dancing—but they're getting a wide berth from all the guests. She supposes that Night Elves are as skilled as Deirdre's usual hangers-on at sensing riff-raff. She feels bile rising in her stomach. Magic doesn't seem to be so much a possibility for her children, so much as another world of privilege they don't belong to. She closes her eyes...no, she'd made it without money or magic before. She'd been born poor, made it into the middle class with her first husband, Alicia's and Joshua's father, and managed to hang onto that after he died. And then she'd met her second husband, William, Cindy's father, in a bereavement group and somehow wound up very wealthy...

...and then the realms had opened up and a deranged Norse God had destroyed several blocks of Chicago. William, their business, and their home had been literally crushed in an instant. She'd lost her husband; the children had lost their father. Money would have been a cold comfort at that time; still, it would have allowed Marcia to take time off to help her children recover from their grief. Unfortunately, insurance policies had exemptions for 'acts of God.' She's just barely hanging on now, with a mortgage for a destroyed home to pay, her rent, and four mouths to feed. But things will get better. She scrunches her eyes shut. No, they won't, because she won't be alive...

Marcia bites her lip. After all that 'magic' had done for her, why has she brought her children here? She'll round them up, and take them home. She looks past Joshua and Alicia for Cindy. In tow with Deidre, Cindy has been fawned over by the vampire prince the whole evening. Marcia shakes her head. He is not a *vampire* prince—he is a Night Elf. Marcia blinks out at the reception area. She sees Deidre, but where is Cindy?

From the veranda, she hears a splash of water, and a laugh that is familiar. Marcia goes cold. The pain in her side is suddenly screaming, but she bolts from her chair, and moves as quickly as she can out the door, and into the warm night.

Down a long flight of steps, she sees Cindy, sitting on the edge of a fountain, the dark hair of the prince a shadow against her neck. It might be the pain in her side, or the earlier hallucinations, but Marcia runs to the top of the stairs, and shouts, "Don't hurt her!"

The prince raises his head. Cindy turns to Marcia and her jaw drops.

Behind Marcia a masculine voice says, "You heard her, Rayne."

A sneer forming on his handsome features, the prince narrows his eyes at the masculine speaker behind Marcia.

"She's only sixteen," Marcia gasps, as though that could possibly make a difference.

The prince's eyes bolt wide, and he gets up hastily. Without a backward glance at Cindy, he hops off the wall of the fountain, runs up the stairs, and bows to Marcia. "Madam, I apologize, I had no idea." To the masculine speaker, he says some words in a strange musical language, and then puts his hand over his mouth and, turning visibly green, runs away. Marcia has a distinct impression he might vomit.

"You ruin everything!" Cindy hisses, charging up the stairs. "I hate you!"

And then she runs for the hallway. Marcia wants to go after her, but she's suddenly dizzy with pain and her own nausea.

The man the prince had addressed sighs. "Teenagers."

Clutching her side, Marcia lifts her eyes. It is the same vampire-Night-Elf-man she'd seen earlier. He looks all of twenty-eight. Maybe. She doesn't see fangs this time. She had been hallucinating, obviously.

"The years my children were teens..." He shakes his head and crosses his arms, looking after Cindy.

The words seem out of place on his youthful face, but Marcia has heard rumors that elves are immortal.

She huffs, and says what she always says at these times. "They have four times the hormones of an adult. That makes them practically insane." She shrugs and catches her breath.

"That is a very generous interpretation of their situation." He smiles wryly and says, "It was the worst century of my life."

Marcia blinks at him, thinking of all the fights she'd had this year with Joshua and Cindy, and all the times Alicia had gone to her room, her face streaming with tears, unwilling to talk about it. "I have never considered the advantages of a short life," Marcia says.

The corners of the man's lips turn up. Bowing slightly, he holds out a hand, palm up. "Madam, you seem to require assistance."

Marcia takes a step back, her hand fluttering to her throat. His eyes follow her fingers, his gaze intent, and she gasps. She sees the fangs, again. Frozen in place, she looks down at the vampire's hand, and she sees...an ending, and peace. And suddenly, that is what she wants so much. Her struggle isn't just with her emotional teenagers. It is dealing with their school, with the teachers who aren't helping Joshua deal with bullies, and with Deirdre, who fills Cindy's mind with tales of how deprived the girl is, but only wants Cindy when it is convenient for her. And it is Marcia's responsibilities to her extended family, her continuing battle with insurance agencies, and the specter of her disease looming over like a dark shadow.

She wants to take his hand, but instead she draws back. "I have to stay with my children," she says. *For as long as I can.* She still feels sick, her side still hurts, but she bolts from the veranda.

In the car not fifteen minutes later, Cindy screeches, "I lost my shoe!"

II

The next morning, Marcia wakes up on the couch to the reek of garbage. Her cell phone is ringing. Seeing her brother's number, she picks up.

"Marcia," Fernando says without preamble, "the assisted living center is saying that you requested that I be given durable power of attorney for Mother and Father."

"Yes," says Marcia. "I need you to do that, Fernando, I'm—"

"My firm is going public," Fernando says. "I'm pulling eighty hours a week right now."

"What about Sarah?" Marcia says, referring to Fernando's wife. "She is staying at home; you have a nanny, and—"

"We can't have Sarah making medical decisions for our parents!" says Fernando.

"I like Sarah," Marcia says. "She—"

"Is too busy with our twins," says Fernando.

Marcia scrunches her eyes shut. "But I have—"

There is a light ping at the other end of the line and Fernando says, "It's my investors, I have to go." And he's gone.

Marcia puts her head in her hands. It's been years since she lost William, and she had thought she was used to it. She loved William. They may not have always been perfect together, but they were always on each other's team. Now she is playing solo, and the weight of his absence is suddenly so heavy she feels like she can't breathe. She sucks in a deep breath, to prove to herself she still can...and is overwhelmed by the reek of garbage.

Throat tight, she gets up and goes to the kitchen. Alicia's and Joshua's doors are shut. Cindy is leaning against the counter, eating yogurt from the container, last night's makeup smeared down her face. She still looks gorgeous, but...

"How can you eat with the reek?" Marcia asks.

Throwing her yogurt container in the sink, Cindy hisses, "Deidre says you were ridiculous," storms out, and slams her door. Marcia should feel angry, but then she hears Cindy break down into sobs.

She feels her stomach churn. If she doesn't take the garbage out, Joshua might, but he'll complain about it the entire time. Cindy will call him a drama queen, he'll say "pot, you're black," and the situation will go downhill from there. If Joshua doesn't take the garbage out, Alicia will. She won't complain, won't say a word...she'll just do it. And for some reason, Marcia finds that scenario worse.

Sighing and holding her nose, Marcia opens the garbage can. A moment later she steps out of their apartment and pads down the hall in her pajamas, her nose wrinkled, her stomach about to heave, carrying a stinking, dripping bag of fermented yuck. She's almost at the door of the garbage chute when a voice behind her says, "Madam, may I help you with that?"

She turns, sees a man with fangs, screams, and promptly drops the garbage. The man swoops in, picks up the garbage, and points to the door Marcia was just about to go into. "Is that the rubbish chute?"

She nods dumbly. It's the same man-vampire she'd spoken to last night, the one with the teenagers, not the one who'd tried to seduce her daughter.

The man-maybe-vampire disappears into the garbage room.

The door to Marcia's apartment opens. Alicia hangs off the door frame into the hallway and demands, "Mom, did you take out the garbage again?"

Marcia darts for the door. Joshua's indignant voice rises from within the apartment. "You made Mom take out the garbage!"

She hears Cindy angrily retort, "She decided to take it herself!"

Joshua roars, "Because you were too lazy and now the house smells like putrid chicken!"

"I'm sticking this piece of bubblegum in your sewing machine!" screams Cindy.

Feeling her stomach roiling, Marcia rushes past Alicia and says, "Shut the door!" Not pausing for breath she gasps, "Cindy, don't you dare!"

"Ah, I see I have come to the right domicile," says the man.

Marcia blinks. Cindy comes running out of Joshua's room with her brother in hot pursuit so fast that Marcia's head spins. She turns and finds the maybe vampire in the doorway. Alicia's lips are parted, her eyes are wide, and she's looking quickly between Marcia and the maybe bloodsucker.

"Mom," Alicia whispers. "I recognize him from the party. We shouldn't slam the door in his face."

Before Marcia can protest, the man asks, "May I come in?" He is definitely a vampire! Marcia can see his fangs when he talks.

Throwing up her hands, Marcia implores, "Don't let him—"

"Sure," says Cindy.

He steps in with a smile, giving Marcia an odd look. Alicia shuts the door behind him. Eyes wide, Marcia backs up. She tries to think of anything in the kitchen that might do as a wooden stake and gestures for Alicia to stand next to her. Alicia just looks at her quizzically.

"How can we help you?" says Joshua, rolling on his heels. Cindy elbows him. He elbows her back.

Marcia wonders if she can hit a wooden spoon against a counter hard enough to break it and give it a sharp point. She starts slowly edging toward the kitchen, motioning for Alicia to follow. Alicia's brow furrows, but she doesn't move. Marcia sucks in a breath. Normally, she thinks of her eldest child as the most perceptive one.

The vampire clears his throat. "I apologize for disturbing you. My name is Darerick Razvano..." A long litany of syllables follows. He must see their slack jaws because he clears his throat and adds, "Please just call me Dare. I'll be working with the Night Elf embassy. First off, I want to return this." He opens a satchel and pulls out a package wrapped in blue tissue paper. Bowing to Cindy, he says, "Your shoe, madam."

Cindy smiles, puts a hand to her mouth, and walks forward to take it. Before she can, Marcia snatches it from his hand, and hands it to Cindy, glaring at the vamp. Cindy gives Marcia a dirty look, but then smiles at Dare and says, "And?"

The vampire opens his mouth as though to speak, and the fangs are there! Can't her children see them? Are they just blinded by how handsome he is, how other worldly?

"If you're here for Cindy's hand in marriage, take her," Joshua says.

"Joshua!" Marcia hisses, edging toward the kitchen.

"Pardon?" the vampire says, eyes widening, and skin flushing all the way to the ears. He's deviously hidden their pointy tips behind his curls, Marcia notices. When her family's bodies are found later, the neighbors won't identify the man who entered their home as an elf.

Cindy doesn't hear Joshua or doesn't care. Blinking up at the vamp, she gushes, "The prince? Did he send you?"

The vampire's jaw drops and he looks at Cindy. "Ah," he says, and Marcia can see the exact moment he catches on to what she's getting at. "He did not send me. I have business this way, and I thought I might return the shoe as well."

Cindy's face crumples. She bows her head, turns on her heel, walks to her room, and slams the door. Marcia has one kid out of the way; now, how to get the other two behind her? She gestures to Alicia again. "Mom, are you feeling alright?" Alicia asks.

The vampire looks at Marcia's eldest daughter, and back to Marcia. "My primary order of business is to speak to you, madam. It is a matter of most urgent importance."

Marcia says, "You're—" She almost says *a vampire*. Catching her breath, she smells garbage, on her, and on him.

It gives her pause. Had she ever seen a horror movie where a vampire helped take out the garbage?

"He's a Night Elf, Mom," Joshua says, in the same tone he uses to say, *you're embarrassing me.*

"—not as dangerous as you perhaps think," the vampire says, gold-flecked eyes on her.

The kids look between themselves and shrug.

The vampire takes a deep breath and adds, "The survival of my species is at stake." He winces. "If you'll pardon the expression."

Marcia raises an eyebrow. The kids' lips purse. After a long pause, Alicia says, "Mom, I think you have to help him."

"Yeah, Mom, I don't think the Sierra Club will ever let you back in if you refuse to save an endangered species," Joshua adds.

Marcia glares at the vampire. He looks...contrite? He's in her home, and if he was going to attack them, wouldn't he have done that by now? Also, it's daylight, and he's out and about. Since the realms have opened up, humans have learned that a lot of the things they believed about magical creatures weren't true. Is it possible, vampire fearsomeness might be another myth? Or maybe he's not a vampire at all. Maybe he sucks the nectar out of flowers, or some such with those fangs. She huffs. No, she doesn't believe that.

Looking nervously to the side, he says, "We need to speak someplace private...if you don't mind?"

Vampires in myths and movies don't talk nicely. They either bite you and drain your blood or use magic to control you and drain you later. Marcia swallows. There is only one place to talk that doesn't entail leaving her children.

"The balcony is private," she says.

He looks beyond her. "Ah, there?" he asks. The apartment is rather small.

Marcia nods. "Yes."

He raises his hands. "May I wash up first? My hands smell like putrid chicken."

More than anything, that makes Marcia think he might not be *immediately* dangerous.

Marcia points to the right. "Powder room right there." She watches him go in, and then glances at the balcony. It's early morning, but the balcony is western-facing, so there is no sun. Putting her hand to her side, she wonders if he gives up his right to entry as soon as he steps out. She also wonders if she can push him off the balcony.

The sun is slipping past its zenith. In another thirty minutes or so, it will clear the balcony above Marcia's and shine on her 'guest.' She feels vaguely sick, and it might be because she is, at a deep intrinsic level, very sick. And it might be because of all that Dare has told her.

"So you are a vampire," she says.

"We like to be called Night Elves," says Dare. He's sitting on the only other piece of furniture on her balcony, a fold-out chair that has a rubber lattice. He's too big for it, and his spotless Armani suit doesn't fit the cheapness of the chair any better. "Vampire conjures too many images of predators..."

"...and you're more parasites."

"We prefer the term 'symbiote,'" Dare says, grimacing.

Marcia narrows her eyes. "You haven't exactly explained how you're symbiotic." He'd said that vampires require mammalian blood for survival, but not enough to be harmful to the host, unless the host is a very small creature, like a mouse. He'd also said, to *thrive* and be healthy, they need human blood. Not very much, he had assured her, and not even consistently —whatever nutrient they need from human blood they apparently can store for a long time. But without access to human blood, they eventually become infertile, ill, and often so depressed that they die. "Are gone" were the words he used to describe it. Still..."Symbiotic implies some benefit to the host species. Not harming the host isn't the same thing."

Dare's face goes blank for a moment. "I am not at liberty to divulge the benefit." He smiles tightly, and gazes out at the parking lot across the street from her apartment. It might be Marcia's imagination, but she thinks he looks sad.

"You can't turn into mist," she says.

He shakes his head. "Though it would be convenient."

"You don't convert anyone you bite into a vampire."

He shakes his head.

Marcia huffs a soft laugh. "I always thought that wouldn't work. The predator-prey relationship would never be balanced."

"We prefer the term sym––we're parasites," he amends at Marcia's sharp glance. "But it works the same way."

Marcia looks at her knees; she's still wearing her pajamas. "And you aren't stronger than a human, faster, or able to enthrall us. And blood drawing is a consensual thing. Vampires feel a bond between themselves and their hosts and so wouldn't want to jeopardize it?"

He's quiet a moment, and then he says, "That all holds true..." He bows his head and steeples his fingers. "...for most of us."

Marcia raises her eyes. He meets her gaze. "All magical creatures: Night Elves, Light Elves, Dark Elves, Fire Ettins, Vanir, Jotunn, Aesir and the Dwarves...they all possess some innate magic they can do without thinking. For Fire Ettins, it is the manipulation of fire; for all elves of all kinds, that innate ability is...usually...immortality."

Marcia leans her head back on her chair. The word itself has weight. And then she bites back a laugh. Forget forever; she'd take just three years.

Dare goes on, "For the Vanir, Aesir, and the rest, the innate ability is more individual. For some, it may be controlling fire or ice, great strength, or longevity, or they might be particularly good at some craft or trade. But all magical creatures, if they learn to harness magic, can learn to do all these things—be strong, control fire, be faster, be charming..."

"No turning into bats, though?" Marcia asks impulsively. She's beginning to feel light-headed.

He smiles. "It would be fun, but no."

Marcia's brow furrows, and she picks at her pajamas. They're too big. She's lost so much weight in the last few months. "In our myths, vampires are—"

"Sadistic and evil?" Dare supplies.

Marcia's breath catches, and she turns to face him.

Meeting her gaze, he says, "There is some basis in that."

Marcia sits up very tall in her chair.

Dare sighs. "There are very few vampires strong enough to walk through the realms. Moreover, it has been illegal for us to do so for nearly a thousand years. The only ones that have come—"

It's Marcia's turn to sigh. "Lawbreakers...powerful lawbreakers." When Alicia was an infant, she'd become obsessed with all news of kidnappings and pedophilia. The network news people love to say, "it could be anyone." That is technically true, but Marcia had discovered that it is a hell of a lot more likely to be a certain type of person: someone who breaks the law is at the top of that list. A vampire that broke the law to get to Earth was unlikely to be a vampire who respected the laws of humans.

"I think..." Dare says, softly. "I think that certain members of my species...who were used to being able not to care nor to love...they sought to kill their hosts so they could loosen that bond."

Marcia's eyes blur. *There is a perfectly good word to describe humans like that.*

He winces. "I only mention this because I want to be completely honest with you."

Grabbing her side, Marcia's brow furrows. There is a gaping hole in his story. "Your prince was about to bond with my daughter."

Dare snorts. "No, he's rash, but even he wasn't about to crack a vein with someone he'd just met."

"Then what was he—"

Dare shoots her a look that says, *really?*

Marcia sags in her chair. "Ah, just some innocent hanky-panky..." She glares at him. "With a *sixteen-year-old*."

"In his defense, she...ahhh...misrepresented her age and he has very little experience with humans. A sixteen-year-old vampire..." He holds out a hand as though to indicate knee-high. "You may have noticed the prince was quite...upset...by what transpired."

Sadly, Marcia can believe Cindy "misrepresented" her age, and she had noticed the way the prince had turned green. She can also believe all the rest of it, and still not find his species particularly...evil. No, she doesn't find them evil at all. She can readily believe a few bad apples could be responsible for all the heinous crimes attributed to a whole race. It hadn't taken many Conquistadors to wipe out the Aztecs. She sighs. Not that the Aztecs were angels, either. She gulps. And there is a vocal, violent minority of humans calling for a reclosing of the realms and the extermination of any magical creatures that might wind up trapped here.

She turns her gaze out to the parking lot across the street, which is almost empty, since it's Sunday. "So how do you keep the strong vamp—Night Elves away from Earth?" Marcia asks.

Dare stiffens in a way that seems almost defensive, but then he rubs his forehead. "We actually have been studying your technology ... We believe that we wouldn't have to send anyone through—well, except for a modest support staff, and the odd procession of dignitaries. You have machines now that would allow blood to be transported without chilling or chemical additives." Head bowing, he nods, as though to himself. "It is..." He sighs. "It will be fine." There is something in his voice, something resigned. But her mind is getting too fuzzy to ask, and so she asks the question at the forefront of her thoughts. "Why are you telling me all of this?"

"So you don't talk," Dare says. Too soon for her to draw away, he reaches over and takes her hand. His fingers are dry and cool. "It is a fluke that you realize the nature of Night Elves; and, if humans know, it will make things more difficult."

Marcia stares down at their entwined hands, too tired to pull away, and it isn't just her illness. It's also from lying. She works in an oncology department—only as their web designer—but she knows enough about cancer to realize that her recent symptoms had warned of something very bad. The scans she had just confirmed it. Now she has to tell her children and her family about what's really going on...she has a meeting with a therapist...right after her next oncology appointment. She'll ask her...She feels tears biting at the edge of her eyes. She's frightened of holding it in that long, frightened of giving it away, too.

"Don't hide it, Dare," she says, staring down at his hands. They are large, heavy, and masculine; and by comparison her own hands look frail, small, and very old. She seldom notices how wrinkled the skin around her joints has become during her half century-and-change on the planet, or how visible her veins are, but next to Dare's magical youth she can't help but notice. She remembers Alicia asking if she feels well, and Joshua's anger at Cindy "making" her take out the trash. "Something will give you away in the end, and lying will make it worse."

He takes her hand in both of his own, and turns it over. She hears him exhale. "How would I even go about that?"

She's slouching in her chair, overwhelmed by life—and him—and this. She glances at him. For most of the conversation, he's maintained an air of self-assuredness that belied the age he looks. But now he does look all of twenty-eight or so, and Marcia feels older than his...centuries? Millennia?

She takes a deep breath, her head clearing. She's worked at an oncology department as their web designer—which really means designer, coder, and *copy editor*. She knows how to soften medical terminology, make it easier to understand and accept. It occurs to her that maybe maturity is based on experience, not years.

She tells him what she would say. When she's done, she feels exceptionally light. She supposes that, if you're going to die, helping save an entire race as one of your final deeds isn't a bad way to go.

"You think, framing it as an inheritable disease, like hemophilia, and our people as in great need of...transfusions...that humans will find this acceptable?" Dare asks, squeezing her fingers lightly. At some point in the conversation, he'd leaned closer.

"You're in need of blood," Marcia says. "Something we give voluntarily, and offering to trade it for tellurium and lithium, things we don't have and need for our new magic power converters and batteries. It will work out." Bless human industrialism and greed, it might just save a race.

She glances over at him. He's leaning sideways in his chair, sunlight covering one side of his face. During their conversation, he'd pulled a pair of aviator glasses out of his pocket and put them on. In the hand not holding hers, he is clutching a small tube that advertises itself as Titanium Dioxide Sunscreen for Baby's Sensitive Skin.

"You don't look well," she says.

He waves vaguely beyond the balcony with the hand that holds the tube. "Perhaps a bit too much sun." He holds the vial up to his nose. "Although this ointment is amazing."

"Let's get inside," Marcia says, jumping up from her chair. She waits for the tide of nausea she expects to pass—but it doesn't even come. Not letting go of her hand, Dare slowly gets to his feet. As she leads him into the living room, he stumbles on the track for the balcony door.

"Why don't you lie down?" Marcia says. "I'll call you a cab." Perhaps seeing him so feeble and in obvious need gives her energy, because as he flops on the couch and she bustles about, she doesn't feel tired at all.

A few minutes later, she's downstairs waiting for the cab with him. He looks so awful she suggests a hospital, but he waves it off with a mumbled, "It will pass."

The cab is just arriving, when she suddenly recalls how resigned he'd seemed when they'd discussed blood banks. "You don't really want to use blood banks...you find it a bit..." She doesn't know what the word is. Distasteful doesn't seem right. The word she wants is sad, or maybe lonely, but she doesn't know why it fits.

For the first time since they left the balcony, he smiles. "What can I say? I'm a romantic."

Before she can ask him to explain, he's stumbling out the door, into the sunlight, to the waiting cab, clutching his side. Marcia's still pondering it when she reenters the apartment.

"Some fairy tale," Cindy says, staring at her shoe.

"See, no such thing as fairy tales," Alicia says resignedly.

Joshua says, "We're still stuck with you, too! Loser."

"Joshua," Marcia growls in warning. She gives her eldest daughter a covert little nod.

III

Marcia stands just outside the official residence of the Night Elves. A dwarven woman stands before her. The woman's head only comes up to her chin. Her face is childlike, round with enormous eyes. But she's broader than Marcia, and the track suit she wears does nothing to disguise that every inch of her is muscle.

"I'm here to see Dare!" Marcia says, stamping her foot.

The dwarven lady blinks up at her. "You call him Dare?" she says, backing up, wide eyes going even wider.

Seizing the opportunity, Marcia storms past her.

"Diamonds, who is that?" she hears Dare say, his voice oddly...whiny. "Make them go away!"

"Madam," the dwarf, presumably Diamonds says, grabbing Marcia's wrist with such force she spins around. "He's not well, leave him alone."

With a move she learned in self-defense classes she took with her children, Marcia twists her wrist away and shouts, "Dare, I need to talk to you!"

"Marcia?" says Dare.

"Madam," Diamonds says. "I've been gentle with you, but—"

"Let her in," Dare says, and she can't tell if he sounds resigned or devious.

Without hesitating, Marcia strides in the direction of his voice, and finds herself in a living room with blinds closed to the afternoon light. He's wearing pajamas, a bathrobe, and fat fluffy red socks that look like Elmo might have been sacrificed in order to make them. It's about 2 p.m., she has a personal day, the kids are safely at school—she's come straight from her oncology appointment. Her doctor's words are ringing in her head. "I don't understand it, Marcia. I think it must have been a glitch with the last scans...or...or...a miracle." His brow had furrowed. "There have been some odd spontaneous remissions since the realms opened—Mayor Rogers has asked to keep track of them. But those are usually blood cancers and I'm not sure this counts. How do you feel?"

She feels great, which is the problem. "Dare, why did you do it? What do you want?" she demands.

"Lovely to see you, too," he says, throwing a hand over his eyes. "Leave me alone, I'm sleepy."

"You made me better!" Marcia exclaims.

He sniffs and replies petulantly, "Made you better? Why, I never had any idea you were sick." There is a sing-song quality to his voice. He's lying. She can feel it in every inch of her body.

"Why did you do it?" Marcia demands. "Do you intend to blackmail me? Is this some sort of vampiric extortion? Do you think I might be in your debt? Because, no way, Mr. Bloodsucker." Is he after one of her children? That always happens in fairy tales, but she won't give any of them away. Not even Cindy, who'd called her a black widow this morning.

He sits up quickly. "If I wanted you to be in my debt, there would have been a contract signed in blood before I healed you." He sniffs. "Don't accuse me of incompetence."

Marcia puts her hands on her hips, and her eyes narrow. "You did make me better."

Flopping back down on the couch, he turns his back to her and curls up in a fetal position...as much as a tall man can on a skinny couch. "Did not." He raises a hand and waves it with a shoo-shoo motion. "Now go away."

"I still have questions for you!" Marcia says.

He sighs. "Oh, bright sunny summer days," he mutters, grabbing a pillow and pressing his face into it.

She blinks.

"Well?" he says. "Are you going to ask? Get it over with. I want to go back to sleep." The last comes out distinctly whiney.

"You have children!" she says remembering that without human blood vampires are malnourished and eventually infertile. "You've drunk human blood." And without the benefit of a blood bank, so directly from the vein.

He rolls over so he's in the fetal position, but facing her. His eyes are glinting, and she's not sure if it's magic or anger. "Yes, Marcia. Before the realms were closed, I lived here and I drank human blood." His nostrils flare, and she feels cold dread settling on her. She raises her hands, suddenly not wanting him to finish, but finds herself unable to ask him to stop.

"I was even married to the human woman in question. She was burned at the stake for being a witch," Dare continues, his eyes *definitely* flashing. "I went home with the closing of the realms, married a vampire in a similar situation, and we had five lovely children."

"Oh..." says Marcia.

His jaw hardens. "But after our fifth...and then the misca—" He takes a deep breath and rolls onto his back. "She was one of those who became...ill. She is...gone."

"Oh," Marcia says. She swallows and walks over to him, as though pulled by a string. "I'm sorry."

He shrugs, and throws his arm over his eyes. "It's all...a very long time ago." For the first time she notices that there is a light sheen on his face. His hair, tucked behind his pointed ears, looks like it needs to be washed, and his eyes are bloodshot. He looks so unwell...she feels something twist in her gut that isn't disease.

"Why did you help me?" she whispers, putting a hand to her mouth.

He sniffs. "I don't know what you're talking about."

Unconsciously, she draws her hand down her throat. His eyes, peeking beneath his arm, follow it. She sees his tongue dart out for just an instant, and then his eyes snap to hers. She knows what he was just thinking, and she knows he knows she knows. She just doesn't know what to do...should she apologize? Or him? Pretend she didn't see?

Curling tight into a ball, Dare screams, "Guards, she has a stake!"

Marcia's eyes go wide. Before she can form a coherent thought, much less a sentence, she's being hauled up and over the heads of seven dwarves. As she's carried away on her back, she can see Dare's back, and his Elmo-sock clad feet, poking out from under his robe.

Next thing she knows, she's being thrown out onto the stoop. "How dare you think of hurting Uncle Dare!" Diamonds says.

Sitting on her butt, Marcia raises her arms so they can see inside her open hoodie. "Where in the world would I hide a stake?" Beneath the hoodie, she's wearing a form-fitting tee-shirt, and below that, she's wearing yoga pants and sneakers.

Behind Diamonds, one of the other dwarves says, "I don't think she had a stake. Uncle's just not feeling well...wonder what he used so much magic on that made him so sick."

Marcia gulps. Oh, no.

"You're speaking English, you dopey 'idget," one of the other dwarves says.

"So are you!" hisses someone else, and then they all begin arguing in what is presumably Dwarvish. "Hmpf!" says Diamonds, and slams the door.

Marcia sits, staring at the door for a long time. Dare is responsible for her miracle and healing her made him ill. She knows it with the same certainty she knows how to breathe. She wants to do something for him, but it's obvious, he doesn't want to acknowledge the gift. She rubs her forehead. Maybe it's completely opposite of what she first assumed. Maybe he doesn't want it acknowledged because he doesn't want anything from her? Well, too bad, she's giving him something.

Climbing to her feet, she looks up at the sun. She used her last personal day for her doctor's visit, and she still has a few hours of free time.

Two hours and forty-five minutes later, she's back at the official residence carrying her gift. It's not an expensive gift, but she hopes that it's appropriately personal: a shiny helium balloon that says, "Get Well Soon," not "Thank you." The balloon is secured to a cute little plush bat that has a picture of the night sky on the underside of its wings; she thought it was more fitting than a bear. She knocks on the door, but no one answers. Without any other choice, she leaves the gift on the stoop. Just before she walks through the official residence's gate, she turns to look back. The little bat and balloon look pathetically small. So little in exchange for a life. She gulps. But maybe Dare wanted it that way? Magic has touched her family's life, but she decides, in honor of his wishes, she won't tell. She heads home. The setting sun warms her face and she smiles. The twisted fairy tale of her family's Cinderella night had an unexpected, but happy ending.

Except the fairy tale doesn't end there ...

IV

Marcia stares down at the letter on the official stationery of the Night Elf Embassy. It came by the post. She couldn't have been more surprised if it had come by owl, or bat. Actually, neither of those would have been as surprising as the contents of the letter itself. And it's not just the fact that Dare might have slightly misrepresented his position at the embassy. He doesn't just work there; he is the *ambassador*.

Picking up the phone, she dials the number on the letter. The line rings three times, there is a click, and then Dare's voice on the other end of the line. "Well, are you taking me up on my offer?" His phone voice is deep and liquid, not sickly, and not young.

"Oh, good, I can tell you're well," Marcia says, refusing to be discombobulated by the lack of preamble or his voice. She's sitting at home, even though it's the middle of the week.

"Well?" Dare says.

She takes a deep breath and licks her lips. "It's very generous." The office manager position he's offering is more than just generous; it's perfect. Fifteen minutes on foot door to door—Cindy will never have a "spontaneous" beer party before Marcia gets home from work again. The health insurance is more than decent, the personal day policy exactly what she needs with three kids and two parents in an assisted living situation. Also, it comes just when her hospital has decided to outsource her job.

"What's the catch?" she asks.

Dare snorts. "Isn't the fact that your boss is a blood-sucking parasite catch enough?"

Marcia sits in stunned silence for a moment, then chuckles. "I thought you preferred 'symbiote.'"

When he speaks again, she can hear his smile through the phone. "We do, indeed. I'm glad you agree it's the right term."

"I didn't..."

"I *didn't* tell you that your plan for divulgement of our... necessity...has worked well."

"Oh, good," says Marcia. She'd seen the article in the paper with his picture in it; it described a genetic disorder plaguing the Night Elves, and about blood banks being set up to counter their society's slow decline. She'd noticed nowhere in the article the mention of "vampires." They are controlling the message, which is good.

"There are a few snags," he says.

"What kind of snags?" she asks.

"Nothing a woman with your sense of diplomacy won't be able to handle," Dare says confidently.

"So you figure I'm diplomatic?" she asks, raising an eyebrow. She knows she is, but she's curious how he came to that conclusion after she barged into his home a few weeks back.

"You went to a gathering with some rather inhospitable relatives while you were dying and managed to hold it together," Dare says.

She shouldn't, but she can't quite resist teasing him a little. "You know, I never told you I was dying." The teasing makes her feel young, and not like the fifty-three-year-old woman she didn't recognize in the mirror this morning.

"You'll need all your diplomacy to deal with our royal family," Dare says in a voice that is so smooth she knows he couldn't have missed the jibe. "Between you and me," he continues, "They've been out in the sun too long. Would you like to come by the embassy tomorrow, say 10 a.m., for the tour?"

"Sure," says Marcia. "What are those snags, again?"

"You'll see," Dare replies, and for the first time she catches the hint of something almost wicked in his voice. "Oh, and thanks for the bat," he adds just before hanging up.

She blinks at the phone. Is she really going down the rabbit hole again?

Later that night, when she tells her children she'll be working for the Night Elf Embassy, Joshua puts a hand to his mouth and cries, "I'll make you a pendant of holy water!"

Alicia says, "Mom, you don't have to do that to protect us!"

Cindy says, "Don't worry, he won't bite her...professional courtesy."

... and Marcia realizes that the Night Elves might not be controlling the message as well as she had thought.

The door to Dare's office slams shut. Outside his office, Marcia jumps up from her desk and darts around it, shouting, "Diamonds!" while whipping out her key.

After three months, Marcia should recognize a "snag" in her plan before he or she enters Dare's office. But this morning she is reviewing applicants for blood donation. Because of the "host bond," donations are mixed and anonymous, but Dare is still very insistent that the donors "not be sociopaths or we may wind up with an Elizabeth Báthory situation...but don't blame us for Attila, Hitler, or Stalin!"

"Marcia!" screams Dare, his voice muffled by the door, as Marcia tries the knob. It's locked...by the reporter no doubt. Inserting the key, she hears Diamonds' and six other pairs of feet behind her. She turns the key, pushes, and the door opens.

Dare is by the window, one arm in front of his face, the other holding the stuffed bat she'd given him. He's waving it at the reporter like a priest once waved a cross at him on the street. The reporter is sitting on his desk, dress open at the front. She's leaning back, exposing her neck and breasts, saying, "Take me."

"Make her go away," Dare whines.

"Let's get her out of here, boys!" Diamonds says.

"Another one?" she hears one of the dwarves grumble. Before the "snag" can protest, she's being carried away on her back out the door, the same way the dwarves had hauled away Marcia all those months ago.

Dare peeks out from behind his arm, and then walks over, puts the bat on the desk, pats its head, and falls panting into his chair.

Without a word, Marcia goes over to the percolator—the device that keeps the fresh pig's blood from coagulating—and pours him a mug of it.

She has learned many things about Dare in the past few months. For instance, she knows that Diamonds is Dare's grandniece, by marriage, of course, not by blood. One of his daughters is married to a very nice dwarf and she has adopted four little baby dwarves. Dare has extolled the virtues of grandchildren over lunch frequently. Vampires do eat. The tiny amount of blood they drink doesn't have many calories.

She also knows that he was—and is—*supposedly* one of the most feared and respected vampires in all the realms. The reason he is the ambassador here is because he has a lot of experience on Earth, primarily hunting down rogue vampires who had disobeyed the travel ban. It's a little hard to believe sometimes. This is one of those times.

She hands him the mug and he takes it with shaky hands. "This is all your fault, you know," Dare grumbles.

He always says that. Vampires have a more devoted following than Marcia had imagined. She nods, and says, "I know."

He finishes off the mug. He has access to the blood bank, but only drinks animal blood, for some reason. Marcia's not sure if it's because he thinks human blood should go to the less fortunate, or if he has some other reason for his abstinence. She's not sure why she doesn't just ask.

Dare looks around his office and then out the window. "What a beautiful foggy day. Where do you want to go to lunch, Marcia?"

Her gut does a little twist at that.

He stands up very quickly. "Oh, but wait. Before I forget..." Walking over to a bookshelf, he says, "I know that Joshua is feeling in need of inspiration for that fashion show, and I thought, perhaps, ah..." He picks up a parcel wrapped in paper, walks over, and hands it to Marcia. He stands too close. She ducks her head and takes the parcel a little clumsily. The paper falls away, and she's staring at a book. Elves in various sorts of glittery attire walk across the cover. It's magic, very literally.

"Elven fashion for the last two thousand years...you'd need an encyclopedia for all the Earth fashions in the same time frame," he says, backing away and sitting down on the desk. "But perhaps it will spark Joshua's muse." Dare knows about Joshua's muse's recent absence because a few days ago, over lunch, Joshua had texted her thirty-one times. Instead of being mad, Dare had read the messages over her shoulder.

"It's beautiful," she says. And priceless. Elvish works of art and literature are still rare, especially originals. She could sell this book to Sotheby's and all her financial problems would be over...forever.

"It's a gift," he says casually.

Marcia swallows. She won't ever sell it.

"So where should we go to lunch?" he asks. "I think I might be in the mood for garlic...does Italian or Chinese suit you?"

How to be diplomatic? "You had Italian yesterday," she says.

His lips purse. "True. But you weren't with me."

"Cindy was with you," she says. Did that sound snippy? She didn't mean it to sound snippy.

"Hmmmm...she seemed to be wandering a little far afield," Dare says, shaking his head.

Marcia huffs. "I hate that open campus lunch policy." Cindy had, according to her, "just bumped into Dare," but Marcia's not sure she believes it.

Dare raises an eyebrow at her. "Is something bothering you, Marcia?"

Marcia looks at the book with the glittering elves drifting across the covers. Many things are wrong. But she thinks...she thinks this might be the way to put them all to rest. Drive a stake through it, so to speak. She winces. "Cindy...well, I think she might have thought...well, the way she was talking to Alicia...I think she may have thought yesterday's lunch...was a date."

She remembers Cindy leaning against the door of Alicia's room, saying, "Dracula took me to lunch...he paid and everything. He's so handsome, and the way he looked at me, it made me feel like I was the only person in the world."

Dare bursts out laughing.

When Marcia looks up at him in alarm, he stops.

"Oh, right, I'm sorry. That is...disturbing, and I shouldn't have laughed," he says contritely.

"It's easy," Marcia says, her jaw getting hard, "to see how she might have gotten that impression."

Dare snorts and rolls his eyes. "Yes, we have so much in common."

"She's a seventeen-year-old girl who lost her father, who thinks she is abused because she is used as a pawn by her god-mother...and she's looking for a father figure to save her!" Marcia bursts out.

Dare's face gets very serious again, and his eyes soften. "Ah..."

"You spend a lot of time with us," Marcia says. This is true. His home is past hers, the kids' bus stop is on the way, and almost every night he winds up walking the three of them home...Sometimes he talks to Joshua, sometimes he talks to Alicia, and sometimes he talks to Cindy. It has been a good thing. Alicia stands a little taller when he talks to her; she says it's because she 'isn't about to show fear to him.' Cindy has started doing her homework more regularly. Marcia is still not sure what Dare said to encourage that. And Joshua no longer gets bullied, because he's met at the bus stop by 'Dracula.' A few times she has wanted to invite Dare into their house for dinner; but, considering how exciting dinners with her family can be, she has been embarrassed and afraid.

Marcia licks her lips nervously. "It might be better...if we, you know, take it easy for a while."

She closes her eyes and exhales. There, that's done. Now she'll just come up with a reason to skip lunch.

"Is that really what's bothering you?" says Dare.

No, it isn't. Marcia wraps her arms around herself and looks at the floor. What's really bothering her is that she is attracted to her boss, who is not just her boss, but out of her league and wrong for her in so many ways. She's not sure how it happened. Usually, with younger men she finds them cute...but a little... well, young. She likes men with silver in their hair and creases in their foreheads, and laugh lines. Men who have loved and lost, and lived, whom she doesn't have to explain things to, about grief, and children, and life, because they *understand*. The problem is Dare understands, too. And two days ago, it had nearly cost her everything. He'd taken her arm in his after lunch, a gesture she's sure he learned during a short visit to New York in the 1800s. She'd looked up at him at precisely the same moment he'd looked down at her, and she almost melted. Worse, she'd stood up on her tiptoes, and then she'd almost kissed him. If that truck hadn't honked its horn...better not to think about it.

"Because if it is, I think I have a solution...to everyone's problems," says Dare.

"Oh," says Marcia, not knowing where he is going with this, but hoping there will be a way for her to wiggle out of lunch.

She sees him wave a hand in the periphery of her vision, and the door slams shut. She gasps and turns her head. "Did you use magic to close the door?"

He puts a hand on top of her left one. Her arms are crossed, and his hand covers her hand and part of her arm...and she goes hot all over. Marcia feels her face go completely red. She looks down at his hand on hers, so he doesn't realize she's blushing like a schoolgirl.

"I could be a real father figure to them, if I became their father."

After those words come out of Dare's mouth, it takes what feels like a century for Marcia to put them together. "What?" she blurts out. She must have misheard, because the words don't really make *sense*.

"We're perfect together," Dare says. "You're diplomatic, and you're brave..."

She blinks at that and he says, "You thought your life was in danger when I brought back Cindy's silly shoe, but you didn't lose your head. I could see you, thinking about where to hide your children, possibly thinking of what sort of kitchen implement you might use as a stake. I was almost expecting you to push me off the balcony."

Her lips part and she feels her heart stop. He had picked up on that?

"Your advice is spot on. Your handling of my royal family's..." He grimaces. "Eccentricities, is inspired."

"Anyone could have told them that asking about potential blood donors' virginity status would bring about a political firestorm," Marcia says.

"But no one did," Dare says. "We make a good team...I mean, I think that I am good for your family."

And hadn't she just been thinking exactly that? She swallows. It's not a speech a young man would give, not at all. It's something an older man would say. And that is what makes it right, and more romantic, rather than less.

She hears him gulp. "We can't get married on Earth with the current state of inter-hominid marriage laws, but in the Night Elf kingdom it would be acceptable. It would make a lot of my fellow elves extremely jealous, but I don't care." He squeezes her hand. "And you don't need to worry about it being a polyamory situation where I have a vampire wife as well. I've had children, already."

"What?"

He winces. "At one time it was practiced. Not just a male vampire and a human woman and vampire woman; it went the other way as well. I've always personally felt with three you tend to triangulate." He shudders. "I have enough of being diplomatic with my job. I don't need that at home."

She stares at him open-mouthed for far too long. "I look like your mother," she stammers at last.

His lips purse, and he pulls her hand to his stomach. He looks to the side, and then back at her. "Nooooo...she has pointed ears, and fangs...and is blonde..." His voice says, *I know this is a trick question. I just don't know what.* He smiles sunnily. "She'll adore you!"

Sometimes he seems old and immensely wise, and sometimes he seems just...clueless. "When we go out to eat," Marcia says in a slow, careful voice, "At least three times, people have mistaken me for your mother. And...you...laugh."

"Because...it's...funny," he says in the same careful voice. He smiles again, and this time it is wicked. "I don't think of you like my mother at all." His voice is just as wicked as his smile. A mouth that just drank pig's blood shouldn't look as sexy as it does.

Marcia still stands frozen. "I'm going to get very old...very quickly...in the grand scheme of things." *Don't kiss him,* she tells herself, *think of the pig's blood, think of the pig's blood...*

Dare stands up, and he's very close, too close. He clutches her hand to his chest. "First off...just as vampires look, I am told, 'too beautiful' to human eyes, humans look the same to us. But...moreover, if you are my wife, my host, you won't grow old. You might even look younger..."

She looks up and finds him gazing down at her hand.

"That's the symbiotic benefit we're not supposed to talk about." Not looking up, he adds, "And you won't get cancer again."

She can see where they might want to keep that quiet. Vampires could wind up hunted to extinction...or something. But then Marcia takes a sharp breath. "I never told you I had cancer."

"No," he says. "But I guessed when I realized you could see our fangs." He shrugs, eyes still downcast. "We have an innate glamour that hides them. Humans who are very close to death...they can see them...and humans in other, emotional, non-death situations."

"You healed me..."

His eyes meet hers, and he looks very old again. "No, I will never say that I did. Please...don't even think of it. There is no compulsion to take up my offer, Marcia."

Marcia looks down at her hand, and laughs softly. "Usually, on Earth, an offer coming from my boss would be considered compulsion."

She feels his hand loosen, looks up, and sees a pained expression on his face, as though she's struck him. "That was the most undiplomatic observation of all time," she says, pulling his hand to her lips and closing her eyes to kiss it.

A coil of hair has fallen in front of her eyes, and he brushes it back. "Does this mean you'll...?"

"I'm saying I'll consider it." She swallows. "But...you should have dinner with my family. You might change your mind."

When she looks up at him, his lips are parted. For the first time since she was ill, she can see his fangs. He doesn't have to explain to her that it has nothing to do with death this time.

He's not the perfect vision of a prince in a fairy tale, but then she's not a princess either.

Marcia doesn't have Dare over for dinner that night. Instead, she broaches the subject with her family first.

"You're so old," says Cindy. "But I guess you're both evil and made for each other." She gets up from the table, goes to her room, and slams the door.

Alicia says, "Mom, you don't have to do this for us."

Joshua, looking at his book, says, "Go for it, Mom. I've been telling everyone at school you've been dating him for months."

"What?" says Marcia.

He waves a hand. "Why do you think all the bullies at school leave me alone now?"

Turning back to Alicia, Marcia says, "I am doing it for *myself*, too. I like him."

Alicia shrugs. "If you're happy."

Marcia looks after Cindy. "Would it help her if I tell her he likes me because I'm old?" And then realizes she's said the thought out loud.

"It might give her hope, Mom." Alicia says. "Joshua's got fashion. I've got good grades…she just thinks she's *only* pretty."

Marcia notices she's not slouching at all.

Cindy hugs Marcia. Maybe grudgingly, maybe shyly, Marcia can't tell. "You look beautiful," she says. "Joshua outdid himself on the dress." The wedding dress, made by Joshua of elven silk that appears to be shimmering water, is beautiful.

Marcia pulls away. "You look beautiful, too," she whispers in her ear. "But you're more than that. You'll figure it out." Cindy nods, and the moment is uncomfortable. Marcia doesn't believe there will ever be a magical moment when it all comes together, but bit-by-bit, maybe someday.

Cindy stands in front of Dare. "You look old."

"He does not look old, he looks older," Marcia says. He's given himself some gray hairs, laugh lines, and crow's feet.

Dare shrugs. "Magic? Is there anything it can't do?"

Marcia hadn't asked him to change his appearance. He had done it himself, saying he was worried about the kids "not respecting him as an authority figure." It's an illusion, and if Dare doesn't maintain it, it will fade. Judging by the way Cindy responds to it, it was a good idea.

Likewise, Dare hadn't asked the first time he drank Marcia's blood; she'd just bitten her lip and then kissed him. Judging by how easy it has become for him to maintain his illusion of age after she started giving him blood, it was a good idea.

Behind them, a carriage drawn by griffins comes to a stop.

"Don't worry," says Joshua, with his hand on Diamonds. "We'll have fun with our dwarf cousins while you start your happily ever after."

Diamonds snorts. "You won't have too much fun."

Dare huffs. "Happily ever after, not at all. I'm literally a pain in the neck, and your mother can be stubborn."

Marcia elbows him, and he elbows her back.

Alicia, quiet the whole time, breaks into sobs at his words. Everyone in the party goes silent.

"Alicia?" Marcia says, going to her.

Her usually stoic, unemotional daughter throws her arms around her neck. "Thank you for giving me a real fairy tale. A fairy tale I can believe in."

FIN

About the Author: *Magic After Midnight* takes place in C. Gockel's *USA Today* bestselling I Bring the Fire universe. The first book in I Bring the Fire, *Wolves*, is available as an ebook, paperback, and audiobook. The series stars Loki, Norse God of Mischief and Chaos. C. Gockel has a healthy respect for Chaos; she has children. To learn more about C. Gockel's books, visit her website at www.cgockelwrites.com.

DANCE WITH THE DEVIL
DONNA AUGUSTINE

I

AGAIN!" MR. BINK SCREAMED FROM THE FRONT OF THE studio. Anastasia avoided looking at him as she went through the motions, hoping she could blend with the rest of the dancers.

From the first moment Anastasia had joined the ballet company, Mr. Bink had criticized nearly everything about her. Her posture was bad, her legs too thick, the arch of her foot too flat, her bun too messy. Nothing went unseen or unremarked upon.

"Faster! Some of you are falling behind the beat!" Mr. Bink clapped his hands loudly. "Anastasia, sloppy, sloppy. And you think you can dance a solo?" Mr. Bink turned, but not before he let out a sound of utter disgust that was loud enough to surely be heard by everyone in the room, even with the piano playing.

Ana blinked rapidly, hoping to keep the tears back as she continued to move in rhythm with the rest of the dancers.

She ignored the looks from her fellow dancers, which varied between disgust and pity. She knew after a year of being with the company, she should be past the point where Mr. Bink could make her cry. Clearly, she wasn't.

"Enough!" Mr. Bink said, the piano player stopping as Bink's hand slashed through the air. "I'm done looking at the group of you. We're finished for the day. You better not perform like this tomorrow. I won't be embarrassed in front of our guest."

Ana's eyes fluttered shut as she stood relieved. Looked like today would be an easier day. There'd be hell tomorrow, though, if they didn't please Mr. Bink when Marcum Hills was there. He was the best-known choreographer in the northeast. Ana never pleased Mr. Bink, so things weren't looking good for her, but that was tomorrow's worry.

She made her way over toward the corner, and settled in beside her bag. She grabbed her towel off where it sat on her bag and wiped the sweat still pouring down her face. With her back partially shielding her from the room, she tugged at the first pointe slipper as she tensed and waited for the pain. The nail on her big toe wiggled with the movement, and she sucked air in through her teeth as she finally got the slipper off. One down, she took a small pause before gathering up the fortitude to tackle the next one, which shouldn't be quite as bad, as she tended to favor her right foot.

She would've heard Mr. Bink approaching if her senses hadn't been muted by the pain of the second slipper gliding over damaged flesh. She smelled the strong cologne and quickly tugged the discarded towel up to her ankles, shielding her damaged feet from view. But it was too late and she knew it.

She turned slightly and looked over at Mr. Bink. His eyes were narrowed as he gazed at Ana, his mouth downturned. His shoe, one of the various shiny black leather ones he owned, pointed at her. This was it, what she'd been dreading since she'd joined the company.

"I'm sorry to inform you, but no matter how hard I try to improve this situation, it isn't going to work out any longer." Nothing about his words or the clipped voice he used to speak them spoke of remorse.

"Please, I'll try harder. I'll practice twice as hard as everyone else," Ana said, not divulging that she already practiced every night after she left for the day.

Mr. Bink's eyes made an obvious travel down toward her now covered feet, and the few gray strands left on his head swayed with the subtle shake of his head. There was a long, slow exhale before he continued. "I took you on as a favor to your aunt, but we both know you aren't cut out for this."

Maybe she should accept it. Give up and realize she'd never be a prima ballerina. She looked around at the dancers close enough to overhear, including Maria, the shining star of their company.

Maria's form was always perfect, her arches high and hair always smooth. Maria was a reminder of everything Ana didn't have. Maria was a born prima.

She saw Maria, and several of the others weren't talking. Their ears were all turned in Ana's direction, and by later tonight, the entire company would have heard some version of this discussion. The humiliation settled a little heavier; her spirit felt a little dingier and worn down.

But dreams didn't die an easy death—not the real kind. She spoke, not caring that it would add to the tale of mortification. "Please, just let me finish this season out."

Mr. Bink crossed his arms, and a single boney finger tapped against the silk sleeve of the other arm. "I'll let you remain until the end of the season because your aunt is a fairly large donor to this company, but you won't be performing. There's a limit to what I can suffer through." He leaned down, hunching over her. "And I wouldn't go complaining to her, either. I know things about you."

Her mouth opened but nothing came out as the pieces fit together. It had been him.

Mr. Bink smiled, and he looked like a rabid dog baring its teeth, before he turned. His heels hit the wooden floor and echoed through the room as he left.

Ana slumped where she sat, the other dancers whispering around her until the room fell silent and she was the only one left.

She knew someone had searched her locker the other day. They hadn't made it a secret, but left her things bunched up and wrinkled, instead of the neat piles she always arranged. The pills she took to keep up her rigorous schedule had been gone.

It didn't matter why she took them. If word got out, she'd be tossed out of the company. Mr. Bink had finally won.

II

The devil walked down the dark avenue just as the clock in the center of town struck midnight. The streetlights reflected off his thick black hair and the sheen of his Italian suit as he approached her. She was sitting on a bench in the darkest corner, her head down as she stared at the cobblestones.

She'd been calling to him for years. She'd been ten the first time, after she'd lost a dance recital. He hadn't come to her then. She hadn't been desperate enough.

She was fourteen the next time she'd called. It had been right after she wasn't selected for the first company she'd applied to. Again, he hadn't been interested.

She'd called to him again tonight. He'd pondered his available amusements before deciding to come. It wasn't as if there weren't other options. Any day of the week, there were thousands of people trying to strike a deal with the devil. He was in high demand and always would be.

The thing most humans didn't understand was that desperation had to age like a fine wine. If it were served too soon, it wouldn't yield nearly the same full-bodied taste. But now she was ready. She was worth the trip.

He sat beside her, reclined against the bench, crossed his legs and rested his arm along the back. There was a second of pause before her body jerked. Her head shot up and she looked up at him, surprised someone had sat beside her and she hadn't noticed their approach.

"I've heard you want to make a deal, Anastasia?"

She shifted away from him on the bench. But she didn't get up. Oh yes, she was ready.

Her chest rose and fell noticeably as she took in his face and then his clothes. He knew how he appeared to her: an attractive man in his twenties, financially well off and confident. The exact type of man she'd met so many times at ballet fundraisers; the kind of man she always hoped to catch the eye of and had always failed.

"How do you know my name?" she asked.

She should have been more alarmed but he could see the appeal of his current form settle in to the rapid rate of her heart. Her tongue darted out to wet her lips—in direct conflict to the logical response to retreat that most humans would have.

"I know everyone's name, but especially those who call me." He reached into the pocket of his suit jacket and withdrew a cigar. It was rolled by Cubans, in a place much warmer than Cuba. He looked over a slight imperfection in the cigar. They were going to pay for that later.

"But I don't know who you are," she said.

"Of course you do." He smiled before he placed the cigar in his mouth. With a flick of his hand, a flame appeared at the tip of his finger and he puffed gently.

"You're... Are you..." Chewed nails went to her mouth as he took in her ratty appearance: drab hair, ashen skin, nothing overly remarkable.

He took the cigar from his mouth and watched her visible discomfort with the smoke. Cancer wasn't going to be an issue for her soon. She'd have bigger problems if she struck a deal with him, which of course she was going to. She'd been calling to him for too long.

"Who else? You've been calling to me for a while," he said, as he felt the strength of her life force. She wasn't much to look at, but she was healthy and strong. Her soul would be worth the aggravation. With all the people in the world and so many of them willing to strike deals, he was much more selective than he used to be. But her soul would be worth it. Not a top-of-the-line recruit, but enough to bother with.

"Can you help me?" she asked. Those were the magic words. She knew who he was and still wanted his help. This would be a quick one. It was going to be almost as easy as pointing her in the right direction to go at a fork in the road.

He rolled his eyes before he answered, "I can do anything I want. I can make you the most famous dancer that's ever lived."

"What do you want in return?"

He hated this part. One drunken night and it'd been centuries of contracts ever since. At least it kept that pain in the ass who lived upstairs out of his business now. Before, it was constant squabbles.

He reached into his suit again, and this time pulled out a single sheet of vellum. With a snap of his fingers, a quill pen appeared in his other hand, and he gave both to her. "All I need from you is a signature at the bottom of this contract."

She held up the vellum until it was illuminated by the streetlight, and squinted as she tried to decipher the Latin. He always wanted to laugh when they tried to figure out what was in it. He might have made a drunken agreement, but there were ways around everything.

"So, what happens exactly?"

"I make all your dreams come true, and when you die, you're mine."

"And what does that mean exactly?"

"Does it matter?" He stood and held out his arm for her. She rose, placing her hand in the crook of his arm, and he began to walk with her. "I know the pain you feel every day, the inadequacy. The way they look at you and talk about you when you aren't there."

As they walked, people appeared as if walking out of the shadows, staring at her, whispering as they walked past. People who looked just like the dancers from the company.

"Imagine yourself on a stage right now," he said, and suddenly they weren't walking on cobblestones anymore but across the wood of a stage, lights shining at them as they moved toward the front. Suddenly, the lights dimmed and a crowd was roaring with cheers, getting to their feet and applauding her. The dark sweatpants and shirt she'd been wearing were now the costume of a prima ballerina. A man approached and handed her a bouquet of roses.

He let her absorb it all for a moment. He'd made it so real that she couldn't help but be absorbed into the scene, feel the crowd's energy flow over her.

"You'll have a wonderful life. You'll be the most beautiful dancer who ever pirouetted across the stage. Every man will want you. You'll have the world at you fingertips." He moved in closer and said softly, "They'll love you.

"Don't you want everything you've ever wished for to come true? And then once you've lived the most wonderful life you could imagine, you'll spend some time with me.

"I'm not so bad. You shouldn't listen to all the things they say about me. Listen to your gut. There's a reason you've been calling me since you were a child. You know what you should do."

She nodded, as she stared into the crowd, mesmerized.

And then they faded away, their cheers with them, and Ana and the devil were back to standing alone in the drizzly, dark evening.

"All you need to do is write your name down," he said as the contract and pen reappeared in her hands.

She held the sheet against her leg in her urgency to find somewhere to sign.

"When will this all happen?" she asked as she handed him the sheet.

He folded it and tucked it away. "Go home and go to sleep knowing your entire life is about to change."

She couldn't leave quickly enough, smiling the whole way.

"So, what do you think, boss? She worth the effort?" the small scaled demon asked as he came to stand beside him. The young man he'd appeared to be minutes ago bearing roses was completely gone.

"I think so, Bobber," the devil said as he smoked his cigar and watched her disappear toward her apartment.

Ana woke the next morning and had to think back to the night before. Had that been real? Had she really made a deal with the devil? Stood in front of a crowd as they cheered?

She grabbed a hairband from her nightstand and pulled her hair into a ponytail, or tried. That was the first sign things were off. Every day, she did the same thing. She got up and put her hair in a ponytail and the band wrapped around her hair three times. Now she barely was able to wrap it twice.

She got out of bed and walked over to the mirror above her dresser. Her hair still looked like hers, but she'd grown more of it overnight. Her skin was glowing like she'd just gotten back from a sunny place that left a warm glow. Her eyes that had always been a dull blue seemed brighter. She still looked like herself, but a much-improved version. Maybe last night had happened.

She showered and changed, wondering what today would bring.

When she got to the ballet company, she wasn't the only one to notice. Her fellow dancers were all looking at her and whispering behind their hands.

"Ana?" She turned to see Scott, one of the lead soloists, who'd never spoken to her before.

"Hi."

"You look...different. Did you do something?" he asked as his gaze kept running over her features, as if he couldn't quite put his finger on the difference.

"Nothing," she said as she tried to repress the smile of attracting the attention of the best-looking dancer in the company.

He nodded and said something about maybe grabbing a coffee after the practice before he left.

"Maybe," she said. She made her way with the rest of the dancers as they went to the stage and prepared for their guest.

An hour later, Ana stood on the sidelines of the stage as Marcum, the guest choreographer whom she'd been hearing about for months, appraised the dancers moving before him.

His ballets could skyrocket a dancer to stardom, but that wouldn't happen if she was never seen. As she stood, watching her chance of being in one of the most anticipated ballets in the ballet corps' history fade, she wondered again if last night's meeting had been a dream.

The group of dancers switched places with another group of names called. It was the last group to go, and she hadn't been called to join them, so she knew it wouldn't be. She saw the looks. They all knew. Mr. Bink would allow her to stay, but it was going to be at a high cost. Marcum would never see her dance.

She heard some scuffling, and the curtain that shielded the side of the stage where she was standing suddenly came down. A group of her fellow dancers seemed to have gotten caught up in it. The material ripped with a horrific sound, and then was joined by Mr. Bink's voice as he demanded to know what had happened.

Mr. Bink glanced over at an annoyed Marcum and told the group to silence and the dancers to restart.

Without the cover of the curtain, Ana couldn't stop herself from looking over at the handsome Marcum, praying somehow he'd notice her, and more convinced than ever last night had been nothing but a desperate delusion.

His dark eyes wandered away from the dancers until he was staring straight at her. She turned away, thinking he must have sensed her staring.

"Who's she?" he asked, loud enough that everyone heard him and Ana looked back.

He was staring at her with an intensity that was nearly unsettling.

"She's not one of my best," Mr. Bink said with a dismissive wave.

Marcum kept staring at her, ignoring Mr. Bink. "There's something about her. I want to see her dance."

"Ana, step forward," Mr. Bink barked. "Do the solo from *Swan Lake*."

Ana's insides tensed. She couldn't do that solo no matter how many times she tried without tripping at some point, and Mr. Bink was more aware of that than anyone.

But this was her chance and she had to nail it. Then she thought of last night. Things were supposed to change. If it were real, this would be her moment.

The dancers cleared the stage, some giggling as they did, since many of them had seen her try and perform this dance before. She took her position and the piano started to play and she let all her worries drop, her lifelong insecurities and every negative word she'd ever heard, and leapt across the stage as if she were born to dance this part. The music took control of her body as if driving her on some other level. She leapt and turned with flawlessness that would've put even Maria to shame.

The music stopped as she finished with her chin tilted up and froze. There wasn't a sound to be heard, not even breathing. Had she botched it? She'd felt so natural, so fluid.

She looked around and saw nothing but shock, except from Marcum, who was smiling. He began to clap.

III

Five years later

"Ana, darling, you look beautiful tonight."

Ana looked up at Marcum's handsome face as he came to stand beside her dressing table.

"Are you ready for your performance?"

She toyed with the engagement ring that he'd given her a month ago. She always left it on until the very moment she had to go onstage. "With you beside me? Of course I am."

He walked over and took the empty chair beside hers. "After the performance, there's some people who would like to meet you."

"I thought tonight would just be us?"

"We're only going to meet them for a quick drink. They might be willing to fund that new ballet I'm creating for you." He leaned in and kissed her cheek before saying, "You know no one can get enough of you, including me."

There was a knock at her door. "Ana, it's time."

She tugged off her engagement ring and handed it to Marcum. "I'll see you after." With a kiss, she left to head to the stage.

In five years, she had metamorphosed from a mediocre ballet dancer with no dating life to speak of to the reigning prima ballerina in the world. She was engaged to a man so handsome and charming that even after a year of dating and having a ring on her finger, she still found herself staring at him.

There was only one thing marring her life, and that was a memory of a night five years ago. What was the cost going to be? Had it ever even happened? What if she'd imagined the whole thing? After all, did the devil really even exist?

She heard her cue to enter the stage, and as she stepped out, she felt the excitement and adoration of the crowd wash over her. She let it take away all of the unwanted memories of contracts and souls.

He took his front-row seat as the show began. This would be her last performance, so he figured he might as well enjoy it. After all, she was his creation. And surprisingly, he'd found he enjoyed being around her.

When the curtain started to rise and the seat beside him hadn't been taken yet, he had a bad feeling he was going to get an unexpected visitor.

God strolled in, so predictable in a suit of pristine white, and sat beside him.

"God," he said to the unwelcome newcomer.

"Lucifer," God replied.

God crossed his arms and settled in, watching as the performance began. Anastasia came dancing across the stage, looking as if she were weightless in her movements. He took a sip of his champagne as he watched her, appreciating the beauty of her lines.

She'd risen to stardom overnight, her brilliant dance form catapulting her to fame, not just within the ballet world but until her name was known by everyone. It was a done deal as soon as she'd signed.

"You did well, Lucifer," God said, leaning in as he said it.

"I did."

"So tonight is her last?" God asked.

Here it came. He really knew how to ruin a good time. He had been raining all over his parade for millennia, sometimes even literally. Hell, they'd needed an ark once.

He turned to watch God. But why her? Yes, she was exquisite now, but only with his help had she become that way. There was really nothing special about her.

"Do you really need her? Another soul when you have so many?" God asked, his eyes still on the stage.

"Yes. I do. What's it to you?"

The devil saw how God was watching her and the sadness there. "Her family has been praying for her. I wanted to try and help them out."

"Why would they pray for her? Her life has been fabulous." Only the devil and God knew the truth behind her rise to fame.

"Her grandmother knows what she did," God said.

The devil did a quick mental search before the woman clicked in his head. That was why Anastasia's soul had felt so strong. She had a small taste of that old woman's strength. Her grandmother was nearly ninety, and what a soul on her. Strong as an ox, that lady was.

"So? What do you think?" God asked. "Maybe let this one slide?"

Devil shook his head. "No can do. I've got a signed contract. I start letting people off because of a few prayers and who knows what crazy ideas they'll come up with?"

God nodded, as if he'd figured as much, and then stood and straightened his suit.

"You're not going to stay for the rest of the show?" the devil asked.

"You know, I've never cared for your endings."

"Just remember—she called me."

"I know," God said, and then walked away.

The devil leaned back and watched the rest of the performance. She was exquisite, but she should be. She was young enough to have another five, maybe even ten years of her career left. He did enjoy watching her dance. Maybe he should allow her to live a while longer. Either way, he wouldn't cut short the performance, so he had time to think it through.

By the time she was done, even he was moved by her. The emotion, love and dedication she sank into her craft was unparalleled. He realized this hadn't been all him. It had always been there. Maybe she hadn't needed him as much as he thought? Maybe she only needed the confidence he'd given her to become what had always been there.

He watched as she stood front and center and a bouquet of roses was placed in her arms. Her eyes scanned her adoring audience and then landed on him. Her smile widened.

He returned the smile as he sat back and waited for her to take her final bow.

Or maybe not.

The dancers left the stage and the audience started to leave. He got out of his seat and made his way back to her dressing room.

She greeted him with a smile as he walked back in, and he dug into his pocket.

"Here's your ring, darling."

Ana took it back, a smile settling on her lips as she slid the ring back onto her finger.

"Marcum, I'll just be a moment to change."

He nodded and settled on a small couch along the wall. He watched her move about the dressing room and realized he couldn't kill this woman. Something strange had happened while he amused himself with her these past five years.

A flick of his fingers and she'd be dead. He had the signed contract that gave him the right. Yet he couldn't do it. He, the devil, couldn't kill her.

She was standing by a rack of clothes when she said, "Where are we meeting these people for drinks?"

He shook his head. "I canceled it. Let's just go home and be alone."

She smiled and nodded. "That sounds perfect."

"There's a couple of things we should talk about," he said, as he wondered how adaptable she'd be. All the humans said that a good relationship was based on trust and honesty.

"About what?" she asked, looking concerned.

"Nothing too big. How do you handle warmer climates?"

FIN

About the Author: To learn more about Donna Augustine and all her books visit her website: www.donnaaugustine.com.

NO GIFT OF WORDS
ANNIE BELLET

THE GIBBOUS MOON HUNG OVER THE CROWNS OF THE baobab trees as Afua slipped from her cot and headed up the cliff road to the house of the witch. Red clay wet with the night rains slapped beneath her heavy feet, her hurried strides belying the fear curling in her belly. It was a dangerous thing to steal from a witch.

But after tonight, she would no longer be called Sahona, the frog. Afua had always brushed off the insults, thinking that she'd grow like her friend Talata had grown, tall and graceful. Afua stayed squat, however, with a pointed face like a chameleon's, blotchy skin, and bowed legs more suited to a lemur than a young woman.

She turned up the steep path above the village, glancing down toward where the moonlight glinted on the rice patties below. The witch, Mpamonka, was said to be the most beautiful woman on the Island, renewed by the magic in her fitaratra, a jug carved from lightning in the beach sands far to the west. Thinking about her half-formed plan, Afua shivered, though not from cold. The forest closed in and the path grew narrower, the red clay turning to coarse grass. Shadows danced, silver and black, and somewhere a night bird called warning.

The witch's hut stood beside a mountain spring that welled from the rock and dropped off the cliffs into darkness. Biting her lip hard enough to taste blood, Afua hovered at the edge of the clearing against a mango tree and listened. The forest shifted and sighed around her, insects buzzing and leaves rustling. No human sounds found her ears. With a deep breath, she walked forward. No more feet slapping against the soil now.

The fitaratra hung from a silk cord on the side of the hut. Once she'd seen it, the vessel seemed to call to Afua, its slender clarity shining as though it were soaking in the moon's light. "No more Sahona," the power whispered. "Become the most beautiful woman in Vazimba." Afua would be Hanuhane, admired, beloved.

Her fingers closed on the thin glass and the cool water beaded on her dark skin. She lifted the vessel down, stepping away from the curtained door, not daring to breathe. Afua backed away until her calves touched the smooth stone surrounding the spring.

With a silent prayer to Zanahary, she tipped the fitaratra to her lips and drank deep.

Fire lit in her belly as though she'd eaten a handful of ants. Afua bit back a scream and dropped the fitaratra. It shattered on the stone, slivers of moonlight flying in all directions. A woman's scream broke the night, coming from the hut.

Afua ran. Warm blood flowed from tiny cuts on her arms and legs and cheek. She held herself as she went, coughing and spitting. Shooting pain burned its way down her thighs and she fell, curling into a ball in the mud. She felt as though someone were pulling on her very skin in all directions.

"Girl! Thief in the night," a woman's voice sounded above her.

Afua forced her eyes open and saw the witch, more like a shadow of a woman than the true form in the darkness. Afua opened her mouth to speak, but only moans came out.

"Why have you stolen my potion? Why have you broken my jug?"

Afua licked cracking lips and shook her head. She wondered if the witch would kill her. She wondered if she were dying anyway. But she clung to the hope that the potion was working, clung with her last sane breath.

"I did not," she said, forcing the words out like stones across her twisting tongue. "I am sick, I came for healing." It was easy to lie to a shadow in the forest.

"Liar," the witch said and she spit into Afua's face. Her saliva was sticky and smelled of vanilla. "Since you like lies so much, I curse you to always tell them. And since you are so clumsy, everything you hold shall slip from your fingers like grains of sand through a seam."

"No," cried Afua, closing her eyes against the horror and the biting pain. She tried to explain. She only wanted beauty, an end to the mean sideways glances and snide words, a way to regain her friendship with beautiful Tatala. The words stuck in her throat and she found only lies rising like bile to take their place.

"I will release you," the witch said, walking away, "when you are able to apologize to me and mean it."

"Azafady, miala tsiny aho," Afua sobbed, curling around her splitting skin, her ant-filled belly. But she knew now the curse had hold, because she could say the words, beg forgiveness but she didn't mean them. The truth coiled like a snake deep in her heart and whispered as the fitaratra had. Any price for beauty.

She slipped into unconsciousness; the false apologies murmured over and over like a prayer in the dark.

The raffia ropes cut into Afua's shoulders as she dragged the plow along another row, slogging through the cracking mud of the fallow paddy beneath the hot sun. Last row before she broke for a meal, but the thought brought her no joy. She reached the end and shrugged the harness off using her elbows and chin to assist.

Talata, Zaza, and Alakamisy were already resting in the shade of the mango grove when she reached it, their clean legs stretched out on the soft grass, passing around a jug of water.

Afua smiled at them with her teeth only. "I wish you an excellent day," she said. Sometimes only telling lies had its advantages.

They three giggled as Talata pointed to one of the trees. "Are you hungry, Anaombe?"

Afua turned, already knowing what she'd find. Her leaf-wrapped lunch sat in the crook of a tree, tied to a branch by the cord she used to carry it from the village. She could use her fingers in small motions to untie the knot, but she'd have to jump up and use her arms to pull the packet down since her hands wouldn't grip long enough to matter.

"Are you thirsty?" Zaza joined in on the taunting as Afua stood with clenched fists, staring up at the food.

She was parched, her throat thick with dust and heat. But all that came out of her when she spoke was, "of course not, I've never been less thirsty."

At home she could just nod or shake her head, ignoring the pursed lips of her mother and her father's unhappy eyes. Here though, she had no such protection or understanding.

The sound of men and cattle on the road drew the girls' attention away from Afua. Around the bend and through the far baobab trees came two white oxen drawing a magnificent cart decorated with yellow and indigo patterns cut into the wood.

"A noble," Tatala said breathlessly. "I wonder if he's a king?"

Afua had taken their distraction as an opportunity and was using her fingers to quickly unhook her lunch, jumping up and down to pull the packet from the branches before the girls turned back again. She got the leaf-wrapped rice down, balancing it on her breasts, tucked beneath her chin.

It slipped down and broke open on the ground as she looked up and saw the man in question leap free of his ox-chair and stride toward their little grove. He was tall as any man in the village, with tight dark curls braided through with silk and glass beads that chimed together as he walked. His face was broad and handsome and as he approached she met his gaze and saw his eyes were brown-gold banded with orange, like the andasibe flowers growing in the groves along the western cliffs. His robes were silk, shining red and yellow and green like a beetle's back beneath the high sun.

"Manakory," he said in greeting, his voice soft and deep. "We are on our way to Jofodiafotaka. This is the correct road, yes?"

"It is," Talata said, tossing her braids over her shoulder and stepping forward. She thrust her breasts out against the bright cloth of her dress.

The king, for Afua thought he must be one of the Ambaniandro kings, ignored Talata and stepped into the shade, looking directly at Afua. She looked down at her muddy feet and the spilled rice in front of them. He was only curious because he didn't know her.

The witch's potion had worked. Afua knew what this stranger saw, why he was so curious. She'd come down from the cliffs in daylight, the pain gone from her limbs but with only lies upon her lips. No more the bow legs and lizard's face, gone her uneven skin and coarse hair. Afua stood graceful and tall with smooth dark skin and golden eyes. She was easily the most beautiful woman in Vazimba.

But the price was too high to overlook. Soon the admiration and surprise faded and the ridicule returned. No man wanted a wife whose hands couldn't grip a tool or hold a child, nor did anyone care to talk to a woman who couldn't speak anything but lies.

Afua bit her lip and looked up. The king still stared, head cocked to one side like a monkey's. He saw a beautiful woman in a rag with muddy feet and thin arms. He didn't really see her, no one did. She stared right back, shame making her angry as next to her the three girls started to giggle again.

"What is your name?" The king asked.

"Anaombe," Talata answered for Afua, glaring at her before moving forward so that she almost touched the king. "She pulls the rice plough like an ox, but different." Talata smiled, trying to draw him into the joke.

I am Afua, who traded truth and skill for beauty, she whispered in her mind.

"I am Ratsibahaka," Afua said aloud, making fists with her useless hands. She couldn't stand the taunts, not in front of the considering eyes of this stranger. "I am queen of the Lemurs and all this land you see is mine."

Behind the king some of his slaves, the andeva, milled about, and they laughed at her words, but the man raised a hand and they fell silent, turning their attention back to the oxen.

"The name fits better than calling you an ox, I should think," the king said with a smile.

"She always lies and cannot do anything of use," Talata said quickly.

Afua glanced her way and wondered that her former friend could not see how bitterness had taken the softness from her own good looks. But now that she couldn't say the truth of anything, Afua felt she saw far more than she'd ever noticed those handful of years ago.

"I wish you luck, then," the king said with a tiny smile playing like a sunbeam across his wide mouth. His eyes still curious and oddly heavy on her skin, he backed away and finally leapt back into his ox-chair as gracefully as he'd descended.

Talata rounded on Afua, kicking the packet of rice at her feet. All the angry words she might have said were lost as Afua turned and ran, sprinting across the rice fields. Some days she almost didn't mind their cruelty, because at least then they talked to her, if only to taunt.

The moment had changed with the king. He'd looked at her, truly looked, as though he'd seen past the pretty face and ragged clothing, the mud and lies and down to the hollowness beneath. He'd seen her truly, and still gazed as a man might gaze on a woman he desired.

The king's gaze had opened a hole in her heart and she refused to stay and let Talata prod the wound. Oblivious to the shouts behind her, Afua ran until her chest felt as though it would break and then she collapsed upon the ground, tears cutting hot streaks down her aching face as she poured her grief into the dust and sunlight.

The lemur showed up two days after the Ambaniandro king had come through, tearing a hole in Afua's carefully constructed defenses. Since that day, Talata and Zaza had avoided her and she them. The mango grove was quiet and Afua tucked her rice cake between her knees, sitting doubled up on the ground so that she could lean forward and take bites. The mangoes were ripening, heady sweetness floating in the air around her, but she didn't even try to pluck and eat one or touch the heavy fruits on the ground.

The mongoose lemur appeared in the trees, the rustling leaves startling her. He was as long as her arm, with sunset cheeks and gold-orange eyes. His curious face leaned out of a tree, blinking at her, and she wished she could offer the funny creature a bit of rice.

He chattered in a friendly way and climbed down closer as she sat very still. When he was almost within arm's reach, Afua dared to speak softly.

"I am the queen of lemurs," she murmured, shoving away the pain in her heart as her words conjured the handsome king's smile. "I can give you all the mangoes in this grove, my loyal subject." She made a loose gesture with her arm indicating such. It was too difficult for her to eat the slippery, juicy fruit, after all. No harm in magnanimity.

The lemur, who she decided to name Komba, seemed almost to understand and immediately dropped to the ground, catching up a ripe fruit in his hands and ignoring the angry bees as he climbed back into the trees.

Afua finished her meal, brushing the grains of rice from her rough smock as she stood. She almost asked Komba if he'd join her again tomorrow, but her cheeks flamed as she realized how pathetic she would look talking to a forest creature. She shrugged her way back into her harness and wondered when she'd grown so lonely. The answer hovered in her mind and she shoved the smiling king away. She couldn't speak the truth, but neither could she hide from it herself.

Komba returned the next day, and the next. She finished the close fields, glad that the men and ox teams sowed the flooded paddies north of the village, leaving her to her work in peace. Her hands couldn't hold the plants or weed the rows, not even guide an ox. She pulled her make-shift plough each day and walked the distance to the mango grove to rest in the shade and tell her lemur stories.

After the first few days she gave up trying to hold her tongue around the inquisitive beast. She wove him stories of her kingdom and adventures among the lemur people. Komba acted like no lemur she'd seen before. Not shy at all and out in the middle of a field in daylight, his wide eyes seeming to take in every word she said, reading every gesture.

In the second week of his strange visits, he came close enough for her to touch. Afua gentle brushed his fur with the back of her hand and Komba didn't spring away. Instead he peeled back the skin of a mango and offered it to her.

She was sitting in her normal curled position, her rice cake tucked between her knees so she could lean forward and chew on it. When Komba turned to her, ripe fruit dripping in his little hands, she froze.

For a long moment she stared at him and the lemur stared back, fruit upheld like an offering. He broke the tension by chattering at her impatiently.

Afua leaned forward slowly, her heart beating like ceremony drums against her breastbone. She stuck out her tongue, the tip touching the mango flesh, tasting the fruit's sharp tang before she pulled back. Komba didn't retreat but held the fruit steady. Braver, Afua leaned forward again and this time took a bite. Juice ran down her chin and she gasped as the warm fruit slid down her throat.

She laughed, the sound rough and startling to her. She was too proud to chew fruit on the ground or make a mess of her ragged clothing with it by trying to eat it on her own, but here she sat, the queen of the lemurs, being fed by her faithful Komba.

Bite by bite she finished the mango, using the back of her hand and her tongue to clean the sweet residue from her chin and neck.

"Komba," she said as the lemur licked his own paws and chin. There was so much more she wanted to say, but the words of gratitude and joy were true and so they stuck in her throat like paste. Inside her heart filled up a little, the hollow ache ebbing. She poured all the emotion she could into her eyes, grateful for any kindness so freely offered even if Komba couldn't possibly understand.

She got up early the next morning and danced her way to the fields, ignoring the disapproving looks of the men rising for their own work. Her strong feet beat a rhythmic joy in the red earth and she shrugged into her harness, pretending the coarse raffia was silken thread and the plough weighed no more than a heavy robe of state.

She left off her harness at midday, after spending the morning working and willing the sun to speed toward zenith. The grove buzzed with insects as more mangoes dropped heavy from the trees. Soon the children would come and gather the fruits away for drying, but she and Komba still had a little time to enjoy those that ripened early.

"Komba, worst lemur in my kingdom!" she called out as she entered the grove.

Happy chatter still the birds for a moment as he swung down from the dark leafy crowns and came to rest on a low branch beside her. Afua tentatively rested her fingers on his back and he leaned into the touch. Thirst pulled at her and she reluctantly broke the contact.

Drinking from the water jug was always awkward, but she'd mastered grasping the smooth ceramic in her forearms and tipping it on her knees much the way she had to eat. Komba came down and she tipped the heavy vessel for him, laughing when he splashed some back at her.

"You are the worst part about my day," she said.

He tipped his head to the side and bared his teeth. She used her mouth to re-stopper the jug, uncaring how awkward she looked in front of her Komba.

Komba climbed part way up the tree as she reached to roll her rice packet up her legs and get into her eating positing. Movement above him caught her eye and she tried to cry out a warning.

Green and brown, with a head like a spear, the deadly vine snake, a fandrefiala, darted down from the branches overhead, disturbed by Komba's playful movements. Afua lunged to her feet too late.

The spear head struck Komba in the shoulder and the lemur screamed, twisting to attack. Blood sprayed crimson on the branches as his teeth cut into the snake. Coiled together, they fell.

Afua grasped at mangos and then fallen sticks, trying to keep hold of something long enough to help her friend. She might as well have been trying to hang onto the stars in the sky or lift her own reflection from water. Every cry, straight and true from her heart, jammed in her throat, jerking and striking like the snake in Komba's jaws.

Then they stilled, Komba's soft body heaving, the snake dead and bloody and still. Afua threw herself to her knees, scraping the dead snake from the lemur's body with her hands and arms, bending low over her friend to see how badly he was hurt.

Fiandrefiala poison was deadly to a man and Komba was so much smaller. Tears burned down her face. She'd seen this before, as a tiny child when one of her uncles had been bit. He'd screamed and screamed until the witch came and offered to heal him. But whatever she'd asked of Afua's family, they hadn't been willing to give and her uncle had died, swollen and ugly.

The witch, Mpamonka. Afua hadn't been back up the cliffs since that night when she'd broken the witch's jar. Even thinking of the shadowed woman sent spikes of terror through her belly.

Mpamonka had offered to save Afua's uncle. For a price. A price too high. But now, for Afua, what price was too high?

No no no no, not my Komba, not my only friend.

She gathered him in her arms, shoving him over her shoulder as she would a sack of rice or her harness straps. Her hands gripped nothing, but her arms and head held his little body well enough.

Afua ran as quickly as she dared in a shambling, awkward gait. Voices called to her as she skirted the village, but the only sound she cared to hear was the soft painful whine of Komba's breathing. He grew heavier as she went, his body seeming to elongate while threatening to slide down her arm.

Afua tucked him in closer, curling her arm up to her head. Her vision blurred with tears but her feet knew the path, climbing upward into the green shadows of the jungle, beating a desperate, uneven tattoo on the grassy path.

The witch's hut loomed and this time Afua showed no hesitation. Her lungs burned and Komba's bulk felt as though he weighed near as much as a man, bending her double beneath his strangely heavy body. She let him down in front of the hut and cried out in a wordless yell for the witch.

The woman who emerged from the smoky hut looked hardly older than Afua's three and a half hands of years, but she wore silks and ropes of necklaces carved from ancestor bones.

"The thief returns," the witch said, her voice like moonlight and running water and gravel crunching beneath cattle feet.

Save him, save my Komba, I'll pay any price. "This is a useless thing," Afua's words came out all wrong. "I hope it dies."

She fell to her knees beside the now man-sized Komba, whose fur was turning from yellow and rust to yellow and green, bright like a beetle's shell. She pushed the truth of her heart into her eyes, begging the witch with every tear to see the truth she couldn't speak.

The witch raised red-brown brows and knelt beside the giant lemur. She touched the swelling snake bites and shook her head. "Fandrefiala?" she asked.

Afua nodded vigorously.

"I can cure this, but the potion requires a sacrifice equal to the deed." The witch had a sly smile on her face which struck deep into Afua.

Anything, she thought. "Az. . ." she tried to say, the word curling like chips of wood over coals on her tongue. "Az... af... ady." *Please.*

"I would need a drop of your heart's blood," the witch said.

Afua hesitated but then Komba whimpered again, the sound deep and almost human. His fur was fading, leaving dark, smooth skin in its wake in places and rich silks in others. Afua touched the silks and recognized the pattern. Her king, the smiling man who'd looked into her eyes and let her be who she was.

Komba. Her loyal subject. Komba, her Ambaniandro king.

"A drop of blood is nothing to me," she whispered, knowing that a drop of heart blood was only gained with death. But her life was useless, chained to a plough and ridicule. If she could do one beautiful thing to make up for her vain act and her wasted life afterward, then perhaps when her spirit rested in the bones with her ancestors and Zanahary, they'd have mercy on her.

The witch rose without another word and fetched a carved chest from within her hut. Afua steeled herself and bent low over Komba's chest, listening to his shallow breathing and the soft whine of pain contained in his throat.

"Veloma," she mouthed in his delicate ear, brushing her lips along the soft skin of his now fully human face. Goodbye.

Mpamonka brought a needle carved of bone and a tiny silver hammer. She pulled Afua away from the king and tore her thin smock down the center. Afua gave her no resistance, closing her eyes instead. She conjured the taste of the mango on her tongue, the bubbling joy of Komba's gift of friendship, given so easily and without price. Afua hardly felt the tip of the needle as it touched her skin, aimed between her ribs, above her full breast.

"Miala tsiny aho," she murmured, in a trance of memory and regret, hardly aware of the words as they flowed like honey across her lips.

The air suddenly turned too bright and white hot sparks leapt from her skin. Her belly felt again like it was full of ants and her tongue twisted in her mouth, curling and uncurling. Her hands made fists so tight she felt her ragged nails cutting into her skin, raising the metallic scent of blood in the air. For a long moment the world was pain and wind and fire and Afua couldn't tell if she were about to burn or fly.

Then it was gone and she heard the burble of the mountain spring nearby. She tentatively moved a toe, testing to see if she still lived. Her toe obeyed. She licked her lips, tasting mango and blood.

A warm hand, big and human, slipped into her own. Afua opened her eyes and found the Ambaniandro king kneeling over her. Her eyes flew to his throat, but it was smooth and clear of wounds. She looked around the clearing and found that the witch's hut had disappeared. Wide-eyed, she sat up.

"Komba," she said, her voice a harsh rasp as she turned back to the king. She flushed then, kicking herself in her mind. That was only a stupid name she'd given to a lemur, not one fit for a king.

He smiled and his fingers twined in her own, gripping tightly. "Ratsibahaka," he said, "my lemur queen. I don't remember much of this day, but I think you saved my life."

Áfua took a slow, deep breath. Then she squeezed his hand, her fingers closing around his own. "As you have saved mine," she murmured, sitting up.

Hands entwined, they smiled at each other beneath the warm and glowing sun.

FIN

About the Author: Annie Bellet is the *USA Today* bestselling author of The Twenty-Sided Sorceress, Pyrrh Considerable Crimes Division, and the Gryphonpike Chronicles series. She holds a BA in English and a BA in Medieval Studies, and thus can speak a smattering of useful languages such as Anglo-Saxon and Medieval Welsh. Her interests besides writing include rock climbing, reading, horseback riding, video games, comic books, tabletop RPGs, and many other nerdy pursuits. She lives in the Pacific Northwest with her husband and a very demanding Bengal cat.

To learn more about her books, visit her website: www. anniebellet.com.

THE GRIM BROTHER
AUDREY FAYE

SOME SAY CHILDREN CAN'T BE EVIL. I KNOW DIFFERENTLY.

I stand here, looking at the fresh mound of earth in front of my sister's gravestone, and know that I have buried evil in consecrated ground. For a priest, there is no greater sin.

For the man, standing in the place where I commended her soul to God, I don't know what to feel. If she had a soul, it had long since been promised elsewhere.

It is not hell I fear, but rather, that my sister waits for me there.

I am long past redemption. Perhaps all those many years ago when we returned from our disappearance—perhaps then the truth might have saved my soul. I'll never know. I only know that as a boy of seven, I saw evil act, and she took my voice.

My sister killed a woman. That's no secret. People still tell stories about the two young children kidnapped and held hostage for an entire fortnight. How we suffered so terribly and escaped only when my sister fought to save me and killed the terrible woman who held us.

My sister lived out her life basking in the deference that comes as reward for such a moment of bravery. I have lived in the quiet shame of an older brother who needed to be rescued by his little sister.

It is not the only reason I sought sanctuary in the priesthood, but the Church's deep relationship with guilt and shame were certainly part of my calling. As a priest, I seek to expiate the guilt of others and bring them closer to our God the Father. I do not expect the same for myself. Some things, even God can surely not forgive.

My friend Gregor would say this is heresy. It is a conversation we have had for most of a lifetime, beginning when we were students with the Jesuits in Olomouc. With all those miles between me and my sister, it was easy to agree with him for a time. He was my first true friend, but even Gregor does not know the whole truth.

It is a truth I have never told anyone, and now the only other who knows it is dead.

In my defense, I did not expect people to believe my sister's story. Who would believe that a small child killed a grown woman, even in self-defense? Or that we wandered around in the woods for days, but my sister managed never to drop the jewels clutched in her hands?

It seems belief is not so hard when the tale is told by a small blonde child with traumatized eyes and a fortune in her grasp.

Our father certainly never questioned her, not even when our much unloved stepmother sickened and died only days after our return, along with the unborn babe in her womb. The story people tell now says she was dead and gone before we got back. It's not true. I don't know exactly what my sister did. I only know that when she held our father's hand at the funeral, her eyes were happy.

No one else seems to see her eyes.

Her eyes were happy when she watched the old woman fall, too.

It was my fault, has always been my fault. I'm the one who took my sister to the house on the hill.

We were hungry. There was little work for my father, and his new wife had a baby on the way. My mother died giving birth to my sister. Perhaps she understood that evil moved in her womb.

The house on the hill was fancy, with flower gardens and real glass in all the windows. I thought the old woman who lived there might have some food to spare. My sister was pretty, so people often gave her scraps instead of the cuff to the head they gave me.

The old woman answered the door herself. I sometimes wonder if that's why my sister always made sure there were servants in her house. Living alone is dangerous—you never know what might come to the door.

She was kind, the old woman. Perhaps my burden would be less if she hadn't been kind to two hungry children. She seated us at her table, fed us bread with real butter and jam. I've never been able to eat blueberry jam since. It tastes of death and cowardice.

My sister told the sad tale of our family, the new baby coming, and not enough food on the table. Our pittance of a house, small and very drafty in the cold of winter.

We were blessed with a moment of uncommon kindness that day. The old woman had a house in the woods, she said. Just a cottage, but warm and dry, with two small bedrooms just the right size for two growing children. It had belonged to her family for generations, but only she remained.

I remember when she smiled at me and asked if I thought we might like to come look at her cottage. I was certain we had met our fairy godmother.

My sister shared my joy. Whatever evil stirred in her, it had not yet awakened when she took the old woman's hand for a walk in the woods.

I believe now that the presence of good simply triggered the need for evil to act. Gregor convinced me of this eternal truth. The forces of evil gathered for the birth of the only Son. It is a story humanity repeats far too often. At seven, however, I knew only that kindness faced down death and lost.

The cottage in the woods was sturdy and well maintained, like the one I remembered from when we were very small, when there was still work for my father. It had a cozy, welcoming kitchen, and three whole bedrooms. Outside were sheds for animals if we had any, and a small root cellar.

The path of some lives is determined by a single moment.

Gregor reminds me often that the doctrine of predestination isn't meant to be interpreted this severely. He wasn't there when the old woman peered down the steps into the root cellar and my sister pushed her. He wasn't there when my sister closed the door of the root cellar and led me back through the woods. He wasn't there when we sat down at the table in the big house on the hill and ate more bread with butter and blueberry jam.

If God intended for one such as I to go to heaven, such moments would never have happened. I do not know if the old woman was dead when she fell. That is perhaps the most heinous of my crimes—I might have saved her. I will never know.

We stayed in the house on the hill for thirteen days. We left only once, in the dark of night. It took us a long time to drag the old woman out of the root cellar and into the cottage kitchen. She was small, and we were strong from hauling wood with our father, but it still took an eternity. I will never forget the cold, papery skin or her staring eyes. In death, they were no longer kind.

I didn't know why we had to move the old woman until my sister spun her lies after our return. I only knew that her eyes were very scary, and I did as I was told.

I slept very little those thirteen days, and I ate a lot. Seventy years later, sleep still eludes me many nights, and food finds me all too often.

When we had consumed everything edible in the house, my sister looked for something to sell. She found the old woman's jewelry and we sat at the table, carefully taking the stones from their settings. Once you've been accessory to murder, the burden of theft hardly ripples your soul.

Those jewels bought my sister a fancy life. You might think she killed for them, but the old woman had been dead for more than a week by the time the jewels were found. In seventy years,

I have never really understood what turned my sister irredeemably from the light.

After disappearing for a fortnight, our return was big news in our little village on the Rhine. My sister spun a story of witchcraft and kidnapping, insanity and escape. The old woman's remains in the kitchen of the cottage in the woods seemed proof enough.

I remember very little of the next year. Soon enough I was sent away to school in Deventer, and after that to the Jesuits in Olomouc, where I met Gregor. That my education was paid for by the old woman's jewels is amongst the more minor of my sins.

While I found some peace at school, happiness was not mine to seek. My small group of friends called me the grim brother. Gregor could often tease a smile from me. Few others ever managed.

It was not an accident, I think, that my schools were too far to permit frequent travel home. I saw my sister but a few times before she married, and then again at the funeral that left her a young widow. She attended my ordination, perhaps needing to witness my vows of poverty and chastity—my obedience had already been well established.

I am a good priest. It does not atone for my sins, but it sometimes gives small solace in the night. Not too many of my congregation fall asleep when I speak, and some come to the rectory to talk. The children listen to my stories, and one or two will often climb in my lap.

My sister never had children. In my later years, this is something for which I have thanked God every day. My friend

Gregor, after many years of work with his pea plants, believes that children inherit the characteristics of their parents. I do not know how much of my sister's blood runs in my veins, but it is good the line will end with us.

I was not there when she died. It was not in me to grant her final absolution. I don't believe God wants her back. In my dreams, when He sits in judgment, Son of Man on His right, and the kind old lady on His left, He does not want me back either.

I buried my sister today, and at the end of a lifetime of blackness and despair, I do not know what to feel. People nod and smile, and repeat the words she wanted etched on her gravestone.

Gretel Nussbaum. Such Bravery.

They have sent a small child now to fetch me back to the rectory. "Come, Father Hansel," she says. "It is time for bread and soup."

Her eyes are kind, as a young girl's should be.

FIN

About the Author: Audrey Faye writes as widely as she likes to read, so you'll find her books in lots of genres, but they are always filled with characters she'd like to hang out with, and some she'd like to be! Try Holly and the siren haunting her dreams in Wanton to the Death, or check out the rest of Audrey's books at her website: www.audreyfayewrites.com.

FAESCORNED
JENNA ELIZABETH JOHNSON

A COLD, SATURATED BREEZE SWEPT DOWN THE GRASSY slope, arriving from the east and setting off a chatter of disquiet through my army of faelah.

"Silence!" I hissed, whipping around to ensure they held their ground. "They will be here shortly, and then, you will be too busy to worry about Eile's discontent."

The noise lessened, but their unease did not. I turned back around to face the hills in the near distance, my eyes narrowed and my impatience growing. Dawn was not far off, the cloud-darkened sky paling enough to make out the shapes of the monsters forming a semicircle behind me. Ten minutes went by, then ten more. The faelah began stirring again, snapping and snarling at one another. Just as I was about to turn and destroy the most agitated ones to keep the rest under control, a dark horse bearing two riders crested the hill I had been watching. I almost missed them, for the animal was nearly the same color as the thunderheads roiling above.

A white shape, my son's wolfhound spirit guide, followed several paces behind, and a shrill cry from above announced another. Ah. The little strayling whelp's merlin. Sniffing, I pushed them from my mind. They were not powerful enough to be a threat to my army, or the Cumorrig who stood by my side. I reached down and stroked the leathery head of one of my corpse hounds, imagining how I might use them if this morning proved more difficult than I anticipated.

"Yes, you will be quite the sight to see should my dear Caedehn choose foolishness over prudence."

A small twinge of malicious delight sparked inside my breast, my powerful glamour eager to begin.

"Patience," I warned it, not wanting to stir the faeduhn magic there as well.

Too late, I realized, as a prick of burning pain flickered beside my well of glamour. I gritted my teeth and drew in a calming breath, willing the Darkness to remain docile.

My Curse, a terrible geis placed upon me so long ago the details of the memory had weathered away like mountains grinding into sand, would surely play a part in what was to come. I could feel the tension in the air and knew this day would not end without a fight. And I, of all people, knew there was no resisting my Curse when it wished to play.

The beat of the horse's hooves grew nearer, and I lifted my eyes, casting my son and the girl riding with him a sinister look. A blast of frigid wind tore through my long hair and whipped my nebulous skirts into a frenzy, making them mimic the roiling clouds above. Of their own volition, my lips twitched into a menacing smile. The imbeciles had fallen for my trap, and so easily, too.

Caedehn leaned forward and murmured something to the girl, the words whisked away by another gust of wind. He cast his eyes on me again, their dark green shade filled with hatred and loathing. I bared my teeth in a menacing challenge. Good. I shared the sentiment, thanks to the Curse plaguing my soul.

Caedehn slipped from his horse's back, then turned to help his little faelorah down. I sneered. The affection brewing between the two of them sickened me and made the Darkness living within snarl with fury.

Not yet, I reminded it, hoping to hold it back a bit longer. I did not need the lancing pain it caused to distract me until I had full control of the situation. The faeduhn magic bristled at my arrogance, but settled back down. It knew blood would be spilled this day, so it didn't press me any harder.

Caedehn and his half-breed female were moving closer now, their steps tentative, the tension pulling them tight like a bowstring. My glamour pulsed again, feeding off the girl's fear.

When they were a few dozen feet away, Caedehn announced in a loud voice, "We wish to pass through the dolmarehn."

All around me, my faelah snorted and growled, their desire to attack these two new snacks grating at my nerves. I lifted my hand away from my dress just enough to send a wave of invisible glamour in their direction. Whiffles of surprise and small squeals of pain assured me they understood my mood. They could complain all they wished, but they would get nothing until I allowed it.

Returning my attention to Caedehn, I said in a dull tone, "I don't see why you would. There is nothing left in the mortal world worth going back to."

The girl's horrified reaction was delightful, causing my cursed magic to purr in delight. If not for Caedehn's close proximity, she might have crashed to the ground. That she believed such an obvious untruth proved what an ignorant little thing she was. Really, what did the boy see in her?

My son whipped around, his eyes darkening with malice.

"You lie!" he snarled.

Rolling my eyes, I sighed and admitted, "Yes, you are correct, my dear Caedehn. Time wouldn't allow it. I'll just have to exterminate the mortals once we're done here."

As much as I enjoyed bantering with him, I was eager to get the girl's glamour and get out of this cursed weather. Goddess of chaos and strife I might be, but thunderstorms in Eile were intolerable. At the very thought of the strayling's potent power, the faeduhn magic lifted its wicked head once again, pressing painfully into my own, natural glamour. Barely, I managed to hide a grimace and resisted the urge to press my hand to my heart. The last thing I wished to do was show weakness in front of those I would soon own, one way or another.

We chatted on, Caedehn and I, trading words back and forth as if neither of us really wanted to admit why we were here, on this barren field, beneath a brewing tempest. I enjoyed tormenting him, for the more I plucked and twisted his nerves, and the girl's, the more the Darkness stayed in check.

The more I initiated discomfort and strife among others, the less my geis was enticed to force me into action. And,

I was not ready for its unbearable wrath just yet. I never was. Casting those thoughts from my mind, I narrowed my eyes and sharpened my focus on those standing, or in the strayling's case, sniveling before me. At one point in our conversation, I learned my son hadn't told his little pet of our relationship. The Curse infecting my soul crooned at the girl's shocked reaction, and I laughed, trying to distract myself from the pain its stirring caused. It wasn't just my emotions the Darkness fed from. Sometimes, those nearby projected strongly enough that it absorbed their unease as well.

That's right, I mused inwardly, *Caedehn is my son, my own flesh and blood.*

Despite the agony ripping through my glamour, I hoped the knowledge alone weakened the girl's resolve. If so, she might be easier to subdue when the time came to harvest her glamour.

I cast Caedehn a sideways glance then, my brow furrowed as I studied the expression on his face. He wasn't looking at me, but at the girl. And his eyes were ... strange. And not just Faelorehn strange. An emotion as unlikely as sunlight touching the ocean floor and just as unfamiliar, tried desperately to claw free of my heart. But, this particular feeling was the one the faeduhn magic despised the most. Before I could even detect its soft caress upon my soul, my Curse snatched it up and devoured it, ripping it apart and morphing it into something ugly.

I glared at Caedehn. The pain and anger of the Darkness driving me to resentment and antipathy.

"I never wanted a son. And here is proof as to why," I spat, indicating the tall, handsome young man standing before me.

Pain lanced through my breast again, that age-old emotion and the faeduhn magic battling for dominance. I knew which would win, in the end, but I did not want to give in. Perhaps, if I pushed hard enough, I could feel ...

"Such a disappointment since birth," I hissed, the Darkness wrenching free of my faltering grasp and lashing me with its poisonous dominance again and again.

Another stab of agony, enough to wipe my memory clean of what my heart so desperately wished to show me, and then, I could breathe again. But the experience left me exhausted and aggravated, and my bitter words reflected my mood.

"All I asked of you, Caedehn, was for you to keep my minions in line and to rein in any lost Faelorehn that might be useful. And here, you have the unwanted offspring of Danua and some Fomorian whelp, a combination you know is volatile and rich with magical potential, and you've kept her away from me all this time. Was that so much for a mother to ask of her son? To bring such treasures back to me? But you refused."

My harsh words and volatile temper lessened my own pain, but only a little. As long as I followed my Curse's direction, it would not hurt me so severely. Caedehn's response further soothed my cursed magic, but then, he said something that sent me reeling, a memory I had tried so hard to erase from my mind tearing free from the place I had hidden it away.

"No matter what I choose to do," he growled softly, "you'll never be satisfied. You'll never stop taking your anger with my father out on me."

I had turned away from him briefly, to catch my breath and give my own glamour a chance to subdue the other, unwelcome power. But upon hearing those words, the Darkness rose again like a battle-hungry dragon.

"Your father," I ground out, "took advantage of my good graces!"

Caedehn, my only son and the near spitting image of his sire, laughed out loud. "Your good graces? He tricked you, plain and simple, after *you* tried to beguile *him*. So really, you have only yourself to blame."

Before I could form a retort, the faeduhn magic swirling beside my own glamour pulsed, seeking my pain and making it worse. It rushed in like floodwater cresting a river and carried me away from that rain-swept field. I blinked once and found myself standing in one of my memories, the one I had tried, and failed, to remove from my mind. Bitter regret and scorn curled in my stomach, and I clenched my teeth. Raging at the cursed magic that tormented me would do me no good, but I could not live through this memory again.

Turning in a near panic, I tried to find a place to flee. Perhaps, I could outrun what was to happen next. Fear spiked in my heart when I noticed the dark mouth of a cave, gaping beneath a hillside covered in ancient oak trees, just ahead of me. Mist clogged the sky above, and the limpid light suggested the time to be early evening.

I can still escape this, I breathed to myself. *Simply turn away from the cave...*

But, it was too late. Like the sun breaking through clouds, a flame leapt up in the heart of the cavern, and a man stepped out. Tall and broad-shouldered, he wore his dark red hair long. His chest was bare, as were his feet. The only clothing he wore was an old kilt that hung loosely around his waist. He looked good. He looked better than good. I knew right away he was more than just Faelorehn. This man had Tuatha De blood in his veins, but whose, I could not tell.

I sneered at him, ready to assert my authority as one of the goddesses of Eile. But then, he smiled, his glamour pouring forth from him like the heady scent of honeysuckle blossoms on a warm, summer morning. I had been known to seduce those men I found attractive, and I knew the feelings they invoked in me, emotions the Darkness consumed before I could recognize them. This was different.

"I thought to spend this evening alone," the man said, his voice rich and deep, "but, here I stand, blessed by the spirits of Eile with such beautiful company."

I had a snide remark ready for this stranger who thought to charm me, but when I opened my mouth to speak, only a sigh passed through my lips.

He moved in closer, his footfalls quiet against the mossy forest floor. With remarkable grace for such a tall man, he reached out an arm and extended it toward me.

I sucked in a breath and took a quick step back. He arched an auburn brow, his changeable green eyes shimmering like the rippling surface of a sun-warmed pond.

"There now," he murmured, not moving any closer, "I will not hurt you."

That statement made me scoff.

"Do you not know who I am?"

The man smiled again, sending heat through my veins. I waited for my faeduhn magic to turn that pleasant feeling into pain or disdain, but it did not. I eyed the stranger again, my brow furrowed. What power did he yield that he could make my Curse remain dormant?

"You are the Morrigan," he said, his voice holding some reverence, "and I am no stranger to you either, I believe."

I crossed my arms and gave him a pointed look. "I'm afraid we have not met."

"I am Cuchulainn."

Ah, yes. I had heard of him. The young, hotheaded half Tuatha De son of Lugh. He had been roaming about Eile, and the mortal world, for the past several years taking on challenges and helping win wars between the mortals. He was skilled in glamour, and he was said to possess the rare gift of riastrad, an ability to transform into a more violent and powerful version of himself in the heat of battle.

But, he was no warped monstrosity at the moment. He was a pristine specimen of a man, even more attractive than most Faelorehn men I had come upon, and they were a race blessed with beauty and strength. Even as I admired the portrait he painted, I waited for my Darkness to punish me, as it always did, when I found myself enjoying any aspect of life. The waves of retaliation never came, though.

"And, as the Morrigan," I finally said, returning to our conversation, "I am very busy."

I had a battle to oversee the next morning, one which would help me reclaim a very desirable portion of my realm and one which would earn me some much coveted and needed glamour. My Curse was always hungry for more, and if I did not feed it, I was punished. Whatever this Faelorehn man was doing to me to keep that punishment at bay could only mean worse for me when I got away from him.

Turning, I meant to leave him behind and forget about this strange encounter.

"Wait," he said, his voice low and breathy.

A heavy hand came to rest on my shoulder. In any other situation, I would have snarled and jerked free, cursing any lout who dared touch me without my consent. I was the goddess of war and strife. I was the one who seduced others to follow my whim, not the other way around. But, the moment his fingers brushed against the sensitive skin on my neck, something happened. Warmth radiated from his fingertips and palm, pulsing through me like a heady drug.

I turned back around, my eyes surely melting to a warm shade of ruby. He looked different now, this renegade hero of the Otherworld. A strange, but not unpleasant feeling wrapped around my heart and the Darkness that never let me be, remained silent. Dormant. As if it wasn't even there.

Before I could protest, his other hand reached out, caressing my face. More of that tingling heat poured forth, and I gasped. Cuchulainn took advantage of my moment of distraction and bent his head, capturing my mouth in a bold, sensual kiss. I had kissed men before, men I meant to use and manipulate. Always, I controlled the situation. This was different. Now, I was the one being manipulated, the one being seduced. My mind knew this, fought against the torrent of unfamiliar and tantalizing sensations coursing through my blood, but I could not tear away from him. Giving up the fight, and in all honesty, relishing in the fact that my cursed faeduhn magic was doing nothing to bring an end to this strange joy, I gave in.

Without breaking our kiss, Cuchulainn swept me off my feet and carried me back to the cave. The awaiting battle be damned, my horrible geis be damned. For once, I knew what it was to be the one desired, the one indulged. And, for once, in my long, long life, that Darkness which controlled everything about me, that poisonous magic I both loathed and craved, that unshakable power which brought me pain every chance it got, was held at bay. For once, I could just feel, breathe, live without the accompaniment of punishment.

That evening, in a small cave tucked into the hills along the edge of my realm, I succumbed to a happiness so many before me had experienced. And for the very first time in my existence, what might have been the first smoldering embers of love kindled within my heart.

I woke the next morning feeling groggy and disoriented, and for a few spare moments, my body forgot what had taken place the night before. Between one breath and another, it all came back in vibrant detail: the handsome warrior, Cuchulainn, my dismissal of his attempts to charm me, his touch, rich with molten, seductive glamour and the passion that followed...

Sighing, I rolled over, reaching out for the man who had chased away my Curse only to clutch at cool, abandoned blankets. The fire which had helped stoke the heat between us had also turned to cold ash.

"Cuchulainn?" I called out tentatively, cringing at the slight sound of desperation in my voice. I was the goddess of war, I was never vulnerable.

No answer came. The cave wasn't very large, perhaps ten feet high and thirty feet deep, so I knew he wasn't in there with me. That meant he was somewhere outside.

I stood, my head pounding and my nerves feeling as if they'd been rubbed raw. Clutching one of the blankets to myself, I stumbled out of the cavern entrance, hoping to find my lover. The sun was bright, piercing its way through the fading mist and thick canopy of oak leaves overhead. Determined to find Cuchulainn, I climbed the hillside hiding the cave. Perhaps, he had gone out to capture breakfast.

When I came to the top of the knoll and glanced down into the wide valley before me, my heart sank and memory came rushing back with a vengeance. My army of faelah and the Faelorehn men and women I had rallied to my latest cause lay dead and broken, scattered upon the ground for over a mile beyond my sight. Ravens, denizens of my own realm, circled above, many landing in the field to pick at the carnage. I grew utterly still, more of my memory returning as the pleasant aftereffects of the night before started to diminish. Years I had trained these soldiers and painstakingly gathered and utilized raw glamour to bring the faelah to life. Hours, days and months of hard work to form an army to regain a portion of my territory from my greedy Tuatha De brethren, and now, it was all destroyed. I had failed them. I had failed myself.

Cold realization flooded over me then, that raw knowledge that Cuchulainn had used me, seduced me in order to sneak away after I fell asleep to destroy my soldiers. Without my power to aid them, they had been helpless, camping overnight in the open until our weaker foe dared stand against them at dawn. Dawn was here now, bleak and grey and tainted with smoke and the rusty scent of spilled blood. My paltry enemy would have no challenger to reclaim what they had taken from me now.

I fell to my knees, a cavalcade of emotions swirling around my spirit. My heart sped up, and my breathing became labored. Sharp thorns pierced my knees through the blanket I wore as a mantle. I glanced down, not caring, but wondering if it was my faeduhn Curse finally stirring to life. No, not the dark magic seeking and wishing to amplify my pain. Thistles. The pale, downy white thistles of the wastes of my realm, their bright scarlet blossoms, bursting forth from the buds like cardinal plumes, matching the heat burning in my heart. A reminder of the sin cast against me, a white flag of truce stained with the blood of betrayal.

Anger, white hot and acrid, poured from my soul and flared out, licking at my nerves and throbbing like an infected wound. Anguish drove me to thrust my hands against the ground to keep from falling over, and the thistles pierced my palms as well. Ignoring the burning pain, I curled my fingers into fists, my own blood now streaming between my fingers. There, on that east-facing slope, I screamed, a long, low-pitched wail I drew up from the very heart of Eile herself.

The ache and rage and hurt swirled together, faster and faster, the faeduhn magic joining it and stoking it, until it became an almost tangible thing I could understand: hatred.

I hated Cuchulainn, more than anything. Not because he had duped me, fooled me into thinking he might love me, but because he had shown me something I could never have. Not with my geis. Any feelings of love or joy or happiness were whisked away and transformed into something evil. But now, I knew what it was like not to be Cursed. For a few glorious hours, I had lived. And because that knowledge would make it even more painful than if I'd never experienced it at all, my hatred had a single target. I would find the man who had done this to me, and I would make him suffer as much as I now did.

Yes, the Darkness crooned, caressing my mind and sending shards of pain through my head. *We will seek the blackguard, and we will make him suffer. Oh! And what delicious glamour he has. Think of the power we'll wield when we have taken it from him!*

Tears of anger stung my eyes, and I stared numbly across the blood-soaked plain.

I learned my lesson, I said to the Darkness. *I will never let such weakness make me vulnerable again.*

In the end, I was not the one to kill Cuchulainn, but I had put the path in motion, and I had been there, watching the events unfold. He died tied to a standing stone. When his spirit was ready to pass into Eile's underworld, I took my raven form and landed upon his shoulder, ready to absorb that potent glamour he had once dared use against me.

For the pain you caused me, I pressed into his mind, *and for taunting me with what I will never have.*

I could not tell if he was lucid enough to hear me, or to understand my words. On his last breath, his glamour rose like a fine mist, and I breathed it in, the faeduhn magic beside my own glamour swallowing it like a ravenous beast. When all his magic was gathered, I cawed once, an anguished cry of sorrow and regret, then took to the sky. My faeduhn Curse capturing my pain and amplifying it to the point of agony. This sting I knew, this torment I could live with. Yet, I flew on, trying to outpace it as I sometimes could, in my corvine form.

The sudden upwelling of chatter from my faelah pushed past the deep pool of memories and jerked me back to the present. I shook my head to clear my thoughts, then narrowed my eyes at Caedehn, the reminder of my regrets scraping against my patience. He looked so much like his father. Anger flared, and I demanded my son turn over the little chit he had grown infatuated with. What a fool he was, for he would call it love, what he felt for the girl. *If only it were so easy,* I thought bitterly.

But, I wanted her glamour. The Darkness wanted her glamour.

"I'll not give her up," Caedehn was saying. "I'll fight your faelah, and if I win, you will forfeit your claim on Meghan."

My eyebrow quirked at his claim. He would risk his life? For this girl?

That primitive twinge stirred in my soul once more, but again, my geis crushed it before I could identify it.

"If they win, I offer you all of my glamour in exchange for her safety. After all, I'm also the product of a volatile combination, and my magic is rather potent as well."

The girl cried out in protest, but I ignored her.

"That might be enough to tempt me," I crooned, my Darkness liking the idea of a challenge. "You do realize the price of your sacrifice, don't you, my boy? There is only one way for me to get to your power."

Caedehn nodded his understanding, his expression hard. "I know. I'll swear a blood oath if I must."

My Curse flared to life at this statement, the sudden upheaval of power causing my faelah to hiss and spit. The instantaneous agony of it drew a gasp from my lips, but I disguised it with a shout which sounded more triumphant than pained.

"Very well, my dearest," I sneered. "Do give me your oath then."

We performed the ceremony, and I gritted my teeth at my son. I called him a fool for his decision, but it had been made, and there was nothing I could do to change his mind. Even if I wanted to bring an end to this madness, my Curse would never allow it. The Darkness, more than anyone or anything else, could sense exactly what I was feeling, and the more anguish it caused me, the stronger it grew.

As soon as the ritual was through, I opened my glamour, allowing it to flow freely into my transformed Cumorrig, now three times their original size and primed for battle. And then, I stood back and watched as my son took on his own battle shape, the riastrad he'd inherited from his father. Beside me, the girl watched, trapped beneath a protective shield of glamour. I tried reaching out for her, my Curse wanting to taste her hidden power and the turbulent emotions stirring in her soul, but the shield was strong, and it easily deflected me. The sharp jolt was nothing compared to what the faeduhn magic meted out, though.

Bored with watching the girl, I eyed Caedehn again, feeling his weakening state like an ache in my bones. That old memory stirred anew, but this time, I didn't have the strength to fight it. Unobstructed, it came flooding back into my mind. I had thought my torment was over when Cuchulainn was through with me, but I had been wrong. Nine months after being spurned by him, I bore his child, a child I did not want, a son I could not love. Alone, in the cavern fortress of my realm, I brought him into this world, reminded during every agonizing minute of that long labor of the man who had been so cruel to show me life, then take it away as if it had meant nothing to him. Because it *had* meant nothing to him.

The child was born healthy, despite my sickened soul and the resentment I harbored against him. For a few minutes after his birth, as I lay holding him and recovering from my ordeal, I allowed myself a glimpse at the life that could have been. If I had not been the goddess of war, if Cuchulainn had not wished simply to use me and cast me aside, if the faeduhn Curse had never coiled around my soul ...

Whatever light that moment had brought was soon snuffed out. That sour, bitter, burning resentment grew once more, fueled by the dark glamour, and I wanted to be rid of the child. I called forth one of my servants and charged her to take the child away and leave it on the boundary of my realm. She obeyed without question.

"Let the elements of Eile kill him," I'd told her, the pain of the Darkness crushing my heart under its weight, "for I cannot bear to look at him any longer. But," I added, remembering who his father was and knowing that I was even stronger, "before you do, let me see him one last time."

Reluctantly, the young woman handed him over. It was painful to gaze into his eyes, so green they conjured memories of Eile's vast fields and the endless canopy of the Weald glowing beneath a summer sun. The pain of my Curse dug into my heart, and I nearly cried out. Whatever peace might have been was dashed away, burned into black ash, choking me as I tried to breathe.

"I place a geis upon you, my son," I rasped, my eyes burning with impending wrath.

I pressed my palm to his chest and conjured my symbol, the mark which tied a Faelorehn life to my service.

"Should you survive after I cast you away, you will someday return to serve me. And should you disobey me, your life, and your glamour, will be forfeit."

A sound of anguish drew my attention back to the rain-slicked battlefield and to the dwindling fight, the memory from so long ago floating away like smoke scattered in the wind. Caedehn had defeated all but one of my Cumorrig, yet his strength and his resolve was failing. Like his father, his pride and warped sense of honor would be his downfall. He would let his supposed love for this fae strayling destroy him.

"Utter fool!" I muttered again under my breath, my eyes burning with impatience and rage. Did he not realize the anguish love would bring him?

In the next instant, my Cumorrig found its opening and plunged its wicked claws deep into Caedehn's abdomen.

The faeduhn magic swelled within me, like a black cloud of smoke and fire, swallowing my heart and any sentiment it might have conjured forth. Agony, like searing mage-fire, coursed through my blood, and I had to fight to keep control. That pathetic whelp of Danua's still watched, screaming my son's name. She would pay me no heed, at least for the next few minutes. I drew in a breath of the damp air and let my eyes close. The dark magic, always trying to overtake me, licked at my senses, its dominance no match for my own. That was my fate as a Tuatha De, a goddess among immortals, cursed to be Faeduihn. Any normal Faelorehn man or woman would succumb and lose all their faculties under the spell of such dark power. But not me. The insidious magic pushed me and warped me to become what I was now, the goddess of war and strife, unable to feel that which my brethren could feel: joy, happiness, love ... But it would never take my mind from me; it would never grant me that one blessing. Instead, I struggled every waking hour beneath its weight and wrath, knowing exactly what I was missing. All because of one night with one man whose glamour had somehow overridden my Curse, a geis I could never break.

I opened my eyes to see Caedehn fall with the last Cumorrig. The dark magic burned deeper, eager to get a hold of his well of glamour. The little strayling broke free of her protective shield of magic and rushed over to him, sobbing as his life drained away.

"Good," I whispered to myself, the dark magic easing back to its place beside my own glamour. "It is done."

I was numb. There had been so much pain this time, so very much.

Somehow, I made my way over to Caedehn's lifeless body. I snarled something at the girl, telling her to back away so I could claim my glamour, and then hers as well. I saw no need to keep my promise now, and I doubted my Curse would let me walk away from this battlefield while such delicious, fresh magic sat in the mud before me.

And then, I saw it in her eyes, that sensation so alien to me, the look Caedehn had given her not too long ago. Somehow, it burned through my defenses and singed the edges of my faeduhn curse, and for a split second, my heart was allowed to experience what it should have this dark morning: love, pride and sorrow so deep, I thought I might fall into it and never arise again. A small gust of cold air brushed against my face, and it felt as though a thread of ice traced down my cheek. Gasping, I backed away as the girl's own glamour burst forth like a thunderclap directly overhead.

I had thought she and Caedehn to be fools, weak for allowing themselves to fall in love. I knew from personal experience that that particular sentiment only led to ruin and pain. Yet, this half-breed Faelorehn woman burned before me, not with the excruciating, punishing scorn of faeduhn magic, but with that same radiance and power I had known only a few times in my life. This Meghan girl, with her brand new glamour and her ignorance of the Otherworld, shone forth like a star, her magic powered not by Eile's magic or glamour stolen from another. Her power came from love.

Never in my life had I backed down from a challenge, for I was always the most formidable opponent anyone would ever face, but this girl had found a way to defeat my cursed magic, and she didn't even know it.

Snarling in frustration, I called upon what remained of my dwindling power and transformed, becoming my animal shape. I beat my black raven's wings and let the gusting wind take me, nearly succumbing to the strayling's attack. I did not care. I had to outpace the punishing vengeance of my geis as the faeduhn magic sought to crush what my heart dared to feel. Cawing out in anguish and rage, I pushed myself higher, blending in with the dark clouds above and disappearing out of reach.

I would not forget this girl and her wrath, and like Cuchulainn so long ago, how she had shown me once more that which I was denied. When I recovered, I would return, my power multiplied tenfold, to rip from her body the one thing that would satisfy my Curse's insatiable appetite, at least for a while. Perhaps then, I would know a small moment of tranquility.

As I streaked across the storm-tossed sky, staying just ahead of the faeduhn's wrath, I allowed myself, for the first time in many, many years, and most likely the last time, to examine that grandest emotion any living thing could posses. I stretched my mind, pushing it past the murky darkness which blocked out all the light, and I caught a glimpse of a shard of a memory: a picture of Caedehn's face the morning he was born, the scent of his new, silky skin, the sound of his tiny voice as he slept, the rapid beat of his heart. And just before the drowning, poisonous pain rushed in to fill all the spaces in my heart, a new torment cut through me: a sorrow far worse than everything my geis had ever thrown at me. And this one hurt the worst, because this time, it was real.

FIN

About the Author: Jenna Elizabeth Johnson grew up and still resides on the Central Coast of California, the very location that has become the set of her novel, *Faelorehn,* and the inspiration for her other series, The Legend of Oescienne.

Miss Johnson has a degree in Art Practice with an emphasis in Celtic Studies from the University of California at Berkeley. She now draws much of her insight from the myths and legends of ancient Ireland to help set the theme for her books.

Besides writing and drawing, Miss Johnson enjoys reading, gardening, camping and hiking. In her free time (the time not dedicated to writing), she also practices the art of long sword combat and traditional archery.

For contact information, visit the author's website at www.jennaelizabethjohnson.com.

DRAWN TO THE BRINK
TARA MAYA

A BRINK HAD ESCAPED FROM ACROSS THE TWIXTING, and when the glamourers drew colors, Sajiana's ribbon came up silver. With an extravagant sigh of resignation, she packed up her linen papers, her scribs and her knots, pretending to a reluctance to leave the stuffy halls of Mangcansten. Once loose upon the moor, with the grouse and the heather and the wind whip-a-man through her hair, she broke into a whistle. She trod no road, and needed none. Upon her back she carried her large, flat portfolio, her scribroll and a smaller rucksack of odds and ends. She pitied herself only because the brink had left a trail a first-year draftsprentice could have followed. In no time at all, she would have the creature's picture in a knot. Once she disposed of it, duty would force her back to dreary Mangcansten.

However, she was in no danger of overtaking the brink that day. When dusk came, she waited through the twixting time, then found a likely spot upon the empty moor to camp for the night. She had a folder of prepared etchings, including many of little cottages. Sajiana had a fine eye for detail. Even these simple sketches included whimsies such as ivy curled over the stones in the fireplace and watering cans sitting upon window-sills planted with radishes. She placed one drawing in the center of a flat expanse of sward, and then set out her knots at a distance around it. Three knots could serve, at minimum, but because Sajiana hunted a brink, she set out four for safety. As she tugged tight the last knot, the glamour caught the piece of paper. Picture billowed into reality. Now a cozy cottage, with potted radishes in the windows and a roaring fire puttering smoke from the ivy-covered fireplace, stood, snug as you like, before her.

The key to a good etching was to fill in the view through the windows. If you hinted at what lay inside, that sufficed. No need to draw *all* the insides separately, as long as enough showed in the picture for the glamour to operate upon it. In the same spirit, if one drew a picture of a cabinet, one must always draw one drawer open just enough to show something inside. Otherwise, when one opened the door of one's house, or the drawer of one's cabinet, one was apt to find a blank white interior.

In the windows of the cottages that Sajiana sketched, one always caught a glimpse of a snuggly bed on one side and a table laden with food on the other. When she opened the blue door to the cottage, therefore, she found a teakettle just coming to boil, a plate of scones, a hardboiled egg and breaded veal cakes. She tucked in with a will. Nothing like a day of walking to whet an appetite! She banked the fire and crawled into the warm bed.

Dawn *almost* caught her by surprise. It had been that long since she'd been on the road. She leaped out of bed just as the twixting of daybreak dissolved the knots on the glamour. As usual, once the glamour vanished, no sign of the piece of paper remained. Bed, table, fireplace, cottage, all misted into the morning fog and left Sajiana shivering in her nightclothes on the desolate moor. Grumbling under her breath, she scurried to her rucksack—no glamour—and pulled on her trousers and jacket of wool felt—no glamour either. She shoved the nightdress into a crumpled lump in her sack and resumed her trek across the roadless moor.

Fourteen drawings later, she reached a town called Paddiglum. The brink had arrived here a few days ago, after taking a much more haphazard route that zigzagged across the moor. The brink would be hungry, and this one was too inexperienced—perhaps it was young—to know that it would do better to lurk out in the wilderness and waylay travelers than risk coming into a human town.

She could have drawn herself a dress of crimson silk, sewn with buckles and bells of gold and a tall moon shaped hat to match. However, Sajiana preferred the anonymity provided by her ragged, rugged, real travel clothes. She tromped through the town, whistling, past villagers dressed no better than she, ignoring and ignored. She had a string in one hand, a scrib and a slip of blank paper in the other. A close observer would have seen that the string did not dangle from her hand, but poked its head out this way and that, gently tugging at her fingers. These were the tugs that led her ever closer to the brink.

The string suddenly jerked her quite hard toward an alley along the cheesemonger's street. Sajiana looked up and met the eyes of a startled young man. His hair tousled about his head all unruly. His eyes were huge in his face, haunted. His lips pressed together under hungry cheeks. Strange that in all this time since he had escaped from the twixting, he had not used his considerable powers to better maintain himself.

Some brinks tried to run. Some tried to fight. The outcome would be the same. This brink looked at her a long moment, hard. He walked away. It was as though he lacked either the humility or the sense to fear her.

His striking face would be his undoing; she could hardly forget a face like that. Sajiana sat down against a wall beside a cheese shop. In feathery, charcoal strokes of her scrib, she began to sketch the face she remembered. It took her only a few minutes to have a likeness. It took her longer to tie the complex knot around the portrait. With her knotted portrait, Sajiana stood and walked into the alley.

"Come to me," she said.

She heard him before she saw him. A scritching and scratching and scrapping sound: he fought each step of the way to answer her call. He could not resist the compulsion, however, and he finally dragged himself into view. His eyes no longer looked haunted. They blazed with hate.

"You would dare draw *me?* Do you know who I am?"

"Just another brink, as far as I'm concerned," Sajiana said.

Whatever answer he had been expecting, it had not been that. He stared at her, flummoxed. "Are you mad? What are you talking about? I'm no brink!"

His surprise surprised her. She had never met a brink who did not know it was a brink. Most boasted of their inhuman superiority.

"Did you honestly think you were human?" she asked, overcome with curiosity against her better judgment. The teachers at Mangcansten universally advised against entering into prolonged discussion with a brink.

"I *am* human," he said. "And the fact you cannot bind me proves it."

He wrenched himself free of the compulsion. This time he did run.

The charcoal portrait had become a smudged mess of meaningless lines. She rolled a choice curse around the inside of her mouth. Because he had not attacked anyone, stolen anything, or wrecked any havoc, she had assumed him to be weak. Instead, it appeared he had a stronger will than any brink she had previously encountered. Sajiana began to worry that a more experienced glamourer should have been assigned to this brink. She had a quick hand, but not the patience for the truly intricate work needed to bind an extremely powerful will. The brink was wrong if he thought that humans could not be bound by a portrait. That was what humans and brinks had in common. However, a strong will could turn a line drawing to mush. She would have to put more effort into it.

She blew air between her teeth. She untied and unrolled her scribroll. It contained an assortment of scribs and brushes. She chose one of the thin charcoal scribs. She peeled back a layer of the wax paper to reveal more nub. She began to draw the brink again, this time his whole body. He wore a kora, a forward-curved sword that broadened at the tip. His cape-coat had once been elaborate but the clasps and bells had been torn off the indigo velvet. Beneath it, the blouse of white silk may once have been pristine. Most brinks were painted richly adorned. However, why had he let the garments wear down to near rags?

"Glamourer!" a cheery shout interrupted Sajiana's concentration. Annoyance soured the smile she flashed to the man who had interrupted her with his salutation. She reminded herself that Mangcansten was surprisingly intolerant of punching locals in the face.

"Glamourer!" He was a portly man, balding, richly belled in silk, with a moon shaped hat that protruded like a horn from the center of his head. Gold clappers cupped his ears, and bangles jingled on his thick wrists. He was seated in an open veyance drawn by massive Tugger hounds. "What an honor to meet one of your mastery! What brings you here to our remote hamlet?"

"Our business need not worry you," she replied coolly. So that no one could see her drawing a forbidden human form—though if he knew she was a glamourer, he would know she had the right—Sajiana filed the paper and scrib back into her portfolio.

"But you must let us assist you. I am the town Honorary, Lord Master Yorch. Have you a place to stay? Oh, I know you glamourers have your own ways of providing shelter, but surely you will permit me the vanity of offering you the hospitality of my house."

Sajiana sighed and gave in to the inevitable. Perhaps it would be better to work on the portrait of the brink inside, on a flat surface, with good light. She climbed up beside Lord Master Yorch and allowed him to babble at her the rest of the trip to his large mansion. She would have to resume her hunt for the brink later.

Most of the houses in Paddiglum were lumped from stone, but Lord Master Yorch's mansion was a warm amber jewel of carven woods. Soldiers in serviceable brown cape-coats and iron helmets stood watch inside the house. A lovely, yet listless maid showed Sajiana to a guest chamber.

Sajiana pleaded fatigue and hid in the guest chamber until supper. The sun set; she lit lamps. She drew and burned several drafts of the brink's portrait. None were true enough to hold him, and there was no point in knotting him just to let him escape again. After a frustrating afternoon, she decided to allow herself to doodle to clear her mental palette before she tried again. She set aside the fine linen canvas she had been work-ing and took out her sketchbook. She always liked to practice upon real rooms, and she especially liked to look at the insides of things because without those views, a picture would lead to a poor glamour. Much heavy oaken furniture adorned the guest chamber. Sajiana sketched the bed, then the casement window and the bronze grill across it, then a clever chest at the foot of the bed, and then a large dresser against the far wall. She opened one drawer...

...Inside it was quite blank. White.

Shocked, Sajiana stared at it a minute. Then she checked under the bed. White. Behind the curtains on either side of the window. White. Inside the chest in the corner. White....

Was it possible? How? The mansion had not vanished at sunset...

"Ah, yes, sorry, this room still has some rough spots," a mocking voice lamented.

Sajiana whirled to face the man in the doorway. Lord Master Yorch.

"I suppose it was only a matter of time before Mangcansten sent someone to investigate," he said. "But the scribblers of Mangcansten are not the only ones who know how to knot a portrait."

He lifted his hands, revealing a painting of a woman. Water colors, hasty and slapdash, they would be possible to escape, except that he had a true talent for capturing detail. He had caught the curve of her neck, the shape of her brow, the way strands of her hair fell across her face.

Sajiana cried out and ran toward him, but she knew even before she felt the searing jab of pain that she would not stop him before he finished the knot around the painting of her. She stumbled to her knees just in front of him. He laughed softly. He reached out and tipped her chin up, forcing her face to tilt to his scrutiny.

"You're pretty enough, and a man tires of paper women. Perhaps I will keep you on my string a while before I end you, glamourer. Take off those rags."

She could feel the binding on her mind, chaining her to his will. Powerless in her rage, she obeyed him.

"Draw a gown for yourself," he said. "And join me for supper."

Though he left, the compulsion to obey him remained. She reminded herself that watercolors were not oils. She should be able to squirm free. However, it would take many weeks filled with long hours of concentration. And he would be most alert for any attempts tonight. So she did as she had been bid. Black silk. Gold bells. Scarlet hat.

The drawing and knotting took her only moments. However, she did not stop. She pulled out of her portfolio another sheet of paper, one of the best quality weave.

Once more, she began to etch the brink.

Perhaps danger honed her concentration. Perhaps the helpless hate that boiled in her helped her to catch the glint of that same emotion in the eye of the brink. The shape that formed under her charcoal nib was truer than any she had ever been able to draw. She tied on the knot, looping each strand with utmost care. When she had finished, she hid the package back in her portfolio.

She could feel Lord Master Yorch tugging at her will, demanding her presence downstairs.

"Come to me," she whispered to the empty room.

All through the farce of dinner, Sajiana sat stiffly by Lord Master Yorch's side while he played the role of genial host. He had several guests, town magistrates and their wives, a few merchants, a guild master. None of them appeared aware that the glamourer who was the guest of honor had actually been imprisoned in the vilest way by her host. The oblivious laughter and meaningless chatter of the other guests made Yorch's know-ing smirks all the harder to bear.

She puzzled over the mystery of Yorch's power. He had knotted a glamour, but tied it to what? Why did the mansion not disappear when it crossed the twixting times of dusk and dawn?

Sajiana saw no sign of the brink. He must have come to the room where she had commanded his presence, and, in her absence, willed his way free of the drawing. As she gave the matter deeper consideration, she felt relief. She didn't know why she had drawn the brink. If Yorch had left her with her scribs and sketchbooks, it was because he knew that as long as he controlled her, he controlled her magic. The last thing she wanted to do was deliver a brink to him.

"Come with me," Lord Master Yorch said to Sajiana after the listless servants took away the dinner. She followed him up the main stairs, across the hall, and up a back stair that she had not noticed before, to the third floor.

"Take off your clothes," he said. He put a key to the heavy door at the top of the stair. "You won't need them for what I have in mind."

Sajiana dropped off the gown. As it fell away, it turned back into a sheet of paper, with the drawing jumbled into uselessness.

Behind the door lay a painting studio.

One huge oil painting, canvas mounted on a wood frame, dominated the room. Sajiana recognized Yorch's man-sion. Years of detail had gone into every minute stroke of the painting. Each room could be seen through the large windows. People, servants and soldiers, could be seen in the rooms. Lord Master Yorch exchanged his cape-coat and the sword belted at his waist for a painter's smock.

He pointed to a couch. "Recline."

Step by step, Sajiana's feet forced her to the divan. She was reminded of the scritching walk of the brink when she had called him in the ally. She did not enjoy the irony of being on the other side of the knot.

"You painted people into the picture with the mansion," she said aloud. Her body contorted into a pose on the divan. "Your servants and soldiers do not *work* for you—they are your slaves."

Yorch replied, untroubled, "As you will be."

He came to arrange her hair around her shoulders and the edge of the divan. He removed her arm from across her breast and tilted her chin so that she must look at him as he painted her.

He went to his large canvas, dipped his brush into a collection of jars on a platter, and began to paint Sajiana into the glamour of his mansion. Yorch painted with oils, and Sajiana could not deny his skill. She might have escaped the watercolor, in time. She knew she would never break free of this painting. The brink would have left Paddiglum by now, and when Mangcansten sent another glamourer after it, the glamourer would bypass Paddiglum altogether. Yorch, with his guilty conscience, had assumed that Mangcansten had detected his illegitimate use of magic. Sajiana knew better. As evil as it was,

Yorch's magic had a limited reach. She had not sensed it from her meanderings around Paddiglum.

"Now, now," chuckled Yorch. "Your tears won't show in the painting, so it's no use crying."

Under the compulsion, she had to take him literally. She could not longer even cry as the minutes crawled her closer to her enslavement.

Absorbed in his painting, Yorch did not hear the door to the studio open. Sajiana heard, but under an order to hold her pose, could not turn. She did not see who it was until the brink walked on soft feet into view.

His dark chestnut hair was still disheveled, his velvet cape-coat torn to expose a tattered white blouse and one muscled shoulder. He gripped his kora sword in his hand. The brink rested the wickedly heavy tip of his kora against Yorch's neck.

"Stand and fight," the brink ordered in the steely voice of one accustomed to command.

Then, as if he were indeed the son of a noble house rather than a foul creature of magic, the young man stepped back and allowed Yorch to stagger to his feet and exchange his paint-brush for the sword he had earlier set aside.

Seconds into the duel, it was obvious that the brink mastered his sword as the greatest painters of Mangcansten mastered their art. Yorch sweated and puffed, trying to move his fat body out of the way more than to fight back. Yet a knowing smirk twisted Yorch's lips. From the divan where she lay, silent and immobilized by Yorch's orders, Sajiana saw the cause for his confidence. Yorch's soldiers, enslaved by his will, stormed up the stair and burst into the room. Six men now pressed the brink. They hacked at him with fierce downward motions of their kora swords, but he dodged in and out, slashing and tearing with his own blade as he swept by them. They began to lose limbs. Here a hand. There a leg. It became clear that they might as easily have lost heads, except that the young warrior did not seem to want to take their lives. Terror crept into their faces, and Sajiana suspected they would have fled, but Yorch's compulsion forced them to keep coming, even when blood gushed out from their wrists or knees.

Meanwhile, another soldier had crept into the attic from outside, through the casement window. Sajiana strove to cry out, to warn the brink, in vain. The newcomer slashed his kora directly into the back of the brink's neck. The blow nearly severed his head from his body.

The brink turned around and knocked the soldier out the window. The brink's head lolled at a silly angle. This development did not distress or slow the brink, but it shocked Yorch long enough for him to forget to maintain his hold over his soldiers. They fled at once.

"You're a brink!" Yorch stammered. "Wait, please! Don't kill me. We can reach an accommodation, I'm sure of it! Besides, all the wealth of this house is a glamour. If you kill me, who will maintain it for you? I will paint you anything you want -- anything!"

"I am not a brink," said the brink. "And I don't want your bribes, you vile dog!"

For emphasis, the brink beheaded Yorch.

The brink finally noticed the odd state of his own head. He yanked out the blade still lodged in it and adjusted his head back on his neck. His skin smoothed over the wound, restoring him to perfect health.

The brink stared at the bloody kora, then turned to Sajiana in panic. "How did I do that?"

"You're a brink."

"How did I survive that wound? It would have killed any man!"

"You're not a man, you're a brink."

"Stop saying that!" He waved his sword.

The death of Yorch had, unfortunately, not altered the magic that bound Sajiana and the other servants of the mansion to the painting. Yorch's last commands no longer held true, so she was able to sit up and try to hide her nakedness with her hair and her arms. Yet, her spirit remained knotted to the house through the painting. She would not be able to leave as long as the painting survived. Since she was in the painting, she could not destroy it herself. She itched to grab Yorch's kora where it had clattered to the floor, but although she expected her swordsmanship a little surpassed Yorch's, she knew it would not be up to par to defeat the brink. Even if a stab would have killed him, which it obviously wouldn't.

"Will you kill me too, brink?" she asked without much hope.

He sheathed his kora. "I can't," he said. "Even if I wanted to. You hold me hostage, even as Yorch held you. I came here because you summoned me."

"You were able to slip out of my other drawing easily enough."

"This one would not let me go. I tried."

Sajiana felt a brief, irrational surge of pride in her work. It passed quickly, as she recalled that she too, remained bound. And there was a simple way for the brink to destroy her and free himself without attacking her directly.

"If I burn this painting, it will destroy this mansion, including the picture you drew," he said, walking to the canvas. "And it will destroy everyone painted into it, including you. That will free me, won't it?"

She didn't answer, but that was answer enough.

"Couldn't you just promise not to hunt me any more? An exchange. I cut the knots on this painting. You cut the knots on the drawing you made of me."

She pushed away the temptation to lie. "I have a duty to Mangcansten."

His huge, moist eyes pleaded with her. "Am I really a brink? How can I be a creature painted into existence when I remember my whole life? Brinks do not grow from childhood to adulthood. They are always as they were first painted."

"You remember being a child?"

"Yes." A thought brought despair to his face. "Could all my memories be false?"

"No. If you were a brink, you would not remember anything before you were brought to life that had not been in your painting."

"Then... I am human."

"No. If you were a man, you would be dead. You said it yourself."

"Am I immortal?"

Sajiana thought she must be a fool to tell him his strength if he did not know it. Yet she found herself answering gently, "No. But you cannot be killed by a man or by a woman, by a manmade object or an unmade object, inside or outside, on the land or on the sea, during the day or during the night. Only a glamourer can destroy you."

He absorbed that.

"Tell me what you remember," she prompted. "Was there anything... uhm, unusual about your family?"

"You might say so." He measured his trust of her, and must have found it small. Perhaps he deemed her no better than Yorch. "For many years, my parents could not have children. My mother said that she was...fortunate...that she finally had me."

"Did you mother paint?"

His pained silence answered her.

Sajiana whistled through her teeth. "No wonder you remember your childhood. Did you..."—it was a ridiculous question to ask a brink, "do you have a name?"

"Drajorian."

She raised her brows. "Your parents were bold to name a brink after the heir to the throne of Cammar."

"Apparently my parents were bold in ways I never imagined," he said dryly. "I knew my mother could be a stubborn woman. But this....You must understand, I was not raised in an isolated hamlet. I grew up surrounded by luminaries. None of them could have suspected, or there would have been consequences years ago."

She wondered how a powerful brink could have gone undetected so long. And what had changed so that suddenly Mangcansten had noticed him? "She must have first painted you as a baby."

"But then wouldn't I have remained a baby?"

"Not if she kept changing the portrait." She glanced over at the large painting that Yorch must have begun more than twenty years ago, that he had been touching up even now. "Year by year... maybe even day by day..."

He bowed his head. "So it is true. I am a monster."

There wasn't much Sajiana could say to that.

All at once, a yowl of despair issued from his throat. He raced to the painting, his hatchet-like kora sword raised over his head. Sajiana braced herself. She wondered if it would feel as though her flesh were being cut if he slashed the painting to shreds.

Instead, she felt a burden lift from her.

He had cut the knots.

The twenty-year old knots drifted away from the painting. From all over the mansion, the glad cries of servants and soldiers burst out. Then the mansion dissolved. Sajiana and the brink and two dozen or so others stood in the middle of a weed-strewn field. Here and there, real objects and pieces of furniture that had not been part of the glamour poked out of the grass. Sajiana recognized her rucksack and ran to it. She pulled on her traveling clothes with a deep sense of relief.

The brink followed her. He recovered her portfolio. The brink pulled out the drawing she had done of him and handed it to her, knot and all.

"Finish your job," he said. "Burn it."

The wind ruffled his hair. He stared at her with those limpid, haunted eyes.

Sajiana took the paper. It trembled in her fingers.

"If I untie the knots," she said, "They'll sense it. They can sense a brink from across the earth. They'll just send someone else after you."

"Burn it."

"I can't."

"I'd rather it be now. I'd rather it be you."

"I can't." She picked up her portfolio and put the drawing, still knotted, into her satchel. "If I don't burn it, but don't untie it, they won't sense you. I won't tug on your will. I won't summon you. You won't even know I still have your portrait."

He stared at her, full of questions.

"Go," she said. "Be free. It's a command."

Long after the brink had gone, and after Sajiana resumed her return trek across the moor to Mangcansten, she took the portrait out again. She studied the tousled hair and large eyes, the shadows on the face, the play of lights across the shoulders, the stance. She did not summon. She did not call. After a time, she sighed, and put the portrait away. She didn't knot a glamour cottage that night. She wanted to sleep under the stars.

FIN

❧ ⟶ ◉ ⟵ ❧

About the Author: To learn more about Tara and find more of her books visit her website: taramayastales.blogspot.com.

THE VARIANCE COURT
ALEXIA PURDY

AYLIN NEVER VENTURED OUT INTO THE WORLD. SHE lived in a land blooming, with greenery and full of shrubs, grasses, and flowers crowding her backyard. She'd never seen any towns or cities, and she barely ever saw other people. This one tiny bubble was all that composed her world in the land of Variance, where she'd heard stories of magical folk who roamed the earth.

She wasn't magical though. It was dangerous to live here with no magic at all.

Aylin and her father had lived in a small cottage at the edge of the woods for all her life. It was a peaceful existence; calm, quiet, and full of nature. It bore the sweet fruits of their labors in their garden and sustained them well. Nothing and no one ever came or went, and the days were all the same, but she was never bored. Aylin loved the land and the solace. It suited her and kept her busy with chores and farming. The place was magical though, and ebbed its curious powers all around her. Even the creatures living amongst the stumps and tiny underground burrows adored her. Her kindness and love blazed from every pore of her body, and every creature in the land knew it. It was almost as if she was a real-life Cinderella.

When Aylin was fifteen, her father died. He'd taken down with a severe pneumonia after a long winter storm had caught him on the way home from the nearest town, where he'd gone for supplies. It had been his annual trip to the city. He'd spent a week with a violent, consistent cough he couldn't shake until one day he did not wake up from his sleep, leaving poor Aylin to fend for herself.

Now she was seventeen and a tall, graceful young lady with alabaster skin, rose-colored lips and deep, earthy eyes. Her long brown hair was always neatly braided and pinned back, for she worked the earth with her hands, and all the animals helped her dig holes in her small garden. They were her friends and lit up the darkness threatening to engulf her with sadness.

Her days were spent peacefully but not without pain or suffering. Alone in the cabin at night was the worst time. There was no one to converse with and no one to read her bedtime stories anymore. All she could do in the waning dusk was read the old books lining the walls of the cabin she'd once shared with her father. She loved reading, and there were dozens of volumes filled with words to comfort her. Flipping through them by candlelight, she could lose herself in the stories, imagining worlds beyond the hills and the mountains, in places she'd never been. Places like foreign cities and towns where castles loomed high above and colorful people walked every street.

People.

She hadn't seen another person in so long. No one knew she existed, and no one cared. She wondered if she should try to go to the city. She'd never been to the nearest town, and she was very low on supplies. She'd been recycling a lot of things and sewing patches on her clothes. Even her shoes were almost as thin as wearing nothing.

Sooner or later she'd have to go. There was money her father had left her, bags of gold coins he'd made sure to save for her and for their well-being. But she wasn't sure how much things cost or if it would be appropriate to take gold. So she stayed on in her cabin, hiding from the world where nothing ever changed. She was too afraid to leave and experience things she'd never tried before.

One day I will, she thought. *One day I will get my wish.*

But for now, she would remain safe in her refuge.

He was a forgotten person, sitting on the sidewalk, worn down, and scuffed. A person nobody cared about and nobody wanted to know, let alone see. To cast a glance his way was to focus on the problems he represented, the problems most tried so hard to ignore: the homeless, the jobless, the hungry, the needy and, ultimately, the greedy, who refuse to share their wealth. I never counted myself as much of a giver; Heck, I could barely keep my own head above water as the college debt mounted and my pantry remained eternally sparse. I kept to myself and hoped the world's problems wouldn't touch me as I tried to make my way in this unforgiving world.

I wasn't blind. I just didn't have the time or resources to make a difference. That was the abysmal truth that helped me sleep at night.

On my way to my apartment, right off campus and near the baking asphalt of the Las Vegas desert, was where I'd see him, under the sparse but lush canopy of decades-old trees. He was always holding out a cup for change, whether sleeping, sifting through trashcans or relaxing under a tree singing to himself. His dusty and filthy trench coat covered whatever he held underneath, and a rugged hat topped the greasy hair that dangled down in stringy strands of charcoal black. He wore it all the time, and it showed. A scruffy beard covered most of his face and looked like it'd last been trimmed a millennium ago. I couldn't tell what color his eyes were. I'd never gotten near enough to catch a glimpse. He was a forgotten person, one people like me rarely noticed... until one fateful day.

After failing my mid-term Microbiology exam, everything changed. I had studied hard for it all week, but the teacher was horrible; she jumped around in the textbooks, never sticking to the syllabus, always confusing the class. I really didn't know what to do anymore. It looked like I would be repeating the course the next semester.

My mood had soured, and the late summer heat was having its way with my head. I swore I'd never take another summer course ever again. It left me with little desire to do anything but get home, plop down in front of the TV, and Netflix it out.

Hurrying on my way, I happened to walk past this man for the hundredth time. Not once had he ever spoken to me. I had never thought him capable of real conversation, what with his incessant babbling and singing. Today, I happened to notice him even more. Whether it was the scuffed, yellowed plastic casino change cup held out with dirt-encrusted fingers or the haunted, far-off gleam in his eyes, I won't ever know, but it dragged me in as I tried to scurry past him before he noticed me.

Not today. Today, I heard him speak for the first time.

"Young lady, why so down?"

I stopped in my tracks, feeling his voice wash over me like an ice-cold shower. I turned slowly toward the man as though he'd been speaking an alien language, confused.

"Excuse me?" I asked.

"There's something on your mind. I asked you what's the matter." He blinked up at me with coherent eyes. I could clearly see their striking, clear-blue color, a translucent hue like the sky. The dark pupil in the center stood out like a blemish in the landscape of his irises.

"Oh, I...." I stuttered. The words refused to come and stuck in my mouth. He was shockingly interesting in a way, because as I stared, he didn't look like the dirty homeless person ignorant of his own needs and oblivious to hygiene I had previously assumed he'd been. I could've sworn I saw flashes of someone else there, someone with the same eyes but with shorter, cleaner dark hair and a charming smile to boot—a handsome man dressed in the finest clothes I'd ever seen.

Like royalty. Only really rich and fancy people wore such things. But the university and surrounding grounds were nowhere near a rich neighborhood and as far from royalty as anyone could get.

"Nothing," I finally responded. "I—I just failed my Microbiology exam. The teacher isn't very forgiving, and I studied all week for it. Either she's terrible, or I'm not very good at the subject. It doesn't really matter, does it? I failed." I felt the sting of tears behind my eyes, but I pressed them back. I couldn't break down here, for goodness sake. Not in front of a homeless person I didn't even know.

Moments passed, and I couldn't move. I felt frozen in place. His face slowly morphed into a half smile, slightly wicked but mostly enticing and terribly handsome beneath the stubble that covered his face. I tried to look away, but it was as if some force kept my eyes glued to the man. How strange that I could see him now beneath the façade of dirt, hair, and sweat when before, all I had ever seen was a pile of human trash.

"No, I suppose it doesn't matter. Such trivial things as school grades, teachers, homework... I never bothered with such things."

"Of course you haven't," I scoffed. "Those things are obviously not high on your list of priorities."

His eyes turned dark, and I felt the icy prick of his stare run along my skin once more. Holding my breath, I wish I hadn't insulted him in such a brazen manner. Stupid, stupid, stupid.

When I could finally rip my eyes away from the man, the freezing air had returned to its previous scorching heat. I turned and began walking toward my apartment, which was just across the street, near the campus, but within walking distance.

"Wait. Wait, miss!" he yelled. "I have something for you."

I paused, again feeling like I couldn't move. Why was this happening? I thought might have to get a restraining order against the guy if he didn't leave me alone. What could he possibly have for me? He had nothing to offer anyone, and owned nothing of worth. Right? What did a man with nothing have to give someone who has a lot more than he did?

He held out his hand, and in his dirt-streaked palm sat a stunning opal and platinum ring. I couldn't take my eyes off it, and I wondered where he'd gotten such a beautiful trinket. Had he stolen it?

"I didn't steal it. It belongs to me. It was my mother's ring, and she was the queen of all the fairies." His eyes shimmered along with the ring. It was mesmerizing, and I fought to swallow down my fear and not get hooked in his hypnotizing words. How was he doing that to me?

"You've got to be kidding, right?" I asked, my voice cracking as whatever hold he had on me remained firm. "Why would you want to give that to me?"

"It's because you're the only one who can see the true beauty in the world where others cannot. Besides"—his frosty blue eyes drilled into my soul—"this belongs to you. Well, sort of."

I almost laughed out loud, but I kept staring at him, hardening my resolve against his eerie spell. I found it hard to breathe, hard to speak, and hard to move away from this person or alien or whatever in the world he could be. No one else was noticing our interaction, and I wondered if I could possibly be home already, snoring away on my couch, dreaming this insanity. I hoped I was. It was a nightmare, and I didn't want to be in it anymore.

"That's not mine."

"How do you know? It's beautiful and light. Made for you, in a way."

"Nope."

He grinned, and it reminded me of an image of the devil I'd seen in an old children's picture Bible as a child. It was intriguing and frightening all at the same time.

"Take it, it's yours. It can give you all you've ever wanted; all you've ever wished for. It's part of you." He cocked his head to the side, and all I could see was his handsome face beneath the stubble. The façade he wore was a mask hiding his handsome face, sharp jaw, strong cheekbones, and perfect smile. He was no homeless person. He had to be something else. Something I'd probably imagined.

No, I thought. To think I was imagining things would be admitting that I'd lost my mind, that failing that test had pushed me to the very edge of my sanity. I couldn't accept that.

"I have to go." I stepped back, relieved to find that the hypnotic hold he had on me was breaking. He frowned and watched curiously as I widened the space between us. I still couldn't laugh. I could barely form words. As hard as I tried not to, my fingers were already at his hand, curling over the perfect platinum opal ring and snatching it from his greasy palm.

Feeling the cold metal against my skin, I moved it to my opposite hand and slipped it onto my finger. I couldn't resist to save my life. There was no more willpower left. All I could do was inch away with all the determination I had left. The metal band called to my blood somehow, and I couldn't leave without it. The odd thing was, the ring fit perfectly, as though it was meant to be on my finger. Like it had always belonged to me.

How odd, I thought.

"How can this be mine? I've never seen it before."

He peered up at me, a satisfied smile flashing back.

"It always was. Make a wish. Anything your heart has ever desired."

"There has to be a catch."

I could swear I saw a momentary twinkle of wickedness in his eyes. There was nothing I wanted right now but to get back to the safety of my apartment and forget I'd ever spoken to this man.

"There is one catch for this power. It'll give you the strength to summon the legions of fairies from the Variance and the ability to grant any wish you desire for yourself or for another." He snickered. "Though I highly suggest caution when granting others' wishes. Most of them don't know exactly what they want. It can turn into a jumbled mess faster than you can blink." He sighed, appearing exhausted for the first time.

"The Variance?"

"It's the place from which all magic flows, the place where fairies live. The rightful rulers live there, but...." He suddenly looked lost in his thoughts, as if he'd transported himself to a long lost memory.

"But what?"

"They've been lost to us." He focused back on me. "If you ever find you do not want this power anymore, find one of the rightful rulers of the Variance and give them the ring. They'll know what to do with it, and your destiny will make itself known."

"Rulers, wishes, and fairies? You're completely insane, you know?"

I stared down at the stone as it sparkled in the sunlight, almost blinding me. When I looked back up, the man was gone.

I spun around, searching the campus for the homeless man, but he was nowhere to be found. In fact, no one was even looking in our direction. It was as if he'd never existed, and I'd been talking to myself.

"The hell?"

I did another turn, studying those closest to me. No one glanced my way, and none looked familiar. Not one of them resembled the man at all.

I groaned, closing my eyes before I reopened them and stared down at the ring once more, amazed I hadn't imagined it. The metal hummed against my skin, full of magic. It was tantalizing to say the least.

"This is crazy."

I turned and ran for dear life, as fast as I could. I didn't live that far; the apartments across from the university were all I could afford right now. Hopefully when I graduated, I would get a good job and get out of the student ghetto hellhole.

The stress of failing my test and the odd encounter with the homeless man was increasing with each hurried step I took. Feeling absolutely defeated, I couldn't wait to get back home to curl up on my couch with all the junk food I could scrounge up and binge watch shows on the TV. As I ran across the street, dodging cars running red lights without regard to human life, I cursed them under my breath while contemplating the events of the day. A person doesn't just give away a precious piece of jewelry without a reason. Something told me I was going pay dearly for it. If that homeless guy came around again, I would have to be prepared to give the ring back to him.

I had a feeling it was going to be hard to do.

Back home, I turned the ring around in my fingers. It was gorgeous, but I didn't know what to do with it. I'd probably take it back tomorrow and return it to the homeless guy. He most definitely needed it more than I did. I had no idea why I'd even taken it from him in the first place. It was strange. It'd been like I couldn't help myself. It had all come down to me not being able to resist the man's present.

Was it a present?

Tired and confused, I placed it on the coffee table, grabbed the remote control, and switched on the TV. I flipped through channels until it felt as if it was just droning on and on. I couldn't figure out what I wanted to watch. Nothing looked interesting, and my eyes kept being averted toward the ring. It was all I could do to not stare at its glimmering sheen in the dim light of my living room. It was somehow begging me to slip it back onto my finger. I was sweating from resisting the urge to do so.

Leaning forward, I snatched up the ring. *What the hell,* I thought. It couldn't hurt just to wear it around the house, could it? Slowly, I slipped it back onto my finger, feeling the nauseating sensation of resisting its charm fade away along with everything else.

The world disappeared.

I gasped. I was still sitting on my couch, but my apartment was gone. Whipping my head around, I saw trees and shrubbery in every direction. A sweet smell like honeysuckle clung to the bark of the trees, beckoning me to taste of their drops of nectar. Dandelion seeds floated through the air while birds chirped and fluttered. Squirrels, rabbits, and foxes ran about, pausing momentarily to study me curiously before heading off on their way into the high grasses or disappearing up the branches into the hovering canopy.

"What's going on?"

My breath caught in my throat, restricting my ability to inhale. This was insane. The sleep deprivation from the long week was getting to me, and now I was hallucinating vividly. I looked down at the ring on my finger and yanked it off.

Bam! I was back in my living room, and everything was the same, as though nothing had happened.

"What the—?" I was definitely losing my mind now. Bringing the ring up to eye level, I scrutinized the simple jewel. It was just a ring, right? Regardless of the pounding in my chest from fear or excitement—I couldn't tell which one it was—I couldn't help myself as I slipped the ring right back on. Just like before, the entire living room vanished, along with my couch this time, since I was now standing.

At least when it happened again, I felt more prepared. I was definitely not in Kansas anymore, or Oz, or wherever the heck this place was, but I was going to find out.

"Hello?" I called out into the open air. There was no answer. I was probably miles from any civilization. I didn't know what I was expecting. The flutter of animal sounds quieted for second as my voice echoed through the trees but then restarted within a vengeance. They appeared to be chattering amongst themselves. Chattering about me. Nothing weird about that.

But wait. How could that happen? They were animals. Dumb things, really. Why would they even be bothered about me? They were probably more afraid of me than I was of them, or so the saying went.

"What is this place?"

I had no idea what it all meant. The location was a pretty forest, full of life and gorgeous vegetation, but that's all it was. I experimented with the ring several more times. It always took me there, but the moment I removed it, I was back in my boring old apartment. I eventually discovered that my apartment was the only place where the magic occurred. It didn't happen outside or anywhere else.

I'd walked around the forest for hours until my feet blistered and my limbs ached, but there were no fairies and nothing overtly magical in that place. I was beginning to think I'd been cheated. It seemed the ring had no special magic other than taking me to that one place in the forest. Why it chose that spot I couldn't figure out, so I did what I did best when stressed out, tired, and disappointed—I went to bed.

Maybe in the morning I would see the homeless guy again and I could ask him more about the ring and its peculiar magic. He had to enlighten me, right? As I twirled it in my fingers, I sighed. This thing had magic, but it sure didn't grant wishes. That was impossible.

I sat staring at the whiteboard, trying as I might to understand the diagrams, labels, and formulas scrawled across it. No matter how hard I tried, it was an alien language to me. The words didn't click, and the diagrams made me want to pull my eyes out and squash them under my shoe. I was completely lost, and my teacher, Mrs. Nathans didn't even care.

It didn't help that I wasn't sure what I was doing there. Nor did I remember walking in or even what day it was. It left me perplexed as I tried in vain to understand the lecture.

I failed my test, and I'm failing this course.

The thought came rushing back to me while I sat in my usual desk chair. Confused, I stood up, feeling sick to my stomach.

"Is there a problem, Miss Peters?" Mrs. Nathans narrowed her eyes at me, and the entire classroom turned to see what the problem was. I felt the weight of their stares sucking the oxygen away, and I choked on my words as I tried to respond.

"I failed the test," I muttered.

"Excuse me? We haven't taken the midterm yet. That's next week." She tightened her mouth, and the look in her eyes told me her concern probably involved calling in the school counselor to examine my head. Was I truly losing it?

"What?" I said. How could this be? "But I failed it. Then I—I was home... sleeping. Um... how did I get here?"

The entire class burst out laughing, and I felt my knees weaken. I slumped back down into my chair, which felt impossibly small. I wanted to bolt out of there.

"You must pay more attention in class, but I'm not sure it would be worth it since you're saying you're going to fail the midterm exam. You might as well toss your tuition into a burning garbage can."

Again, the whole room roared in a maniacal laughter that dug under my skin with a thousand pins. There was no air, and I couldn't think. What was I doing there? We hadn't yet taken the exam? How was that possible?

Had I wished it in my sleep? *Oh no....*

"I—I think I need to get some air," I whispered, feeling my chest tighten. I couldn't stay there. It was... wrong somehow. I knew it. Maybe it was a just a nightmare.

I felt for the ring on my finger, and lo and behold, the silvery thing was there, like it was wedged on me forever.

I wish they'd all shut the hell up, I thought.

Immediately, the incessant chatter and chuckling stopped. The complete silence caught me off guard as I stumbled out of my row and slid to the bottom of the carpeted steps. The whole room was up out of their chairs in a desperate panic. Most were pointing to their mouths, their lips gaping open and shut like dying fish out of water.

What was happening?

Even the teacher couldn't speak, and her eyes bulged out like goldfish suffering from hypoxia.

I reached down to my finger, twisting the ring. It had worked! But how? I watched as some girls near me began crying as they tried in vain to speak. They were now desperately texting to each with their smartphones, trying to make sense of what was happening.

I can't talk!

Me neither!

What's going on?

Can you talk?

No! Help!

I shrank against the wall. The students were now leaving, rushing out, even more frightened than I had ever felt. The teacher, Mrs. Nathans was on the floor, passed out from shock.

Oh... I wish they could all speak again.

The room erupted with noise, and everyone stopped in their steps, shocked once more. Their chatter died down for a few seconds as they all shared a moment of confusion then rose up once more. No one seemed to suspect that I had anything to do with their temporary muteness, but I wasn't going to stick around, just in case. Before I left, I paused outside the door and snuck a look at Mrs. Nathans, who was being held up by some students and fanned back to consciousness.

I wish my grade was an A on the Microbiology midterm, and I wish it was that day again.

I walked out into the hallway, but nothing seemed changed. I pulled out my cell phone to look up my grades online and check the date. My grade was no longer an F but now a shiny A, and it was again the day of the exam.

I was giddy with excitement. The stupid ring worked! Who knew such a pathetic piece of possibly counterfeit metal had such magical properties? I was going to have to thank that homeless guy for the gift.

What if he wanted it back? Would he? I paused as I placed my hand on the main doors of the building and peered through the glass, across the lawn, and toward the busy street. I didn't see him anywhere. That didn't mean he couldn't just pop up out of nowhere and demand his gift back. Nevertheless, he'd said that if I wanted to get rid of it, I'd have to find some kind of ruler to give it to. Why would I want to do that?

I turned away and headed toward the back exit of the building. I'd take the long way around to get home today. That's what I'd do. Whatever happened, he couldn't have his ring back. At least, not yet.

Back in the overly bright sunlight of the Las Vegas day, I squinted and wished for sunglasses. Immediately, a dark, over-sized pair was on the bridge of my nose. Grinning like a fool, I began to think of all things I needed, wanted to do, or had to have. It was a long list, and I'd have to write it all down once I got home. Hurrying there, I kept one eye out for the homeless guy and another on the shiny ring.

Too bad I hadn't notice the Cadillac turning the corner with a bit too much speed. The screech of tires woke me from my daydreams and sent my heart racing. The guy behind the wheel laid on his horn as the smell of burnt rubber surrounded me in a nauseating cloud. I cursed at him and slammed my palm on his hood. I finally stopped my stream of curses and moved to the side of the road.

"Move it, lady!"

"Watch where you're going!" I yelled, giving him the finger. He threw back a trail of obscenities along with a matching middle finger as he slammed down on his gas pedal, squealing away. I almost wished him a nice car crash but managed to nip that thought in the bud.

I had to be careful. It wouldn't be prudent to filter my thoughts a bit more. I could wish terrible things on people, and they would happen, whether I'd really want them to or not.

With this ring on me, there was no telling what could happen or what sort of wishes could slip from my subconscious mind.

I quietly made my way home, clearing my thoughts until I got somewhere safe. No matter what, I had to keep things under control.

That was the understatement of the year.

I jumped. Had I just heard someone yelling for help? I was back in the clearing of the forest where the ring took me whenever I wore it in my apartment. Why it didn't do that when I was at the university or even outside my apartment was a mystery. I liked this bubble of forest. It was soothing to me somehow, and it was the one place I couldn't wish someone would turn into a pile of steaming poo for being rude to me. Even subconsciously, my mind was wreaking havoc on everything and everyone back in my real life.

I'd turned the neighbor's cat into a cactus, the neighbor now had hives covering her body, and her demon child son was now bald and wearing wigs to cover up his shiny pink scalp. Childish wishes—no, curses—I had muttered under my breath. I couldn't think anything anymore; it all came true. I was dangerous, and I had to be contained. That or get rid of this ring, but the homeless man remained elusive. I'd not seen him for weeks, and I had no idea where to find the ruler to give the ring to. I had tried throwing it away, but it would return to my hand in an instant.

"Help!"

I spun around. The voice had sounded like it had come from right next to me, but it had to have been farther away, for there was no one nearby.

"Who's there?" I called out. Whoever was out there needed help, and I was the only person there, so it was obvious I was going to have to throw on my superhero panties. I headed toward the direction of the voice, hoping I'd find something sooner or later.

Soon enough, I found the source of the voice, but I was also sliding down into a deep, dark Alice-in-Wonderland-like hole and wondering if I was ever going to stop falling. The hole was a lot deeper than I'd imagined, and I kept sliding down the dampened tunnel of earth. If I hadn't been so terrified of falling to my death in the dark, I would have had fun sliding down this tunnel. But I definitely wasn't having any fun. Moments later, I landed right on my bottom and felt my tailbone sting as it bruised from the hard thump.

Crap, I thought. How was I supposed to get out of this?

I peered around, but I didn't have a flashlight on me, and all I could see was the tiny little halo of light high above me. It might as well have been miles and miles away. I had no rope and no one who knew where I was. There was no hope of rescue in this forlorn place.

"Some rescue."

I startled at the voice. Someone had spoken right next to my ear. The voice had sounded like the one I'd heard calling for help. Could it be the same girl?

"Who are you?" I asked. I was ready to pummel her if she was going to be a threat. I felt around in the darkness for a rock or something to hit her with just in case she attacked me. All I could hear was her shuffling and the grinding of shoes against the pebbles while she shifted her weight around in the darkness.

"I was hoping for a rescue, not a companion."

I wished for a flashlight, and it popped into my hand. I flicked it on, but it shorted within a millisecond.

"Oh, you're from the other side of the Variance. Your special instruments don't work here."

Great.

"How do you know that?" I asked.

"I read it. In books. I read a lot."

I heard something scrape against something else, maybe a knife or a stone. I wasn't sure. The girl lit a match and held it up so I could see her face and then held it out toward mine so she could see me.

"Ouch!" She blew it out as it scorched her fingertips, and we were back in the darkness along with the stench of the match.

"Well, I thought you were going to rescue me, but obviously I was sorely mistaken." She sighed melodramatically.

"So," I began, "how did you end up here?"

"I was chasing Runner. She's a rabbit. I caught her stealing a bunch of my carrots, so I chased her. I only wanted to give her a good scare, but she's quick, and I found this hole."

"Oh, okay." That sounded like the truth to me.

"And you?"

"And me what?"

She groaned. "How did you end up down here?"

"Oh." I squirmed, wondering if she was entitled to the truth. I figured there would be no harm in it. She was from this weird bubble of forest, so I wanted to ask her a bunch of questions about it anyway.

"I fell in trying to find you. I don't know how it works, but when I put on this ring I end up here in this patch of forest. It's this stupid ring. It always messes things up and sometimes turns my wishes into things I don't want."

I heard her shuffle around before lighting another match, illuminating the darkness with a sudden flash. It was just enough for her to see my ring gleam in the firelight before it went out.

"Oh, that's magnificent!" she exclaimed.

"Yeah," I mumbled as I twirled the ring on my finger. "It's beautiful, as was the guy who gave it to me. I don't know why he did; he was some homeless guy who could've gotten more use out of it than me. Make some cash off it, you know?"

I could hear the girl scratching her head, probably pondering if my story was true or not.

"Why don't you just wish us out of this place?"

"Um...." Yeah, why didn't I? It made me realize how tired I was. Taking tests and going to college was no joke. After changing my midterm grade, I'd made a decision not to use the ring for school. It felt too much like cheating. So I was usually up at the crack of dawn and got home when the sun was setting, only to burn the midnight oil studying. I was gone all day, and it was hard work.

"Well, maybe it's dangerous. Things are never what they seem here."

"True. This ring doesn't do exactly what I want it to. Wait... what do you mean by things aren't what they seem?" I asked.

She didn't reply right away, and my suspicions rose.

"Well," she said slowly, "there's this one legend I read about of a man who goes around and tricks people. It sounds like your homeless man. He lives in the Variance, but he probably went where you live and tried to trick you."

"Who is this guy that you're talking about?"

"Oh, he's some sort of prince or something like that. I'm not really sure. It's been so long since I read that story."

I settled back against the cold tunnel wall, sighing. She made no sense—no more than the homeless man did—but I really didn't want to use my ring now. I even worried that taking it off might not return me home at this point. The girl had filled me with doubts, and I was ready to go melt the infernal thing if I ever did get free.

"Do you know of any other way we could get out of here?" I asked.

"No, but I'm sure someone will come along sooner or later, and we'll be rescued before dinnertime. We're near a town."

"But it's already dinnertime," I pointed out. I could almost feel her frown.

I had heard her sigh and settle back too. "Well in that case, it's going to be a long night until the morning wagons appear. Then we can call out to them."

Soon enough, I heard her soft snores in the darkness. I peered up at the fading circle of light above me. *There's no way I'm going to die like this,* I thought. If someone didn't come soon, I would start on my way back up, clawing if I had to. I'd only use my ring if the situation got desperate. Whatever happened, it would be better than dying of starvation and dehydration. In the meantime, I decided I might as well take my cue from the girl and get some sleep. I settled back even more, leaning my head against tunnel wall. Even though it was hard and uncomfortable, something about the cave was comforting, so I curled up into a tight ball, leaned on my side, and went to sleep.

Aylin was the girl's name. We'd both slept through the night, but once we were awake again, we began talking to pass the time.

"So you've never left the Variance or been anywhere else?" I asked her.

"No. I've never gone anywhere nor ever seen anything truly amazing, and now here I am stuck in a hole where I will surely never see anything ever again." She sighed, and I could almost see her rubbing her face and wiping gritty tears away, but it was so dark I didn't think I could even see my hand in front of my face.

"Look, if you're really worried, I could make a wish and get us out of here," I offered. "I just hope it goes the way I'd want it to."

The silence that followed didn't tell me much of what she was thinking. In fact, I wondered if she had fallen asleep again.

"How do you do it? How do you make wishes?" Her voice finally cracked the quiet pressing down on us.

"I just wish, out loud or even in my head. Anything I wish for happens, but I have to be careful. Sometimes things that I never mean to happen do, and sometimes the wish comes out all wrong and goes haywire."

"Haywire?" Aylin had apparently never heard the word before.

"As in crazy. Mad. Not the right way."

"Oh." The girl sighed. "So you won't wish us out of here?"

"I don't know. I've tried to stop wishing. It's a curse, really. Not any kind of fun anymore. But I guess if you really want me to...."

She let out a delighted little sound, and I gave in.

"Okay," I said, "but I want to do everything possible to make sure it doesn't go wrong. Why don't you hold on to me when I make the wish? Maybe that'll help make sure we both end up out of the hole together. Hold on tight."

"Okay."

She reached out and gripped my arm as tightly as she could, digging her tiny, sharp fingernails into my flesh. I winced but bit my tongue. I didn't want to spook her. I felt for the ring and touched its cool surface. I couldn't see it, but I knew the jewel was gorgeous. I was thankful I'd not lost it sliding down into the abyss.

I wished that both Aylin and I were no longer in the hole and instead in the forest above. I squeezed my eyes shut, hoping the wish would turn out right and not mutate into something obscene. Nothing happened.

"It's not working!" I panicked. What if we were to die down there? No one would know where to look, and this would become our grave. My chest seized.

"Can I try it?"

I sucked in a breath, wondering if it would work. I had to give the ring to a ruler of some kind, not just anyone, or I'd never be released from this curse. But I didn't know anything about Aylin. There was a possibility.

"Are you... royalty?"

"Not anymore, but my father did once say my mother was a queen or... something. He didn't talk about it much. She shed the title to marry my father. I suppose that makes me a princess, but I have no lands, no people, no castle."

I could have jumped for joy. How had I gotten so lucky to meet this girl? She was just what I needed. I hoped.

"Here, put it on," I said, deciding that there was no way my situation could get any worse. I took the ring off, only half surprised that I wasn't flung back into my living room. I had remained in the earthen pit with Aylin. I handed it to her, and she quickly slipped it onto her finger. The air moved about us like something had changed. Something was going on, but it stopped as quickly as it had begun.

"I hope this works," I muttered. "Wish us out of here, Aylin."

She nodded and grabbed onto me again.

"I wish us to the surface, back in the Variance forest."

The moment she wished it, something happened. The damp, earthen scent of the hole faded and gave way to a warm breeze enriched by the familiar scent of honeysuckle. I could feel the warm air circle around me, feeling more like a hug than just wind. I couldn't have been happier.

"I did it! We're out of the hole!" Aylin shouted.

"Then you must be a queen," I said, smiling at her. The coincidence of it all was crazy, but I was relieved to be free of the ring. It had been nothing but trouble and had never given me what I truly needed.

Aylin smiled and peered down at the gleaming ring on her dirty hand. "It's beautiful."

"I've finally found you," said a strange voice, cutting through our joy.

We both turned to find the homeless man standing in the middle of the clearing, but he was no longer dirty or wearing torn clothes. He was dressed regally, cleanly shaven, his skin white and gleaming. He was breathtakingly handsome, and we both held our breath as he approached.

"You—you're that homeless guy who gave me that infernal ring." I pointed toward Aylin's finger. "It was a curse, not a gift. There are no legions of fairy or wishes. They all get messed up. Why did you give that to me?"

"Because, sister, you're the one who could find Aylin with this ring. The only one."

My eyes widened. Sister?

"What are you talking about?"

"I'm Prince Axlon of the Variance Court. My sisters disappeared long ago, taken for protection by the man who married my mother after our father died in the war our family waged against the darker courts. He hid one in the human world and one in the Variance to keep them safe. Aylin has no magic without her ring. You"—he pointed toward me—"were the only one who could wield the ring to find her, even though it would cause chaos wherever you went. I am the ruler now, and I want my sisters back in our court, safe and sound."

"Wait, what?" I stepped back. I was adopted? My parents had never told me that. "What's my real name then?"

"Ainsley. Your name is Ainsley." Axlon held out his hand, and in it was another blasted opal ring. "And this is your true ring. It will restore your powers. It won't be chaotic or unpredictable. It is pure power and will help you rule our kingdom."

I shook my head. It didn't make sense. I turned to Aylin, who was grinning ear to ear, like she'd always known she was meant for something more. I had never thought that. I never could have imagined anything like this.

"What if I don't want it? What if I want to return to my human world?"

Axlon's face fell, and he took a tentative glance toward Aylin before staring at the ground.

"It will be difficult to rule without the triumvirate. We are nearly powerless without each other. Our kingdom has suffered without us all to help balance the power of the Variance. It is a difficult job, but there must be three to succeed in keeping it at full power. It is how we defend against the dark courts and evil magics of the Variance."

I swallowed hard. It was a big decision to make, and I wasn't sure I could do what he asked.

"I—I don't know what to do."

"Join us, Ainsley. You and I can learn together." Aylin reached for my hand, and her warm fingers felt familiar against my skin. Somehow I knew these two, and the desire to learn more about them and this world, the Variance, grew tenfold just by hearing her say my real name.

Ainsley. My human name had been Anna. So close, yet so far off.

Axlon handed me the ring, and I slipped it on, half expecting to be jetted off to another weird world. That didn't happen. In fact, the power of it surged through me like a natural high, soothing all my bruises and whispering my history to my mind in flashes of memory. My mother, my father, the kingdom, they were all there for me to look over in my own time. It felt warm and inviting, and I suddenly felt more at ease with all of it.

I nodded. "Okay." It was better than learning more Microbiology. "I'll give it a go."

Axlon bowed slightly. "Thank you. Our battles against the dark courts are ever ongoing. They are rising up again, growing stronger. You will not regret taking back your seat on the throne. This is a promise I will forge in blood."

"No more wishes or promises, please." I shook my head. "I've had enough wishes to last a lifetime."

He gave me a nod and grinned as he offered his hand. "To the Variance Court."

FIN

About the Author: Alexia currently lives in Las Vegas, Nevada—Sin City! She loves to spend every free moment writing or playing with her four rambunctious kids. Writing has always been her dream, and she has been writing ever since she can remember. She loves writing paranormal fantasy and poetry and devours books daily. Alexia also enjoys watching movies, dancing, singing loudly in the car, and eating Italian food.

Visit the Alexia's website to find all her books: www.alexia-purdybooks.com.

THE MORRIGAN
PHAEDRA WELDON

OAK & ASH & THORN

I

OH CRAP.

That was the thought running through Tam's mind as he watched the group of thugs form a threatening circle around him. It was after midnight, and he'd just left a drumming circle inside one of the dormitories at Harvard Yard. Since he didn't live on campus and it'd started out as a nice spring day in Cambridge, Tam had decided to forego his Harley and walk the grounds.

Big mistake.

Some of the other folklore students, like himself, had filled him in on some attacks on campus, all suspected to have been from the same group of guys in matching black hoodies and carrying pipes. And not the kind to make music with. The victims had survived, but all had ended up in the hospital.

"You should be really careful, Tam," Janet Bostwick said as they packed their drums before he left.

"Why me? Do I look like a victim?"

Harold Jamerson, a psyche student, but Irish folklore enthusiast, had chimed in. "You look like the other victims. Five in all and they all had your general look."

My general look? "They're attacking short, dark-haired guys with funny names?"

"Same build, same hair and face shape." Janet had nodded.

"I have a look?" The serious expressions on Harold and Janet's faces came back to him as he stared down what he suspected was the same hooded gang. The single light from the building behind him wasn't strong enough to break through the shadows created by their hoods. They'd picked the perfect place to surround him, less than a mile from his house. Didn't accidents always happen less than a mile from one's house?

Tam wasn't totally defenseless. He had a backpack full of library tomes, all of them weighing a hefty amount. He also had his bodhrán's hard case, something he was now happy he'd paid more money for instead of the soft case. At the time, he'd felt anxiety for spending so much, but given the bodhrán had belonged to his mom; he'd do anything to protect it.

With the backpack and case on his shoulders, and dressed in a thigh-length peacoat that would constrict his movements, Tam held up his hands. "Hey...look, guys. I've got nothing of value."

"You think it's him this time?" the tallest one to Tam's right said. The guy's voice surprised Tam. It was gravelly and deep. Not usually the tone of a college kid's voice. Unless these weren't college kids.

"So what if it ain't? We're to keep looking till we find him, and then take it from him." This voice came from Tam's left, from a medium-height hoodie. The voice had the same graveled timber. *What is up with these guys? They smoke too many cigarettes?*

"I'm bet'n it's in that case. That's where he keeps it."

Oh hell no. Tam turned his body so the case was furthest away. "There's nothing in the case of value." He surprised himself when his voice didn't shake, though the same bravado that kept his timber even wasn't talking to his knocking knees.

Adrenaline pumped furiously into his system. Everything he'd learned in defense classes told him this would end in a fight. He had to be ready. Of course, he'd paid more attention to his Irish step dancing classes lately, mostly because of a particular young woman. He doubted he'd be able to dance his way out of this.

"So why you protect'n it, huh?" Still another voice, graveled and with a slight accent that sounded vaguely Irish, but it'd been polluted with something else. Tam knew what a purer accent sounded like because of his own family and their ties to Ireland. He couldn't tell which of the dark hoods spoke.

"Let's do it quick," the first one said, and to Tam's horror, pulled a metal pipe out of his jacket.

They all pulled metal pipes from their jackets.

Janet and Harold had said the victims were beaten with hard, blunt objects. One of the victims remained on life support.

"Look...guys...I really don't have anything of value. You don't have to beat the crap out of me."

"Oh, yes we do," the smaller one said. "We have orders to kill after we relieve you of the prize."

Kill? He narrowed his eyes. "You left the other victims alive."

"'Cause they weren't what we was look'n for."

"They didn't have the prize?" Tam shifted his feet into position for one of two options. Fight or flee. What they did next would determine which he chose.

"No. But we're pretty sure you do." The smaller one slapped his pipe into his other hand. "So, we can do this easy...you give us the case and we kill you fast, or we take the case and kill you slow."

"What's the prize?" He figured it was a lot to ask, but now curiosity had its grip on him. That was something all the Kirkpatricks in his family had. An abundance of curiosity.

"The shill—" the smaller one started to say, that is, before the one next to him knocked him in the face with his pipe. The smaller one flipped in the air and rolled into the empty road.

Tam took that moment to make his move. It was the diversion he'd hoped for. One thing he could do well, besides playing his bodhrán, was run. Fast. He wasn't a tall man, standing at five-foot-seven without shoes, but he was lean and he kept in shape. It was something his stepdad had instilled in him when he was younger, after his mother ran out on them. "Keep healthy, keep fit, and one day your body will be your greatest asset."

Now it was time to validate that advice.

He heard their yells and the following pounding of their feet on concrete as they came after him. Tam pumped his arms and legs hard as he retraced his steps toward campus, the backpack and case beating against his sides and back. If he could get them to follow him back to Harvard Yard, then the campus police would see them, and maybe even arrest them.

He heard metal slide against concrete seconds before one of their pipes tangled in his feet. Pain lanced up his right leg as the pipe cracked his ankle. He went down with some speed behind him, and forced himself into a roll to make the impact less painful. Tam wasn't sure if that worked or not, because the agony in his ankle overrode every other rational thought he had. He also felt the burn on his exposed skin, especially his left cheek, where he scraped it against the concrete.

The group descended upon him before he could get back up on his feet. They shoved him over on his side, holding his arms and legs, as they wrenched his backpack and case from his shoulders. One of them struck him repeatedly in the stomach with a pipe. The pain caught his breath, so he couldn't get in enough air to cry for help.

Through the pain-induced fog, he heard their voices, as well as the sound of ripping vinyl and the cracking of the case around his bodhrán.

"It's just a drum!"

"Don't be break'n it, Tolen." That was the voice of the tallest one. "That might be it. They can shape shift."

"Och," another said. "Is it him?"

"Check him."

Tam fought back as they attempted to strip off his coat and t-shirt. He wrenched his left arm, his playing arm, free and delivered a hard right cross into the hood of the closest one. He let Tam go and fell back as Tam clenched his jaw at the bone-shattering pain in his fist. What the hell? Was that guy wearing some kind of iron mask?

Even with one down, there were still four more. He managed to kick one of them holding his legs just before a pipe struck the side of his head. The sound rang in his ears and slowed his reflexes. The pain didn't feel right. Tam had been hit in the head plenty of times in his life, scrapping with friends, at the dojo, and even with his sword master, but never had the impact caused such a warp in his sense of reality.

He no longer had control of his body as they finished removing his coat and shirt, though he did react to the cold temperature. It might be March, but it was still cold at night in Massachusetts.

"Look at his arm!"

"It's the mark, you see it? This is him!"

Mark? My arm? Does he mean my tattoo? He had a Celtic knot tattoo around his upper left arm. How was that a mark? And more importantly, a mark for what? Certainly not a gang, unless there were secret Irish gangs. So secret, in fact, that they hid their tats? Tam tried to speak, but his words slurred, and his vision just wasn't working right. For starters, when he looked up at the one holding his bodhrán, the tallest one, he thought he saw...

No...it wasn't possible. The guy's hood was back and his head... *I've got brain damage. That's it. They knocked my brain against my skull, 'cause that guy looks like a troll. A big, horn-wearing, tusk-sprouting troll.*

"Boys, we found our prize. Put the torque on him and bring the van around."

Torque?

His question was answered when someone put something cold and burning around his neck. His body went limp and his thoughts spiraled into a dark, confusing place. He could see and feel, but he wasn't in control. He heard squealing brakes, felt himself being lifted over someone's shoulder like a sack of potatoes and then dumped onto a cold, metallic floor.

The tall one with the troll head spoke, "Clean up the street. Don't leave any trace. And send a crow to the Morrigan. We have the Unseelie Prince."

Tam's next waking thoughts were something he wanted to put back where he got them. They hurt. Bad. And he shook. Cold seeped in through his skin and made his bones brittle. Nothing prepared him for this.

They'd hung him from his wrists in what looked, and smelled, like a basement. His feet were bound at the ankles with chains, and only his toes, if he pointed them, brushed the floor. A few bulbs hung from the ceiling, illuminating the room. Tam still couldn't speak or really control his movements. Just small things like making sure his head rested against his arms and didn't drop forward so the only things he saw were his feet and the floor, and pointing his toes. A dull ache plagued the muscles along his shoulders and neck as he swayed.

His body was little more than a connect the dots of bruises and cuts where they'd taken turns striking him with their pipes. And with each hit the pain intensified. So much so that the impact of the hit wasn't what hurt, but the touch of the pipe against his bare skin.

His ankle burned where the pipe had damaged it. Missing a month of step dancing was the least of his worries.

They'd left him alone again, for a while. But he knew their questions would start again. *Where is it? How do you make it shift? We'll end your pain if you just give us the secret.* Tam hated that if he knew what it was they were after, he'd have given it to them long before it got to this point. He was little more than an isolated island in an ocean of pain.

If he moved the right way, he could see his attackers huddled over the contents of his backpack and the drum. They treated the bodhrán as if it were gold.

What frightened Tam the most wasn't death so much as what he kept seeing as the instrument of his demise. He thought when he came to again he'd see them as people. Just regular people out beating up on college kids. But when they all removed their hoods, they all looked like trolls.

They varied, from the size of their tusks to the size of their horns. Some horns curled back to meet their pointed ears, while others stuck straight up before they sloped backward. Their features were different. He'd had long enough to look into their faces and memorize them. Their skin tones were different shades of gray. Just...slate gray.

I'm hallucinating. I'm dying. And my mind wants me to think I was killed by mythical creatures from fantasies so I won't be so upset to die at twenty-two. That's it. That's gotta be it. Because if this is real...

The big one, called Magnus, moved from the table and strolled over to Tam. He made sure Tam could see his face. "I'll admit. You've held up longer than the others. But we know it's you, Tam Lin. You can see us for what we are, and only the Unseelie can do that."

Tam hadn't been able to talk the entire time, not with the torque around his neck. He simply stared, mute, and waited for the blows to start. He tensed when Magnus reached out to him, but he didn't strike.

The troll took off the torque, and as he pulled it away, Tam could see what it looked like. He'd seen them before, in museums and at the local Renaissance Faire now and then. A semicircle of metal, carved like the heads of two dragons with the same tail, facing each other.

That simple half-circle of iron is what kept me helpless?

Not that removing it did him any favors. The volume of pain increased by a thousand, and he moaned before he could stop himself. It was odd to hear his voice again.

"The torque dulls the pain as well as your wits. It's what keeps the Unseelie in line. You have one more chance to tell me where it is, Tam Lin."

Tam took in several deep breaths and used that opportunity to look around. He took in more of his surroundings. He was pretty sure they were in a basement, he just didn't know where. And he didn't know if the stairs on his right led up to a house or perhaps a business. And if he were at all successful at getting out, where would he go? He was pretty sure the ankle had swollen and was unusable.

"My name…" he said, as he winced again because the damage to his chest interfered with breathing, "is Tamberline Kirkpatrick, not Tam Lin."

Magnus struck his face. It was a good, hard knock against his temple. Tam saw stars as his body swayed back and forth from the impact. "The pain won't stop until you tell us how to shift it."

Tam tasted blood and spit it out. A tooth was loose. "Wh-what are you looking for? I don't know what it is." He expected another blow.

And he got it. This time, he blacked out for a few seconds before the shock of cold water woke him. He reacted to it, and then screamed out as his body answered in pain.

"If the Morrigan takes you, your life will be much harder. We can give you peace. Kill you and burn the body. You'll never have to be her bonded."

Tam had no idea what that meant. He'd heard them talk about this Morrigan, and he knew the name from folklore, but that's what she was…a myth. *But then again, I'm talking to trolls, right?*

A tune went off somewhere in the room. Tam assumed it was a phone. He had to laugh internally at the idea of trolls carrying cell phones. The smaller one stepped away as he pulled a phone from his pocket. "We have company. Upstairs."

"Ignore them," Magnus said.

Tolen answered, "Better to turn them away than to feed their insistence."

Magnus gave him a harsh growl. "Then go turn them away. And take Poot with you."

The smaller one stomped his foot. "No...I want to see it shift."

"Go." Magnus pointed to the stairs.

Tam watched as the two went up the steps. The wood creaked under their weight.

Magnus placed the torque back around Tam's neck. "Best to keep you quiet, just in case."

And once again, he was mute and unable to move.

They all waited for a signal. Two stomps on the floor. Magnus smiled. "All clear. Now we can start again, and you can tell me where it is—"

The basement door opened, and Tam expected to hear Tolen and Poot come down the stairs. So did Magnus and the other two. What Tam didn't expect to hear was a *swump* sound and another thud. He could only focus on Magnus as the troll roared at something to Tam's right. He brandished his pipe and ran out of frame.

Tam heard the sounds of battle. Heard the cries of pain. And more of that odd *swump* noise.

Then nothing.

Until...

He recognized her face. He'd watched her in step dancing class, all while dreaming of asking her out, but also feeling embarrassed because she was a good few inches taller than him. It was Áine (pronounced Awn-ya) McCuill, the lead dancer in the troupe, only instead of being dressed in jeans; she wore what looked like leather pants, boots, and a tight-fitting vest. She had her red hair pulled back, and sticking up over her shoulder, he could see a quiver and arrows. She had a bow in her hands, and she looked like a cosplayer.

He blinked as she put her arm through the bow and rested it on her shoulder. She pulled a cloth from her pocket and used it to remove the torque. Once it was off, Tam gasped and bit back a yell. He had no idea what was going on, but he sure as hell didn't want to show weakness in front of Áine McCuill!

He followed her with his eyes to one of the slumped trolls as she retrieved a long knife. That's when he saw all of them were on the floor, some with arrows protruding from their backs.

"I—" he said.

She put a finger to his lips. "Sshh. First, we get out of here." Áine stepped away for a few seconds before he was lowered to the floor. He didn't stand because his ankle gave, and he fell with a thud and rattle of chains to the hard floor.

"Sorry...my bad," Áine said as she scrambled to his side. She had a key, and still holding the cloth, used it to unlock the shackles from his wrists and then remove the chains from his ankles.

Tam blinked hard as he looked at the burns on his wrists. "What—happened to me?"

"Iron. It's what the torque is made of. Something the Unseelie can't tolerate. No...no more questions. We don't have time. They're not dead, Tam. My arrows can't kill them. It takes a lot more power than that. So let's get you on your feet."

"My ankle..."

"I know." She picked her way over the downed trolls and gathered everything back in his backpack and grabbed the bodhrán. Tam wiped at his mouth and came away with blood on his hand as she put the drum back in its case (thank goodness they hadn't destroyed that!), and with those added items on her shoulders, made her way back to him. She put the backpack on his back, and he kept his mouth shut at the pressure against his bruised shoulders. She helped him push himself up on wobbly legs. He put his weight on his good ankle as she moved under the shoulder of the bad side and wrangled the case strap over his good shoulder. Her height practically lifted him up, and he stumbled as the room tilted at a fairly wrong angle.

"I...always wanted to put my arm around you..." Tam winced. *Why did I say that? Out loud?*

"Sshh. You're in pain, and you've had the torque on too long. Let's go."

"But how—"

"I'll explain everything. Please, Tam. We have to go. I had the element of surprise, but if we linger and they wake..."

She didn't have to tell him twice. He took in a deep breath, moaned at the pain in his chest, and worked with her to get up the steps. They emerged in a hallway, and he looked to his right. He saw two doors that said "Ladies" and "Gentlemen." Beyond them was another door. But Áine led him in the opposite direction to a larger door. An exterior door.

They pushed it open together and stepped out into cool night air. Shivering, he tried to move with her down a sidewalk. He looked back to see they'd been in...

He had no idea where he was, but it wasn't in Cambridge.

A very, very loud roar stopped them both.

"Crap," Áine said. "I'd hoped they'd stay out longer, but Magnus is a strong one."

"You...you know him?"

"I know of him. I need you to move to my back."

"What?"

She sighed and stepped out from under his shoulder, then presented her back to him and knelt down. "Put your arms around my neck."

"I'm not sure—"

"Swallow that human pride and do it!"

He did it, the muscles in his shoulders screaming the whole time. Instantly, something shifted, and it wasn't him. His dizziness increased, and he almost let go until a voice in his mind said, *Hold on!*

That's when he realized he wasn't on Áine's back anymore, but astride a huge, red mare. It turned its head to look at him and snort, and he grabbed hold of her mane seconds before the door to the building slammed open and Magnus appeared. The horse took off.

II

Something tickled his nose.

Tam reached up and batted it away, but whatever it was, it was persistent. "Stop," he muttered as he rolled over and buried his head in the sheets. "Just let me sleep."

"You've been asleep for three days," came a sort of familiar voice. "I think it's time you woke."

Wait...three days?

He opened his eyes again and looked at the sheets. They were blue, and dirty, and not his. He turned back to his right and looked up at the ceiling. Definitely wasn't his room, unless he lived in a trailer. His uncle, Bogs, lived in a trailer, so he was intimately familiar with what they looked like.

In fact...that ceiling looked at lot like his uncle's trailer.

He snapped his head to the right and stared up into the grisly face of Uncle Bogs. "What—"

"I said"—Bogs held up the feather he'd been teasing under Tam's nose. He spoke in his old diluted accent—"it's time you got up, boy-o."

"So where..." Tam pushed himself up and then stopped. "Ow!" he said in a rush of air as his body protested the sudden movement.

"Aye. You're going to be a bit sore, laddie. But you've got your mum's genes and your da's tenacity. You've healed up nicely."

"My what?" Tam stared up at his uncle's face. He hadn't seen the man in what...ten years? And he looked exactly the same. "How did I...what did I..." And then he looked down at himself. He was pretty much nude except for the occasional bandage, covered in just the brown-stained blue sheets.

"Let's take this a bit slower, shall we?" Bogs let the feather fall to the bed, and Tam picked it up. It was black with an iridescent sheen. "That's a crow's feather." Bogs pulled up a chair and sat in it as he crossed his legs and his arms. "I'm afraid there's bad news to be had with that feather."

"A crow?" Tam turned the feather between his fingers. "Bad news?"

"Take a minute. Your memory will catch up in a second or two. But while it's reboot'n, have this." Bogs turned and lifted one of his sturdy mugs from the nightstand. "This is the best thing for what ails you."

"What is it?" Tam set the feather aside and took the mug. He remembered this mug from his childhood. And he remembered his uncle drinking some crazy stuff from it. "This isn't your old grog, is it?"

Bogs laughed. "I see your memory's on the mend. Good. Never know when it comes to Faery healing. But we Leprechauns"—he beat on his chest—"we got stamina. Makes us hardy folk."

Staring into the amber liquid, Tam processed his uncle's words. At first, they didn't make any damn sense, but as he watched the liquid swirl and move, he remembered... everything.

Unfortunately, he sloshed the mug as he yanked the sheet up to look at his ankle. Bogs grabbed the mug and held it back as Tam did a quick body check. His last memory was that he'd been covered in bruises and scrapes and he had broken bones. That he was sure of. A look at his wrists showed no burns, and he put his hands to his face.

"I see you've come back," Bogs said and set the mug back on the table. "That's good. We have a lot to talk about, you and me, and not a lot of time to do it. I'd hoped to have this conversation when you were younger, but your da wasn't having any of what he called my nonsense filling your head."

"My da—you mean my dad?"

"Your stepdad. Phil. The Kirkpatrick who raised you." Bogs sat forward on his chair. "You remember the trolls?"

"Yeah," Tam nodded. "But that had to be fake, right? I couldn't have seen real trolls."

"Do you remember how you got out of that place?"

He did. "One of the girls from my step dancing..." Tam stared wide-eyed at Bogs. "She had a bow and arrow, and she turned into a horse!"

"Aye, she did. Because she's one of the Clurichaun."

Tam blinked. "The what?"

"Damn, child. I thought you were a student of folklore. The Lin protectors? They're the soldiers that guard the lineage." Bogs pursed his thick lips, and his mustache poked out like bristles. "This is going to be a bit harder than I thought. Do you not remember anything from your mother?"

"I can't even remember my mother. I barely remember you." Tam ran his fingers through his hair. "So, you can tell me right now, was my mom crazy? You said I had her genes, so crazy is in our family, right? Because you just sounded like you believe trolls are real."

Bogs didn't say anything for a few seconds, then he stood and walked across the room. The floor creaked and the trailer swayed as it always did with his uncle's weight. Bogs returned with a mirror and held it out to Tam. "Take a look for yourself. There's a spell that covers this world, one that prevents us from being seen by the regular folk. I think with what you've just gone through, or perhaps the wearing of a torque, your Faery sight's finally broken through that spell. It allowed you to see the trolls for what they are, and I'm sure you'll be able to see yourself now."

"What are you talking about?"

Bogs nodded to the mirror. "Have a look. I think they're more fetching, but you're going to have to learn basic glamour if you want to go back out in the waking world."

Tam glanced at himself in the mirror, just to check for bruising, and he was pretty sure he'd suffered a busted lip and broken nose. His face was bruised, there was no getting around that, and a closer look at his neck exposed a light ring around part of it. *That's where that torque thing had been.*

And then he looked at his cheek—

He saw them. Sticking up out of his hair. With his jaw hanging open, Tam reached up and traced the points of his ears to make sure they were real. "What...what did you do to me?"

Bogs laughed. "I didn't do anythin' to you, boy-o. That was your mum and da."

"My ears..." He checked the other one. And other than that, he looked fine. In fact...given the beating he'd taken, he looked... "I'm okay."

"As I said, we have a hearty constitution, and since you were given time and this is your first regeneration, all's well. But like I said, your true nature's peeking through."

"True nature..." Tam dropped the mirror and pushed back. "I'm...I'm a..." He blinked at Bogs. "What am I? You said Leprechaun."

"Half, because your real da was human, and your mother is the daughter of the former King of the Leprechauns, Seamus Lin. Unfortunately, you being an Unseelie didn't sit too well. So now you're here. And your mum was here. Came to stay with your da, who was human."

"Unsee...wait, wait." Tam put his hands on his face. "Like you said, I'm a folklore student at Harvard. I know what Unseelie means, and I'm not an evil Faery."

Bogs roared with laughter. When he finished, he slapped his knees. "No, you're not. And that's not what an Unseelie is, boy-o. The Seelie are the pureblood. Complete and all Faery. Like myself. But, the hybrids, the halfsies like you, you're the Unseelie."

"That's..." He wanted to say ridiculous. But Tam realized all too quick his idea of ridiculous had now gone through a shocking shift of perspective. "I'm...a Leprechaun."

"Aye."

"You're a..."

"Leprechaun."

"But we're not three feet tall with red hair and green suits..." He closed his eyes with a long, frustrated sigh. He was thinking of the stereotype, the image and cultural identification that kept the idea of Leprechauns in the realm of fiction and fairy tale. What he saw in the mirror was based on the reality. "That's a...what they call a red herring, isn't it? The short, fat red-haired man dressed in green with big buckled shoes?"

"Aye, but don't feel bad, Tam. That's the way we want it." Bogs stood, grabbed a stack of clothing, and tossed it at Tam. "Get dressed. You know where everything is. And drink that mug. It'll finish the healing and clear your head. Áine should be back any minute."

Tam caught the clothing and waited until Bogs shut the door. He started to bound out of bed and stopped, remembering his ankle. Looking down, he couldn't see any damage, and when he stood, it didn't hurt.

He slipped on a pair of jeans and a t-shirt, but not the dark green hoodie. These were his clothes, so someone went to his house to get them. He sniffed the mug, and then downed it all at once. It was both bitter and sweet and left the aftertaste of bark in the back of his throat. Tam meandered through the stacks of things his uncle Bogs liked to collect to the kitchen at the other end of the trailer.

Bogs motioned for him to sit at the table and set a plate of his famous heart-stopping fried breakfast in front of him. Eggs, sausage, bacon, hash browns, and a cup of black coffee. Tam devoured it as fast as he could, not stopping to breathe or talk, as Bogs leaned against the counter.

When Tam finished, he smiled. "I really, really needed that."

"Aye, you did. You've been out of the world for nearly a week."

"Out of the world?"

"Off the grid." Bogs came forward and sat at the table with his own mug. "You'd been missing for two days when Áine tracked you down. And you've been here for three. That's five days and no one's seen you. You've been on the news. Luckily I let your stepda know you were with me. You'd been attacked by thugs and I came in to help, though I made sure he didn't know that. That way he didn't cut his trip short. Figured while this mess went on, it was best he stay out of town."

Five days? Tam sipped his coffee as he thought back over his experience in the basement. "The trolls...they really were trolls."

"Aye."

"I don't understand what it was they did to me. I mean they put this thing on my neck. Called it a torque, but I've read about those."

"Forget what you've read and use that knowledge only as a reference, Tam. A torque is what the Morrigan uses against the Unseelie. Because you have Faery blood, and yours is particularly strong, the iron in it won't kill you immediately like it would Áine or myself. For you, it lingers and keeps you in a fugue state, not living nor dying. In constant pain and willing to do anything the one who places it on you wants you to do."

Tam rotated his coffee cup on the table. "You just said a whole bunch of stuff that didn't make much sense to me. When you say the Morrigan, you mean—"

"The exact one you've probably read about in your books. She's been the Queen of Faery for several hundred years now. But only in the past hundred or so was she able to gain control of the Unseelie court."

"Why? If they're not evil like you say and just hybrids... why try to control them? Why come after me? Just because I'm a half-breed?"

Bogs moved his mug out of the way. "There's several answers here, and you're going to have to listen carefully. I wasn't kidding about the time issue. About a century ago, the Morrigan had a dream. Now, she doesn't dream often these days, so when she does, she's convinced herself they're prophetic. Do the rest of us believe it?" He shrugged. "I think she's mad. But the danger is *she* believes it. And in that dream, an Unseelie defeated her. Unseated her from the throne. Stripped her of her power. That's why she's gone out of her way to destroy and enslave the Unseelie. The problem with that plan is the Faery are, by nature, a very lascivious lot. We like to breed."

Tam snorted. "Uh huh. Which is why I'm alive."

"Aye. Remember the spell I mentioned? The one that keeps people from seeing things? Spirits, Faeries, all those things that worked their way into culture as myth and legend? Now, this also made it harder for the Morrigan to find Unseelie like you. She has to know you exist to look for you."

"And she knows I exist. Why does she know this?"

"We're not sure who told her. But she's particularly invested in you because you're a Leprechaun."

Tam rubbed his chin and noticed it was smooth. No growth at all for five days. "I'm not following. I never thought, or read, of the Leprechaun being that important in the Faery World."

"Of course not. And we'd like to keep it that way. Tam, we're descendants of the Tuatha de Danann. We have power and abilities the Morrigan doesn't. We're also mortal enemies." He pointed at Tam. "And you have something no other Leprechaun still possesses, and she wants it."

"What? A pot of gold?" He laughed and then stopped when he noticed Bogs wasn't laughing. "Oh crap...are you serious? I have a pot of gold?"

"Och...think with your heart, and not that learned rot. What is it that a Leprechaun possesses that no other myth does? Besides the gold?"

He had to think hard on that since he'd never really given Leprechauns much attention in his studies. He's always been more interested in the families, and the kings and queens, of Ireland, the mythic fights and land grabs that, until five days ago, he believed had been turned into myth and legend.

Tam thought back to the basement, the trolls demanding he make it shift. They thought his bodhrán was something important. "It's not my drum."

"No, but your drum is a part of your particular heritage. Your mother made it?"

"Yes."

"Thought so, it feels like her. And don't worry, it's safe. We put it away."

That was a relief. "They said"—Tam pointed to the table—"they wanted me to give it to them. Make the bodhrán shift into it. But I had no idea what they were talking about."

"Ah"—Bogs slowly nodded—"they believed your drum was your shillelagh."

Tam did a double take. "My...they want my shillelagh? They think I have a walking stick?"

"Oh Tam, it is no mere walking stick. There was a time before the Morrigan when the Leprechaun ruled the hills. Even the Daoine Sidhe paid homage to us and called upon the magic of our shillelaghs to smite their enemies." He gave Tam a crooked smile. "The Morrigan stole all of the shillelaghs in the Faery Realms, Tam. Sent her crows all over, and like the thieves they are, they took them. Robbed us of our power. Our gold turned to lead, and our influence over the land waned."

"You're saying...I have a shillelagh?"

"I'm saying you have the *last* shillelagh. And the Morrigan wants it. We have to find it before she finds you. Or your hope of survival, and ours, is lost."

III

Áine knocked on the trailer door at that moment, but stepped in before Bogs could answer. When she saw Tam, she smiled, and then frowned. She pointed a finger at him. He noticed she wasn't wearing the leather anymore. She looked like she always had in jeans, sweater, Vans, and a jacket.

"Why in the hell did you go out alone that night?"

Tam sat back, unsure of what to say. He also noticed her ears weren't pointed. He reached up and touched his own. They were once again round.

Bogs waved his hand. "Sorry. But we don't have time to teach you glamour right now, so I fixed them."

"Oh, ah..." He noticed Áine still had her finger pointed at him. "Because I've walked that same route home before. I didn't think it was dangerous."

"That's the first mistake." She lowered her hand and set a bag on the table next to Tam's empty plate. "Routine. They'd been watching you, just like they watched all those others. They memorize your routine, and they wait until you're vulnerable. If you'd had your Harley, that might not have happened."

"You know I ride a Harley?" Tam rubbed at his chin. "I didn't think you even knew I existed."

"I'm pretty sure your uncle's filled you in on what I am."

"Yeah, and I can't pronounce it."

"Regardless, I was assigned as your protector over a year ago."

Now that was interesting. A year ago was when she showed up in his class. "And I'm the only reason you're here?" He couldn't help but smile. "Me?"

"And the college has a decent folklore department, but it's sorely lacking in facts. Which is just the way we like it." She pushed the bag to him. "Here are more of your clothes."

Peering inside, he saw jeans, socks, shirts and... He blushed scarlet. "You went through my underwear drawer?"

"Get over yourself, Kirkpatrick."

"You could have grabbed the gun."

Now she snorted. "I didn't think you knew how to operate one of those, and given the last situation I rescued you from, I didn't want to induce any more bodily harm."

"What the hell?" He put his hands on the table. "I can shoot. I've been trained to shoot, and I'm a damn good shot. So get off my back."

She smirked and looked at Bogs. "I stayed there a good three hours. Inside and then on the street. I don't think they're watching the house."

"But they were there," Bogs said.

"Yeah. I could smell the troll dung in the back. Nasty creatures." She moved to the kitchen and leaned against the fridge.

It was a small enclosure, so they were still close together. "Tam, I got the sense you don't know where your shillelagh is."

"You'd be right. I didn't even know I had one till like...ten seconds ago." Tam put his hands in his lap and leaned back in the chair. "How can I have something I don't know anything about?"

"It's part of our magic, boy-o." Bogs leaned to his left. "As a Leprechaun, you're born with it. It's like a...part of you that connects you to the Earth. To spirits, like nymphs and dryads. And usually, when a Leprechaun comes of age, their forebears help them find theirs."

"Forebears?"

"Fathers. Mothers. Family," Áine said. "But you didn't have either, not of your own. I didn't realize the one you lived with wasn't your natural father."

"So this is bad?" Tam asked. Avoiding discussion about family was something he'd always done, so moving on seemed natural. And he was really, really interested in this shillelagh.

"There's always the possibility the Morrigan will find it first, since she and her crows can sense magic. But given the dampening spell..." She shrugged. "It makes it hard on any of us. The best way for you to find it is to let it call to you."

"Call...to me? What, you mean like some mysterious message?" He was trying to be funny, so when they both nodded, Tam sighed. "Guys, I don't know what it is, what it looks like, and I wouldn't recognize it if it walked up and punched me in the face."

"This is true." Áine nodded. "The boy's got no magical talent."

"Hey"—Tam frowned at her—"that's not fair. You probably grew up knowing you were...whatever that word is."

"Yes, I did. I'm Seelie. I was raised in Faery. Not like this." She scratched the back of her head. "From what I read, your shillelagh is usually close to you. It manifests in something, or by something, or around something familiar and comforting to you."

A phone went off. Áine pulled hers out of her pocket and checked the face. "Looks like the trolls were spotted."

"Where?" Bogs asked.

"North of the campus. They're staying there, keeping an eye out for the Prince."

"I am not a prince!" Tam ran a hand through his hair. He needed a shower. Clean clothes didn't help the gooey feeling he had, not to mention he'd bled all over that bed. He should wash those sheets and get them back to Bogs clean.

"Can I at least go home?"

Both of them turned to look at him. "No," they said in unison.

He moved back toward the stacks of things in the middle of the trailer.

"Sorry, Tam," Áine said. "But you need to stay out of sight. You want them to take you again, knowing what they'll do?"

"There's no guarantee they'd be able to do that again. They had the element of surprise."

"Look, it's not a big thing, okay? Just stay here. I'll be back in a few hours." She smiled at him. "Just get more sleep, okay? You've still got circles under your eyes."

Tam watched her leave and plopped down on the chair. "I can't stay cooped up in here. Bogs, I need my gun."

He remained by the fridge. "Can you really shoot as well as you say?"

"Yeah. I don't know if bullets can hurt trolls, but I'd like to have some kind of weapon with me."

"Oh, bullets can hurt them. They just don't stop them. Not like spelled weapons, such as Áine's blades and her bow."

He remembered seeing those and the way she'd used them. Or rather, he'd seen the aftermath. He knew if he ever got out of line with her, she'd kick his ass. "So...can my gun be spelled?"

"No. Too much iron." Bogs narrowed his eyes at Tam. "So how is it you can touch it and use it?"

"The grip's pearl, and most of the gun's an alloy. I'm not sure how much iron's even in the thing. So how is it that I never noticed iron before? I mean I saw their troll heads. Is that right?"

Thunder sounded in the distance, and Tam felt a chill run up his spine as Bogs pursed his lips, his mustache once again bristling out. "You saw their true faces when they took you, or after?"

"When they took me."

"Interesting." He patted his sides and grabbed a wallet off the counter. "Let's go."

"Where?"

"To your house."

Tam hesitated. "Why the sudden change of heart? And don't tell me it's because you think me having a gun is important."

Bogs shrugged. "Áine's right. Your shillelagh should manifest as something close to you, something that gives you comfort. I suspect whatever that is, might be in the home you grew up in. Looking around for such an item seems...reasonable? And...you can get your gun."

Tam smiled and followed his uncle out the door. "Won't Áine be angry? She said I had to stay in the trailer."

"Aye. But she also said they weren't watching your house." He looked up at the darkening sky. "The lightning will cover your scent. But let's hurry before we get wet. Nothing smells worse than old, wet Leprechaun."

They took the train to Cambridge, and then walked the two blocks from the station to the house where Tam lived with his stepdad. It looked like every other two-story house on the road. Close beside its neighbor, and painted beige with a screened in front porch.

Tam led Bogs around the back where he lifted a key from a fake rock and went inside. Bogs pulled Tam back and stepped out in front of him with his hand up in a warning. Tam was pretty sure nobody was in the house, but he stayed put in the kitchen, grabbing a drink from the fridge and waiting until Bogs came back. "She's right. I smell troll."

"I don't smell anything." Tam headed to the stairs a bit too enthusiastically. Once he reached the stop step, he decided he wasn't going to do that again because it made his ankle flare.

"Hey Tam," Bogs yelled up.

"Yeah?"

"You don't have a favorite stuffed teddy, do you?"

Tam made a face. "No. Please don't tell me that's what your shillelagh was?"

"I won't be admitting to that, no."

Tam pulled the tin box from under his bed and retrieved the Desert Eagle his stepdad bought him for Christmas when he turned eighteen. He kept it well cleaned and unloaded. Setting it on the bed, he pulled the ammo out of his nightstand drawer and slipped in a full magazine. He had two more ready to go and slipped those into his pockets. But as he reached for the pocket watch on the nightstand that his real dad had left him, he froze.

Panic set in. He was locked in place, staring straight ahead at the watch, focused on the vine-like etchings over the surface, his fingers inches from it, but he couldn't move forward or backward. This wasn't the same as having the torque placed on him. This was something completely different.

"Leprechauns," came a deep, gravelly voice from behind him, "cannot move when focused with a gaze of intent, Tam Lin." Magnus put his hand on Tam's shoulder. "No more playing around. This time, I'll take you to the Morrigan herself."

IV

Tam couldn't believe this was happening. *I'm being held in place because he's looking at me? How in the hell is that possible?*

The troll's beefy paw brought the torque around so Tam could see it. "I want you to look at this long and hard, Leprechaun. This is going to be last independent sight you'll see. Because once I give you to her? She'll place her own torque around your neck and you'll think, say, see, and do anything she tells you to. Including giving her your shillelagh."

Tam swallowed. It was about all he could do as Magnus brought the semicircular-shaped band closer.

"Hey! Dipshit!"

Áine! Run!

"Run! Get out of here!" Tam had been straining his muscles so hard to move that once the hold on him was severed, he pitched forward, slammed into the nightstand, and rolled onto the carpet. The watch slipped off with the motion and struck him in the back of the head. Tam grabbed it and put it in his pocket.

"You little witch!" Magnus's attention was focused solely on Áine. Tam reversed directions and rolled under the bed as he watched the troll's boots stomp out of the room. Áine had broken his gaze on Tam and was leading Magnus away. He didn't plan on losing the advantage.

After rolling back out from under the bed, he grabbed the remaining magazines, stuffed them into his pockets, and then he ran down the steps as he heard shouts and felt the house vibrate. The air became thick with the smell of burnt hair and smoke as he quickly, but carefully, descended the stairs. He spotted his uncle hiding behind his stepdad's bookcase in the living room and frowned at him.

Bogs pointed to the kitchen and then put his finger to his lips. *So Magnus is through there. Where is Áine?*

In answer, he heard her yell, and then another slam. He recognized the *swump* of her arrows and then a thud. Descending the rest of the steps, Tam put his back against the wall next to the doorframe leading from the living room stairs into the kitchen. He peered around the frame to see Magnus holding Áine by her neck. Her boots kicked underneath her as he raised her toward the ceiling.

Blood dripped onto the linoleum. Áine's blood.

"Now we will see just how long a Clurichaun witch can last without air," Magnus said as he snarled up at her.

Tam fought the urge to run out and just start firing. His stepfather had taught him better than that. Bullets were a commodity and not something to be squandered in a fight. Every strike, whether using a knife, a gun, or even an arrow, should be directed toward a purpose.

He didn't know a lot about trolls, other than they were big and strong. He didn't know if they carried the same allergy to iron as himself and other denizens of Faery. He didn't know their weakness as a race. So, it was time to go for the obvious.

What was the best thing to shoot at when the opportunity presented itself? What was the one thing all defense teachers told possible victims to go for? The softest, most vulnerable advantage an attacker had.

Their eyes.

And without his eyes, that bastard can't lock me in place like that again. Tam grinned.

He leveled his gun, aimed at the bastard's face and remembered to breathe as he fired three shots. At least one of the bullets hit true as blood splattered Áine and the floor, and Magnus dropped her. The troll roared out and spun around as he slapped his hands to his face and blundered into the kitchen table, which promptly collapsed under his weight.

"Tam, look out!"

Tam started to dive for Áine just as something grabbed his left leg. Burning pain preceded him being yanked from the doorway where he slammed into the hardwood floor. Or rather, his head did. He lost his grip on the gun as his vision blurred just a bit, and he thought for a second what he was seeing just wasn't real.

A huge, gray wolf loomed over him, its barred fangs dripping with blood. Tam's blood. He realized the thing had bitten his calf and used it as leverage to bring him down. The wolf growled just before it opened its jaws wide. Tam knew the beast planned on taking out his jugular.

A shot made Tam jump. One of the wolf's eyes exploded. Tam felt something warm and sticky spray his face. The wolf cried out as it swung its head back and forth and backed away. Tam turned over to see Bogs in the center of the living room with one of his stepfather's shotguns in his hands. Smoke slipped from the barrel.

"Thanks," Tam said.

"Oh, I think could grow to like this." Bogs held up his hand to show Tam the burn marks on his palms. "Though I'd like mine in plastic." His smile fell. "Tam, duck!"

Tam was already on the floor so he brought his head down and covered the back of it with his hands. He felt the air over him move as another shot rang out, and a second wolf collapsed in the hallway beside him. He lifted his head to look. *It's time to get out of here.*

He pushed himself up and would have collapsed back down when his leg gave, but Bogs was there, helping him up. Tam looked down to see— "Oh, wow..."

"Aye. Faery wolves. You just have to catch 'em before they—"

"Look out!" Áine's voice shattered the brief respite.

Another wolf bounded out of the hall toward Tam and Bogs. It was moving too fast for Bogs to reload and take aim, and Tam couldn't get to his gun quick enough, until an arrow fired into the thing's head and it went tumbling over them, knocking Bogs out of the way.

Tam pushed himself to the side, favoring his bleeding leg, and grabbed his gun. When he turned to look back at the kitchen door, Áine stood there, her bow in her hand, breathing heavy and bleeding from a wound on her arm. But she was alive. "Thanks," he said.

"No problem. Can we go now? Before the troll wakes up—"

At first, he wasn't sure why she stopped mid-sentence. Tam frowned at her as her eyes widened and she looked down. His gaze trailed down her front, and locked on the cylindrical pipe protruding from her stomach.

He didn't want to believe what he was seeing, until Magnus's shadow solidified behind her. His left eye was little more than a ruined hole where Tam's bullet had made contact, but the right eye was still very much whole. The troll wrenched the pipe out, causing Áine to collapse in a heap in the doorway.

"Let's see how well you escape me again, Leprechaun, with your protector *dead*."

Dead? Tam held the gun in his trembling left hand as he used his right one to pull himself closer to Áine's unmoving body. "No..." he said as he reached out for her.

"Iron. Deadly to the Seelie." Magnus stepped over Áine and reached down for Tam. "Now, it's time to go, Prince. Your master is waiting."

Tam couldn't take his eyes off of Áine. He willed her to get up. Silently screamed for her to rise and stab this bastard with her knives. He'd only really known her for a few hours, but he'd watched her for nearly a year, as she danced, and smiled, and had good times with her friends. All the while, he'd never known she was there for him.

Just for me. To protect...me. And what am I? I'm nothing. I'm some Faery freak who can't do magic.

His terror at the thought of losing Áine twisted into a boiling rage inside his gut. It spun into a ball of burning energy that ping-ponged around his body, igniting his limbs to move, urging his leg to heal, and finally resting inside his mind. It told him to grasp the thing he wanted. To take control of what was hidden. To take back what was stolen.

That rage, that anger, that feeling of helplessness coalesced into single point, a pulsing, spinning spur of power that moved faster, and faster, and faster, and faster...

Magnus touched his arm.

...And then it released.

At first, Tam wasn't sure what happened. He was on the floor, his calf a bloody, chewed mess, and then he was looking directly at Magnus, standing up, and brandishing a huge wooden stick in his left hand. The gun was gone. The stick glowed a bright blue and white light from its center. Vines grew from the wood and shot out like darts into Magnus's skin. The troll raged and flailed about. He took out the wall beside him and backed into the kitchen, but Tam followed him, careful of Áine at his feet, his attention fixated on the troll.

"Stop!" Magnus shouted.

But Tam pressed the power harder, heard nothing but the spinning, storming rage in his ears as the power created a whirlwind that rooted around in his memories and brought back the pain he'd endured at the hands of the trolls. It reminded him of the agony he felt as they laughed at him, called him a puppet, and beat him endlessly with their pipes.

Tam...

And then he saw the pipe sticking through Áine's stomach, and he released that power with a yell. It spun out of control, traveling down the vines and entering Magnus. Tiny explosions from within sent bits and pieces of the troll's hide out to coat the kitchen walls. Tam and Magnus were caught up in a whirlwind of power that shut out everything else.

Tam, please...

Finally, the troll disintegrated into ash and the whirlwind stopped. Tam, panting heavily, felt his knees give as he collapsed on the kitchen floor. The wooden stick vanished as he stared at the ceiling. He started shaking violently, as if burning with fever.

Bogs appeared above him, his expression an odd mixture of sadness and joy. "You've done it, Tam. You've found your shillelagh."

He nodded to his uncle. "Yeah," he said, as he closed his eyes and settled in for a long sleep.

V

The room was warm, and the sheets soft. Tam turned over, and once again opened his eyes to find himself not in his bed. When he pushed himself up, he looked at his surroundings. *I'm not in Kansas anymore. Hell, I'm not in Cambridge.*

This room, unlike the cramped clutter of Bogs's trailer and the sparse furnishings of his own room, appeared to be filled with the latest in tech and modern conveniences. Tam got out of bed and realized he wore a pair of soft loungers. Where were his clothes this time? He pulled the legs of the loungers up to look at his calf. All he saw was a long, healed scar where the wolf had bitten him.

Is this my healing power again? He stood by the bed and took in the long wall of closed blinds, the enormous flat screen on the wall opposite the bed, the smooth, modern dresser with its handleless drawers, and two doors to his left. The door to the right was a bathroom, complete with a tub, a six-nozzle shower enclosed entirely in glass, and a separate toilet room.

An assortment of bags sat to the right of the shower. He found clothing inside, all in his size. New jeans, sneakers, underwear, socks, a gold shirt, and a green hoodie. As he held up the hoodie, he noticed something on his left arm that hadn't been there before.

He dropped the hoodie and turned to the mirror over the sink. Vines had been woven into the knots of his original tattoo. They traveled down his arm, wrapping around it, with four leaf clovers added here and there, some large, some small. The vines ended on the back of his hand as they twisted into a point just at the middle knuckle.

His bird finger.

The design looks so familiar. I've seen this before, but it was in gold. In fact, he'd just seen the vines—

This is the same pattern on my dad's pocket watch! He ran out of the bathroom and found his old hoodie hanging on the back of a chair. Tam shoved his hand into each of the pockets. *I know I put that watch in my pocket. I remember doing it!* But a thorough search of his clothing proved he didn't have it.

Tam ran back to the bathroom and looked at the new tattoos under the bright light.

The vines moved as if they were traveling down his arm to his hand, but once they covered his hand they sprouted out from his palm and created the same walking stick he'd seen earlier. It formed in midair and would have fallen to the floor if he hadn't grabbed it. He put it in his right hand to make sure it wasn't still attached by the vines.

It was separate.

The stick itself was maybe five feet in length. It looked like someone had ripped a tree branch down and smoothed off the bark. It was irregularly shaped, with a larger knot at the top and tapered to the bottom. *Or...is the knot the bottom?*

Carvings exactly like the ones decorating his dad's pocket watch were expertly worked into the wood. And the wood was warm.

The pocket watch had been the most comforting thing he had. The only thing left to him by his real dad, and it was something Tam kept at his side since his dad died. Until that night at the drum circle. He'd left it on his nightstand, probably the first time he'd forgotten it in fifteen years.

And now...it was part of his tattoo?

"So, you're my shillelagh," he said, and felt a bit odd talking to a stick. "You're what that harridan wants."

He felt a sort of...impression from the wood. Something akin to agreement, but not in words or in images. Just a...*knowing. Is the thing sentient?* He looked at himself in the mirror, saw the pointed ears and the remaining band of the tattoo on his arm. But the vines were gone.

"I'm...a Leprechaun. Well...what the hell."

But now he wondered how to make it disappear.

The stick wrenched and lurched in his right hand. He held on to it at first, until a burning pain in his entire left arm opened his right hand. The stick disappeared, and the tattoos reappeared. The burning faded, but it made his arm sore. Had he interrupted it from returning by holding onto it? That was good to know.

He heard loud voices outside the bedroom door. He stepped out of the bathroom and put his ear to the door. He recognized Bogs's voice, but not the other one. It was deep and commanded authority, not that Bogs had ever succumbed to someone telling him what to do.

Tam took a quick shower and dressed, deciding that he wanted to install a multi-nozzle shower in his own bathroom. *That is, once I clean Magnus's troll guts off the floor.*

A quick look in the mirror didn't do anything for the ears, but Tam trusted that whoever that was, he knew about Bogs and himself. He thought of Áine and hesitated before he opened the door and stepped out...

Into a wonderland.

The place looked like a cross between a lab and a home. He stood on a ledge overlooking a circular living area. A waist-high glass partition prevented him from falling as he leaned over and looked down. A circle of Celtic knots bordered the room, and he thought he heard something humming, like an engine somewhere.

Glass stood in for most of the walls, and the view of Boston was breathtaking. It was night, and the city was lit up like a sea of precious stones against a black backdrop. Modern styled sofas and chairs littered the space inside the circle of knots, spiraling into a fountain in the center. From this height, he could see more knots in the face of the fountain.

The arguing voices carried upward. He could hear them, but he couldn't see them, so he moved around the side till he found a set of steps and descended as quickly as he could. As he turned the corner into the round living room, he spotted Bogs standing on the far side, facing down another man.

There was no mistaking who this was, and Tam was petrified with nervous energy.

"This is ridiculous, you poor excuse for a dethroned ruler," Bogs said as he pointed at the taller man. "You think holding us hostage is the way to win over the Prince's trust?"

"I think, dear Bogs, that we're no longer alone." The taller man turned and strode toward Tam. Bogs followed, albeit with a far less open attitude. "Mr. Kirkpatrick, I'm very glad to see you up and about." The man's accent wasn't as pronounced as Bogs's, but it was there. A touch of Ireland.

Tam took the offered hand and shook it. He was a little unsure what to say, so, "Thank you," was the only thing he got out.

"You look very well. It's good to see your Leprechaun half is awakening nicely. Allow me to introduce myself, I'm—"

"Dian Cécht," Tam blurted out, making sure to pronounce it the way he'd seen it, *Dee-yun Kehcht*. "Oh, I know all about you, Mr. Cécht. I just read the article in 'Forbes' and I'm a bit of a gamer."

Dian smiled. "I'm flattered to hear that, Mr. Kirkpatrick."

"Please, call me Tam."

"And you may call me Dian." Dian Cécht was as sharply dressed in real life as he was in every commercial and advertisement Tam had ever seen. He was thin, with soft, sharp features, and long blond hair he kept in a neat and tidy ponytail braided down his back. His suit looked like it was custom-made and fit him perfectly.

There was just one small difference, something Tam hadn't seen in the magazine pictures.

Dian's long, elegant pointed ears.

Bogs held out his hands. "So...aren't you going to hit him with the real gut puncher now?"

"Patience, you old Leprechaun," Dian said, though his tone was more playful. "Tam—"

"Where's Áine? Is she dead?"

Dian's smile broadened. "No, she's not dead. She's very much alive and in good hands."

"Can I see her?"

Dian's expression shifted just a bit. "Can you call your shillelagh?"

Being more than happy to impress Dian, and hoping doing so would allow him to see Áine, Tam looked askance at his uncle. At Bogs's nod, Tam repeated his actions in the bathroom. But this time the moving vines went faster, as if their path to his hand was smoother. Within seconds, he held the shillelagh in his hand.

The look of adoration on Dian's face was almost alien. Tam frowned at Bogs as Dian took a few steps closer, his fingers inches from the shillelagh.

"I wouldn't do that—" Bogs started.

Too late. A spark in the shape of a vine and clover shot out at the Faery's fingers and did a combo of shock and slap. Dian pulled his hand back, and for a second, Tam feared he'd made Dian angry.

Instead, he shook his hand and laughed. "This is amazing. Do you know it's been ages since I've actually seen a shillelagh in the hands of its rightful owner?"

"Really?"

"I was a minor king back then, the healer to the three. An advisor no one listened to." He turned and moved into the center of the room. Tam dismissed the shillelagh; this time releasing it so it could disappear into the tattoo once again, and then followed alongside his uncle to the fountain.

"Why didn't they listen to you?" Tam asked.

"Because they were fools, boy-o," Bogs said. "All of them. Thought they were untouchable. Dian here had seen the wounded in battle, and knew that the Morrigan was on the move."

"Aye." Dian nodded, but he faced the expansive view. "It was a terrible war, but it was a swift one. Within a year, we were disposed and the Morrigan held the power. The kings and queens were imprisoned. Bogs and I and several others escaped through a Cairn into this world and hid ourselves under the protective spell"—he glanced back at Tam—"before she, too, stepped into this world and committed the ultimate sin against the Morrigan."

Tam figured he knew this one. "She had me."

"With a human. Bogs has told you how the Morrigan has hunted down and either killed or controlled the Unseelie throughout the world. But she can't see into this world easily, so she sends her trolls, her wolves, and her crows—all of them impervious to iron. Which is why they can wield it against us."

"You're not a Leprechaun." Tam shoved his hands into the pockets of his jeans.

"No. I'm Daoine Sidhe by birth. Same as the kings and queens. Leprechauns were our connection to the mounds in stories you've probably learned in your folklore lessons, though many of the tales have been obliterated to a point of silliness." He turned to face them. "You represent one of two things, Tam Lin Kirkpatrick. The means for us to take back what was stolen, or the end of our time."

"End of our time?" Tam looked between the two of them. "I don't understand."

"He means, boy-o," Bogs said, "that the prophecy that frightened the Morrigan into controlling the Unseelie could be flipped on its head. If she gets her hands on you."

"You mean if she gets the shillelagh?"

"No," Dian said. "That time has passed now that you found it. As you've seen, no one can physically take it from you. It belongs to you."

Tam held up his hand. "But Bogs said the Morrigan had her crows steal all the shillelaghs. Can she not touch it and they can?"

"They can. But only if it's manifested. Yours apparently comes and goes."

Tam looked away. *Is it possible they don't know the shillelagh is my new tattoo?*

"I'm not sure why it does that," Dian said. "I don't think I've heard of that happening before. Shillelaghs were always something the Leprechauns kept on them. Perhaps yours adapted with the times. Either way, even if she can't get to the shillelagh, there is always the torque."

Tam looked back at Dian. "Magnus threatened me with that. He said once the Morrigan put her own torque around my neck, I'd be her puppet."

"This is true." Dian tapped his chin. "My intel informs me that the Morrigan doesn't know of Magnus's demise, and my people have cleaned and disinfected your home. Without direct proof or witnesses, she can't track that death with magic."

"What about the wolves?" Tam asked.

"You dispatched three of them. As far as we can tell, that was all Magnus brought with him. This also means she doesn't know you found your shillelagh. My guess is, after Magnus fails to answer her call, she'll form another raiding party to capture you, or kill you."

"Why kill me?" Tam shrugged his shoulders. "If she kills me, she couldn't find the shillelagh."

"If you died before you found it, it would die with you. So her reasoning would be, if I can get it from him, then I can take it. And if I can't—"

Tam sighed. "Then kill him and the threat goes away. But what if there are other Unseelie like me?"

"There will always be," Dian said. "But the magic protects them. By oak, and ash, and thorn."

The repeating of those three trees stirred something inside of him. Some small bit of something he either knew or forgot or...just learned. "Those are the trees of magic."

"Aye," Bogs said. "You'll not find them in Faery. They were used to make the spell that hides us."

Dian reset his gaze on Tam. "You've learned your weaknesses."

"Iron, and if someone stares at me. That's how Magnus attacked me in the house."

"It's not just any stare. It's one with the intent to keep you still. Any person's gaze won't do it. So if someone hits you with an idle stare, you won't freeze."

"Well, not him," Bogs said as he settled himself on a couch. "But for me? All stares become nuisances."

"Because you're Seelie?" Tam asked.

"Aye. Lucky for me, in these past few decades, kids stare at phones and not at people." He chuckled to himself.

Dian took up the conversation again. "Do you understand the weaknesses?"

"I think so. And my strengths are that I can turn a troll into ash?"

Dian slipped his hands into the pockets of his suit pants. "Your shillelagh acts as a focus of your will. It will have the same limits you have. Meaning belief is key. Your want and need have to reflect your heart's desire. For instance...you may want to elicit vengeance for someone doing a wrong, but that's a surface want. Your heart knows it's wrong to kill, if it detects there could be other factors involved in you being wronged, the shillelagh will sense that conflict and it won't act."

"He's right," Bogs said. "In fact, if you make it do something your heart disapproves of, you'll feel the consequences. So always be careful, boy-o."

"But...I *destroyed* that troll." Tam looked at each of them. "I mean I obliterated him. And I knew I was doing it."

"Because he tortured you." Bogs sat forward. "He broke your body and tried to control your mind. He hurt you, and you'd never touched him or done anything to make him hurt you. Your heart knew Magnus acted on pure selfish wants and needs. And"—the old Leprechaun gave Tam a half-smile—"he hurt your Clurichaun. But she's not only that, she's your friend. Your heart knew the command was true, so the shillelagh did its job."

Tam looked at his arm and imagined the vine tattoos beneath the sleeve of the hoodie. It did indeed. "So...you said Áine was alive. Can I see her? Will she live?"

"Here we go," Bogs said.

Tam ignored Bogs and looked at Dian. "What?"

Dian took in a deep breath and released it as he turned back to the window. Tam joined him and looked out over the city. He could see their reflections in the glass. "I'm a healer. In fact, at one time, I was considered a god."

"That was a long, long time ago."

Tam gave Bogs a dirty look before he looked at Dian's profile. "Go on."

"But over time, living here in this world, my power has waned. I am able to heal one thing, others I can only patch, but not mend completely. The Clurichaun's wound with the iron pipe should be fatal. I've halted her life, but only for a time." He turned toward Tam, and for a moment, he thought he saw the man's true age in his eyes. "There is a well I blessed some time ago. A well of healing water. It still retains a great deal of my power. It was a place the Daoine Sidhe could go and heal anything."

"Anything?"

"Except a missing head," Bogs piped up. "Don't forget that little mishap."

Dian's lips twitched. "A severed head is a problem and nothing I know of will breathe life back into friend or foe who loses theirs. But it is a place that will heal Áine."

"Then let's go there." Tam pulled his hands from the hoodie's pockets and started to head to the door, but stopped when he saw neither Dian nor Bogs moving. He moved in front of Dian, blocking his view of the city. "What are you not telling me? Is the well in Faery? Is that it?"

"No. It's in this world. I just can't..." Dian finally shrugged. "I can't get to it."

"No..." Bogs said as he stood up. "No lies, Dian. Tell the truth."

"Come on, you two! We have to save Áine." He looked from one to the other.

Dian looked angry, and Tam thought he saw his eyes flash red. "No, Bogs. Some things should be left in the past. And don't give me the same schtick about reliving it if we don't face it. I've faced it. Every waking hour since that old crow took everything from us."

"Does it have anything to do with healing Áine? This past thing?" Tam asked.

"No."

"Then *screw* it. Just tell me what you want. It has to do with me, doesn't it? Otherwise, you wouldn't have given us help, and you wouldn't have asked to see the shillelagh. You want something, Dian Cécht. What is it?"

Quiet crept into the room and brought with it a cold, icy feeling that moved over the tiled floors. Everything stopped in that moment as Dian turned a stony face to Tam. "You."

VI

This time the shillelagh manifested unbidden in his hand as Tam felt a surge of power and a basic need to protect himself. He held it out in front of himself and took a step back. "I think you need to explain that a bit better."

Bogs got on his feet, laughing. "Easy, boy-o. Calm down. Dian's not like the Morrigan. He doesn't want to control you. He just needs...favors."

"From time to time." Dian visibly shrank away from the shillelagh as Tam held it between them. The thing pulsed with a subtle green light. "I have one in particular right now."

"The well." Tam figured that one out pretty quick. "What does this have to do with the well?"

"The well is in the middle of the Morrigan's human gardens," Dian said. He relaxed. A little. "She takes a dip in that well from time to time. It prolongs her life and zaps the Earth of her strength. Not because the magic is weak, but because the Morrigan takes too much. Controlling the entire Unseelie population takes a lot out of her on a daily basis."

Tam raked his fingers through his hair as he turned away from Bogs and Dian and looked out over the cityscape. He caught a glimpse of his ears in the reflection as he lowered the shillelagh and put the fingertips of his right hand on the glass. It was cold, hard, and soulless. "We have to put Áine in that well."

"Yes."

"And the only way to get to it, has to do with the shillelagh."

"Again, yes."

Tam refocused on Dian's reflection. "But you don't want to just use it. You want to take it back. You want to run the Morrigan out of there and reclaim the well."

"No."

The answer stunned Tam. He turned away from the window and stared at Dian. "No?"

"No. I don't want anything that old crow has touched. What I want is much more...complicated. And I'm not sure you're up to the challenge." Tam cleared the room in a blink and stood inches from Dian.

It was only a second before Tam raised the shillelagh and the tall Faery was thrown back. He sailed through the air and crashed into the fountain, knocking it over and cracking it into several pieces.

Bogs jumped up as the door opened and an army of black-clad men with machine guns filed in. They formed a ring around Tam and pointed their guns.

"Wait," Dian called out from behind them. "Stop. There's no need. You're dismissed."

The men in black lowered their weapons and filed back out of the room. Tam, still holding the shillelagh in front of him, saw Bogs fishing Dian out of the rubble of the now destroyed fountain. "That...was quite a show."

"I apologize. I told them to remain on standby, but not to come until called." Dian was more than wet; he was drenched. His blond hair was plastered to his head, and his suit stuck to him, making him appear even thinner.

"But...I attacked *you*." Tam narrowed his eyes.

"No, I came at you, and you reacted, just like you're supposed to. The fight to survive is built into the shillelagh. As I said before, it is your will. And having been kidnapped and tortured recently, your will to survive has grown. I think you would have reacted slower if this event hadn't happened." He brushed Bogs off of him and stood dripping in his living room. "We can save Áine's life. The well is the key. But we have to do it before the Morrigan discovers you have the shillelagh. If she knows, she'll build her defenses against you, as well as triple her offense to capture you. There won't be a better time to get to the well."

Tam wasn't sure he believed everything Dian said. He wanted to. After all, this was a figure of authority, someone he'd looked up to for a while in the electronic and gaming world. But this guy wanted to breach the garden of what everyone was telling him was a crazy, powerful Faery whose only connection to Tam was the desire to take, destroy, or control his shillelagh.

"It's a big task, boy-o," Bogs said. "You don't have to do this."

"I have to save Áine." Tam lowered the shillelagh as it vanished from his hand. "I was just getting to know her. I mean, think of how great it'll be if I can rescue her? But if you don't want to take the well back, then what do you want to do with it?"

"I want you to destroy it. All of it. Without the well, the Morrigan can't keep regenerating. And without replenishing her power, she'll lose it, and her hold over Faery."

Tam couldn't argue with that. If Dian Cécht wanted to destroy one of his own creations, then so be it. The only thing worrying him, now that he had his shillelagh, was healing Áine. "And you believe the shillelagh can do that?"

"Oh. No. Only I can destroy it. I just need you to get us to it. Now, if you'll excuse me, I need to change before we get going." He turned away.

"Now?" Tam said.

Dian paused. "Would prefer to wait until Áine dies of her injuries? Get ready, Leprechaun. You're about to test your power and your weaknesses."

VII

Apparently, Dian Cécht had been planning this day for a very, very long time. He knew exactly where the well was, down to the longitude and latitude. He knew the Morrigan's schedule down to the minute. He'd watched her for years, sent all manner of spies to gather intel, and burned through large sums of money, just to keep an eye on her.

If I didn't know why he was doing it, I'd think he was pretty creepy. Tam studied the maps Dian had drawn, and memorized the surrounding landmarks at least fifty miles away. Apparently, shillelaghs, according to Bogs, were capable of transporting a Leprechaun instantly to a known location. But that was the key—known. Tam had never been in that part of the world.

That part being Connacht, Ireland.

The plan was to transport himself to the well, and if he was successful, come back to get Áine and Dian. They would slip Áine into the water, allow her to heal, which Dian said was an instant process, and then Dian would destroy the well.

It all sounded easy enough, but something about the idea bothered Tam. It nagged at him as he sat in Dian's round library amidst ceiling-high shelves of books. Old books, new books, books in languages Tam was pretty sure he'd never even heard of. He periodically got up and walked around to stretch his legs as the night wore on and the time to try Dian's plan arrived.

"Hasn't this guy heard of eBooks?" he muttered to himself as he moved about the room. He ran his left hand along the books as he made his sixth, or tenth, or hundredth pass around the room.

Tam...

He stopped because he thought someone had come in the room. He turned to answer, but no one was there.

Tam, please...

Wait... Tam turned around again and looked at the shelves of books. *I've heard that voice before. Recently. Heard it when he... When I...*

Tam...don't do it...

Now he was creeped out. The voice sounded like Áine's. He'd asked Dian several times if he could see her, but the Faery mogul put him off, telling him she was in critical condition.

Listen, Tam...

"Áine?" he said aloud, and his voice echoed in the room. There was no answer. No voice in his head. He moved to the pages of maps on the table and picked up a pen. "I gotta be dreaming. This is just nuts." And it was nuts. The whole idea. Not just popping from place to place, but doing it to destroy something as rare as a healing well seemed...wrong.

He started using the pen as a bodhrán's tapper, softly striking it against the table, just as he would if he were playing his drum. But the angle was off. It wasn't the same. His routine since he was eight had been to pull his bodhrán out and play when he found himself in a tough situation, having difficulty with a decision, or if he couldn't think through a math problem.

He needed the rhythm to think. Bogs said he'd put the drum where it was safe, but Tam hadn't seen Bogs since Dian stuck him in the library to memorize the location. He dropped the pen on the table and held out his left hand as he summoned the shillelagh. If it was possible to go to a place and back, was it possible to bring something to where he was? What was it going to hurt to try?

Uh huh, and what if I end up bringing something to me that wants to kill me?

He dismissed that thought and closed his eyes. Using his imagination, he formed an image of his bodhrán in his mind. He saw the curve of the wood, the studs around the edges, and the felt the texture of the skin. He thought of playing it, sitting in his room at home and striking out a beat.

Something thudded on the ground at his feet. He broke the image and opened his eyes to see his bodhrán's case. Tam set the shillelagh on the table and knelt down to open it up. His drum was there, as were his tappers in their velvet sleeve. He pulled the drum out, selected a tapper, and sat back down on the stool with the bodhrán on his right knee, his tapper poised at the relaxed, ready position in his left hand.

Tam began to play.

He closed his eyes and lost himself in the music, in the beat of the drum, the whisper of the tapper's brush against the skin, the glide of his hand as he moved the edge of his right palm along the inside of the drum to change pitch. He saw a well in his mind, but not the stereotypical kind with rounded brick, or stone sides, and a wheel and pulley for a bucket.

This image showed only a hole in the ground, in a diameter much larger than he'd imagined. Grass grew long around its borders, so long it fell into the water itself and bloomed lilies of purple, pink, and white. It didn't have a muddy bank or a sandy beach, just the roots of a nearby tree...no, three trees.

The ash.

The oak.

And the thorn. A blackthorn tree.

They grew in the shape of a triangle, a root system in each corner. And in the middle rested the blessed well. He reached out in his mind to touch the roots, to feel their bark, and listen to the song of the Earth inside of them and felt hundreds of whispers against his mind. Name after name of Leprechaun, Seelie, and Unseelie alike. With each whisper, he saw the root of a tree as it formed the shape of a staff—

Shillelaghs. He was hearing the teaming voices, the joined song of hundreds of shillelaghs, singing out to him.

That's it!

Áine's voice shattered the vision. He dropped the tapper, and would have dropped the bodhrán if he hadn't moved to the table. He breathed hard as he reset his awareness back to the library, back to Dian Cécht's home. With the drum in his lap, sandwiched between his chest and the table, he reached out for the shillelagh and moved his hand along its surface.

He knew in that instant his shillelagh was made of blackthorn wood. And the trio of trees, the sacred trees surrounding the well, was the rebirth of the stolen shillelaghs.

The trees... "Dian's well keeps the shillelaghs alive," he said aloud as he finished his thought. "Áine...I think I figured it out. She's keeping the shillelaghs alive. But...why?"

Take me there.

"Where are you?"

Above you.

Tam looked up. He hadn't noticed the ceiling. It was domed, much like the one over the living room. Two circular rooms. How odd was that? But Dian was a billionaire a billion times over. He could have anything he wanted. He could buy... anything he wanted.

He stared at the ceiling as he clutched his bodhrán. Was it possible there was a room there? Above the library? Tam put his drum back in its case along with the tapper. Grabbing the shillelagh, he ran to the door, thinking he could do a bit of exploring.

It was locked.

He jerked it back and forth, but the door remained locked. Dian had locked him in the library? Why? They were supposed to go to the well. Heal Áine. Unless...that wasn't the real plan.

"You're above me. In a room?"

I don't know. I can't see.

He looked at the shillelagh. Dian said he could only go where he'd been before. So what happened if he tried going where he hadn't? What would be the outcome? Bogs hadn't said what it would be, only giving his usual shrug. Was his uncle aware he had been locked in the library?

"I'm going to try."

Think of my bow. Think only of my bow.

Tam closed his eyes and thought about the bow. He'd seen it in her hand, on her back. He imagined her firing it, touching it, and he heard it singing to her...

No, it sang to him!

"*Taistealaí!*" he said, releasing the shillelagh, and using the word for traveler.

Tam felt the floor drop out from beneath him seconds before he landed on something hard again. He dropped and rolled, then came up with the shillelagh in front of him. Not that it mattered. He didn't think he was in Dian's fortress anymore. Not unless he'd installed a hospital wing.

The bright lights made him squint as he came up on his feet. He stood in a hospital room, intensive care by the looks of the machines surrounding someone in a bed. Dark red hair on white sheets. Tam moved closer and looked down at the encumbered person.

"Áine," he said softly.

"How did you get in here?"

The voice startled him as the shillelagh vanished. He turned and faced a nurse in scrubs with a very prickly expression. "Sorry...I didn't...I was looking for Áine McCuill's room."

"Well, you found it, but she's not receiving visitors. Her uncle gave strict instructions she wasn't to see anyone."

"Oh?" Tam didn't know if she had an uncle. He hated the fact he barely knew her, and yet she was in this mess because of him. "Was her uncle tall, with long blond hair and very thin?"

"Yes."

Dian.

Tam kept his hands in front of him just so she could see them. "I'm sorry. I just...I'm her boyfriend. I've been out of town, and I just heard she was here. Can you tell me what happened? I promise I'll leave with no problems. I'm just...concerned." He smiled at her and leaned forward, thinking only thoughts of cooperation and kindness.

The nurse sighed and seemed to think it over. "We don't really know how it happened, but she was injured from a pipe. Her uncle said she fell onto it, but with her other injuries—"

"Other injuries?"

"Yes. She's got multiple contusions, which could be from a fall, but there's a lot that seem to have been made before the injury from the pipe."

"What?"

"I shouldn't get into it, and you need to leave. Just know her uncle's paying for the best care and security for her. So whoever is trying to kill her can't get in here."

I got in here. Tam licked his lips. "One more thing...has her uncle been in to see her?"

"Yes. He just left. Should I stop him?"

"Oh, no. I don't want to cause a problem. Is that the door out?"

"Yes."

Tam smiled and stepped out of the room. The main station was empty, so he ducked inside the closest empty room and called the shillelagh. *What the hell is Dian playing at? He locked me in his library, and now I find Áine's across town on life support in Massachusetts General Hospital?*

Feeling a bit more confident about his traveling abilities, he thought of the coordinates Dian had made him memorize and honed in on there—

"*Taistealaí,*" he said, but didn't shout it this time.

Again, the floor dropped out from beneath him, and he landed on soft, grassy ground. Sun sifted through a thick canopy of trees overhead as he rolled on the ground. He smelled the earth and felt dampness caress his cheek. This was the place in his dream. The three trees surrounding a center well. He moved to his hands and knees and looked at the water, at the reflection of the swaying green leaves overhead.

Tam pushed up to just his knees and looked around. A forest surrounded the well, and as far as he could tell, there was no one for miles. He needed to test the water before he brought Áine here, but he didn't have an injury he could use.

"You're early," came a deep, sultry voice overhead. "Remind me to kill that son of a bitch Dian next time I see him."

He jumped back and brandished the shillelagh. A note echoed in the forest, and to his surprise the trees answered in harmony. Tam looked around for the voice, but he didn't see anyone, or anything.

A single crow's feather swayed in the breeze as it fell at his feet.

He jumped back as something very large, and very black, landed close to where he'd been beside the well.

It was a woman. A tall, blond woman with large black eyes and enormous black-feathered wings. She spread them out behind her, obscuring the well from his view. Her lips were as black as her eyes and her teeth white as snow. "So you are Tam Lin."

"And you're the Morrigan."

"You don't have to use the honorific. Morrigan will do." She smiled at him, and Tam felt...oily. "You were supposed to bring me a Clurichaun."

"Bring you?" He kept the shillelagh between them. "I was supposed to dip her in the water."

"Yes. I know. It was my plan. We figured if I could get inside that witch's head, I could get closer to you. Interesting how Dian neglected to tell me you'd already found your shillelagh."

"Dian made a deal with you."

"That's what we do, boy. We're a people of promise dealers."

Tam licked his lips. "So you were going to use my Clurichaun to control me."

"No, to prod you to find your shillelagh. Seems I'm too late. But no matter, it's just one more piece of wood to add to my garden." She moved away and tucked her wings against her back. "Now you can be a good little Leprechaun and behave. Give me your shiny toy, and I'll let you save the life of your Clurichaun. Or," she paused and faced him, "I can take you now and let your little witch die. Either way, you become mine and your shillelagh is added to my collection."

Collection?

Morrigan held up her hand and a torque appeared. This one was different than the one Magnus had. This was more elaborate. Thicker. The skin around his neck prickled at the memory of the iron's burn. He kept his eyes locked on her, unwilling to let her get behind him. He wasn't going to let her do what Magnus did.

His mind continued to race ahead. Tam was told how the Morrigan stole all the shillelaghs in Faery and put torques on their owners. If that was true, and if his uncle didn't have a shillelagh, then had he worn a torque as well? Come to think of it, he hadn't seen Bogs's neck, and before recently, he hadn't seen Bogs in nearly a decade.

"This is where you put the shillelaghs. You bring them here and put them in the water, and they become part of their original trees. Why?"

Morrigan laughed. "A shillelagh is not only the will of a Leprechaun, but a part of their soul. It also has the power of prophecy for their owners. Combined, I can see the futures for all the people of my kingdom when I surrender myself to the water."

"That's how you knew about me."

"Of course. And that's how I know you will submit to me, just like all the other good little Unseelie have. I am the Mother."

And then she was gone. No lift of a wing, not even a stirring in the air. Holding out the shillelagh, he spun around looking for her. She laughed behind him.

Too late.

His muscles locked and he found himself staring at the three trees, unable to speak or to will his shillelagh away.

"Pretty," Morrigan said as she brushed her talons along his cheek. "So very handsome. It's amazing how the world paints your kind as tiny bearded creatures. When in truth, you have always been the most pleasing to the eye." She pressed her hands down on his shoulders. "You will be mine now, Tam Lin. My aid. My right hand as I search the world for more Unseelie and bring them under my wings."

He scoured everything he'd learned in the past week, everything Bogs, Dian, and even Áine had said. Bogs's words, though they might be said under the guise of Morrigan, felt the most true. When he talked about his shillelagh, he spoke with emotion, revelation, and honest envy. He missed his power.

He missed his tie to the Earth.

The shillelagh was a Leprechaun's will. *If this is my will, then I will myself a way to break her gaze.*

Think...the way Áine had done it was to distract Magnus. But Tam had no one here to distract Morrigan. He'd told no one he was going. So if he had to have a distraction, he'd have to make it himself. And if so...could he? Was it possible?

The gaze might trap his body, but it didn't trap his mind. He stared straight ahead and thought of Áine. Her body, her shape, her hair, but he thought of her dancing. Step dancing in a line of people, arms at her sides. He heard the music, the beat of the bodhrán. He focused everything on that image, and then projected it into the trees.

To his surprise, a grayish image of Áine appeared, dancing, and on the breeze he heard the beat of a drum as it struck an old familiar rhythm.

"Who's there!" Morrigan said.

Her gaze broke. Tam could move.

He flipped the shillelagh around, turned with a yell, and shoved the small end into Morrigan's belly. "I have a will of my own, and my path is not yours to control!" He continued shoving until he skewered her, mirroring what Magnus had done to Áine.

Morrigan screamed, and the place where he pierced her lit up like a roman candle. She exploded in a flurry of crows that flew at him, scratched at his face, and then disappeared into the trees.

Tam went down on his knees, his face stinging and his arms and shoulders burning. His shillelagh was covered in some kind of black ocher. With a smile and a numbing feeling in his gut, he dipped it into the well. The water glowed blue and as he pulled it out, it was pristine again. It looked like it had a few more carvings on it.

When he cradled it to him, he felt it vibrate and thought he heard a laugh. "Just a few more things to fix"—he smiled—"and then we both can rest."

VIII

Getting back to Áine was easier the second time. Getting her untangled from the wires and tubes—that was a whole different matter. He knew if he unhooked the heart monitor, the nurses would be in the room and all over him. So he decided to wing it with his hand on her arm and traveled back to the well.

He felt lucky that just Áine came with him and not the entire hospital apparatus. But the moment she wasn't on life support, she gasped for air. Tam dismissed the shillelagh as he lifted her in his arms, and then holding her, slipped himself into the well.

The water bubbled, and felt a lot like a mineral spring he'd once visited. He held Áine close to him and smiled as he felt her body shift and change against him, until finally her eyes opened wide as she gasped one last time for air and then she moved on her own. In fact, she scrambled away from him and fought to climb out of the well.

"Hey, relax," Tam said as he put his hand on hers. "I'm not trying anything. I promise. I just wanted to make sure you wouldn't drown."

"You...you can't drown in a healing well," she muttered as she continued to climb out. "And...I'm barely dressed."

That much was true. The thin hospital gown with no back did nothing to cover her body, and Tam had to admit it was a nice body. He turned away and waited until she was out before he climbed free and offered her his soaked jacket.

They sat to the side of the well for a few minutes, enjoying the warm breeze and the sound of birds. Tam listened to the whispers of the shillelaghs. "They're here, you know."

"Yeah...I got that from you. So, how do you get them out? The shillelaghs?"

"I don't know. And even if I could, where would they go? Their owners are still under Morrigan's control."

"She isn't dead?"

Tam shook his head. He was pretty certain a simple stab to the gut for someone like her wasn't fatal. He was sure he'd wounded her, though. "She'll be back. Freeing the shillelaghs has to come after we free the Unseelie. What good would it do to release their wills when they were being controlled by iron?"

"We?"

"Or me. This isn't your fight."

"It's not yours either. You have a chance to lead a normal life."

Tam frowned at her. "Seriously? Áine, I have pointed ears, I can summon a magic stick, and I have a legendary monster after me. Where in there is normal?"

She smiled at him and shrugged. "Conceded. So...what about this place? You want to take it from her?"

"There's no need. I proved to her that the prophecies of the shillelaghs are just shadows of the future. We can change that future if we will it. That's what she stole." He leaned his head to the right and smacked his left ear as he tried to dislodge water out of his right. "Keeping the shillelaghs alive like this does give hope for the future. The trees know this. That's why they grow here. And no matter how many baths that bitch takes in this water? She'll never be able to bend the future to make it hers."

"So...we just leave it? Under her control?"

Tam stood and offered her his hand. "That's the secret, Áine. It's never been under her control. That's a lie, one she chooses to believe. Let her continue to believe it." Once Áine was on her feet, he summoned his shillelagh. Looking at it, he thought, *I'm getting pretty good at this.* "There is one shillelagh I can sense, louder than the rest."

Áine's lips pulled into a thin line. "Your uncle's?"

"Yeah. The Morrigan admitted she struck a deal with Dian. There's something about Dian, something Bogs has on him. I agree with her that we're a race of promise dealers. My uncle in particular. I think he's got something up his sleeve with Dian, otherwise why make himself a player in whatever game Dian's got going? I just can't make sense of the idea that he wants to destroy this well." Tam narrowed his eyes at her. "That was you I heard, right? Before? In the library?"

"I didn't know you were in a library. I was in a dark place, but now and then I could see, and hear, you. I think it has something to do with my duty to you and your family."

"About that...who sent you to protect me?"

She smiled. "Your mother."

Tam took several steps toward her. "You...you know my mother? She's alive? Where is she? Why did she leave? Does she know my dad died of a broken heart—"

Áine's strength returned as she summoned a knife and held it out between them. "Stop right there, Prince. I can't answer those questions. I shouldn't have told you as much as I have. But...I thought you should at least know that if your uncle is dirty, and Dian's the ass we suspect he is, you do have someone on your side."

On my side. Tam was pretty sure he wasn't going get any more out of her, at least not right then. But if he played his cards right, he might be able to wear her down over time. He smiled to himself as he waved at her knife. "Put that away. I'd never attack you."

"Not now. But who knows what the future brings." The knife disappeared. "The Morrigan's not going to stop coming after you. She's probably more pissed than ever."

"Yeah. I figured."

"Your house has been cleaned, and Dian set up new wards. I'd like to take those down and set up some of my own."

"Sure, sure." Tam looked around at the woods as a breeze moved the hair over his forehead. "I don't know whether to confront Bogs and Dian now, or just wait. I'm sure Dian's going to be pissed as well, seeing as how I did this without letting him destroy it."

"And I don't think he can get here without you." Áine took a step forward. "We carry on as usual?"

"For now. So it's been a week?"

"Yes."

"And I'm currently listed as a missing person?"

"Yes."

"I think I should start by assuring everyone I'm not missing. Then I have to resort some priorities."

Áine shifted into her horse form. A beautiful red mare. *Yes. And I'll be watching you like a hawk in step dancing. Might even make you my partner.*

Tam laughed as he jumped up on her back and held on to her mane. "Go right ahead, if you want some broken toes."

I might. You ready to head home?

"No. Wanna go for a run?"

I thought you'd never ask.

FIN

❦

About the Author: : If you want to learn more about Phaedra and be notified when her next novel is released and get free stories and occasional other goodies, please visit her website: www.phaedraweldon.com.

ALICE
JULIA CRANE

TICK. TOCK. TIME. TIME. TIME. IT WAS MOVING MUCH TOO fast.

With the Red Queen always breathing down her back, pushing the issue, Alice was going to have to act soon.

In an attempt to soothe her frayed nerves, Alice rocked back and forth. It was going to have to be something drastic. But what? Could she really kill her own flesh and blood?

A prophecy was a prophecy. Wasn't it?

It wasn't fair! Why couldn't she have been the only one?

Needing something to keep her hands occupied, Alice grabbed one of the glass figurines off the mantel. As she walked in circles, her mind raced with potential solutions. Why wasn't a good alternative coming to her? There must be a way...

In frustration, Alice flung the statue across the room, shattering it against the wall in a thousand pieces.

One of the maids scurried in, head down, avoiding eye contact. Attempting to avoid her wrath.

Curiously, Alice watched as the woman dropped to her knees, efficiently brushing up the mess with movements mastered from years of practice. Alice was widely known for her temper tantrums. They'd only gotten worse as she'd gotten older. In many ways, she took after her mother, the Red Queen.

Too bad her mother hated her guts. She saw Alice as a disgrace. No matter what she did, it was never good enough to please her wretched mother. All Alice had ever wanted was her approval, but her hope was in vain.

And in less than three months, she would be forced to marry some fool from Wonderhills in a show of solidarity for the dimensions. Ridiculous. Her mother was insane if she thought she was going to go through with this madness. There was only one person Alice would ever dream of marrying, and he wanted nothing to do with her. In fact, he thought she was cold, ruthless and disturbed. Why did everyone she care about hate her?

"Get out!" Alice screeched.

The maid rushed out of the room. The door shut softly behind her. Alice dropped into one of the chairs, staring off into the emptiness, seeking an answer to her dilemma.

Suddenly, she jumped to her feet. Maybe the old crone could help her.

Closing her eyes, Alice called forth a portal. She jumped through the dimensions, emerging into another realm. This realm wasn't much different than her own; the main difference was the darkness. It was dreary, where hers was bright. But for some reason, Alice felt more at home here than in her own dimension.

She continued down a dark, wooded pathway, until she reached her destination, the shabby cottage. Without bothering to knock, Alice pushed through the front door. The old woman, seated at a table at the center of the cottage, glanced up. "Nice of you to drop by," she said sarcastically.

The Oracle was the only one who dared speak to Alice without deference. And for that, Alice respected her. "You knew I was coming before I even made up my mind."

The woman smiled, flashing her crooked teeth. "Of course. But I can be of no help. I've seen no change in the prophecy. I told you I would contact you if any new information became available."

Alice dug her nails into her palm. "Tell me what to do."

The woman set down her spoon, giving Alice her full attention. "You know I cannot play with fate in such a way. Do not ask me to do so. I will die before I disregard the rules of the realm. I'm the last Oracle of our time, and I refuse to be forced into anything that does not align with my divinity."

A deep sigh escaped Alice. She wasn't about to kill the Oracle, and the woman knew it. But the woman had foreseen the outcome of her future, a fate Alice was desperate to know.

The Oracle held up her hand before Alice even got her words out. "You're wrong. I do not know your future. I see possibilities. That is all. The ultimate decision is up to you."

"But I don't know what to do!" Alice cried. She'd never admit such a thing to anyone else.

"Then let it run its course. When the time comes, you will know how to act. Child, I know you have a heart buried under all that darkness. Someone will have to make a sacrifice; it's the only way."

Annoyed, Alice crossed her arms over her chest. That was not what she wanted to hear. She was the one that had endured Wonderland her whole life, and she had no intention of further sacrifice.

"You're of no help," Alice spat.

The woman picked her spoon back up and continued to eat her soup. "I will give you one kernel of insight."

Alice raised an eyebrow, waiting.

"The one your heart longs for is not as far out of reach as you think. I will say no more. The rest is up to you."

It took all of her self-control not to throttle the old woman, but despite herself, Alice felt a stirring of hope. Could it be true? Did she have a chance with Landon after all?

Without another word, Alice left the Oracle and stepped back through the shimmering portal to her home.

Her body flooded with a mixture of emotions. It was not an experience she enjoyed. Every little sound put her on edge; even the air was too loud. Deep down, she knew she was mad, but Alice couldn't bring herself to seek help. Instead she lived her life always on the edge of a meltdown. The simplest things would set her off.

Everyone thought she was just spoiled, but she knew it was more. Insanity lurked at the edge of her awareness.

After several moments of deep breathing, Alice felt composed enough to search for Landon.

Why she had feelings for him was beyond her. He was of a lower class, and he barely gave her the time of day. If anything, he was borderline rude. Oh, he was never outright insolent – that would cost him his life – but there was something in his eyes when he spoke to her. Just the sight of her irked him.

In a huff, Alice stormed down the long hallways, not making eye contact with any of the help. When she finally stepped outside, a sense of relief washed over her, but it was short lived.

Her mother was coming up the staircase. They met midway.

"Mother," Alice greeted her mother without emotion.

"You're not really going out dressed like that are you?"

Alice glanced down at her gown. It was stunning, and they both knew it. "I was being thoughtful, I didn't want to outshine the Queen, so I'm downplaying myself a bit."

The Queen's face remained neutral. She lowered her voice. "We both know your beauty is your only redeeming quality. Do not concern yourself with my appearance. My beauty will always shine brighter than your own, because your soul is withered and black, and people can see that my dear."

Alice smiled serenely. "Like mother like daughter."

The Queen's eyes narrowed slightly. "Were you my *true* daughter, I wouldn't have so much trouble sharing the same air with you."

Her words cut deeply, like they always did, but Alice was determined not to show her feelings. "If you weren't so flawed, perhaps you could have borne your own children." Alice's voice was sickly sweet.

In a rare display of emotion, the Queen's face clouded over. She didn't say another word as she continued up the stairs.

Why would a woman want a child if she couldn't stand the thought of it not being her own flesh and blood? Alice never wanted to have children. She refused to bring a child into this cruel world.

With a heavy heart, Alice made her way to the stables. She wasn't dressed for riding, but she'd think of some excuse.

There was a young boy carrying water to the horses. When he glanced up, fear was evident on his face. With haste, he looked down again.

"Where is Landon?" Alice demanded.

The boy pointed behind him, his arm visibly shaking.

With a curt nod, Alice strode down the pathway. As she entered the stable, Landon's head came up, and their eyes met. His light brown eyes were unreadable. "Princess."

"Have a horse ready for me within two hours, and I demand that you join me for a ride." The words surprised her as they flew out of her mouth.

He looked as startled as she felt. "Excuse me?"

"You heard me. I want to travel to a place I've never been and I know you know the trails better than anyone."

He scratched the top of his head, and his brown hair remained standing on end when he lowered his hand. On anyone else, it would look ridiculous, but she found that, on him, nothing looked bad. A part of her longed to reach over and smooth the unruly hair down, but she knew better than to do such things.

"Shouldn't you take one of your guards?" he asked warily.

She knew he'd rather do anything than spend time alone with her. When they were children, he was forced to play with her. She'd even made him play dolls, but he'd never enjoyed himself. It was always a chore, and those times ended many years ago.

"Who are you to question a princess? I'll be back in two hours, and you *will* be ready."

He stood up, dropping a dirty hand towel onto the table. "I'll be ready."

Alice couldn't help but take in his massive frame. He'd grown so much over the years, he was bigger than some of the knights. His shoulders were broad, his waist narrow, his legs appeared muscular even through his pants. Masculinity oozed out of his pores.

If he noticed she was staring, he didn't acknowledge it.

She cleared her throat. "I'll be back after I change and have lunch."

He gave a slight bow. "I'll be humbly awaiting your return."

She heard in his tone he was being facetious. Anyone else would have been whipped, or worse, for such a sign of disrespect, but she acted as if his words were respectful. "Don't make me wait." She spun on her toes and walked away, head held high, back erect.

As she walked, she inhaled deeply, waiting for her heart to return to normal. Landon always had that effect on her. She had no idea what it was, but he made her feel things no other man had ever come close to.

Maybe it was the fact her mother would have a heart attack if she ever found out she was attracted to someone like Landon, or maybe it was more.

Soon she would be forced to marry another, so there was no sense in wasting any time. And the Oracle had said there was a chance. The woman was seldom wrong. If there was a chance, Alice was going to take it. After all, she deserved some happiness in this dreadful world.

Now it seemed as if time passed too slowly for her liking, so Alice changed into riding clothes and hurried back to the stables. It was not uncommon for her to go to the stables, because horseback riding had been one of her passions throughout her life. However, the real reason for her love of horses was Landon. Okay, maybe that was not completely the truth. She did feel a bond of sorts with animals. They understood her in a way that humans could not. Horses had no trouble allowing her to be free and run wild without any rules. There was a peacefulness that came over her, with the wind on her face, and her hair blowing behind her. Freedom.

Once she got to the stables, she was annoyed to see the horses were not ready. "Landon!" she yelled.

He came around the corner, his jaw set in annoyance. "Yes, Your Grace?"

"Why aren't you ready?"

"Because you said two hours, and it's only been one."

"Well I've changed my mind. I want to go now."

He yelled out for one of the other stable hands to bring around the horses.

Alice watched in dismay as he walked away from her. He glanced over his shoulder. "I think Jim will be a better guide for you, since you're in such a rush, and I haven't eaten."

Alice stomped her foot into the ground. "No. That is not an option. You *will* accompany me, or I will see you whipped in the courtyard."

He stopped mid-stride. "Well then I guess I better get cleaned up."

Impatiently, she waited while he took his time getting ready. When he came back into view, she was surprised to see he was carrying a bag. When he noticed her stare, he shrugged. "You might be able to force me to go with you, but you're not going to force me to miss my meal."

He strode toward the horses without waiting on her. Anyone else she would have had drawn and quartered. Instead she took a deep breath and followed him. He could be infuriating at times, and yet her heart leapt to her throat at the thought of being alone with him.

When one of the other grooms tried to help her onto the horse, she shoved him away and jumped on by herself. Landon took off, and she urged her horse to catch up. *How dare he!*

Once they were beyond the castle walls, Alice slowed her horse to a steady trot. Landon heard the difference in the hoof beats and reined in his mount. For the first time, he looked over his shoulder at her. It pissed her off that her breath caught at the intensity of his gaze. He'd always been able to see through her, even when they were children.

"Why are you like this?" she asked, as she eased her horse beside his.

A smirk crossed his handsome face. "Like what?"

"I'm a Princess. You can't treat me the way you do."

He laughed. "You're no Princess. You're a tyrant."

Alice sucked in a breath.

She watched his lips form a lazy, arrogant smile. He knew he was pushing her patience. It was almost as if he took pleasure in it. The same as when he was a young boy.

Pulling the reins, Alice brought her horse to a standstill. With ease, she jumped off the horse and started walking towards a trail in the woods.

"You're just going to leave your horse out here?" Landon called out, the annoyance clear in his voice.

Alice didn't bother to reply. She knew he would make sure their mounts were safely tethered. He loved those horses more than he loved his own life. She needed to create some distance between them; the day was not going at all as she'd hoped. How could she bring things back around? Why did she desperately want him to see her as something other than a spoiled Princess, and yet whenever she opened her mouth she acted exactly the way she knew he hated?

It didn't take long for him to catch up with her. Without turning, Alice said, "You really don't like me, do you?"

She could feel his presence. He was close enough that if she turned they would be nearly touching. It was another thing stable hands were not supposed to do: invade the space of royals. Even though she was warm from the heat of the sun, Alice knew the flush she felt was from being so near to Landon. It was strange the effect he had on her. She could have any guy she wanted, but she wanted the one who despised her.

"No, I guess I don't much care for you, Alice. You're mean as a snake. You spread your venom around, infecting everyone you come into contact with."

She hadn't expected him to be so honest. His words didn't really sting, at least not much, because she knew he spoke the truth. Her whole life had been living on the attack.

Alice turned, tilting her head up. His eyes snapped to hers, and a muscle in his cheek twitched. It was useless to demand he take back his words or even to threaten to punish him. For a long moment, they stared at each other.

"You know you're my only friend," Alice said, dropping her gaze. Why did she keep saying the things she was thinking?

Landon's abrupt laugh turned into a frown. "If I'm your only friend, you're in a sad state of affairs. I've thought many things about you, Alice, but not once have I thought of you as a friend."

"I know." Her voice was sad. She turned and continued down the narrow pathway.

Cursing under his breath, Landon followed after her.

It'd been a long time since Alice had returned to this particular area. She wasn't even sure what lead her to go there. The last time she visited was when she was about twelve years old, and she'd tried to run away. There was a portal nearby with access to the dimension of Wonderhills, but she'd never made it. Her mother's guards had chased her down. She'd been locked away for nearly two weeks in the dungeon for disobeying the Red Queen. During that time, Alice learned to access her own magical powers. It quickly became apparent that she was equal in strength to, if not stronger than, her mother. Once she freed herself, at the expense of several of the guards, Alice and her mother came to an agreement of sorts. The Queen would stay out of Alice's way, and Alice would remain in Wonderland and take her place on the throne once the Queen's lifetime was over.

Life had been going rather smoothly, until The Red Queen insisted that Alice marry someone from Wonderhills before her eighteenth birthday, all because of that damn prophecy. It wasn't a bad pairing. In fact, the man she was supposed to marry was gorgeous, but he wasn't Landon. He didn't make her stomach drop or her heart pound like a jackhammer. If anything, he bored her to tears. The idea of spending the rest of her life with someone like that was not acceptable. However, the Queen was not open to discussion. Of course, Alice could flat out refuse, but a part of her was also worried about the prophecy.

The Oracle was seldom mistaken.

The rustle of the tree branches brought Alice back into the moment. It was not that she'd forgotten Landon was nearby; she'd just gone into that quiet place in her mind where she could think without being distracted.

Half-turning, Alice gave him a side-long glance. "I hope you brought enough food for two."

One of Landon's eyebrows lifted. "I thought you went back to the castle to eat?"

"I couldn't stand one more moment being cooped up in that dreaded castle. If you don't have enough food, I'll conjure my own."

"I've got plenty." Landon glanced around before moving toward a large boulder. He was tall enough to just drop down on it. Alice had to hoist herself up.

"I never understood why you hated that castle so much," Landon said while opening his bag and pulling out sandwiches, fruits and a canteen. "When I was a boy, I used to dream of living in a big-ole castle instead of the small one room hut I lived in with my parents."

Alice reached for an apple. "Did you? It's funny how, no matter what we have in life, we're never satisfied."

"Speak for yourself. I'm quite content these days."

Her head came around abruptly. It didn't surprise her to feel her stomach twist and jealousy rear its ugly head. "Why's that? Have you met someone?" Alice cringed at hearing the anger in her voice.

Landon shot her a skeptical look. "What gave you that idea? Can't I be happy on my own?"

Alice reached for a drink from his canteen in an attempt to regain her composure. "I don't know. Is that even possible?"

"Come on Alice, it can't be that bad living up on the hill with all those servants. You literally have anything you want at your command. No offense, but it's a little hard to feel any sympathy for you. I know your mother is psycho, but you could rise above that. Nothing says you need to act like her. You could be nicer. It might surprise you to find out there are some decent people in this world. If you wanted, you could even leave this realm and go to another to live. Your past doesn't define you."

As soon as she felt the tears well, Alice dropped the canteen and jumped to her feet, turning away from him. There was no way she was going to let Landon see her cry. Not now. Not ever. "I'm ready to go back. Now."

She heard the shuffling of him cleaning up the lunch. Alice blinked her eyes several times, pushing away the sadness that was coming down on her like a thick blanket. *Please, not now,* she wanted to scream. Dammit, she hated when this happened! It usually came out of nowhere and she had no control over it. Closing her eyes, she tried to center herself, but all she could see was the walls closing in on her.

"Hey." Landon touched her shoulder from behind, instantly sending a jolt throughout her body. "I didn't mean to upset you, Alice."

Forcing a smile, Alice turned. "You didn't. You're right. I've got everything a girl could ever what. Power, money, long golden locks that guys seem to love. Soon I'll be married to the perfect match. What more could I want? I need to get back home. I have a lot to take care of."

What she really wanted was to lock herself in her room and rock back and forth until she calmed. Right now, she felt like she was going to come out of her skin or kill someone or something.

"So, it's true then?" he asked, hoisting his bag over his broad shoulders.

"Is what true?"

"You're going to marry him? The guy from Wonderhills? I've seen you two together. Neither of you looks very happy."

"It seems that way. Believe it or not, Landon, some things are out of my control. Even magick can't break a thousand-year-old prophecy."

"What does the prophecy have to do with you getting married? If anything, I'd think your mother would want you dead by your eighteenth birthday, not married off."

Alice had thought the same thing many times. "The Red Queen couldn't kill me if she tried. And believe me, she has tried. Plus, Mother doesn't believe the prophecy is valid with my twin presumed dead. She believes it would only go into effect if there were two, as is stated. She thinks this marriage uniting the realms will be proof to the world that she is invincible, prophecies be damned."

"Do you think she's dead? Your twin?"

Alice looked off into the distance. "No, I don't. I think she is alive and well."

"If you believe that to be true, aren't you concerned about reaching your eighteenth birthday?"

A slow smile spread across Alice's face. "Not at all."

Twirling around Alice sang the words she'd learned when she was locked in the dungeon.

"When two moons meet, twins will be born
How many lives will we mourn?
The loss of one?
The loss of two?
If they reach the age of eighteen it will be quite a few
Red Queen
Black Queen
Will be no more
Time will tell and days will pass
You never know if it will be your last."

Her mood was suddenly lifted like the fog. "I will not shed a tear if the Queens of the realms die because of my life. If there's collateral damage, that is out of my control."

Landon shook his head in disgust. "You really are self-centered aren't you?"

Alice's temper flared to life. "You have no idea what I've been through! Don't you dare judge me. Why should I feel responsible for others' lives? It's not like I asked to be born into this godforsaken realm. Tell me, Landon, do you believe I should die, in case the prophecy is true?" Alice conjured up a blade, holding her hand out toward him. "Why don't you have the honor? Or should I do it myself?" Alice flipped the blade around, holding it with both hands. A wild look in her eyes, she drove the blade toward her torso.

Landon knocked her hand aside before the blade could make contact. He grabbed a hold of her wrist. "Gods, you really are crazy!"

Alice struggled to be released. The more she struggled the tighter he held her, until a wave of sobs broke through. She was mortified, but she had no control. Her body heaved, and the tears soaked her face. Landon's grip around her wrist loosened as he pulled her into his strong arms. She fought him, but it was useless. He was too strong and she needed the comfort. Even though she'd put on a façade, inside she'd been crumbling for years. Ever since she found out about having a sister, the emotions that were stirred and they were not always good. One moment she longed to have a sister to play with, and the next, she was green with envy that her sister had made it out alive.

When her chest stopped heaving, Landon pulled away and looked down. Alice was too ashamed to meet his gaze. Finally, she glanced up and was taken aback by the intensity with which he was watching her. "Tell me the truth. Why did you want me to come with you today?"

Alice bit the side of her mouth. She thought of a million different excuses to give him. Instead, she spoke the truth. "I wanted to be alone with you. I've always wanted to be alone with you, even though you can't stand being near me. There I said it. Are you—"

He kissed her.

His lips were warm and gentle as they parted hers. Surprised, Alice stilled, her heart thudding in her ears. As his tongue probed, her body relaxed, she leaned into the kiss. It started out slow but soon increased in urgency. Greedily, Alice kissed him back. There was a desperation to the kiss, and their hands hungrily roamed and explored one another. His fingers sank into her hair, as if trying to pull her even closer. The intensity was almost as frightening as it was exhilarating.

Eventually, they finally broke the kiss and pulled away to catch their breaths.

"Sorry." Landon ran his hand over his jaw and mouth, as if he was just as shocked as she was.

Stunned by his apology, Alice just stood there staring at him. "You're sorry? You didn't mean to kiss me senseless?"

A crooked grin spread across his face. "Senseless, huh?"

Face flushed, Alice found herself grinning back. For the first time in as long as she could remember, Alice felt happy, giddy almost. But that quickly turned to apprehension. What if he really did regret kissing her? At least she knew he was drawn to her as she was him. That kind of passion couldn't be faked.

"Kiss me again," Alice demanded.

Landon moved towards her. "Doesn't work that way. Not with me." He continued stepping forward, causing Alice to retreat, until she found herself almost pressed against the trunk of a very large tree. "I'll kiss you when I'm good and ready." Landon dipped his head, his mouth once again covering hers. She melted into the kiss. It was even more searching than the first, as if both of them were trying to figure out what in the hell was going on. She sensed confusion in him, but also an undeniable attraction. His large hand rested on her shoulder, his thumb caressing her jaw, his mouth devouring hers. She groaned beneath his touch.

This time when he pulled away, he said, "You have no idea how long I've wanted to do that."

Alice's head dropped back against the tree. "Me, too." Her voice was nearly a whisper. All this time, it had never dawned on her that Landon was attracted to her. He never gave himself away, not even a wistful glance. Every time they were near each other, he became agitated, as if he couldn't get away from her quick enough.

"I thought you hated me." Alice dropped her hands from around his neck, resting one on his chest. The material of his shirt was coarse against her skin, a silent reminder of why they weren't supposed to be together. They were from different classes. The Queen would have a fit if she knew Alice was spending time in the arms of a stable hand. Good thing Alice couldn't care less what her mother thought.

"Oh, I've hated you all right." Landon's calloused fingers traced the length of her neck down to her collarbone. "But I've hated myself even more for thinking about you all the damn time. It hadn't occurred to me you could be interested in me. Or that I'd ever be able to feel your skin beneath my hands."

Alice's chest rose and fell at his touch. In a little over two months, she was supposed to marry another. How could she possibly do that now?

The sound of hoof beats drawing near startled them apart. Within moments, a team of guards appeared. Landon leaned against the tree and Alice walked across the greenery toward the men. "How dare you invade my privacy!"

The main guard dipped his head. "The Queen has demanded your return to the castle."

Alice rolled her eyes. "Tell the Queen I have no intention of returning until nightfall."

"She says it's urgent," the guard said, his voice almost pleading.

Alice glanced toward Landon, who shrugged.

"Very well, I'll return shortly."

"We were commanded to return with you."

Alice was not in the mood for her mother's charades. But she knew very well if the guards returned without her, at least one of them would lose his head. "Fine. Ride ahead. We'll catch up shortly."

The relief was evident on all of the guards' faces.

She turned to face Landon. "She knows," Alice said, her words hollow.

"What do you mean?" Landon's eyes widened. "How could she know?"

"She's the Red Queen. She knows everything. But don't worry. I will deal with this. I'm not about to give you up."

Landon absently rubbed the back of his neck. Alice knew he was imagining his head in the guillotine.

"She wouldn't dare touch you. I would scorch the realm if she even tried."

A smile flashed across his face before turning into a frown. "I never know when you're joking."

She wasn't joking, but knew Landon wouldn't approve of such hostility. "I'll take care of my mother. Can I see you tonight? We could meet at the pond where we used to catch frogs."

His face softened at the memory. "I'll be there. If you can't make it, I'll understand. We need to talk about this, Alice. I'm not naive enough to think it can last, but I'm not stupid enough to turn you away either."

"Let's just see where this goes. I have a feeling things will be very different two months from now," Alice said, looking off into the distance. She wouldn't lose him, even at the expense of her sister.

FIN

About the Author: Julia Crane dreamt of elves and teen androids long before she captured them and put them on paper. She's written and released over fifteen young adult and new adult titles over the past two and a half years. This story-line will be continued in *Down the Rabbit Hole,* to be released Fall 2016. If you would like to be notified of its release, please sign up for her mailing list at www.juliacrane.com.

STILL RED
SABRINA LOCKE

THE STENCH FROM A STINKING HULK FILLED EMILY'S nose, thick and deep with rot. Her throat closed and her over-taxed lungs screamed for air. She halted, panting a little while she surveyed the thing. Nature had been busy. It was hard to tell now exactly what sort of critter had decided to die on this stretch of Oregon beach. Seal probably. It was losing shape and started to liquefy. Grayish slabs of fat and flesh slid down thick yellow bones that jutted skyward like flagpoles. The smell had an overlay that was fishy and ordinary, but beneath the surface scent floated rich streamers of decay.

Familiar scents.

She'd learned the smells of death before she could draw her ABCs. Long ago and far away it had been, in the woods with the hunters in the time of stories. She remembered, and she was grateful for that fact. There was so much she'd forgotten, days and weeks, entire stretches of her long life had vanished into the treacherous depths of her mind.

But not the story, never the story.

She had lived with the story so long she'd forgotten where it ended and she began, or if there was such a thing as a borderland between story and history, between fantasy and reality. Her story was the singular constant of her lonely life, the thing that gave her purpose.

She clung to the memory as fiercely as she gripped her walking stick. The doctors said mini-strokes were erasing her memories bit by bit, that it was only a matter of time now before she forgot even her own name. What did they know? Doctors. They were little boys and girls in white coats who thought they could protect people with charts stuck to clipboards because science explained everything.

Fools.

They knew nothing of the way the world truly worked. She knew that life—the whole crazy mess of it—was made of bits and bobs of this and that, cut apart with round-tipped scissors and thrown high in the air only to settle to the tile floor where clever little hands sorted the pieces, arranged them on wide sheets of colored construction paper and pasted everything, taking care to press out each and every bubble until it was smooth and dry and flat.

What a pretty picture, Emily! I love all the colors you used. Is that you with your doggie?

No, bitch. Don't you know a fucking wolf when you see one?

No, they never did.

That was another lesson of her long life: wolves offered death on a platter, all gleaming fangs and lethal claws. Most fools never recognized the danger until the very last second, when it was too late to do anything but scream and bleed and die. She'd seen that too often, and hated the way they bargained for their lives, all dignity abandoned in a frantic bid to save their cowardly skins. Critics could say what they wanted, but Emily had never begged—or, God forbid—blubbered.

Never that.

Blubbering was not only useless; it wasted precious energy. If, through sheer dumb luck, the fools managed to escape the wolf, they were still not safe because a hunter would track them down. Wolves and hunters: one followed another and that was the way of things.

Thighs burning and her feet sinking deeper into the sand with every step, she trudged toward the rocks at the foot of a sheer basalt cliff. About twenty feet away, the beach turned shiny with hard-packed sand where the tide rolled and foamed. She wouldn't sink there, but she'd be closer to the water, closer to danger from the sneaker waves the activities director from the home had warned them about before she'd let them get off the bus. Lectured them in that serious-but-concerned tone young people used with their elders. Like they cared.

Emily was almost to the cliffs when she glanced over her shoulder and spotted the activities director, Becca, trotting after her, one slim arm in the air waving like she was trying to flag down a rescue helicopter. Emily's stomach tightened. *Should have moved faster. Too late now.*

"Miss Flannery, wait up!" Becca called.

Emily halted, leaning on her walking stick, breathing a little harder than she would have liked. Becca jogged to a stop, her pretty, tanned face flushed from exertion. She propped her fists on her hips and shot Emily a look that said, *you're not behaving.*

Emily pasted a bland, and what she hoped was a slightly dotty smile on her face. "Is there a problem?"

She watched Becca glance around the beach. The campfire with the rest of the folks from the home was far enough away to look small in the distance. A man and a woman walked together under the cliffs and big yellow dog loped around them in circles, ears flapping and tongue lolling. An older man in a baseball cap and baggy shorts stalked along the shoreline swinging a metal detector back and forth in wide sweeps. Business as usual.

Becca looked perturbed. "Where do you think you're going? I thought we all agreed to stay together."

It was the way she said it that was so irritating. As if Emily had no more of a right to independence than your average toddler with Becca standing in for Mommy. As if Emily hadn't been a woman grown since before the birth of Becca's own mother. As if there was anything that could happen out here that Emily couldn't handle.

She tightened her grip on the walking stick. "I'm just taking a little walk."

Becca reached and started to put an arm around Emily's shoulders, but Emily stepped back. Becca reached for her again, but Emily stopped her with a hand. "I'm fine, really."

"Let me help you back to join the others. You're missing the S'mores."

"I'm not ready to go back yet." Emily gestured toward the cliffs. "I set myself a goal to walk all the way there and back. The doctors say exercise is important."

"You've made it quite a distance. Far enough to count for exercise, that's for sure. Why not come back now?"

Emily cranked up the wattage on her batty old lady smile. She'd been told that smile could scare small children. She'd never tested it before on twenty-somethings. "I brought my journal."

Mentioning the journal seemed to have worked because Becca's expression softened. Emily's journal was a fat thing, the pages thickened with layers of gesso, acrylic paints and all sorts of collage materials. As activities director, Becca had spent weeks encouraging the residents to draw, paint and record events and stories from their lives.

Emily was proud of her journal because it detailed her story—the real story—not the lie she'd lived the past seventy years. She let the walking stick fall to the sand, opened the volume and flipped to the page she wanted then turned it around so Becca could see.

The art spread across both pages and featured a drawing of a cave set into a sheer black cliff face. Just inside the mouth of the cave, a small girl sat with her knees pulled up to her chest and her long red hair streaming over her body like a cape.

Becca's hand drifted over the colored pencil on gesso image. "You finished that page just the other day."

"Yes," Emily said, "it's the last one."

Becca frowned. "Why the last one? You've got plenty more pages in your journal and we have four more sessions."

"I know, but I've finished my story." There was one more step left, but explaining that would only confuse Becca. She didn't know how the world worked.

Emily pointed again. "Up ahead there's a cliff that looks just like the one I drew. I'd like to go there and sit for awhile with my journal and look through it while the sun sets." She shrugged. "I know it's silly, but if you'll humor an old woman, I promise I won't stay long. I'll be good."

A shout rose up from the group back by the campfire. Becca glanced over her shoulder then back at Emily and shook her finger. "One hour, no more, or I'm coming after you."

"One hour," Emily echoed.

Before she set off, Becca bent and reached toward the ground. "I'll take this back with me."

"No, I need my walking stick. It helps keep me steady."

The muscles in Becca's trim arms flexed as she hefted the thing, clearly unwilling to return it to Emily.

"Please, Becca. I need it. The only way I can hurt myself with it is if I fall down. You don't want that to happen, do you?"

Becca hesitated for what felt like a long time before finally handing it over. "Don't make me regret this."

Emily mumbled suitably appreciative nonsense until Becca headed back toward the group.

It took her another fifteen minutes to reach the cave. There she found a flatish sort of rock where she sat, leaving the walking stick close at hand, and placed her journal in her lap. The sun rode low on the horizon and the tide, while still out, was beginning to turn. When her hour was up, the waves would be rolling about her ankles. The timing was a guess at best, but there was nothing left to do but hope she'd got it right.

The wind whipped her hair and lifted her skirt.

"I am not afraid of the dark places," she whispered, "and I am coming for you."

She opened her journal and read her story for the last time.

This is the true story of a girl named Red. In some times and places she was called Little Red or Red of the Hood. Stupid names, you ask me. Nevertheless, I am that girl; rather, I was that girl once upon a time in a land far, far away.

Or not.

I don't expect you will believe my story nor do I expect you to place any trust in my words. Go ahead—call me a liar—I won't be offended. After all, it's only a story and a few pictures, badly drawn. Nothing more.

I was called a liar long before a hunter tossed a hood over my head, and I don't care about names. Now that I am no longer young by any definition, my only allegiance is to the truth because there is no truth but the whole truth.

So take what you will, I am still Red.

My woodcutter mother and evil stepfather abandoned me in the woods with some hunters from whom I managed to escape.

Eventually.

But not before I learned things no child should ever know, the things men do in the dark, and long after I learned how a big man's hands fit about my small neck. This is the truth I learned in the woods: vision dims and blood roars in the ears when precise pressure is applied. The little girl body goes limp until she wakes again, and he is still there with his big hands.

These are the true things I know. This is the true story that is mine to tell, paid for in blood and pain and time.

The important thing, however, the thing storytellers always forget or gloss over in their rush to get to the sexy part about wolves and girls is that I was never stupid enough to be fooled by a disguise. I was never a pushover, never the little ninny, tra-la-tra-la, prancing through the woods with a basket.

I fought back. Always. Even when I was very small and my puny fists and pitiful kicks only excited the hunters.

In time, I grew. I waited for my moment, and in time, it came.

One night while the hunters snored, their naked bodies stacked like thick white logs, I escaped through a rip in the tent and ran through the dark woods. A dog collar flapped about my waist. Sticks and thorns tore at my feet until they bled.

I ran and ran.

A pack of feral trial attorneys found me and took me in. They raised me as best they could, although they really didn't know what they were doing. They'd spent much too long in the dark woods themselves and had forgotten the ways of civilized people.

At least, that's what I told myself. In reality, I think they were afraid of me.

You see, during those long nights in the tent with the hunters, I'd learned to kick and fight and scratch and bite. Later, whenever anyone tried to discipline me, I fought back no matter what the infraction. I fought back because for me, nothing had changed. It didn't matter that I'd escaped and was no longer chained with the hounds.

I was still in the dark woods.

Still hiding under the dark green canvas.

Still smelling rotting leaves and mud.

Still and listening for the squeak of rubber boots. Dreading the rising shadow of a man's shoulders against the firelight and his hard hands, and then when it came and no, oh no, it came no matter what, it came, and I was nothing against that tide, the wave of sensation that dragged me down and down, down deeper still, deeper than breath into the dark places where there was no more breath, no more air, no more...

And then from the stillness, breath came again, and the dreaded light. Another day followed by another night. Again and again.

Still, I fought.

Even after I escaped, when anyone came close enough to touch, I transformed into a whirlwind of elbows, feet and nails. I snarled and screamed like a wild thing. No one touched me without a battle.

The pack tried not to blame me for my feral ways because they understood: little girls lost in the dark woods fought back or they died. The trial attorneys had been hunted themselves. That was how they'd been exiled to the wild, however their memories of it had faded with time. They longed to go back to the world they'd lost. They dreamed of returning to the bright cities of their youth and how their friends would exclaim and throw lavish parties to celebrate their arrival.

When it came right down to it, they only had one problem: how to explain the girl. She was out of control. A broken child, dangerous and unpredictable. Something Must Be Done.

Although the glory days of the trial attorneys were long past, they were not without influence in the Greater World. Regarding the girl called Red, they searched for options. That meant they whispered amongst themselves, scratched their hairy chins and muttered over stubby glasses of scotch rocks.

There was a great deal of coming and going, but in the end they decided I was too hard to handle, which was no different from what they'd thought the day they found me in the woods with blood and filth dripping down my legs.

What changed was their opinion.

In the realm of trial attorneys (feral or not), opinions count more than truth. Opinions are enshrined in glossy leather books with long and impressive titles stamped in gold. The volumes are passed from one generation to the next with critical citations read aloud with great pomp and ceremony.

You see, from the beginning the pack had never talked about me to authorities or anyone who could have done anything. Doing so would have required them to lift their long snouts from study and actually tell the terrible story. They would have had to remember it and replay in detail the condition in which they'd found me (which would be annoying considering the effort they'd put into forgetting that day). Besides the fact that the trial attorneys had been too long in hiding themselves. They'd forgotten how to tell the truth—if they ever knew in the first place—but that's another story.

In the end they decided to consult an old woman who lived on the other side of the forest. They led me through the woods to her cottage. After the trial attorneys left, I followed her into the kitchen and watched while she rolled white dough flat and sliced it into long strings to make noodles. I lifted the noodles carefully and draped them over wooden rods propped between chairs.

She asked me questions.

I told her my story.

Because she was calm and gentle and her breath did not stink of scotch, I told the truth. She never called me a liar.

Later, she made hot, black tea and poured it into a saucer and blew on it to cool and spread thick, brown apple butter on fresh bread. The kitchen was quiet and clean. I sat by the fire with a stack of books. I could have stayed there forever. The whole afternoon, the old woman worked and hummed under her breath. Occasionally I would look up and see her watching me with her flat gray eyes.

That evening when the trial attorneys returned, I listened while she reported that, in her opinion, the hunters had damaged me beyond all hope of repair. She said it would have been better if I'd never been born, but the damage was done and there was nothing anyone could do. Then she zeroed in on the real problem: I had lived.

The filth and horror can never be removed from the child, more's the pity. Death would have wiped the slate clean, however it is not for us to know why she survived when compassion would have sent her to a better place.

At that, the trial attorneys exchanged looks I did not understand. Something had changed, but I knew not what. They thanked the old woman for her advice. Before we departed, she handed me a basket containing a loaf of bread, a jar of apple butter, and a sharp, sharp knife.

The walk home to our den was long. Along the way the trial attorneys talked about the hunters for one last time, as if the tale belonged to them now. It was all very sad, they said, a tragedy the things that had happened to me. It wasn't fair, but it wasn't their fault. They'd done their part, put a roof over my head and clothed me, but I'd shown no appreciation. I'd continued to fight. They could not understand my shameful aggression in the face of their kindness.

Next followed a recounting of my many failings—a lengthy list by any measure. (I'll not bore you with it now, however, feel free to take a break to jot down relevant items as they occur to you. Brainstorm, if you wish. Have fun. No matter what you come up with, I'm certain the items on your list will be similar to what I heard that night.)

We walked and walked. They said more things, a torrent of words that rushed over the tromping of their big feet and the swish of their bushy tails and the clacking of their fearsome teeth.

In summation, the trial attorneys were hurt and disappointed by my attitude along with the whole being difficult part, which led them to their final point that it was my fault for allowing myself to have been taken by the hunters in the first place. This fact brought them to the most important truth: the safety of others must be assured. It was their solemn duty to protect others from me.

Granny herself couldn't have tied it up with a neater bow.

When we reached the den, I returned to my small room. There we completed our last conversation where they said the surest solution was always the simplest one. Thinking too much inevitably led to complexity (which was always trouble), and trouble was the one thing they could not tolerate. It was the very reason they'd abandoned their careers in the city. Trouble must, above all things, be avoided, and that is how it happened.

A shove on the shoulder, the swing of the door, a snip of the latch and it was done.

They locked me up.

For my own good.

I pounded on the door and yelled loud and long to no avail. At length they sent an emissary, a hapless junior partner who commanded me to stop causing trouble or else I would be Sent Away. *Think on that, young lady.*

As it turned out, I had a lot of time to think.

Years later I learned that some in the pack had argued for me to be sent away because the old woman said I needed professional help. This is why most of the Red stories start with Granny sending the girl into the forest. It is also why I have never trusted storytellers. The only reason to start the story there is if you think that old bitch had a point.

What she had was an agenda. Why do you think she gave me the knife?

To the credit or damnation of the trial attorneys, they did not send me away. I am not certain now from the vantage point of age which choice would have been better: being locked up or sent away to parts unknown. At the time, the mere mention of being *sent away* terrified me. I knew only too well what happened. I also did not ask for clarification because I'd learned that words were useless things—excuses, wishes, hopes, and sometimes promises—the stuff of stories.

And what was the point of a story? I'd told the old woman the truth and look where that had gotten me. The only way to make a point was with my fists and my feet, but even that choice had been eliminated.

By now you must have realized that my truth, my story, is nothing like the familiar version. Girl, cape, basket, woods, wolf. Perhaps you'd prefer it if I made Granny into a kindly old thing? Or shall we transform her into a wily and clever woman? (Dream on.) Perhaps you'd like my story if I turned it into an action-adventure thriller where I picked the lock and escaped. Or how I disguised myself as a wolf...

I do not trust stories. For me, all memory begins in the dark, in the woods.

Here's the truth: I dreamed in my little bed while locked in my little room inside the wolf den. Dreams that helped me pass the time while the trial attorneys held the threat of exile over my head like an axe strung from an exceedingly thin thread. It was for a good cause, they said, so I would stop fighting and learn to be good and behave. It meant *be quiet, don't talk, don't cause trouble, and above all, never, ever tell anyone what you did in the woods.*

Not what the hunters had done.

What I had done.

Things so bad they must never be spoken aloud, let alone remembered. A story so terrible the very telling of it became a weapon that might harm others. Like the knife that rested in my basket.

But I was still Red, and Red's story was my story. It was the only story that mattered, and it was the only story I could never tell. From this knot there was no escape.

Alone in my room, I tried to forget, but it wasn't easy. I pushed the memories away, but every night they rushed back in. In my dreams I fought back, but the hunters always came for me. Over and over. I ran and they caught me, overwhelmed me with their cruel strength until everything went mercifully black.

Then it would start. All. Over. Again.

This was how I did my time. Some people call it childhood. I watched endless hours of television until the shows and characters blurred one into the other because I feared sleep and the evil that rolled along behind.

When I'd lain awake for days, my body tight as a prowling wolf, an unseen door opened in my mind. From it came a little girl who looked remarkably like the three-year-old I'd been, once upon a time. Her feet were bare and bloody and a dog collar hung about her waist. She carried the basket to me, pulled away the red checked cloth. We both stared at the long and wicked knife. We both knew why the old woman had put it there in the first place and what was expected of me.

Still, I could not behave.

But I found a use for the knife, certainly not what Granny had intended and not as final, at any rate. I used it to chop up my memories into tiny bits. When I was done, I folded the knife carefully in the cloth and slept. I did not wake up for a long time.

When my keeper finally opened my little door, I emerged a pale and quiet girl who never fought and rarely spoke. The trial attorneys were pleased with the result. Their solution had worked.

What remained of my childhood was spent alone. It wasn't so bad because I wasn't outdoors in the rain and there were no hunters about in those days. The cave was clean and dry. I had a television and a lot of books. I was allowed out for meals and to go to school. I didn't have many friends because the other kids were afraid of the trial attorneys, and I didn't have much experience relating to people outside of books or a good fight. I kept my nails sharp.

About the time I was supposed to graduate from high school, the trial attorneys worst fear came true: a hunter came for me. He was a boy instead of a man. When he walked out of the dark woods he looked like any other hunter because he carried an axe, long and wicked looking with a red handle. No one particularly noticed the axe. What interested them was that he also carried a notebook, which meant he had a plan.

He had something to prove.

He had to kill a girl.

He chose me. I don't know why.

Over the years, I have wondered if the hunters who'd taken me later told the story of the girl who ran, the one they'd lost. Perhaps in this version, the boy heard the story around the campfire and vowed to find the girl who had shamed his elders. Vowed to find her and succeed where the other had failed so long ago.

Perhaps this happened.

Or not.

I will stick to what I know for sure: the day he walked out of the woods there were names scratched in his notebook in blue ink.

The name on the first line of the first page was Red.

The hunter tracked me, and when the trial attorneys learned of the threat, they promptly left me alone in the remote and lonely cave and waited in hiding for the inevitable. The inevitable took awhile, but hunters are patient.

Since I am here to tell this tale, you have logically assumed the boy hunter failed. That is, you must assume the boy failed if you believe I'm telling the truth because I cannot be, like the poor physicist's cat both dead and alive at the same time. I cannot be Red and not-Red. It must be one or the other. The two ideas fit together like a hand to an axe.

One evening I returned home from school and found the hunter waiting for me. I ran, but he was faster. He threw a hood over my head.

Blinded, I stumbled and fell. He scooped me from the ground and threw me over his shoulder and set off at a furious pace. Soon the crunch of boots smashing through the crust of snow gave way to a thump and slide that slowed to a soft, gravelly amble. We had reached the lake with its frozen expanse frosted with delicate layers of fresh snow. His pace slowed even more, and I could feel his body tense as he picked his way across the ice. Fear radiated from his broad back with the stench of unwashed skin.

Fear told me what to do.

When he slid right, I rolled in the same direction, throwing all my weight against his grasp, letting momentum set him off-balance. We lurched sideways. His knees buckled, and I tumbled across the ice. I yanked off the hood, pushed away from the cursing, floundering hunter, scrambling until there was distance between us.

He growled and struck out after me, lean and lethal against the flat white. I was lighter and faster and reached the center where I knew the summertime waters rippled over rocks far below the surface. The lake was deep here, but the current made for thinner ice, thin but strong enough to hold one smallish girl, I hoped.

The hunter was only a boy, but tall for his age with big arms and legs padded with dense muscle. He could not touch me here, not without breaking the ice and plunging to certain death in the dark waters. If that happened, he would take me with him, this was true. Down into the deeps, past air and light and all hope of life, into the night tide, but that was a place I knew by touch.

When he stood there stinking of blood and death and roared his fury, it came to me that I should feel pity for him. Some measure of compassion for a boy raised by brutes in the wild. They'd fed him cruel stories and handed him an axe and set him on a course that led to me. There were other stories, more true, if only I could make him believe. Faint hope bloomed that the truth might save me more surely than any blade.

"Have you killed a girl?" I asked.

He took a step and the ice cracked.

Silence then, across the frozen lake. I shoved my hand into my pocket and brought out my knife. If he came close enough for me to strike him, would it matter? We would surely fall through the ice and die together.

"Have you killed a girl?" I asked again, louder this time.

"No," he said, "but I will this day and in so doing, become a man."

He took another step and the crack widened.

I held my ground, this act of being cold and quiet something I'd mastered during the long years I spent locked in the den, and called to him, "They told you lies. There are other ways to prove yourself and become strong."

"Shut up," he shouted. "I'll have none of your tales." And with that, he charged.

The ice gave way, huge jagged shards raking skyward as we fell, sinking into the deep black. The lake swallowed the boy's dark form. I waited for my mind to go, for the endless cold to steal my breath, for death to take me one last time.

It did not come.

What happened is that hands like claws, bony and hard, gripped my legs and dragged me up and up until my head plowed through wet sand that clogged my nose. When I could breathe again and my body stopped shivering, I scrubbed my eyes. I lay on the floor of a cave. Somewhere nearby, waves crashed against rocks.

"You've got about fifteen minutes." The voice sounded like gravel on sandpaper, sharp and full of acid. Familiar.

I pushed myself upright and stared into the ancient and ruined face of the old woman.

"Fifteen minutes for what?" I asked.

"To decide if you want to live or not."

"I don't understand."

"Don't be stupid, child."

You cannot trust her, whispered a voice that might have been inside my head or come from the walls of the cave. *You told her your story. You told her the truth and she betrayed you.*

"I will not kill myself no matter what you say."

"Is that what you thought?" She chuckled with cool amusement. "I gave you a weapon, girl."

"I was a child. What did you expect me to do with it?"

"I expected you to grow and bide your time and learn the strategy of patience."

I stared at her in the shadows, the mass of frizzy white hair blown wild by the wind and her small, reddened eyes. "What are you?"

She grinned a wolfish smile and her teeth were like sharpened bits of yellowed ivory. "I am the girl who ran."

I shook my head and backed away from her, a low moan escaping my lips.

She advanced toward me. "I became the woman who went after those who hurt me. I became a hunter. I am the girl who lived."

"No."

"I am the girl who fought back. Always."

She is death, whispered the voice in the cave. *She will kill you with the very knife she gave you long ago.*

I stood there unable to move, trapped as surely as a rabbit in the hunter's snare. *She is the old woman who betrayed me. She is the woman I might become, a bringer of horror as surely as those who took me into the woods.*

"I gave you a knife, a worthy blade, but you became a girl who felt pity for that odious boy who fancied himself a hunter. You might have saved him, pulled him from the water and then where would we be?" Her mouth twisted into a sneer. "You are weak, and I cannot have that."

I said, "I am not weak. I survived."

"Because of me. I saved you."

"And what of it?" I asked. "If we are the same, aren't you saving yourself?"

"You know nothing of the way the world works," she said. "The way it slices things and puts them back together in different ways. Choose strength and I'll let you live and teach you to become a hunter."

"If I make another choice?"

She smiled, a goofy thing that made me shiver. "Why would you do such a thing? If I wanted you to die, I could have left you in the icy water with the boy."

The boy. I had forgotten about him.

She's afraid of the boy, whispered the voice in my mind. *She is afraid you might make a different choice than she did.*

She rushed toward me then, holding the thick, heavy stick in her hands like an axe, and she came at me. Again, my hand found the blade, but instead of striking her, I let it fall and turned and ran. Her screams followed me into the tide that swept me back into icy waters...

...where the boy's dead white face floated in the darkness.

With all the fight and fury of the girl who never gave up, I grabbed him, kicked my way to the surface and dragged his leaden body onto the gravel-strewn beach where he gagged and vomited.

There was no sign of the old woman. I found the gnarled length of polished driftwood she'd used for a walking stick not far from the entrance to the cave where a set of footsteps in the sand abruptly stopped. I traced the footsteps back inside the cave until I came to where the knife had fallen, but it was not to be found. It was as if it had vanished with the old woman.

When I came out, the boy's eyes were open. He stared about him in wonderment. "I was going to kill you," he said.

"I know."

A hank of wet dark hair fell across his forehead. Blood trickled from his nose. "You saved me."

"I know."

"What do we do now?"

I turned away from the cave entrance and faced the length of the beach and the clusters of houses piled along the shore with their shining windows.

"We go home," I said, and held out my hand.

FIN

About the Author: "Still Red" is Ms. Locke's second published short story. You can find her other short story, "The First to Fall," in *Beyond the Stars: A Planet Too Far,* a science fiction anthology on Amazon and Barnes & Noble.

THE FINAL STRAW
JENNIFER BLACKSTREAM

"ANOTHER TEST?"

The soft, seductive tone whispered over Milly's skin, wrapped around her senses in a way that sent shivers spiraling over her nerves in tingling waves. She spun around, banging her elbow against the cold stone of the windowsill and hissing as pain shot down her bones.

"How do you do that? I was really watching for you this time."

Her voice was breathier than she'd have liked, and she crossed her arms, trying to summon a glare for the man who'd snuck into her prison—again. Maddox smiled at her, and his grey eyes twinkled with amusement. His long black hair slid over the smooth, pale muscles of his shoulders as he tilted his head at her.

"I told you last night, I am a sylph. Until I take physical form, you can no more see me coming than you could watch the approach of any other gust of wind."

He approached her with light footsteps as silent as a gentle breeze, the faint rustle of his soft cotton shirt and pants barley audible over her own breathing. He took a lock of her hair between his fingers, smiled softly at the golden curl as he looked from it to the piles and piles of straw that filled the cavernous tower room around them.

"How can the king be so immune to your beauty, your charm, that he tests you still?" He let go of the curl, cupped her jaw with one hand.

Milly's throat went dry and it took her two tries to find her voice. "How could the prince of Sanguennay threaten to disfigure a face as handsome as yours?"

Maddox laughed, a raspy chuckle. "I dare say he was in a poor position to appreciate my appearance. I imagine few men would be, considering he'd just found me in his private chambers with his wife." He shrugged one shoulder. "My fault entirely. I should have known better than to fly about after imbibing that much wine."

His deep chuckle vibrated things low in Milly's body and she bit her lip to keep from leaning further into his touch. Maddox lowered his hand and part of her mourned the loss of his warmth.

"It was an innocent mistake and he should have guessed that from the fact you were passed out lying on top of the dresser," she pointed out. "Besides, you tried to make it up to him. You gave him half of the siren's treasure when you found it, even though you almost lost your leg to that sea monster trying to get to it."

Maddox quirked an eyebrow. "Do you remember every story I've told you with such detail?"

"Yes," she answered immediately. "I have no adventures of my own to remember. I must live vicariously through yours." Her chest tightened and she looked at the locked door that kept her a prisoner in the tower, surrounded by heaps of straw. "Ironic, isn't it? After my mother died, my father barely let me travel twenty feet from our mill for fear that something horrible would happen to me. And yet it was his outrageous boasting that's put my life on the line. Not once, but three times."

"Milly."

Maddox's voice caressed her senses like a physical touch, a soft blanket drawn over her skin. She couldn't help but look at him, look into his beautiful silver eyes.

"Your father made a foolish mistake," he said gently. "One poor choice that brought on consequences he will have to live with for the rest of his life."

There was something in his voice that said he wasn't just talking about Milly's father anymore. As one, they both turned to look at the spinning wheel in the center of the room, its polished wood perfectly framed by the monstrous piles of yellow straw.

"Spinning straw into gold," Milly murmured.

A muscle in Maddox's jaw tightened, but he dragged his lips into a smile. "Fate then, that my mistake and your father's should align so nicely."

Wood creaked as Maddox lowered his large frame onto the stool in front of the spinning wheel. The spark had left his eyes, and the shining silver was now the heavy grey of a rain-swollen sky.

"He will demand a price." His voice held the edge of a growl, the faint stirrings of anger.

Milly's stomach bottomed out and she fisted her hands at her sides. "I know."

Maddox put his right hand on the spinning wheel, scooped up a small bundle of straw with his left. He met her eyes then and there was a ferocity there that left her breathless. "If it were within my power to do this for you, I would. I would not ask for anything in return." The lines around his eyes deepened, pain shining in his gaze now. "It is my power that let me hear your cries on the wind. But spinning straw into gold...that is him."

A lump rose in her throat, barring any words from escaping. She nodded.

He opened his mouth as if he would say more, but suddenly his left hand closed around the straw, crushing it in his grip. Black pupils swallowed his pale grey irises, until there was nothing but darkness staring back at her. A second later, red irises appeared, began to glow softly. Milly held her breath, her veins full of icewater as she watched the demon rise, pushing Maddox away from her, deep into his own subconscious.

"So, you are in need of my help again, are you?"

The demon's voice came from Maddox's vocal cords, but it sounded nothing like him. There was no hint of Maddox's strange cadence, that whispering quality that reminded Milly of the wind through the trees. There was no trace of his smile in the macabre spreading of lips that bared white teeth at her now.

She faced the intruder and stiffened her spine. "Once again, and then no more."

"Once more you have to prove yourself, and then the king will make you his queen." The demon looked her up and down, a leering scrutiny that made her skin crawl. "And what do you offer me in payment this time? Another necklace? Another ring? You had such pretty little trinkets..."

"You will have your choice of treasure once I am queen." Her voice wavered despite her determination, her resolve weakened by the sight of Maddox's lips cradling the demon's taunting words. The tiny voice that had been screaming in her ear these past two nights chose that moment to screech again. *You cannot marry the king! Before you is the man you love!*

The demon narrowed his eyes and Milly's stomach rolled as he looked her up and down again. Unlike Maddox's appreciative gaze, the demon's inspection left her skin feeling cold and clammy, unclean as if she'd just been rolled in filth. She groped behind her for the ends of her thin cloak, drew the faded green material more tightly around her.

"No," the demon said slowly. "No, I do not think that will do at all. What guarantee do I have that you will be queen?"

"I will be queen," she said firmly. "The king has promised. All that is left between me and the throne is this room of straw."

"And the bag of flesh I wear that draws your traitorous eye so," the demon sneered.

Milly looked away, realized her mistake, and looked back. The demon was staring straight into her eyes now, and its smile had grown even more frightening.

"So typical of a woman. You are all such fickle, fickle creatures." His right hand lashed quickly against the spinning wheel, sending it into a blur of motion. "I will spin for you. But the price will be no less than your first born child."

"No!" The word exploded from Milly's lips before she could think, but it didn't matter. There could be no consideration of such a demand.

"Very well. Then I will inform your guards. No sense forcing them to stand in the hall all night when you've made your decision." He let the straw in his hand drift to the floor like feathers plucked from a struggling bird. "Better for me anyway. This evening was so much more promising when I was watching through Maddox's eyes as he mounted a supple young nymph. Returning to her arms will be so much more fun than sitting here all night doing your work."

Images sprang to life in Milly's brain. Maddox entwined with an otherworldly creature far more beautiful than she could ever be. Bitterness coated her throat, rose up to splash against her tongue. She bit her lip until it bled, shoved the images away.

"I want to speak with Maddox." She'd meant it to be a command, but it came out more of a plea.

The demon snorted. "No. I rather like my bargaining position as it is. You will agree to my terms, or I will call the guards."

"That's blackmail!"

The demon closed the distance between them so quickly and silently he may as well have been a shadow cast by a raised lantern. The large hand that had toyed with her hair so gently a moment ago now wrapped in her curls up to the base of her neck, twisted her head painfully to the side so he could lean in and press his lips to her ear.

"Make your choice, little one," he whispered, his breath hot on her skin, carrying a hint of sulfur. "The time has come to work or play, and the choice is yours. Will I do your work for you? Or will I return with Maddox to play?"

Milly pressed her lips together, biting back the protest she knew would do her no good. "Fine."

The demon didn't give her a chance to reconsider. He half flew to the stool, set the wheel spinning furiously with one hand, using the other to feed the straw into the madly whirling wood. Milly stared at him, her hatred for the demon burning inside her like a pile of white-hot coals.

I will never have a child, she promised herself. *I don't want to bear the king's children anyway.* It was easier said than done, but Milly refused to think about that. Instead, she watched the demon, waited for the telltale signs that it had lost itself in its work, had relinquished consciousness to Maddox.

There. Tension sprang back into his muscles, his head jerked up, gaze flicking around the room with panicked speed before finally landing on Milly. She held her breath, fighting to keep her composure long enough to walk over to the spinning wheel and sit on the floor in front of it before her weak knees gave out.

"What did he ask of you this time?"

Maddox's voice was calm, but the question hurt as badly as if they'd been written on parchment, tied to stones, and hurled at her unprotected body. Milly wanted to look away, hide the shame she knew must be etched across her face, but she stopped herself. If this was to be her last night with Maddox, she would not waste it talking about the wretched choice she'd made to save her own life. With every ounce of self control left to her, she waved her hand in the air, attempting to sweep away his concern.

"Let's not talk about him." She looked down at her cloak, wrapped it more tightly around herself as if it could protect her from the cold chilling her from the inside out. "Tell me more about your adventures."

Maddox's shoulders twitched as if he'd tried to face her more fully, but the tension in his body betrayed the demon's lingering control. It wasn't present enough to keep him from speaking, but it was still there in his body, manipulating the wheel and feeding it straw. Manacles on the inside.

"Adventures." Maddox spat the word as if it tasted foul. "It's too grand a name for them. Foolish escapades, that's all they were. Perhaps if I'd been less infatuated with adrenaline-induced exploits, I would be sharing my body with a wife instead of a demon."

Without permission, Milly's mind painted a tempting picture of her as the wife Maddox spoke of sharing his body with. She cleared her throat a little too loudly, as if the sound could somehow also clear the image from her optimistic imagination. "You didn't tell me that story." She hesitated, not wanting to bring him more pain, but somehow needing to know. "How you came to be—"

"Possessed." He flung the word from his lips like a stone hurled into a still pond, sending ripples of agitation through the room. His teeth clenched and he stared at his hands flying over the wheel. "It was my own ignorance, my own *arrogance*. The rumors were everywhere about the prince of Nysa. Rumors that he'd died, that his body was now moved about by a demon and not the queen's son. They said Aphrodite herself had plucked an incubus from the astral plane and put it into the prince's body, had done it to protect the royal family from the war that would come if it was learned that their only heir was dead."

Milly leaned forward, uncaring of the cold stone floor beneath her palm. "I heard no such rumors."

"You wouldn't. You are human, and such matters are rarely spoken of outside the circles of the otherworld." He paused. "Except Dacia. But then again, I suppose it is much harder to ignore otherworldly beings when the royal family is massacred in a coup and then continues to rule afterwards."

Vampires. Milly shuddered. Yes, everyone knew about the vampires that ruled Dacia. If it weren't for the machinations of Prince Kirill, the cold man with eyes like a winter sky, trade would likely have stopped entirely. Milly didn't know how the vampire had kept trade going after his family's terrifying transformation, let alone urged it to such thriving heights. And she didn't want to know.

"I wanted to find out if it was true," Maddox continued. "And like a child, I didn't think beyond the satisfaction of my curiosity. I learned how to separate my mind from my body so I could travel to the astral plane myself." His face darkened and the spinning wheel spun faster, golden thread glittering as it flew through the air to land in a growing pile next to him. "No one told me about the dangers of leaving my body unattended. And I didn't bother to ask."

Milly dug her fingernails into her palms. "The demon entered your body when you were on the astral plane."

Maddox nodded, a stiff bob of his head. "I found out later that I was lucky. A greater demon would have been able to keep me from returning to my body at all, could have claimed my flesh for himself and left me an incorporeal spirit forever." He stared at his hands, at the wheel spinning faster and faster, at the golden thread spiraling through the air. "At least this demon is merely my match. I cannot force him out, but neither can he get rid of me."

Milly wrung her cloak in her hands. "Isn't there any way to exorcise it?"

"Not without knowing his name." Maddox's shoulders fell, as much as they could with the demon still controlling him, still using him to work the wheel. "I'm not an exorcist. I don't have the power or the expertise to cast him out, and so far, I have not found anyone who can. There are rumors of men and women powerful enough to do it, but every time I try to find them, to get word to one of them, the demon takes over and..." He set his jaw and tilted his face away from her.

Suddenly Milly felt like a wretch for complaining about her boring life, for complaining that her father had refused her control over her own destiny. At least she had control of her body, her mind. She wasn't demon-ridden.

"I'm sorry," she whispered.

Maddox looked at her then, and there was a smile on his face, even if it didn't reach his beautiful grey eyes. "Don't be sorry. At least now I can take some small comfort that my burden was of use. Without the demon, I would have heard your plea on the wind, but been unable to do anything to help you." He looked at the golden thread. "Perhaps I can find some solace in knowing that I helped put a good queen on the throne of this cursed kingdom."

Something sharp stabbed at Milly's belly, dread honed to a fine point. *I don't want to be queen. I want to go with you.* The emotion was so strong that her lips parted, her vocal cords vibrating with the intention to speak. She made a choking sound as she swallowed them back, humiliation burning her cheeks at the thought of how Maddox would react to such a declaration of love. How many human women had thrown themselves at him? Had seen his beauty, heard that voice like a whisper in a dark bedroom, and wanted to listen with her head pressed against his lean, muscled chest?

"As much as this land can know a queen," she said weakly. "There hasn't been a true king in Midgard for centuries."

"Your husband-to-be's family has done their best." Maddox was back to watching the wheel, and there was more resignation in the set of his shoulders now than anger. "They control this valley, which is more than anyone else has managed."

"They control it because they are ruthless mercenaries who don't care what they have to do to maintain their power. They've been up in this castle for too long, looking down over the valley from their high and mighty position. What sort of king threatens death for failure of an impossible task, then in the next breath promises marriage for success?"

Maddox jerked his head to look at her and only then did Milly realize she'd voiced those thoughts out loud, voiced her anger and derision for a man she supposedly meant to marry. Flustered, she opened her mouth before she could think of something to say, but then closed it when her gaze locked with his. There was a sudden intensity in his eyes, a directness that seemed to bore right through her to read the words written on her soul.

You called him here, begged him for help. He's sitting there with the demon moving his body as if he were a puppet—all to help you marry a man you just slandered. You may as well tell him it's all been for nothing.

"I have a treasure box," she blurted out.

Maddox's eyebrows rose, stealing some of the intensity from his eyes. "A treasure box?"

Heat scalded Milly's cheeks. "Yes. Sort of." The blush grew hotter and she fisted her hands at her sides to keep from covering her face with her hands. "It is to me. It's where I keep the things I've collected. The things..." She trailed off miserably, her chin falling to her chest in a pathetic attempt to hide her face. *This is so embarrassing.*

"What kind of treasures?"

Maddox's voice was soft and encouraging. Gentle enough that it almost took the sting out of her cheeks. Almost.

"I don't have much, just what I was able to barter for with the traders who came through the village. I have feathers from a golden bird that a sailor found in the kingdom of Mu, a silver coin from Dacia, a silk scarf from Nysa, a spear's head from

Meropis, and a strange little doll from the southern corner of Sanguennay."

Maddox smiled, a real smile that crinkled the corners of his eyes. "That is, I think, the greatest treasure box I have ever heard of."

Milly sighed. "It's not as good as traveling to those places myself, I know. But it's as close as I can get." She looked at the door as if she could see through it, see the guards waiting there. "Somehow I doubt I'll have any more freedom when I'm queen. The king of Midgard doesn't have your passion for travel."

As soon as the words were out of her mouth, she realized how they sounded. Her mouth went dry, the voice in her head screeching in panic. *You might as well have proposed to him, you idiot! Do you want to hear him laugh in your face?*

"But I guess that's a small price to pay for being queen," she rushed to add, not looking at Maddox. "I'll have power, and money. I'll be able to take care of my father."

Maddox didn't say anything, and Milly couldn't look at him, couldn't bear the thought of seeing what emotion must be etched across his face. What a fool he must think her.

"Please tell me more stories," she said finally, her voice quiet and pathetic.

Again, Maddox was silent. Milly clasped her hands together, her heart hammering in her chest. *Please, just start talking. Forget everything I said.*

Maddox took a deep breath and a moment later, launched into a story about sailing on a ship and seeing an angel kill a merman who was trying to drag a sailor off the ship to his death in stormy waters. Milly sagged with relief. She could listen to

Maddox talk all night, listen to the unique, breathy quality of his voice. He described his adventures with such vivid detail that if she closed her eyes, she could pretend she was there. Pretend this tower and its piles of straw were just a horrible nightmare.

Just as with the previous nights, the time passed too quickly, the straw vanishing with impossible speed. After what felt like mere moments, the first rays of the sun reached through the window, touched the golden thread that lay in piles where once there had been only straw. Milly watched with the threat of tears warming her eyes as the sunlight traveled the length of the golden thread, lighting it up until the entire chamber was filled with shining gold. As if the entire tower was burning.

She stayed where she was, seated on the dusty floor with her back against the wall under the window. The cold of the stone had seeped into her body hours ago, but it hadn't bothered her until now. Nothing could have bothered her while Maddox was talking. But now he was levering himself up from the stool, his hands falling away from the wheel as the demon's control melted away. It was time to say goodbye.

Maddox wouldn't look at her. His last story had ended with first light, as if the magic of his stories was too delicate to withstand the harsh light of the sun. The previous two nights, he had smiled at her before he left, had wished her well. But this time as he walked to the window, he said nothing. Wouldn't meet her eyes even though she sat less than a foot away from him. He might have just been tired, but Milly couldn't help the foolish voice in her head that whispered maybe this last goodbye was going to be hard for him too.

He's going to leave now. He's going to leave, and you'll never see him again. If you don't say something now, you'll hate yourself forever. Say something. SAY SOMETHING.

Milly shot to her feet, almost falling over as her sleeping legs protested, threatened to pitch her to the floor. Her lips parted, but before she could speak, his hands closed around her biceps. The world tilted and suddenly she was staring into his stormy grey eyes from mere inches away.

"I know you've already promised payment to the demon." His fingers dug into her arms, then quickly gentled. "And I know you don't owe me anything. But if I could be so bold as to ask for one thing before I go?"

His voice was even huskier than usual, a sound that started at the base of her spine and swept out along her nerves like a velvety caress. The delicious sensations that voice inspired nearly stole her voice, left her next words breathy and thin. "What do you want?"

Grey eyes darkened with hunger, his attention falling to her mouth. "A kiss. Just one kiss."

She would have said yes if her body had given her the chance. As it was, her willingness was all too clear in the way she dove for him, so eager to grant the request that she could scarcely breathe. He made a sound deep in his chest that was pure masculine satisfaction and her legs trembled, her body dipping as her knees gave out.

One strong arm banded around her waist, dragged her against his body. His lips slid over hers, a soft kiss that ached with restraint. Before her courage could fail her, she threw her arms around his neck and pulled him closer, pressed herself more tightly against him until she could feel the outline of his solid muscles through the rough material of his shirt and the thin cotton of her dress. If this was going to be her last chance, their last meeting, then there was no reason to hold back. Let him think her a foolish human, one of the many who had fallen for his charms. At least she would have this memory to last her through the sham of a marriage that waited for her.

Maddox groaned and deepened the kiss, swiping his tongue between her teeth, teasing her into playing with him. Tension sang in his muscles, a tremble of promise that made Milly wish the king wasn't coming for her, made her wish they had more time, that she'd had the courage to ask for this kiss herself when he'd first arrived. Before she was facing a life without him, before she'd made her final deal with the demon...

The kiss ended far too soon. Maddox pulled back slowly and with effort, as if the sun had melted them together. As he retreated, he pulled words from deep inside Milly, words she'd never intended to speak.

"I don't want to be queen."

Maddox froze. The hands that had been slowly sliding away from her suddenly tightened, fingers digging into her hips with bruising force. "What did you say?"

"I don't want to be queen." Her eyes widened, but she couldn't stop speaking, not now that she'd started. "Let the king keep the gold, I don't care. I want another trinket for my treasure box—I want to find it myself on a beach or in some far off shop. I want to see the world, I want to get out of this miserable little valley." She couldn't breathe, couldn't stop the words scrambling to escape through the chink in the wall of her self control. Her hands fisted in his shirt, holding him as tightly as he held her. "Take me with you."

"You would never be safe with me." Maddox's voice was hoarse and he glanced down at his body before meeting her eyes again. "With us."

He didn't let go of her, his grip still unyielding as if his bones and muscles themselves fought to keep her. Milly's confidence swelled and she jutted out her chin.

"If you leave me, I will be forced to marry a man who threatened to have my head not once, but three times if I did not fill his coffers with gold spun from straw. Do you really think I will ever be safe with him?" She pointed out the window with a shaking finger. "This is not one of the five kingdoms. This is Midgard, land of chaos. Eventually, someone will try to take this valley from my would-be husband, and when they do, they will need a miracle to keep it. I cannot be that miracle. And we both know what will happen to me when they realize that."

Anger flashed in Maddox's eyes like moonlight on a churning lake. He didn't speak for several moments and Milly would have lost heart if he wasn't still holding her so tightly.

"The king will not give you up easily," he said finally.

The protest was weak, robbed of its force by the passion that left his voice low and gruff. Milly's spirits soared. "Then run away with me. Let us have another grand and terribly foolish adventure."

Maddox raised a hand to brush her hair back, a faint laugh falling from his lips as the tension eased from his shoulders. "I had thought I would never desire another adventure again.

But you, my enthusiastic little miller's daughter...you make me want to live again."

Milly returned his smile with every ounce of her being, closing her eyes and leaning forward to accept the kiss she could feel coming.

Then suddenly she felt it. The shift, the cool shadow of the demon roaring back into stolen flesh. Her eyes flew open as Maddox stiffened, an enraged protest choked off a split second before his eyes smoldered with reddish light. She cried out and tried to pull away, but the demon tightened his arms around her waist, held her in a perverted mimicry of Maddox's passionate embrace.

"I knew it," he hissed. "Did you think I wouldn't come back? Wouldn't be certain that you held up your end of the bargain? I may not be able to hear the sweet words you share with this fool, but this is my body now, and I can feel what it does."

He leered at her then, and her skin grew cold and clammy in the wake of his lingering assessment. Again she tried to break his hold, but the demon chuckled and held her tighter.

"Such a sweet kiss goodbye," he taunted. "If you weren't so pathetic, I may have enjoyed it along with him." He jerked her against him, closing his grip until she couldn't breathe. "I held up my end of the bargain. The straw is gold, and the king will marry you. I don't know what promises Maddox made, or what you promised him, but know this. I *will* have your first born." He leaned closer, whispered the next words in her ear. "No matter who fathers it."

Her firstborn. *Maddox's* firstborn.

Fury burnt her fear to ashes, infused her with a rush of much-needed adrenaline. Milly bared her teeth and shoved against the demon, giving herself just enough space to get the breath she needed to speak. "No. You won't. We will find a way to get rid of you. There are those who can help, those who can force you out of his body for good. You may be able to keep Maddox from them, but you can't stop me. I will find them and I will bring them back. Call the guards if you like, Maddox will only come for me later. You can't fight him forever."

The demon snarled, twisting Maddox's handsome face into something hideous, like a candle left too close to a hot stove. "I will kill you, girl. Do not think that Maddox—"

A snarl of pain from his own lips cut him off and the demon released her, half hurled her back. Milly fell, hitting the stone floor with a grunt of pain. She watched, mesmerized, as Maddox's body contorted, muscles twitching as if they would peel away from bone. It didn't last more than a few seconds, and when it was over, the demon glared at her with hatred burning in his red eyes.

Milly swallowed her fear, forced herself to smile at him. "What's the matter? Ride getting a little bumpy?"

"You will not get rid of me," the demon growled. "One of you—or both of you—will die first."

Milly's smile wilted, but she kept it pinned to her face. The demon wasn't as confident as he seemed, she could see it in his eyes. But neither was she. What if that brief struggle was the summit of what Maddox could do? The hardest he could fight?

"You might be able to kill one or both of us," she agreed slowly. "Or you might be wrong. It might be that we will find a way to not only banish you from Maddox, but to imprison you permanently." She sat up with forced nonchalance, tapped a finger against her chin. "It seems to me that there have been cases of demons being trapped in bottles, or even enchanted objects. A sort of firefly in a jar, perfectly harmless."

The demon said nothing. He stood there, staring at her as if she were a fly that had just landed in his soup. Milly's confidence rose with every second that passed, every second that kept him standing there, offering no threat. Then something slid through the demon's red eyes, and he nodded.

"Very well," he said finally. "Then I propose another deal."

Milly's heart leapt, but she fought to keep her face calm. "I'm listening."

The demon strode over to the spinning wheel, trailed one finger over the spindle. "I will give you until sundown. If you can guess my name, I will leave Maddox forever. If you can't, then our bargain proceeds as intended, with the added stipulation that neither you nor Maddox will do anything to try and stop me, to try and be rid of me, before I get the child that is rightfully mine."

Dear gods. He means to possess my child. Milly shook her head as she stood, brushing off her skirts to hide the trembling of her hands. "No. Let me give you something else for your help. I can get you gold, or I will find you some treasure—"

"Nothing you could offer me would be as valuable as the life you already promised. I *will* have the child."

"Be reasonable. You gave me gold. To ask for a life—"

"I gave you more than gold, and well you know it," the demon snarled. He flicked a hand over the wheel, sent it spinning with a low, steady hum. "That gold is all that stands between you and death. I gave you your life, and I will have a life in return."

Milly ground her teeth. It was no use. The demon wouldn't budge, wouldn't withdraw his claim on the life she'd been such a fool as to promise him. The opportunity he'd offered her to guess his name was as far as he would go. Her only chance. "Fine. Till sundown."

The demon fled Maddox's consciousness so quickly, Maddox stumbled and nearly fell into the spinning wheel. His elbow hit the tip of the spindle and he hissed, arching away from the cursed thing as a bright red droplet of blood beaded on his skin. He was still rubbing his elbow and getting his bearings when his gaze landed on Milly. Immediately he straightened and he took a breath to speak.

The sound of the door's lock being disengaged cut him off. Milly's eyes widened and without thinking, she ran into his arms, too upset to relish the way he embraced her without hesitation.

"We're too lat—"

Before she could finish her sentence, Maddox's body changed. One minute she was cradled in his warm, solid arms, the next he was gone, and only a strange undulating pressure marked where he'd once been. The door hinges creaked and she looked toward the door, her heart in her throat. The pressure around her increased and the room tilted madly. She barely had time to draw breath to scream before she was flying, hurtling out the small window and into midair. Shouts sounded behind her, but they faded quickly as she was carried off at dizzying speed.

Milly didn't have words to describe the sensation of flying in what she was increasingly sure were Maddox's arms. Her nerves danced with exhilaration, the caress of the air against her skin firm enough to hold her, but still remarkably gentle. The land flew by below her, but as she adjusted to the sensation of flying, she could concentrate enough to make out landmarks. The land opened up into a yawning green field, and the pressure against her eased. Maddox spiraled down in lazy circles until her feet touched the grass.

He let her regain her footing, and before she could turn, he'd taken the physical form she'd known him in since that first night. His black hair floated around him on the remnants of a breeze and his grey eyes were sharp with concern as he ran gentle fingers over her face, down her arms.

"What happened? I felt him grab you."

And just like that, the thrill of flying evaporated, and the sinking feeling returned to her stomach. Quickly, and with as little despair as she could manage, she told Maddox about the new deal. It was difficult to speak past the lump in her throat, and she scanned his face the entire time, waiting for the inevitable moment when he would realize how foolish it would be to tie himself to her and her terrible, terrible promise. For the gods' sakes, they'd known each other for less than three days. Any minute now it would all sink in.

When she was finished, that look still hadn't come. Maddox merely pressed his lips together and shook his head. "I've tried to find out his name. I can't." He looked away then, the shadow falling over his features out of place with the sunny field around them.

Milly put a hand on his arm, trying to summon a confidence she didn't feel. "But that was when you were trying alone. This time you'll have me to help."

He rested a hand on hers, turned back to face her with only the ghost of an attempted smile. "Milly, it's impossible. The demon comes from the astral plane. It would take me far more than twenty-four hours to search that realm for someone who might know his name."

"There has to be a way." An idea struck her and Milly grabbed his shoulder. "Wait a minute. What about Prince Adonis?"

"What about him?"

"You said he's from the astral plane. And Aphrodite chose him to help the Nysan royal family, so he must have a good heart. Maybe he could help us?"

Help us. We're an us.

The thought made her lean closer, testing. Maddox immediately put an arm around her, as natural as if they'd been together for years instead of days. Milly couldn't help the smile that spread over her lips and she gave into the urge to lay her head on his chest, let the warmth of his body chase away the last of the tower's chill.

Finally, Maddox nodded. "It's possible." He leaned back and Milly tilted her head to look into his eyes as he feathered a hand over the side of her face, cupped her jaw. "It's well known that Prince Adonis has a soft spot for lovers. He might be willing to help us."

Milly leaned into his touch, her heart soaring with hope despite the obstacles looming before them. The word "lovers" echoed in her head in Maddox's seductive voice. She almost missed the muscle tightening in his jaw, almost didn't hear him when he spoke again.

"But we'll never get to him in time. The demon can sense anything I do physically. He didn't stop us from leaving the tower, but I doubt he would sit by idly and let me go for help." He looked away again, and a tightness crawled into his voice. "I cannot fight him the entire way there. I have no way of knowing where I might end up. And I would have to leave you alone." He looked back in the direction of the castle, still visible high up on the mountain. "The king will send people to look for you."

Milly fought back a sudden surge of doubt. She would not give up now. Not when she had a chance at a happy life with Maddox.

"Can't you travel to the astral plane?"

Maddox stiffened. "Yes, but if I left my body, that would leave you here alone with *him*."

The pleasure of being held close to him distracted her from the task at hand and she had to force herself to concentrate enough to argue. "He wants my child, he's not going to hurt me."

"You don't know that."

He pressed his lips to her forehead in a gentle kiss, and Milly released a small sigh of contentment. "What I do know is that if you don't go now, then someday I'm going to be holding our child in my arms and that horrible demon is going to come for him. Or her." She pressed her forehead against his chest and for just a moment, hopelessness threatened to swallow her whole. "I don't think I could live with that. Not when I would know that my weakness, my willingness to offer up my child's life in exchange for my own, was the reason for it all."

Maddox tightened his arms around her and nodded. "All right. But for the love of the gods, be careful. I'll be back as soon as I can."

Despite her show of bravado, Milly had to bite the inside of her cheek to keep from calling him back as his physical form thinned, grew more and more translucent until she couldn't see him, could only feel him pass her as a gust of wind. Her interaction with the demon to this point had been limited to bartering for his help. For whatever reason, the demon had always allowed Maddox to be in control while he worked. Now it would be just the two of them for as long as it took Maddox to find Prince Adonis.

Please hurry, Maddox.

Maddox's body twitched and shivered as the demon rose, as if the demon's consciousness were a different size. Blackness consumed the whites of his eyes, shining crimson replacing his beautiful silver irises. The demon blinked and looked around, regaining his bearings before turning suspicious eyes on Milly.

"I am alone in this body. Where has our Maddox gone that was so important he would leave me alone with you?"

He took a step closer to her and Milly crossed her arms, barely resisting the urge to back away. "He left so I could talk to you. I'm ready to start guessing."

The demon arched an eyebrow, studying her for a long moment as if assessing the truth of her words. Instead of fighting her nervousness, Milly used it. She swallowed hard, pretended to struggle to meet the demon's eyes. "I get unlimited guesses, right? I can keep guessing till sundown today, no matter how many times I guess wrong?"

A smile slid across the demon's face, twisting Maddox's mouth into something hungry and monstrous. He crossed his own arms, mimicking her position. "Guess wrong as many times as you like. I look forward to putting all of this nonsense behind us."

Keep him busy. Just keep guessing until Maddox gets back.

She started with family members' names, then went to other people in her village. She named the members of the royal families she knew, and the traders who'd passed through the valley. She fumbled for fairy tale names and the names of legendary warriors.

The demon shook his head every time, the smile on his face growing, stretching wider than it should have been able to, until his mouth was a slash across Maddox's handsome face. Milly got more creative, started repeating names, but saying them backwards. The demon snorted at her ploy, but kept shaking his head.

Time passed, and the sun made its way slowly but steadily across the sky. Milly's mouth grew dry, her throat scratchy as she kept guessing. The demon seemed to tire as well, settling down on the grass and propping his head on his hand as he continued to shake his head at every guess. His obvious discomfort pleased Milly and gave her the strength and will she needed to keep going. Just to be difficult, she started repeating names if he didn't shake his head, sometimes shouting them in his face as if he'd gone hard of hearing.

She drew out the space between her guesses, trying to give her throat what little relief she could. The sky turned pink and the demon sat up a little straighter, the irritation bleeding from his face, replaced with a broadening grin. Milly stared into his eyes, praying for the black and red to shift, to become the white and silver of Maddox's true eyes.

Please, Maddox. Please.

A shadow passed overhead, barely perceptible in the fading light. Milly ignored it, too focused on Maddox's eyes to pay attention. Then the demon looked up, and his face contorted, nose wrinkling in disgust, eyes burning with sudden hatred. Milly looked up then, and her lungs froze.

Another demon.

Her heart pounded furiously, a bruising rhythm. The demon was large, great leathery wings cradling the wind, soaring with the grace of a falcon. He circled lower, giving Milly a good look at the thick horns forming a crown around his head, eyes that held sparks of red like burning cinnamon. He landed less than ten feet away from her with barely a sound.

"Are you Milly?" he asked.

Speech seemed beyond her for the moment, the combination of her tortured throat and the sudden lump that had risen conspiring to steal her voice. She bobbed her head, wheezing as she tried to breathe through her panic.

The newly arrived demon gave her a surprisingly gentle smile. The light in his eyes faded, red irises turning to a rich hazel and the black bleeding to white. His horns and wings melted away, the loincloth around his hips spreading to form a rich tunic the color of a fresh plum, a sash of pale lavender falling over his shoulder, fastened by a silver brooch. A curl of dark brown hair fell lazily over one eye and he huffed out a breath to blow it out of his way.

His new appearance was less frightening, but Milly was all too aware that danger could come in beautiful packages. She looked from the new demon to Maddox's possessed form, distracted from the new demon's approach by the hiss that came from Maddox's mouth.

"You have no business here," the demon snarled.

The new arrival ignored him, smiled at Milly as he came closer, leaned down to whisper in her ear. It took more nerve than she wanted to admit not to jerk away, but something about the fury on Maddox's face kept her still, made her listen very carefully to the words being spoken so softly in her ear. A smile pulled at the corners of her mouth and she met Maddox's eyes.

"Rumpelstiltskin."

She flung the name at the demon, not even the sound of her poor ragged voice enough to steal the triumph lifting her soul. The demon's eyes exploded into flame, the light from his crimson irises painting his face a bloody red. He threw back his head and screamed his rage to the sky, a sound that shot down Milly's spine, seized her muscles in a painful, agonizing grip. She choked, trying to draw breath, her lungs aching in feeble protest. Her nerves crackled painfully as she forced herself to stand, to face Rumpelstiltskin as the sun's final rays trailed over the howling demon.

Rumpelstiltskin looked at her then, and she could taste his hatred in the air between them. He lifted one of Maddox's hands, the fingers curled into claws. Fear threatened to drive Milly back, but she steeled herself against it. The darkness was coming. For the last three nights, darkness had brought her Maddox. It would bring him again, she knew it would. She had Rumpelstiltskin's name, and his word that he would leave forever. There was nothing to be afraid of anymore.

The demon took a step toward her, raised his hand as if he would strike. She jabbed a finger into his chest. "Go away, Rumpelstiltskin. Go away, and never touch this body again."

The hand slashed through the air, but before the blow landed, something buzzed against her fingertip. It hurt, but it didn't, there and gone so fast she couldn't decide. Rumpelstiltskin's eyes widened, his jaw going slack with shock. He started to scream, but the sound ended abruptly, and Maddox's body slumped against her.

Milly let out a grunt as she found herself under Maddox's full weight. The other demon was suddenly there, helping her support Maddox as his head lolled from side to side and he blinked blearily into the growing darkness.

"It worked," Maddox said hoarsely. "I can't feel him anymore. He's gone."

"And good riddance to him," the other demon said.

He snapped his fingers and suddenly a ball of golden light appeared, hovering over his shoulder. It bobbed as if alive, fluttering between Milly and Maddox, lighting up his handsome features and reflecting in his perfect silver eyes.

Milly blushed, suddenly shy without the adrenaline that had kept her going all day. She took a step back as the demon steadied Maddox on his feet, let him regain his bearings. Maddox's eyes followed her and Milly's breath stilled in her chest, her heart leaping into her throat. A second later, Maddox threw himself across the distance that separated them. He grabbed her, stumbling about a few steps as he dragged her into his arms and held her tight. Finally he steadied himself, stood there clutching her to him as if she were the last solid thing on earth.

"I thought I would be too late," he whispered into her hair.

She struggled in his arms, fought to hug him back, hold him as tightly as she could. "You are never too late. You have always been there exactly when I needed you." Her throat was raw, and her voice cracked on every other syllable, but she didn't care. It didn't matter, not when she had Maddox safe and sound in her arms.

"Save your voice." He nuzzled her forehead, planted a kiss on her temple. "We will have plenty of time to talk later."

Plenty of time. No more dreading the morning light, no more waiting for darkness to fall. They could be together now, for as long as they wanted. Milly curled her fingers into his clothes, holding onto him even as she asked the question buzzing around in her head like an annoying insect. "No second thoughts?"

"Never." He stiffened, pulled back so he could look down at her face. "Are you having second thoughts?"

There was a wariness in the lines of his face that wrenched at her heart, told her more than words that she wasn't the only one feeling a little vulnerable now that the excitement was over. She shook her head and put a hand on his face, brushing her thumb over his high cheekbone. "Never. This was my first adventure, and I can't imagine a better ending."

Maddox chuckled and caressed the line of her jaw with the tip of one finger. "And there's more where that came from," he promised.

"That is precisely what I wanted to hear."

Maddox's arms tightened around her, and the growl in his chest rumbled against her skin. He angled their bodies to put himself between her and the speaker, but then relaxed when his gaze landed on the man who had brought Milly Rumpelstiltskin's name. The demon stood out of their way, waiting patiently with a knowing smile on his face and a sparkle in his hazel eyes.

"Prince Adonis." Maddox tipped his head down in a gesture of respect, his grip loosening around Milly, though he didn't let her go. "Forgive me, I—"

"Don't apologize." Adonis waved a hand, almost swatting the will o' wisp that had floated back to dance in front of him. "I would think less of you if you'd taken the time to speak with me when you had this lovely lady before you."

Milly blinked, her jaw dropping as she realized who the demon was. "Prince Adonis...of Nysa. It's really you."

"In the flesh." Adonis winked, then laughed as if enjoying a private joke. "I won't take too much of your time as I can only imagine how much you have to talk about after that stunning whirlwind of events. I just wanted to take a moment to extend...an invitation."

"Invitation?" Milly echoed.

"Yes." The demon prince plucked something out of the air and held his fingers to his lips. A soft red glow illuminated his features and he dropped his hand, trailing smoke from the glowing tip of the cigarette he now held. "It has come to my attention that King Midas may be a bit put out with you for some time." Smoke crept out of his mouth as he spoke, infusing the air with the scent of cloves. "As it happens, some companions of mine and I are looking for some adventurous couples to settle a recently founded kingdom. We're starting from scratch, and we're looking for men and women who don't mind a little... excitement. We would be most pleased if you would join us."

A new kingdom? Milly looked at Maddox, uncertain how to respond. Her nerves danced beneath her skin, but she wasn't sure if it was fear...or anticipation.

"We owe you a great debt," Maddox started carefully. "If this is what you ask for repayment—"

"There is no debt." Adonis's eyes glowed to match the tip of his cigarette, a hot undertone of anger heating his voice. "Banishing Rumpelstiltskin was a pleasure. He had a disgusting penchant for helping along miserable marriages. Anything he could do to support a marriage that had nothing to do with love, and he was there with bells on." He raised the cigarette to his lips, inhaling sharply as a shadow passed over his face. "And planning to possess a child. That is unforgivable." He brightened, exhaling another cloud of smoke as he looked at Milly. "If anything, I feel I owe you another favor. Taking his talent for spinning gold was a stroke of genius. Not to put too fine a point on it, but it will also make you a much more desirable candidate in the eyes of a certain vampire. It always pleases him to find another means of funding."

Milly furrowed her eyebrows, trying to follow the demon's rather rapid train of thought. "Taking his talent? I didn't..."

"He threatened you when you beat him, tried to offer violence instead of honoring his bargain. You were within your rights to demand recompense." He grinned. "You called him by his true name, touched him as you banished him. You didn't specify what you demanded in payment, so the magic chose for you."

"I... I didn't know. You mean I can actually spin straw into gold now?" Milly swayed, leaned against Maddox for support as she processed this new information.

Adonis nodded. "Indeed. Which brings us back to my point. King Midas is not going to let you go willingly. I do hope you'll consider my invitation."

Maddox looked down at Milly and smiled. "Well, what do you think? We can blow through your former abode, get your treasure box? Perhaps purchase a few more to hold all the wonderful treasures you're going to find?"

Milly returned his smile with her own, her heart swelling until tears warmed her eyes. "I can't wait."

FIN

About the Author: Jennifer Blackstream is a paranormal/ fantasy romance author planning to extend her repertoire to include urban fantasy. She is routinely attacked by plot bunnies and does her best to splatter the pages of her books with their inky blood before the little fluffers can escape. She firmly believes that no playlist is complete without Alice Cooper, no library is complete without Terry Pratchett, and no recipe is complete without garlic. (Side note: "Garlic" always means a minimum of three cloves. Any recipe instruction that calls for less than that is obviously a typo and should be ignored.)

Want to learn more about the kingdom Adonis invited Milly and Maddox into? Meet the werewolf prince of Sanguennay? See the full story behind Adonis, the demon prince of Nysa? Start the Blood Prince series now. If you would like to sign up for Jennifer's mailing list and receive alerts about new releases and other goodies, visit: www.jenniferblackstream.com.

The Unicorn Hunter
Alethea Kontis

THE DEMON WAS WAITING FOR HER WHEN THE HUNTS-man brought her into the forest. He knew exactly who she was and where she'd be and when she'd come and how she smelled and what she ate and the size of her slippers and the sound of her voice and exactly how far her chest rose and fell when she drew in a breath. From the tiniest needle on the smallest tree to the oldest dragon in the mountains, the denizens of the forest had been whispering about her for weeks now: the poor, beautiful young princess whose horrible jealous mother was sending to her death. The whole of nature waited with bated breath for her arrival, wondering at what adventures might arise from this terrible occasion. There hadn't been this much drama in the Wood since the last time his brethren had crossed the storm-tossed threshold into this accursed world.

He killed a doe while he was waiting, in part because the princess would eventually want for sustenance, but mostly because the idiot creature was too distracted by all the excitement to have the sense to stay away from him.

He knew the moment she entered the forest, for everything in it smiled at once and sighed, like a chorus of tinkling bells. The cold winter sun broke through the gray clouds and bare branches to kiss her alabaster cheek in reverence. The gold thread in her dress and golden ribbons in her ebony hair caught the light and danced like fire. She was young for her height, slender as the willows, and as yet untouched by the first blush of womanhood. Perfect. The four winds, dizzy and drunk with happiness at her arrival, caught up the dead leaves of the forest floor and spun them in a frenzy of dried applause. The ecstasy was short-lived, however, and the forest caught up a collective gasp when the huntsman tore the sleeve of her dress, scratched the pristine flesh of her arm, and forced her to the ground.

It wasn't supposed to happen this way. But there were demons in the world now, making the evils that men do far easier to reach. So the Memory Stone had taught him and his brethren, and so he knew what he must do to correct the situation.

He had hoped not to make his presence known so soon, but he needed her purity intact, and if he waited much longer all his efforts would be for naught. Her scream ripped through the now-still air. The ice pansies at his feet wept in terror. In a few long strides he crossed the clearing and kicked the huntsman with an ironclad foot, lifting his body off that of the princess and sending him sprawling in the dirt.

"I was ordered to kill the child," the huntsman said after spitting out a mouthful of teeth and blood. "What use is the rest to you, beast?"

"None of your concern," said the demon. "You have new orders now. Be gone from this place."

The huntsman came to his knees, withdrawing both a knife from his belt and a box from his cloak. "Not without claiming what's mine," he said. "I'm to return to the palace with her heart."

The demon went back to the body of the doe and sliced open her chest with one sharp claw. He plucked the tiny heart from the cavity and dropped it at the huntsman's feet. "Be glad it's not your own," said the demon.

The huntsman nodded. He snapped the heart up into the box and limped away from the demon as fast as his legs could manage.

"Oh great and honorable beast," the young princess addressed him without looking directly at him. Her voice shook and hiccupped with tears. "Thank you for saving my life. My kingdom owes you a great debt."

"The same kingdom that just sentenced you to death? I doubt they'd sing my praises at the moment." She might have been a princess, and the most perfect human female form this world had ever seen, but she was still a young girl and far sillier than she looked. He'd forgotten how closely ignorance walked in the footsteps of innocence. The memory was less amusing than it was annoying. "You, however, owe me your life, and that life I will take. So stop your sniveling and get on with you. We have work to do."

"Work, my lord?"

He snorted at the address. As if her ridiculous feudal society would function longer than five minutes in his world. He felt the compulsion to explain, but knew the words would be wasted. "That's right, *work*. Are you at all familiar with the term?"

"I've heard of it," she said in earnest.

"Excellent. Your highness"—a ridiculous honorific as he was roughly nine feet tall, before the horns, and the top of her head came to just above his navel—"you are going to help me catch a unicorn." Actually there were three unicorns, and he intended to kill them once he'd caught them, but the demon felt it wise to omit these details.

"Oh, that does sound lovely," she smiled. "I accept."

Yes, indeed. Stupid as the day was long. Just as he'd suspected. He waited what seemed like ages for her to compose herself. She finally stood, adjusted the torn sleeve of her gown, collected the small silken purse she'd brought with her, and squared her shoulders. "I am ready," she announced.

"Fantastic," said the demon. "Let's go."

The demon kept a steady pace through the trees, through bushes and over streams, straight to the Heart of the Wood. The Heart was the oldest part of the forest, where the trees had forgotten more than the world would remember, where magic ran wild. There were no paths there, for only a handful of human feet had sullied those hills and valleys in the last few centuries. The Heart was where the demon had first appeared in this world. He assumed they would also find the unicorns there.

The demon looked back over his shoulder periodically to make sure the princess was still following, and slowed his pace accordingly. Every time he looked back, the forest had given the princess something else. There were flowers in her hair, she wore an ermine as a neck ruff, and the shoulder of her dress was now firmly anchored with what looked like cobwebs and a vine of some sort. She sang or hummed or whistled as they walked. She even skipped sometimes. And every time he turned back she smiled at him warily with those full, cupid's-bow, blood-red lips. He tried not to turn back very often.

He tried not to stop very often either, but her feet were small and her legs were short, and there was no help for it. Every time he stopped, the princess asked him a barrage of silly questions that had no doubt occurred to her while singing or humming or whistling and were now burning to be answered.

"Do you live in the mountains with the dragons?"

"I am from a different world, a world very unlike this one."

"How did you come here?"

How to explain using the fewest words? "The same way the unicorns did. There is a place, deep in your Wood here, where our worlds meet. The storms there are sometimes so powerful that they rip a doorway between the worlds. One creature gets pulled from my world and one from the unicorn world, and we end up here."

"How do you know all this?"

"The Memory Stone tells us so," he said. "The spirits of our demon brethren past are drawn home to the Memory Stone. It is how they share their knowledge with us."

"Do all the demons have big horns and black-red skin where you come from?"

"Most have horns. Size and skin colors vary by nature."

"Why do you wear iron boots? Are your feet like a horse's?"

"A little, yes. And I am a being of fire, so cloth or leather would do me little good."

"Why don't you wear any clothing?"

He was glad his loincloth had remained intact to avoid further such questions. "I am a being of fire. I do not feel cold the way you do. Plus, a creature who can kill anything with his bare hands has no need to be modest."

"Why didn't you just kill me?"

Not that it hadn't crossed his mind. "Because I need a living innocent to lure a unicorn. I've had little success with dead ones."

"Have you seen a unicorn?"

"Once, briefly." One had arrived at the same time he had. Such was the balance.

"What are unicorns like?"

"Like giant white puppies of happiness."

"Do you think the unicorns will like me?"

"They will think you are the best thing they have ever seen."

Like everyone else, it seems.

"Do you like me?"

"Only when you're quiet."

"Why are we capturing a unicorn?"

"Because it's the only way I know to get home." Again, he thought it wise to omit the rest.

"Do you have a family back home? Do you miss them?"

"I do need you alive, but you don't need your tongue." The answer was enough to curb her examination until the next time they stopped. It wasn't a planned rest, but the girl collapsed on the crumbling stones at the foot of an ancient well. It was as good a place as any. A bear cub snuggled up to the princess's back and a warren of rabbits cozied up to her front, keeping her warm. The demon thought it a bit ridiculous that nature here should fawn all over a little girl just because she was beautiful and a princess. He felt bad for any poor ugly pauper girl who stumbled into the forest unawares. She'd be that bear cub's breakfast for sure.

Every time they stopped there was always one animal or another in the princess's lap. The demon noted their bravery. In all his time in the forest, he had never before had the pleasure of any beast's company; they sensed what he was and stayed far away. The more intelligent creatures still did, but it seemed some of their children were young enough to tempt fate.

Turning the tables, he asked her one question before her heavy eyes escorted her into sleep. "Why aren't you afraid of me?"

"Should I be?" she asked.

"I'm a demon," he said. "I could drink your blood to warm my feet and grind your bones to make my bread."

"But you won't," she said. "You need me to capture a unicorn."

"I could burn all your clothes so that you might freeze. I could spit in your face and you would lose your beauty in a heartbeat."

"Will you?" she asked.

"Perhaps, if you make me mad," he said.

"Then I will endeavor not to anger you." She yawned. "We have tales, old stories from long ago of benevolent beasts who were really kind souls, or princes in disguise."

"I am no prince," he said.

"Pity," she mumbled. "I could use a prince." And with that, she slept.

Perhaps the queen was not mad, and in sending her daughter away she had done her kingdom a favor. This child, though a rare beauty, was too happy and silly and gullible and kind. Her subjects would riot and her advisors would rob the coffers bare and her castle walls would be breached within a fortnight. She would make a terrible queen.

Even still, he could not imagine sending his own daughter, or any child, to her death. And he was a demon.

He leaned back against the stones of the well, safer from his body heat than a tree, and closed his own eyes in relief. This world was so cold—not to his skin, but to his heart—and it wasn't just the winter season having washed all the colors with the stark dullness of mud and snow. What little fire existed in this world was buried far underground, so far that being away from it tore at his mind, trying to free the madness there that would be all too happy to escape. His brethren had succumbed to that madness, and eventually so would he. Even now he could taste the princess's pulse beneath her skin, imagine his claws marring her perfect flesh, smell the fear of the wild animals who dared accompany her. He wanted to destroy the forest around him, dead limb from dead limb, and set it ablaze so that there might be color and warmth filling this world, if only briefly.

If he did not destroy the unicorns soon, their presence would tip the balance too far. It would cause another storm and rip another of his brethren from his world. He needed to kill those unicorns now, all of them, the first two for his brethren and the last one so that he could escape this prison and end the dreaded cycle...for as long as Chaos would let it be ended.

He woke and realized he'd fallen asleep. The stones beneath him had melted away into the dead earth. On the far side of the well the princess sat, quietly singing and gently combing the hair of the latest beast in her lap with a jeweled comb. Of course the princess had taken a jeweled comb into the woods. Then again, she hadn't expected to survive this long.

The animal in her lap seemed to be an albino fawn or a large goat, and then the demon realized that what looked like an ice shelf behind them was actually an icicle protruding from the animal's forehead. The first unicorn. The demon would have laughed if he hadn't been afraid of scaring the beast away. There the princess sat, shimmering like magic, her skin darker than the unicorn's by a mere blush, the curtain of her ebony hair like a waterfall of shadow between them. From her blood red lips came a nonsense song about flying dishes and talking pigs. A rainbow of feathers fluttered in the trees around her; a cacophony of birds had flocked just to hear her sing, and the unicorn was mesmerized. Its eyes were closed and it suffered the princess's combing without complaint, completely still. Too still.

The demon crossed over to the princess in a few steps that shook the ground and caused the myriad of inhabitants in the bushes to explode into the air. The unicorn did not move. The demon reached down with a large hand, the skin of it as red as her lips, the claws as dark as her hair. She stopped singing when that hand came into view, and she stopped combing, but the unicorn's head in her lap held her trapped.

The demon swept back the unicorn's silken white mane with a claw; a few stray hairs stung his skin. The perfect flesh beneath the mane was crisscrossed with layers and layers of angry red lines.

The princess looked confused. The demon gently took the jeweled comb from her hand. Its aura of bile taunted him. "Poison," he said. He melted the trinket into slag with the heat of his palm and tossed the little golden ball of it into the well where it could do no more harm. "Did your mother give that to you?"

The princess nodded silently. One big, fat, shimmering ice-drop of a tear slid down her cheek and fell onto the unicorn. Into the unicorn. Another tear fell, and another, deeper into the unicorn's flesh as it turned to snow in the princess's arms. When she realized what was happening she jerked, startled, and the shape of the unicorn crumbled to cold lumps of nothing in her lap. She lifted her arms slowly, reverently, and the rising sun made the rime on her forearms sparkle. Dazed, she raised a shining finger to the tongue that waited between her blood red lips. The demon slapped her hand away. He pulled her up by the wrists and began dusting and melting every bit of corpse-ice on her that he could see.

"Stupid girl," he muttered.

"What would have happened," she asked when she found her voice, "if I had tasted the unicorn?"

"You would have screamed with delight because it would have been the most delicious thing you've ever put in your mouth. But after unicorn, all other food to cross your lips would taste foul. You would wander the world for the rest of your life, starving, forever trying to taste something, anything, that comes close to that divine perfection."

"Oh," she said, and clasped her traitorous fingers behind her back. "Thank you," she added, but sounded unsure.

"Come," said the demon. "We should leave this place. Other unicorns will sense that one of their brethren has died here and they will not come near it."

"I'm sorry," was all she said.

"Why?"

"I did not let you capture the unicorn. I killed it."

"No matter," said the demon. "There are others. Let's go."

The princess was navigating the melted stones of the well in her thin, inadequate slippers, when something occurred to her. She brightened and reached for her tiny clutch, pulled a small object from it and held it tightly in her hands. She squeezed her eyes shut and scrunched up her face, as if in pain. The demon held his breath, waiting for a magic spell or another bout of weeping to burst from her. Though possibly more trouble, he hoped for the former.

"I wish my handsome prince, my one true love, would find me and save me and take me away from all this," she said, and she tossed the coin in the air.

The demon stretched out a hand and easily caught the tiny gold disc before it hit the well. His palm, still hot from the comb, melted it, too, into slag. He tossed the thin, swirling, misshapen bit of metal into the snow at her feet.

"Why did you do that?" the princess asked.

"You didn't want to make that wish," the demon replied.

"I didn't?"

"You don't want any prince who would have you right now," he said. "Trust me."

"But I always make that wish," she said.

"Then I hope he takes his sweet old time finding you," he said.

"Wishes are magic and wonderful," said the princess.

"Are they now?" said the demon. "'Skin as white as snow, hair as black as ebony, lips as red as blood...' How'd that wish work out for you?"

Those blood red lips formed a thin red line, and the princess stomped away from the well. The demon chose to enjoy the silence.

They marched through the forest as before, with a varying menagerie of wild animals keeping pace. The princess was distraught when the demon picked one new friend at random to be their lunch, but once cooked her growling stomach betrayed her and she ate with relish. She apologized to her friends when she finished; they seemed to accept it easier than she had. And so she frolicked with them as the day and miles through the endless forest stretched on. The meadows gave way to hills and then mountains, and at times they had to skirt sheer cliff sides and rocky terrain, but still they walked. The princess had long since shredded and discarded her delicate slippers, her ebony hair was as stringy as the limp ribbons still woven through it, and her golden dress trailed behind her in muddy rags, but she maintained her posture and addressed her wild friends with all the pomp and circumstance of royal courtiers.

They did not stop again until they came to a stream that sliced a deep crevasse through the forest and rushed swift with icemelt water from the mountains. The princess was far ahead of him, singing a harmony with a family of larks and dancing with a fluttering collection of moths and butterflies, so she did not spot the unicorn refreshing himself in the stream until she was almost upon it. The demon noticed at once; he had felt the chill presence of the unicorn emanating from the water, far stronger than icemelt.

The princess stopped her dancing, though the circus around her did not, so she still appeared to be a flurry of move-ment. She lifted her mud-heavy skirts and curtseyed low to the unicorn across from her, on the opposite bank of the narrow-est part of the stream. The unicorn noticed her, lifted his head from the water, and bent a foreleg as it bowed to her in return. Without taking her eyes from the animal, she reached into the silk purse at her belt and withdrew the most beautiful red apple the demon had ever seen.

It occurred to the demon to wonder why the princess had not mentioned the apple during her passionate fit at lunch-time. It did not occur to him to wonder why she was possessed of such a remarkable fruit in a season where similar apples had long rotted into memory. And so he did not stop her when she offered the apple to the unicorn with both hands, and it munched heartily. For a moment they were a mirror of snow white skin and blood red lips, a picture of innocence and perfection.

When the unicorn started to scream, it sounded very much like how the princess had screamed when she'd been attacked by the huntsman. Its cry cut through the oncoming twilight and pierced the heart of any living thing within earshot. Some of the smaller animals in the glen did not survive the terror of that scream. The demon thought it wise not to mention this to the princess.

She was already crying, screaming in fear as the unicorn screamed in pain. She leapt into the icy stream and threw her thin young arms around its slender neck, mindless of its spastic hooves and rolling eyes and blood-frothed mouth. She ceased her cries and began to sing to the beast, a lullaby, in an attempt to calm it.

There was magic in her voice, whether she had willed it there or not. The demon saw several animals curl up in sleep as they heard the song. He yawned twice himself. The unicorn's thrashing slowed with its heartbeat, and it laid its head in her lap, far less gracefully than the previous unicorn. She rocked it back and forth, back and forth, all the time singing it to sleep. Singing it to death. She held the unicorn until long after it had turned to snow at her feet and the wind had blown its form into tiny drifts around her.

The demon approached her gently this time. He did not want to disturb her, but he also did not want her to freeze to death, so he loosened his fire essence through his iron-shod feet and into the ground, warming the earth around her. The corpse-ice of the unicorn began to melt away.

"I am sorry," she told him again when the tears were gone. "I killed the unicorn."

"No matter," he replied calmly. "Can I get you anything?" He found himself surprised at his concern for her welfare.

She untied the silk purse at her waist and held it out to him. "A drink of water from the stream, please," she said. "There is a golden cup in my bag." Her voice was ragged and hoarse with strain and sadness.

The demon snorted. "You humans and your gold." He was careful with his giant claws so that he only untied the small bag instead of ripping it to shreds. He withdrew the ridiculously ornate cup; like the comb, it, too, burned at his eyes with its sick aura. "Your mother gave you this." It was not a question.

"Yes," the princess affirmed. "She gave me the bag to take with me on my journey."

He cursed himself for his own stupidity and immediately immolated the bag and all its contents at his feet.

"No!" cried the princess, the unicorn now all but forgotten.

"Why would you want any of that?" he asked. "Every bit of it was meant to kill you."

"It's all I have," she said over the blackened mark of singed earth. "It's all I had to remember her by."

"You have your memories," he told her. "Those should be painful enough."

She stood tall and glared at him, her whole body rigid, her hands in tiny fists at her side. "How many more unicorns are there?"

"One," he answered.

"How many more demons are there?" she asked.

"One," he answered again.

"What happened to the others?"

"I killed them."

She relaxed a little in sympathy. "How could you do that?"

He could just as easily ask her how she could have killed two unicorns, but he thought it wise not to mention it. "We are not meant to be here in your world. Not us; not the unicorns. Our presence makes the spectrum of your world larger. We make the waves taller, the valleys lower. We turn bad into evil and good into divinity. The longer we are here, the more we lose control of our minds. Demons become savage. Unicorns, I imagine, become more ephemeral. Our souls belong in our own worlds, and they return to these worlds after our death."

"So you hunted down your brethren and killed them for the sake of my world."

"And to save their souls. They were easy for me to find; evil begets evil. I would not have found the unicorns without your help."

"And how would you have killed them?"

"I don't know," he answered honestly. "You did that for me."

The princess exhaled then, deflated, and sat again. She hugged her knees to her chest and looked out over the rushing, icy stream. Apart from the burbling of the water the woods around them were blessedly silent. The demon sat beside her, only close enough to warm the ground beneath her and the air around her.

"Is that why my mother is so evil?" asked the princess. "Because there are demons in the world?"

"Perhaps. I don't know."

"I don't think you are evil."

"Then you are a silly girl."

"Are unicorns demons too?"

This was certainly an avenue of thought the demon hadn't considered. "What makes you say that?"

"They have horns, and hooves, and they are elemental, and they are the polar opposite of you. They are ice where you are fire. You said that demons are all different colors based on their nature. Are there ice demons where you come from?"

"I have not heard tales of any."

"Perhaps they were exiled from your world. Or you from theirs. Or perhaps we were the ones exiled. We might have all been part of the same world once."

"That would be a remarkable history," he said.

"What will happen to you when you die?"

"My soul will be returned to my world and I will tell my tale to the Memory Stone, so that others who might follow this path will know how to act."

"I don't want you to die."

"I have to. My continued presence here will only tear your world apart."

"I know," she said matter-of-factly. "I just wanted you to know."

"Thank you," said the demon. Her declaration both pleased and frustrated him. She was growing too mature too fast. He hoped it didn't affect her ability to attract the unicorns.

"Shall we go find this last unicorn then?"

The demon stood, offering one large, clawed hand to help the princess to her feet. She took it. "We shall."

Just beyond the stream was another small mountain, more of a large hill, with a gaping maw before them that appeared to be the entrance to a mine. "Up or down?" the demon asked her. He imagined the unicorn would find them either way.

"I want to see the stars," was all she said before she started climbing.

They climbed to the summit in the long hours of the early evening. In the spring, the demon suspected this ground was covered in wildflowers. What crunched beneath their feet now was only dirt and dry grasses hiding sharp rocks. The princess stumbled a few times, but she kept on climbing. The demon could not see the blood on her feet, but he could smell it on the wind, and so long as she said nothing, he wondered why he cared.

Once atop the small mountain, the princess skipped and jumped about joyously under the bright heavens. She ran around the summit as if the wildflowers still surrounded her. She spun and spun and threw her head back and held her hands up to the sky to catch the flakes of snow that had started to fall like little stars all around her. And then the stars themselves began to fall from the sky and dance with her. The princess pulled the golden ribbons from her hair and tied them all together in one long strand, and the stars leapt and swirled and twirled the ribbon as she spun it around herself. Her giggles and laughter sounded like bells. The wind around her whooshed and whistled and sounded like whinnying.

And when the whirlwind of flurries took a unicorn's form, she quickly tied her ribbon around its neck, fashioning it into a crude golden harness. The great white beast bowed his head to her, accepting his defeat, and allowed her to lead him to the demon. With one quick hand, the demon snapped the horn from the unicorn's head; with the other, he slit its throat, deep and deadly. Without so much as a snort the unicorn burst into a flash blizzard of snow, covering both the demon and the princess in blood and ice.

The demon lifted the unicorn's frozen horn to his lips, and the heat from his breath melted it quickly down his throat. His stomach clenched and his muscles spasmed; the poison was quick.

There were tears in the princess's eyes. The demon held a large, warm hand to her small, cold cheek. "I'm sorry," he said. "I killed the unicorn."

"I cry not for a beast I never knew. I weep for the beast who was my friend."

"Where will you go?" he asked, no longer surprised at his concern for her welfare.

"I will find whoever mines this mountain and seek shelter with them." She was above him now; he did not remember lying down. Her ebony hair curtained her face, erasing the stars from the night. From her neck dangled the melted coin she had almost thrown in the well; she had woven one of her golden ribbons through a hole in the design. He reached out to touch the medallion, but his arm did not obey.

"Perhaps your prince will come," said the demon.

"In time," she said. "Perhaps in a very long time, when we are worthy of each other."

"Very wise," said the demon.

"Will you tell your Memory Stone about me?" she asked.

"Yes," he whispered. "I will tell it all about the smart and brave princess I once knew."

She laughed and fought back the tears that no longer fell. "There is no need to lie."

He laughed too, but his breath had left him. "And what stories will you tell your world?"

"I have"—she screwed up her beautiful face in an effort to maintain her composure—"I have my memories," she said. "Those should be painful enough."

He nodded in reply, but his head would not obey. He fought to keep his eyes on her face, but he suddenly went from looking up at her to looking down upon them both. He watched her as she hugged herself to his chest, then shifted herself around his horns so that she might cradle his head in her lap. She held him until he turned to ash in her arms, until all that was left of him were his iron shoes. He watched her until his corpse-dust flew away on the wind, until his soul was drawn so far away that she was only a golden speck on the dark mountainside, another star in the sky.

He had been wrong. She would make a great queen.

FIN

About the Author: Alethea Kontis is a princess, author, fairy godmother, and geek. She lives and writes on the Space Coast of Florida with her teddy bear, Charlie. Experience Princess Alethea's joy and magic on her YouTube channel, all the social media, and at www.aletheakontis.com.

HUNTER'S HEART
CHRISTINE POPE

THE QUEEN IS ANGRY.

This is not an uncommon occurrence. She is an expert at finding fault—the roast joint is cold, her bed linens have not been aired properly, the hem of her new gown is uneven.

But all these things are trifles, and I know at once that whatever has raised her ire this time, it is not a trifle. Her magnificent bosom heaves beneath its covering of embroidered gold bullion, and the faintest of lines appears in the perfection of the ivory skin between her arched brows. The line is gone so quickly it is possible I imagined it, but the queen herself briefly raises a finger to the betraying flesh, as if to reassure herself by touching the skin there that she left no permanent mark.

"Huntsman," she says, and I bow my head.

We are alone in her sitting room, a bower with walls of rose-tinted marble and numerous softly upholstered divans and chairs, all in shades of blush and pink and coral intended to flatter her complexion. Despite its rosy-hued clutter, the chamber might as well be bare of all furnishings, for one's eye is always drawn immediately to the mirror framed in intricately wrought brass on the wall behind her.

She stands, and I kneel before her. "The princess, I have learned, is a traitor."

At this I raise my head, shock making me forget the expected decorum. The queen's dark eyes flash at me, and I immediately direct my gaze toward the rose-worked needle-point rug beneath my knees.

"A traitor," she repeats. "I will not belabor how shocking this is to me—I, who have always looked on her as my own flesh and blood."

Knowing that the queen desires no comment from me, I remain silent. She must have her stage, even if I am the sole member of her audience.

A pause, and then I feel her hand on my shoulder. The faintest scent of roses emanates from those long, elegant fingers as they alight there, delicate as butterflies, before she lifts her hand once more.

"I would not have a public trial. The people, misguided as they might be, love her, and I wish to avoid scandal."

Still I wait in silence, although my heart begins to pound in long, sounding strokes, as if it has divined some truth my mind has yet to grasp.

The queen places her hand beneath my chin and lifts my head. At any other time her touch would have wakened hopes I dared not acknowledge, but now as I meet her gaze I sense only a chill, as if those dark eyes are not windows to a soul, but only gaping holes hinting at the utter emptiness within.

"You are brave, my hunter." Now her voice is a purr, warm and inviting as a soft bed at the end of a long day. "Brave, and loyal, and true. Can I trust you to do as I ask?"

"Anything, my queen," I manage. How can I protest, when my acquiescence may coax her to continue touching me even for a few seconds longer?

But she removes her hand from my chin and smiles, as if she knows she need do nothing else to earn my blind obedience.

"You will take the princess," she says, and now her voice is hard, cold and brilliant as the mirror hanging on the wall behind her. "Take her into the forest, far from prying eyes. Once you are there, take the fine dagger you carry at your belt and cut her heart from her breast."

I cannot say why this pronouncement surprises me. Its root has been there for some time now, increasing with every compliment paid the princess, every admiring gaze sent in her direction. Jealousy, the dark vine growing at the heart of the kingdom.

My voice comes in a harsh whisper. "And then, my queen?"

"Bring the heart to me." She turns to an elegant little gilt-topped table and retrieves a box of carved ebony, black as the princess's hair. "Place the heart in this box, and bring it to me as proof of your loyalty."

I say, "It will be done, my queen." For what else can I do? If the price of jealousy is death, then the cost of disloyalty is more than I wish to pay.

She presses the box into my hands. "Rise, noble hunter. See that the deed is done before the day is out."

The dismissal is obvious. I wrap my cold fingers around the box and rise to my feet. A bow feels foolish and superfluous after agreeing to such a request, but I make my obeisance, as I know she expects it. Then, with the sharp edges of the box still biting into my chilled flesh, I leave the room.

She is not known for her patience, no, not this queen. I dare not tarry, as I know she is all too likely to find another to carry out her dark errand if I am slow to follow her instructions.

It is a bright day, warm with the promise of coming summer. The little princess walks in the garden, the sunlight finding flickers of copper in her long black hair. She raises her face to me and smiles; I have been in the household all her life.

She has no reason to fear me.

"Come, princess," I say. "There is something in the forest I would like you to see."

"Have you made a great discovery?" she asks, a teasing lilt in her voice. Her eyes are bluer than the forget-me-nots in the garden border, bluer than the sky.

"A very great discovery," I reply, forcing a smile.

We go on foot. The great forests come almost to the castle walls, and for the first mile or so the way is well-trodden, used often by the members of the royal household when they want to go out into the woods and play at rusticating. But the path then grows more narrow, the trees crowding on every side, jealous of man's encroachment. It is here that I hunt the deer and the boar for the queen's table. Would that my intended prey had their fleetness of foot.

"Is it very much farther?" the princess asks. She is too sweet-tempered for complaint, but even so I hear the edge of weariness in her voice.

"Not much farther," I tell her. I find I cannot look at her directly.

We come then to a clearing, a hidden place of green grass within the crowding fir and pine. With a happy sigh, the princess sinks down onto a fallen log.

"I can see why no one else has made this discovery," she says, and wriggles her feet within their tiny slippers. "For I doubt anyone else but a huntsman would come this far into the forest."

I do not bother with a reply. Now that we are here, I know I must harden my heart for the task ahead. Best to make it quick.

The knife is very bright as I draw it from its sheath. I had not thought so much sunlight could penetrate the forest canopy, but the steel sparkles under its rays, brilliant as the diamonds in the queen's crown.

At first the princess does not understand. Her smile grows uncertain as I approach, but it is only as I raise the knife for the killing blow that realization enters those sky-colored eyes.

She lets out a cry and falls to my knees. "You cannot!"

"I must," I say. I look everywhere but at the tear-stained perfection of her face. "It is the will of the queen."

"Why?" she sobs. "What have I done?"

Nothing, I want to say. *Nothing but grow more beautiful with every passing day, until you are the brilliant sun eclipsing her waning moon.*

I know I cannot make her understand the weariness of the ever-encroaching years, the slow tide of resentment toward those younger, stronger, more vigorous.

More beautiful.

I say instead, "It will only hurt for a moment." And I raise the knife.

Only to find some invisible force staying my hand. I stand there, blade glittering in the sun, as the princess weeps at my feet. For how long, I do not know, but after a time, my arm, strong as it is, begins to waver. At last I lower the knife.

She does not move. Her hair is a curtain of black silk, obscuring her features.

Again she asks, "Why?"

I have no answer. I could tell her that there is little enough beauty in the world, and I find I have no desire to take her from it. Or I could say that the queen is wrong, and evil, and in conscience I cannot do as she bids any longer.

But I say neither of these things. For a moment I reflect on what my punishment might be, should the queen learn of my unexpected treachery. Then the princess lifts her head and stares at me, and in the wondering innocence of her face, I see something of why I let her live. One death cannot halt the slow, steady flow of time. The queen might wish to stop it, or at least try to pretend that she is forever changeless, but I know better.

"Run into the forest, little princess," I say. "There is no life for you in the palace now. God grant you grace that you might find a better fate somewhere else in the world."

She rises to her feet. I see an almost queenly grace in her movements as she takes my free hand in both of hers and says, "Thank you."

And then she is off, blue skirts gathered in her hands as she disappears down one of the paths that lead into the clearing. Her gown is a wisp of fallen sky between the darker green of the forest. The trees shelter her fleeing form. She is gone, lost to me forever.

On my way back to the palace, I bring down a young buck and carefully remove the heart from his breast. It pains me to leave his carcass on the forest floor when it might have provided a handsome meal, but I know the queen must never suspect my treachery. The heart fits very well within the box she has given me.

It is my secret, my quiet rebellion. And if I should die because of my duplicity, so be it. The princess lives, and within her, some part of me lives on as well.

FIN

About the Author: A native of Southern California, Christine Pope has been writing stories ever since she commandeered her family's Smith-Corona typewriter back in the sixth grade. She is the author of the bestselling Witches of Cleopatra Hill, Tales of the Latter Kingdoms, and Djinn Wars series, among others. She now lives in Santa Fe, New Mexico, with her husband and the world's fluffiest dog. For information on all her books, including her novel-length fairytale retellings, Tales of the Latter Kingdoms, visit her website: www.christinepope.com.

CPSIA information can be obtained
at www.ICGtesting.com
Printed in the USA
FSHW021941181119
64266FS